BLACK LIGHT: SCANDALIZED

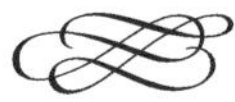

LIVIA GRANT

Published by Black Collar Press

Black Light: Scandalized
by Livia Grant

e-book ISBN: 978-1-947559-17-2
Print ISBN: 978-1-947559-18-9

Cover Art by Eris Adderly, http://erisadderly.com/
Editor: Sandy Ebel, Personal Touch Editing

First Electronic Publish Date, October 2019

First Print Publish Date, October 2019

DEDICATION

So I have a confession. There were many days this year that I wasn't sure this day would ever happen. It wasn't because I didn't love this story. On the contrary, I am going to have a hard time saying goodbye to these characters. I love each and every one of them, not only because they shared their personal stories with me (and by extension you), but because they all spent the last year rattling around in my head with me as I've struggled hard to keep my author career moving forward.

In case you didn't know it, being an author is fucking hard. I don't say this to garner any sympathy because I truly LOVE being an author. It is my passion. My dream. The only thing that could make it better is if I got to do it full time.

But, you see, I am also blessed to have a fabulous day job/career that I also love. This year my day job exploded on me (in a great way) and I have found myself struggling every single day to juggle all of the things I have on my plate. Even for a certified Type-A workaholic like myself, I know I've bitten off more than I can chew.

My family and friends have taken the biggest hit. I am so grateful for all of the help I get from so many people in my life, both in real life and authorlandia for their support and understanding behind the scenes as I do my best to get things back under control. I always worry when I list names because by definition, I'm leaving out so many others who have been there for me, but I would have lost it long ago without Niki Roge, my awesome PA, helping me so much every single day. And my alpha reader, Katie Reads, did triple duty on this book - part alpha reader, part cheerleader, part psychiatrist. And of course, my BFF, Jennifer Bene. In spite of having one of the hardest years of her life, she has always been there for me.

I am so excited (and a tad nervous) to turn ***Black Light: Scandalized*** *out into the world. Any author will tell you that some books are just more special than others. We know it as we're writing. Maybe it's the characters, sometimes it's their story. This one has it all.*

I can't wait to see if you agree.

To you wonderful readers, from the bottom of my heart, thanks for you support and patience as you waited for me to rip this baby out of my heart. Sorry if I left a few tears and drops of blood on your kindle.

Love,

Livia

CHAPTER 1

"Look what the cat dragged in. You're almost an hour late."

Nalani Ione teased as her good friend and boss, Madison Taylor, sauntered into the second-floor Runway office. The normally stylish manager was looking a bit crumpled in an outfit that looked suspiciously like the clothes she'd had on the day before. Nalani was pretty sure the crusty-looking white stain on her boss's wrinkled skirt was a leftover *deposit* from one Trevor McLean.

Madison plopped down into her office chair with a whoosh, almost knocking over the tall cup of aromatic coffee from a shop on nearby Rodeo Drive. "Then I guess it's a good thing I'm salaried and not hourly," she snapped.

"Whoa, seems like someone woke up on the wrong side of the bed," Nalani joked.

Her friend grabbed her coffee and took a long drag of caffeine before replying. "That would imply that I actually got some sleep." Despite her disheveled state, Madison couldn't hide the sly grin slowly lighting up her face. "The man is a sex god. I've never met anyone who comes even close to his…" Madison paused, a twinkle in her eye as she chose her words carefully. "Let's just say he is very *gifted*… and he is very generous about sharing those *gifts*."

A pang of longing threatened to put a damper on Nalani's sunny Saturday as she realized how lucky her friend was to have found one of the good guys. Trevor McLean was everything a man should be in Nalani's dreams—tall, dark, and oh so sexy. Most importantly, he was a gentleman who would treat Madison like the Valley Princess she was.

Madison took another swig of coffee and added, "Thank goodness I have another outfit here to change into, or I would have been even later."

The mammoth grandfather clock in the hall outside the club office chimed one regal bong telling Nalani she was running late. She motioned a quick wave to the tired manager of Runway as she headed out of the office and down the long hall toward the walk-in closet where she stored the tools of her housekeeping trade.

Like every lock in the building, Nalani leaned in to provide her retinal scan to gain entry into the spacious closet, lined with shelves of linens and cleaning supplies. In the middle of the space waited her rolling cart, already stocked and ready to tackle the afternoon's work.

All eight guest rooms in the mansion had been occupied the night before and were expected to be fully booked again that night as well, which meant she had just a few hours to return the messy suites back into the pristine and elegant rooms rich people gladly paid up to five-grand a night for on weekends. A couple VIPs from the band performing a live concert in the ballroom-turned-dance-club would be arriving in just a few hours. And since it was a Saturday, every unspoken for room would be snapped up by the end of the night, taken by horny couples unable to wait the short drive home before consummating the sexual dance they'd started in one of the two clubs on the floors below.

She waited until she'd arrived in front of the first suite door to pull her smartphone out of the deep pocket of her neat uniform dress. It only took a moment to pull up the housekeeping app they used to track arrivals and departures of their guests. While the mansion wasn't a traditional hotel, the trio of owners—Jaxson, Chase, and Emma—spared no expense to make sure their employees had the tools they needed to do their jobs.

Not for the first time, Nalani said a silent prayer of thanks for the steady job. Since starting at Runway, she finally felt like she was in control of her life again… no small feat, considering where she'd been just a few short years ago.

Determined to knock out her work on this floor as quickly as she could, she let herself into the London suite recently vacated by the major-league baseball player who'd slept there the night before. A quick scan of the spacious room made her suspect he'd invited half his team to party with him. She sighed as she went to work, cleaning up the dozen empty beer bottles scattered on every flat surface of the space. The number of spent condoms piled into the small wastepaper basket near the desk told the story of the debauchery that had taken place just a few hours before.

A familiar tingling sensation sprang to life in her pussy. She considered her perpetual sexual frustration a small price to pay for landing the job working for the Cartwright-Davidson's. As if caring for the well-used bedrooms didn't present enough sexual fodder for her imagination, cleaning in the BDSM club, Black Light, had been eye opening. She could feel her cheeks flushing red just thinking about the odd pieces of furniture, sexual equipment, and erotic artwork on display a few floors below her.

A piercing cry broke her out of her daydreaming. It had been muffled and short. She stood stock still, listening hard, finally deciding she'd been hearing things since music playing in the distance was the only sound flitting through the space. She'd just resumed scrubbing the bathroom sink when a much louder, sharper scream unmistakably rang out.

Peeling off her rubber gloves and throwing them into the sink, Nalani rushed through the suite and out into the hall. The screaming had stopped, but she was able to follow the muffled cries down the hall until she stopped in front of the Hong Kong suite. It was the last room, farthest from the grand staircase, and the most opulent.

She didn't need to check her app to know which guest was registered in the room. Henry Ainsworth, Hollywood's moneyman—and as best she could tell, resident asshole—loved this particular suite. In fact, he often paid a premium to secure this particular room on the weekends he was in town. He said it was because he loved the views from the balcony out onto the spacious grounds, but Nalani suspected it was the added privacy of being at the end of the hall.

This wasn't the first time she'd heard crying behind the French double doors of the Hong Kong room and suspected it wouldn't be the last—and she hated it. She knew she should mind her own business, after all, the privacy afforded the rich and famous while in the mansion was exactly what kept them coming back to dump their money, again and again. She'd watched the fans flock around the celebrities, selling their soul for a brush with the rich and famous. Being chosen to accompany someone like Henry Ainsworth to his expensive suite was considered a score for most women. They just wouldn't realize the high, very personal price they would be paying for the privilege until it was too late.

The crying behind the door stopped. Nalani should leave. It was none of her business what two consenting adults chose to do in the privacy of their own suite. Since Mr. Ainsworth had rented the suite for the entire weekend, perhaps she'd be lucky enough to be able to avoid cleaning his room today. As handsome as the older gentleman was, he creeped her out.

She had just turned to walk away when a rhythmic pounding filled the hall. She didn't need to use her imagination to picture what was happening on the other side of the French doors. For the briefest of moments, the thrum in her pussy returned, reminding her it had been entirely too long since she'd even been on a date, let alone been close enough to anyone to be intimate. But all thoughts of sex vanished when the pounding was drowned out by the long wail of "Stop!" screamed from behind the locked doors.

Nalani halted in her tracks. She was tempted to throw her hands over her ears to block the escalating sounds of distress from inside the suite. The walls weren't thin, which meant the sharp sounds of a hard banging accompanied by escalating panicked sobs alarmed her. Unable to ignore her conscious, she spun and returned to the door. Her hand itched to pound on the wood, but she forced herself to respect the promise of extraordinary privacy for their VIP guests like Mr. Ainsworth. She froze, indecisive. Maybe she should run get Madison to see how she would like to handle….

The renewed piercing scream of "It hurts!" followed by what sounded like rumbling laughter helped her make up her mind. She stepped up to the retinal scanner to the right of the door, and the lock clicked. Before she could lose her nerve, she barged through the door, determined to help the poor woman crying out.

She rushed through the tiled foyer, rounding the corner into the open floor plan of the opulent suite. Too late, she realized just how different it was to *see* a woman in distress rather than *hearing* it. The bravado she'd felt to rush in to help fled as quickly as the breath in her lungs when her brain caught up with the scene in front of her. The vision slammed into her, making her sway on her feet.

The redheaded woman in front of her couldn't be more than twenty-one years old. While she may qualify as a woman, she had a child-like vulnerability compared to the much older man who presently had his hands wrapped around the young woman's throat from behind.

It wasn't that the crying woman was naked that shocked Nalani the most. It was the absolutely obscene position she'd been tied down in, coupled with the bright red stripes sprayed across her otherwise milky-white skin that upset her. That and the fact despite him looking directly at Nalani, Henry Ainsworth hadn't slowed his thrusting hips at all. A devious smirk lit his otherwise handsome face as he raked his hungry gaze up and down Nalani even as he dipped his cock again and again into another woman's body.

The redhead choked out another sob as tears and snot fell down her face to plop into the pool of wetness already waiting on the seat of the chair below her.

Why isn't he stopping? I know he sees me.

"You'll have to just wait your turn, honey. I'll be done with this one soon, then we can have some fun."

It took a full five seconds for his words to register in her brain. The asshole thought she'd come to join him, not stop him.

Well, of course, he thinks that. You haven't said a word.

"You're hurting her."

The asshole had the nerve to grin, keeping his thrusts hard and fast as he stood behind the woman draped over and tied-down to the tall-backed chair in the middle of the room. He'd spread her legs wide to the outside edge of the chair while her arms and hands were tied to the armrests of the chair. The hand printed breasts swayed under her to the brutal rhythm of the fucking in action.

"She likes it." He slapped the woman's asscheek as he added,

"Don't you, slut?" He punctuated his question with an extra hard thrust that drew a renewed cry out of the abused woman. The resulting volley of swats against her ass increased until she was sobbing.

"Stop! Can't you see you're really hurting her?"

"Of course, I see, and I'm telling you she likes it, don't you whore?" His voice had turned menacing as he grabbed the long red locks and yanked his partner's head back with a snap.

Red fingermarks circled her stretched neck where the older man had squeezed too hard. The woman's panicked gaze met Nalani's as she cried her lie, "I like it! I like it!"

The asshole had the nerve to bark a laugh as he simultaneously let go of his grip on her hair, letting the woman's head flop, pulled down by gravity and defeat, finally stepping away from her body.

Henry Ainsworth stalked around his captive, beelining his way toward Nalani in all of his naked glory. His sudden movement caught her off guard, distracted as she was by the sight of his engorged, ugly cock, jutting out from his manscaped groin. The veined shaft bent to the side at an odd angle.

He was almost all the way to her when her fight-or-flight instincts kicked in. Nalani spun around and took off, running toward the exit. When she'd entered the room, she'd only thought about the safety of the woman tied to the chair. It had never dawned on her that her own safety might be at risk if she intervened.

Her hand was on the handle, the door opened a few inches, when Henry Ainsworth slammed the weight of his body against her back, crashing them both forward against the wood door, slamming it closed with a loud bang.

She fought to be free of his pressing body, alarmed at how hard the penis was poking against her lower back.

"Shhh. I'll show you a good time. Come join our party."

"Are you crazy? I'm working!"

"I'm sure Jaxson won't mind you taking extra good care of one of his VIP's. You can start by telling me your name."

"I said, let me go!" Truly panicked, Nalani flailed as hard as she could to be free of him. He leaned in close enough, his bad breath almost made her gag.

"Now, now. If you don't settle down, I just might be forced to let Jaxson and Chase know about your major mistake today."

"What mistake? You're the one making the huge mistake," she shouted.

"No, little voyeur. I was having consensual fun with my guest. You, on the other hand, broke an important policy by letting yourself into my room without knocking first and without identifying yourself as housekeeping when you entered. Then you stood there, uninvited, spying on me having sex. I'm pretty sure you'd be in a lot of trouble with the owners… if they ever found out about it that is."

His veiled threat wasn't lost on her. He was right. What a fool she'd been to enter his room without at least knocking first. Oh, how she wished she'd gone to get Madison before confronting the asshole.

Righteous anger helped her lift her foot, crashing it down on the asshole's bare foot at the exact moment she flailed in his arms, thrusting out her ass in an attempt to make him release her. His own grunt of pain brought her almost as much joy as her freedom. Distracted by his discomfort allowed her the time to fling the door open and rush out into the hall. She took off running as fast as she could toward the Runway office.

She didn't make it far. Just a few doors down the hall, she crashed into the hard chest of none-other-than Shane Covington, her number one celebrity crush, as he exited the Paris suite.

"Whoa, there, little lady. Where are you off to so quickly?"

~

IRONICALLY, Shane Covington was used to women, and a few men, throwing themselves at him — literally. He was even used to them crying, trembling, and even fainting when they met their celebrity crush for the first time. It went with the territory of being an international celebrity.

What he wasn't used to was women falling apart, knowing it had nothing to do with meeting him. That was exactly what was happening as he held the shaking woman up in front of him. Her legs had given out under her, and he suspected she'd crumple to the ground in a heap if he let go of her. Her breathing was erratic as if she'd just finished running a race. The rosy hue on her olive cheeks shone with perspiration, but it was the sheer panic in her eyes that told her story.

She was afraid.

And beautiful.

But afraid.

"What's got you spooked?" he asked after his assessment.

Her frantic glance back down the hall gave him his first clue. He followed her gaze to see the double doors at the end of the hall open and none other than Henry Ainsworth exit. He was in the process of closing the thick Runway robe provided to guests in each suite, but he hadn't bothered to hide his erection, even after his robe was closed, tenting the terrycloth in a telltale sign of his continued arousal.

An unexpected pang of jealousy surfaced before Shane tamped it down. It was ridiculous to be jealous of the older man. Sure, the woman in his arms was beautiful, but beautiful women were a dime a dozen in Hollywood—at least for men like Shane.

"There you are, sweetheart. I know you love to play hard to get, but I really would like you to come back to our room so we can pick up where we left off."

Lucky bastard. Shane had heard many of the hushed rumors in Hollywood about Henry Ainsworth's notorious sexcapades. Words like orgies, swapping, and sadistic were common themes of the wagging tongues. He understood, when you are one of the richest and most powerful men in a glamorous industry, you get to make your own rules.

With regret, he prepared to release the woman in his arms, but when he glanced back down at her, fear remained etched on her face. He felt her struggling in his arms, trying to wiggle her way behind him, careful to keep Shane between her and the approaching man.

He had no idea what was happening between the two people in the hall with him, but the soft whimper from the dark-haired beauty as Ainsworth advanced triggered a fierce urge to protect her.

"Sorry, Henry. Looks like this one might be second guessing your date." Shane kept his voice light, not wanting to make an enemy out of one of the most powerful men in the industry. He didn't miss the hardness in the older man's eyes as he responded.

"Oh, we aren't on a date, are we naughty girl?" There was nothing playful in his tone.

Shane was confused until Henry continued.

"You'd better be careful. This little bitch let herself into my room while I was… predisposed. I caught her spying on me, like a stalker. For all I know, she was trying to steal something while I wasn't paying attention."

His accusation finally convinced the shaking woman to step out and be seen.

"That's a lie! I would never steal from a guest!"

Shane had been so distracted by her beauty before, only now did he notice she was wearing what looked like a housekeeping uniform. Pieces of the puzzle were starting to fall into place.

"I'm sure she didn't know the room was still occupied," Shane interjected, trying to defuse the situation, only the woman was not helping.

"Oh, I knew the room was occupied. I only went in because I

could hear a woman crying out behind the door. She was telling him she was in pain and asking him to stop!"

Fuck. I don't need this kinda drama. I need to just mind my own business.

Even as he thought it, the protective wall he'd constructed between the housekeeper and Henry Ainsworth solidified more. While he was pretty sure Ainsworth was harmless, there was no denying the woman hiding behind him had thought she was helping someone in need.

"I won't deny things can get loud when I'm playing with my… dates… but when I stay at Runway, I expect to have my privacy respected. Did you break into my room to take photos?"

"No! I would never…"

"Am I going to see video of this on TMZ tonight?"

She was flustered by his accusation. "I was just trying to help…"

"Well, you didn't help. You interrupted me. Inconvenienced me. I demand to know your name. I have Jaxson Davidson on speed-dial. I think it's time he heard about how rude some of his employees are."

"Oh God… I can't lose my job…" Her words were soft, under her breath. The beauty was almost hyperventilating at Henry's threat to call her boss.

Shane didn't know her story, but that didn't stop him from continuing to play the role of her protector.

"I'm sure this was just a misunderstanding. I'm sure you're really sorry, right?" He'd turned to stare down at her, waiting for her to look up into his eyes. She was a full foot shorter, so when she did look up, she had to crane her neck.

She looked so lost… so vulnerable, triggering every protective bone in his body. She opened her mouth several times as if she were going to speak, but no words came out. Wanting to bring the awkward silence that had descended on the hallway to a close, he instructed her again. "Say you're sorry, young lady. Tell Mr. Ainsworth it will never happen again."

He'd used his best Dom voice, the tone he used in scenes as he dominated willing submissives at Black Light. He was sure he'd never seen the woman in front of him at the club in the basement of the building. If he had, he would have remembered. She was a real beauty—even without makeup or designer clothes.

He nodded, urging her to follow his lead. When she spoke, her quiet "I'm sorry" was almost a whisper. He felt a stir as blood rushed to his own cock. He felt like a prick, getting turned on at her obvious distress, but considering humiliation was his kink of choice, it was impossible not to be affected by the vulnerable submission etched on the beauty's face as she followed his command.

"And…" he urged.

"It will never happen again," she answered, the tears in her caramel eyes threatening to spill over and down her cheek.

"Damn straight, it won't. If it does, I'll have your job. You got that?" Henry Ainsworth threatened. When she didn't answer, he added a stern, "I didn't hear you."

Confusion clouded her gaze. She must have replayed Ainsworth's threat again before she added a simple, "Yes."

Ainsworth was a real dick. "Yes, what?"

The combination of anger and embarrassment in her eyes turned Shane's semi-hard erection to rock. Damn, she would be fun to dominate. He found himself wishing her quiet, "Yes, sir" had been directed toward him instead of the older jerk in the hall.

He hadn't realized she'd been holding her breath until the door slamming closed at the end of the hallway had her exhaling like a balloon that had been popped. Whatever bravado she'd mustered to confront Ainsworth had fled, and he could feel her trembling again.

He was tempted to pull her into the room he'd just left to try to comfort her but refused to take further advantage of her distress. Glancing around the wide hallway, he found a padded bench just a few feet down the hall. She was like putty in his hands as she let him lead her to the seat.

"I think you should sit down," he instructed, turning her, so her back was to the wall.

She tried to resist, "I need to get back to work. I've wasted...."

He cut her off with a simple command, "Sit."

She complied immediately.

Once she was seated, he squatted down in front of her, putting them at eye level. She broke their eye contact to glance nervously down the hall, making sure they were alone, and Henry Ainsworth had indeed gone back into his room.

"Now. Let's try to sort things out, shall we?" He asked although it wasn't really a question.

"There is nothing to sort. I made a mistake. It won't happen again."

He watched her carefully, picking up on the defiant edge to her response.

"Why do I not believe you're agreeing you made a mistake?"

"Well, I did." Her reply was abrupt and stronger now that Ainsworth was gone.

"And what was that mistake again?" He expected her to answer going into a guest's room without knocking.

"I forgot rich and powerful men get to do whatever the hell they want to do to defenseless women," she snapped defensively

He wasn't entirely sure if she was referring to herself or the unseen woman still in Ainsworth's suite. He suspected it didn't matter.

"Listen, I'm not really sure what was or wasn't happening down there, but I think it's best if you try to steer clear of Henry Ainsworth for a while, don't you?"

"Oh, you'd better believe I want to be as far away as possible. There's just one problem. I work here, and he stays in that suite several weekends each month."

"That'll make it more difficult, but I'm sure he'll want to avoid you as well." She didn't look the least bit convinced of that assertion, and he had to admit, what little he knew about Ainsworth told him she was right. He decided to change the subject.

"Now, why don't you tell me what your name is?"

"Why? So, you can report me to Jaxson and Chase?" The panic in her voice was back.

"Not at all. I'd just like to get your name. I'll go first. I'm Shane Covington."

"I know who you are, Mr. Covington. I'd have to be living under a rock to not know who you are."

He was used to people recognizing him, yet it still pleased him knowing she knew his name.

"Then it's not fair. You know my name, but I don't know yours… yet." Little did she know, he wouldn't be letting her leave without it.

She hesitated, before quietly answering, "Nalani."

"What a beautiful name. So unique."

"Thanks. It's a family name."

"Spanish?"

"Hawaiian. My mom's family was from there." He detected sadness in her voice.

The dark hair and eyes… olive skin… it made sense. She looked Polynesian.

"It's great to meet you, Nalani." He'd been headed out to meet friends for a late brunch. His sudden urge to invite her to go along was ridiculous—she was a housekeeper, and he was an iconic movie star.

The blush in her cheeks as she wiggled under his stare, embarrassed, reminded him of how long it had been since he'd played. He needed to get laid. It was the only explanation for the uncharacteristic intimacy he felt with the petite woman in front of him.

He stood tall, holding his hand out like a gentleman. She yanked her hand back as soon as he'd helped her to her feet. For several long seconds, they each stood awkwardly, reluctant to say goodbye, yet unsure what else there was to say. It was Nalani who put an end to their standoff.

"I really do need to get back to work. I believe you're staying over again tonight, right, Mr. Covington?"

"Call me Shane, and yeah. I'm staying over for a few weeks, actually. I'm having some work done at my house, and I didn't want to deal with it."

"Okay… Shane. When will you return? I'll be sure to have your room cleaned before then."

He wasn't sure why it bothered him she would be the one to clean his room. On the one hand, it pleased him she would be in his room, intimately touching his personal things. But in the same breath, he had to acknowledge his disappointment she was a housekeeper and not a submissive on her knees in front of him at Black Light.

"No need to clean my room."

"But…"

"No buts. I'm good, and I'd rather you take off a little early and do something fun for yourself tonight instead of working so hard."

"Well… okay. Thank you, Mr. Covington. I mean… Mr. Shane." The blush was back in her cheeks, and he was happy to know this time, he'd been the cause. He enjoyed watching her squirm as he raised his right eyebrow in disapproval until she finally tacked on a quiet, "Shane."

"You're very welcome, Nalani."

CHAPTER 2

What a long day. Nalani couldn't wait to get home and take off her uniform—mostly her bra—and slide into a hot bath. She usually finished up work by early evening when the clubs were getting busy, but she'd stayed late that night, helping Avery clean out the walk-in pantry. There was a big shipment of food arriving early next week, and the chef had asked Nalani to help her free up some space.

Normally, that was the sort of project she didn't mind—she loved the people she worked with and enjoyed helping out where she could—but today had been anything but normal. Her brush with Henry Ainsworth, then Shane Covington hours before had left her rattled. Nalani couldn't wait to lock herself in the privacy of her own apartment so she could unwind and think through all that happened.

One thing she already knew with clarity—she'd made an enemy today. And not just any enemy—a powerful enemy. It was clear Henry Ainsworth didn't like nor was he used to being told no. She wished she could just forget about the ugly encounter, but Nalani couldn't help wondering if the redhead was okay. She'd purposefully avoided being in the public areas of the mansion where she might run into the older guest, which also meant she had missed seeing him or the young woman leaving. She hoped the restrained woman had not been lying when she had assured Nalani all was well.

Nalani had just grabbed her purse and pulled her car keys out when a text chimed on her smartphone. Since almost everyone who texted her worked at Runway or Black Light, she hesitated before digging in her bag to pull out her mobile phone. When she saw the text waiting for her on the screen, she wished she hadn't heard it. As much as she'd love to ignore the incoming message, her conscience and work ethic wouldn't allow it.

~

Text from Elijah:

Sry to bug U. If U R here, come 2 BL. Accident. Help!

~

The brief message was so typical of the Master Dom. At least she was able to understand this message. Half the time, she had to ask for clarification on his crazy abbreviations.

~

Text back to Elijah:

Still here. On my way!

~

She threw her keys in her bag and dropped her purse on the office desk just as his return of a simple *thx* came through.

Her feet ached as she headed toward the small elevator that

would whisk her several floors below the Runway office. She'd been on them all day and had been looking forward to taking a load off. She prayed whatever accident they'd had would be quick and easy to clean up.

"Hey, Nalani. Good to see you down here on a Saturday night. You here to play?" The question was posed by Tyler, Elijah's second in command at Black Light, as soon as she got off the elevator in the heart of the club.

"Oh, hell, no. I'm just coming down to help Elijah clean up something. He didn't give any details."

The music was pounding, and she had to lean close to his ear to be heard. Despite the dim lighting in the main dungeon, Nalani could make out several couples already getting started on their sexy scenes for the night. Always curious about the BDSM lifestyle, she did her best not to stare.

"Does he ever?" Tyler grinned as he asked the rhetorical question.

"Do you know where he is?" she asked, tearing her gaze away from the couple going at it on the stage closest to the elevator.

"Last time I saw him was in the bar around the corner."

"Okay, thanks." Nalani pulled the velvet curtain aside as she teased the dungeon monitor. "Have fun. Not everyone gets to watch people have sex all night while getting paid."

"Don't I know it. I'm living the dream," Tyler teased, genuinely happy.

The lighting and sounds changed on the other side of the heavy velvet curtain. She'd spent a fair amount of time in the social area of the club over the year she'd been working in the mansion. Madison and Avery liked to come down on slow nights in the middle of the week for a night cap, and if Nalani was still around, she'd join them.

Tonight, being Saturday night, the place was packed. She pressed through the crowd, making her way to the bar to see if

Susie knew where Elijah was. The crowd waiting for drinks was several people deep. At five foot three, she was too short to see through the crowd and knew she had to weave her way around behind the bar if she was going to find Susie.

She had just broken through a split in the crowd as she neared the back stairs where Black Light members could come down from Runway. Finding Susie became a moot point when she rounded the end of the bar to find a huge debris field on the back bar that had spilled onto the floor. Susie was bending over, a small garbage can in her hand, picking up the largest shards of glass from the mess on the floor.

"What the hell happened? Did someone start throwing bottles of booze?" she asked, trying to figure out what had caused the mess.

"I wish. That would have at least been entertaining." The head bartender stood, stretching her back while waving her glass-filled hand toward the mirrored back wall of the bar. "A whole fucking shelf broke. Not only did it drop all the bottles from that shelf, but it crashed into the bottom shelf as well. We've lost thousands of dollars of inventory, not to mention I've been ignoring the waiting guests, trying to clean the shit up enough, my crew and I don't cut ourselves to shreds on the shards."

"Okay, well, let me deal with the cleanup. You go take care of the paying customers."

"No fucking way. I'm not making you clean this up on your own. It's a goddamn debacle."

Nalani smiled at Susie's normally colorful language. Tonight, the bartender was right, though. It was a Goddamn mess. She almost didn't know where to start. Still, she persisted.

"Seriously, the natives are getting restless. Go take care of them and let me handle this."

Her friend looked unsure but finally gave in. "Fine, but I'll be back to help as soon as I get the line down. I hope everyone is happy with beers, soda, and water since most of my high-end booze just went down the drain... literally."

Nalani busied herself with the cleanup, starting with a trip to her cleaning supply closet, coming back with a large rolling garbage can and all the other supplies she'd need for the job. Most importantly, she donned long rubber gloves and got to work picking up the largest pieces of the broken glass.

It took her almost twenty minutes of bending and reaching to get the space cleaned up enough to be ready to mop and do the final wash down. Her back was aching, and her feet were on fire. That soaking bath waiting for her at home was more welcome than ever.

She'd tried to tune out the buzz of the crowd while she worked, in part, because she kept catching snippets of sexy conversations that made her feel like a spy, listening in on things that were none of her business. More importantly, she was ultra-aware, in her housekeeping uniform, cleaning up the broken bottles and spilled expensive booze, she wasn't one of them—one of the privileged.

As a glass half-full kinda girl, most days, she was more than grateful for her steady job and good friends. She knew things could have turned out very differently for her and was determined to remain grateful for the opportunities she'd been given after a very rough start in the world.

But the downside of working for the Cartwright-Davidson's was the daily reminder, she didn't really belong in the opulence found under the roof of the mansion. Oh, they never once tried to make her feel like less. In fact, they went out of their way to make her feel needed and valued—as an employee.

Fuck! She'd been so distracted in her own little world, she hadn't been careful enough. Not one minute after she'd taken the rubber gloves off, thinking she had the glass cleaned up, a stray splinter found the palm of her hand.

"Shit," she said to no one in particular. The din of the

compressed space was so loud, she assumed no one would hear her curse.

She was wrong.

"Here, let me see that."

The voice behind her was familiar. Muscular arms wrapped around her from the back, reaching out to grab both her hands as red blood dripped down to the recently cleaned floor.

"Let's get you over to the bar sink and run some cold water over that cut."

The man's voice was deep, authoritative—yummy. She connected with his gravelly voice at the same moment they stepped up to the sink, and she could see their reflection in the mirrored bar wall, him a full head higher than her.

All thoughts of her bleeding hand flew out of her mind the second she realized it was Shane Covington who'd rushed to help her. Shane Covington who was triaging her injury like an emergency technician.

Shane Covington who had his arms wrapped around her, his muscular body pressed into her back intimately. Nalani's brain scrambled while her tongue-tied into knots—being hugged by an international superstar would do that to a girl.

The shock of the cold water hitting the open gash on her left palm broke her out of her paralysis.

"Owie! That stings!"

His grip on her left wrist tightened as she tried to yank her hand free.

"Leave it under the water. I don't want you to get an infection."

"But, it hurts," she protested, wiggling in his arms.

"Sorry, but in case you missed it, you're at Black Light. I hate to tell you, I'm a sadist. Does it make me an asshole if hearing that kinda turns me on?"

His question caught her off-guard. She glanced up from the sink to see the sexy grin spreading across the actor's handsome face. He was teasing her. She wasn't sure if it was the sight of her own blood or his feral look that was responsible for her light-headed wobble.

"Whoa, there." With ninja reflexes, Shane's right arm wrapped around her waist to hold her steady while his left hand remained outstretched, holding her wound under the water. His gaze penetrated her in their reflection as his lips brushed the shell of her ear.

"You aren't one of those people who faint at the sight of blood, are you?"

"I'm not fainting," she defended.

"Uh huh. That's why I'm the only thing keeping you from face planting right now."

Her heart fluttered under his intense glare. Nalani was used to fading into the background—never in the limelight. His heated scrutiny warmed her. She felt the full-body blush spreading head to toe as their eyes remained locked in their reflection. Her tongue felt heavy in her suddenly parched mouth as her brain tried to process what was happening.

It had to be a misunderstanding. There was no way *the* Shane Covington was flirting with her—not a housekeeper. He was an actor, she reminded herself. He was used to flirting with everyone. That could explain his smile and willingness to help her. It didn't quite explain the erection she felt hardening against her lower back, however.

Embarrassed, she thrust her ass out in an attempt to push him backward, but he remained molded to her like locked puzzle pieces, turning her thrust into an R-rated dance.

Was that a flash of disappointment in his eyes just before he broke their stare to glance down at the running water?

Well, of course, he's disappointed. I'm not a famous model.

"Let's have a look at this now, shall we? We need to decide if you need stitches," he added, pulling her hand out of the water to inspect it.

The gash was about an inch-long right in the middle of her left palm. It was definitely more than a scratch, but there was no way in hell she was going to the hospital for stitches.

"I'm sure it'll be fine," she assured him, embarrassed at the continued attention.

"I don't know. It's borderline. We need to see if we can get it to stop bleeding. Stay here."

It was an order, yet the second he stepped away, her fight-or-flight instincts propelled her into action, turning to escape. Two hands clamped down hard on her hips, yanking her back against his hard body. Droplets of blood dripped from her outstretched hand onto the floor.

"Was I unclear, little girl?" he asked, his voice as hard as the appendage at her back.

The man personified every sexual fantasy she'd ever had. Still, there had to be a mistake. Her accident must have interrupted him in the middle of a date with a rich socialite or maybe a fashion model. That was the only explanation for his continued arousal. Men like Shane Covington could snap his fingers and have any woman he wanted. He didn't need to slum it with the help.

His fingers dug into her hips, holding her tight. The only good thing was she'd turned to leave, so they could no longer see each other's reflection in the mirror. She did her best to pretend he was just a random guy and not a larger-than-life celebrity rocking her world, but her name on his lips made that impossible.

"Nalani… what did I tell you?"

Her brain told her he was overstepping. Who the hell did he think he was, giving her orders? The rest of her body, however, recognized him for what he was… a dominant.

"Stay put," she whispered as another few drops of blood dropped to the floor. She wasn't even sure if he'd heard her over the noise of the bar.

His "good girl" against her ear was a powerful aphrodisiac, which was ludicrous since there was absolutely nothing sexy about getting injured. Still, as she allowed herself to be lifted up like a rag doll by those strong hands on her hips, then redeposited back in front of the still running water at the sink, she couldn't stop the clenching at her core.

"Now, don't move. Understand?" he pressed, still holding her as if he were afraid she would try to bolt again.

She couldn't resist looking up at his reflection again. The hard set of his scruff-covered jaw took her breath away. She could tell he was waiting for her to answer, despite having no idea what to say.

She finally went with a simple, "Yes, sir."

The sexy smile that lit up his face should be outlawed.

"Man, I do love the sound of those two words directed my way, especially from those full lips of yours. Let's get your hand fixed, and we'll see if you can tell me *yes, sir* a few more times tonight." He paused before sternly adding, "Now I mean it. Don't take your hand out of the water."

Her brain felt scrambled. He was really flirting with her—Nalani, the housekeeper.

Adding to her confusion, she felt a chill when he stepped away. It was ludicrous, but she missed his heat… his strength… his masculine smell.

She closed her eyes, taking deep breaths, willing herself not to read too much into the innocent encounter. He was just being a gentleman, stepping in to help her when she was injured. He'd get her wound wrapped, then go back to seducing any number of women present who would gladly drop to their knees to service Shane Covington.

A pang of something close to jealousy hit her at the thought of him moving on to play with someone else that night, which was completely insane. She already had a great story to remember later in the privacy of her tiny apartment. Nalani knew she'd be replaying tonight's events over and over for many nights to come. When she turned her lights off and was alone in her bed… free to pretend his attention was more than him just being kind. To pretend she was one of the rich members of Black Light, there for a date with the larger-than-life action hero.

He was only gone a few minutes, and when he returned, he had the stocked first-aid kit they kept behind the bar. He flung open the container and started rummaging through the supplies, picking out the items he wanted.

Around them, the crowd chattered on, some shouting drink orders to Susie and the other bartender on duty while others chit-chatted with friends and lovers.

She hadn't finished cleaning up the spill before she injured herself, and Shane was having trouble finding a place to lay out his supplies. Before she knew what was happening, he'd thrown everything back into the kit and slammed the lid closed. Grabbing a nearby towel, he turned off the running water and wrapped her hand in the cloth before reaching out to take her uninjured hand.

"Come with me. We need to find someplace better to work on this."

"But… I can just wrap it when I get home."

He was pulling her behind him, out from behind the bar and through the throng of members hovering in the bar area. Once they broke out of the crowd, she almost had to jog to keep up with his long strides as he headed for the double doors leading to the theater. An odd electric charge emanated from where their hands remained locked together.

The second they got into the dimly lit room and the doors closed behind them, the crush of the people talking in the club gave way to an awkwardly quiet theater where the only sounds were from the X-rated movie playing on the huge screen, along with the equally steamy sex scenes playing out by the handful of couples spread out in the space.

She'd always known the sticky deposits on the expensive leather seats were very personal body fluids, but tonight, watching the action, she had a new appreciation for the fun members had while making the messes she cleaned up.

Shane pulled her along toward the front of the room, where there were several open seats together. About halfway down the aisle, Nalani started to pull on their link, trying to get him to stop. She was barely brave enough to watch porn movies at home in the privacy of her own bedroom, she sure as hell wasn't going to watch one in public… with Shane Covington watching *her*.

"Come along, little girl. The sooner we get started on patching you up, the sooner you'll be able to escape since that's clearly what you're obsessed with doing."

He wasn't wrong, yet his playful glance over his shoulder got her heart racing faster than any sexy movie ever could. She stopped pulling, allowing herself to be led to a plush lounge seat at the front of the theater. The screen was only ten feet away, making the thick cock of the actor presently plowing the ass of a tied-up submissive huge.

Shane motioned for her to sit, then shocked her by kneeling, facing her while placing the first-aid kit on the floor. The room was dim, but her seat was close to one of the small wall sconces, providing light for him to see the supplies he needed.

"Now, let me get a look at this hand and see if the bleeding has slowed down." He pulled her left hand toward him. "You just sit back and enjoy the entertainment."

SHANE WAS THOROUGHLY ENJOYING the best show in town.

And no, it wasn't the X-rated porn flick on the screen at his back. It was the plethora of emotions playing out on the face of the beautiful woman sitting in front of him. He'd known Nalani was pretty when they'd met earlier that day, but tonight, he realized just how gorgeous the natural beauty really was.

The golden flecks in her deep brown eyes caught in the flickering light of the theater. She had thick, long, dark hair he would love to thrust his fingers through as he pounded her from behind like the action on the display behind him. But it was her flawless complexion, currently blushing pink as her attention remained riveted to the on-screen tryst, that had him wishing for a chance to re-enact the on-screen scene with her in the privacy of his suite upstairs.

Even as he thought it, he dismissed the idea. As much fun as it had been to flirt with the housekeeper, he could tell she was a novice. A small pang of guilt tried to wedge in, putting a damper on his enjoyment watching her wiggling in her seat. Still, she worked at Black Light, so just how innocent could she really be? It could be fun, trying to get to the bottom of that particular question.

He took his time cleaning her cut, wrapping it in gauze and applying enough pressure to stem the bleeding. She wouldn't need stitches, but by the time he'd finished bandaging her up, he could smell her arousal, telling him her petite body might need some other type of attention.

Dare he? Surely, it wouldn't hurt to have a bit more fun with the Polynesian beauty. Considering his kink of choice was humiliation play, he just couldn't resist seeing just how red he could make her cheeks—both sets.

He had a front-row seat—literally—as Nalani's breath hitched, quickening as the guy behind him pounded his onscreen sub like a jackhammer. The faster the scene played out, the more Nalani rocked in her seat, subconsciously trying to scratch her very personal itch.

Suddenly remembering she wasn't surfing porn sites alone

in the privacy of her home, she turned panicked eyes, as wide as saucers on him, blanching from beet red to pale chalk when she realized he'd been studying her. Her mortification fanned his own hunger. His already erect cock throbbed for release from his confining jeans.

Forcing restraint, he settled for teasing her verbally. "I'm used to kneeling at Black Light, but I confess it's usually the woman on her knees, not me. But I like the view from down here... and how close it puts me to that sexy smell of yours."

Christ, the embarrassed humiliation in her eyes was his kryptonite.

It was his only complaint about playing at Black Light. The club provided unprecedented privacy, which was so important to men in the public eye like him. It even gave him the opportunity to connect with experienced submissives who came ready to play. He'd found great sex partners in general, but none of the women he'd met had been able to feed his deepest need—the one he kept on a tight rein.

Watching Nalani's embarrassment turn to a feral-like longing tempted him to throw off the reins and see how far he could push her.

"I've taken care of your cut. Now, I'd like to take care of another part of you."

The full lips he'd admired earlier fell open, forming a cute little 'O,' yet she didn't speak, so he pressed her further.

"Do you know what a safeword is?"

Confusion clouded her heated gaze, threatening to extinguish the tenuous thread between them. He reached out to place his hands on her bare knees, enjoying the smooth touch as he pressed her verbally.

"I'm waiting for an answer, Nalani."

"Not really... well, sort of..." Her voice started as a whisper but trailed off to silence.

"A safeword works like magic at Black Light. A safeword brings all play to a halt. No matter what's going on."

"Okay," she whispered softly, not pressing him for more.

"I like to use the traffic light system. It's nice and easy. *Green* means you like what's happening and want more. *Yellow* means you want things to slow down a bit. Maybe have some time to regroup. But *red*... well, that's the magic word that makes everything stop." He stopped to let it all sink in with the novice in front of him. When she said nothing, he quizzed her. "What could you say to make me take my hands off your knees right now?"

Her breath hitched, but she was finally able to squeak out a pinched, "Red?"

"Very good. Let's make the question a bit harder." He paused, enjoying the cocktail of anticipation in her expressive eyes before pressing her. "What color are you feeling right now, Nalani?"

He waited thirty long seconds while she struggled to answer. Her wiggling in her seat had resumed, and the smell of her sex wafted up to tease him. Still, he held, waiting for her consent to proceed. It came in the form of a whispered, "*Green*."

He hadn't realized he'd been holding his breath, waiting for her answer. His "Good girl" brought a small smile to her lips. He found himself wishing he could test her reaction to being called a *naughty girl* or better yet, his *dirty girl* after she'd enjoyed him fucking her sure-to-be tight ass.

And she would enjoy it. He didn't know how, but he just knew she'd make a perfectly reluctant anal slut. It took all of his iron control not to dive in to test his theory. He'd love to have her kneel on the padded theater seat, facing the couples behind them so they could watch her face as he raised her skirt, ripped off her damp panties, and fucked her pucker while she cried out in equal measures of pain and pleasure.

He was getting ahead of himself.

Shane settled for squeezing her knees, massaging them lightly as he ever-so-slowly tested her resolve by applying enough pressure to begin spreading her legs as he inched his fingers higher on her thighs, kneading her lightly, willing her to relax her tense muscles.

It wasn't until he reached the elastic of her panties, she snapped her legs closed, trapping his thumbs between her squeezing thighs.

"I forgot… I can't… I mean… you shouldn't…" Her shaky voice trailed off.

He didn't know what had spooked her, and he sure as hell didn't want her to leave. Still, he reminded her, "I didn't hear a color, Nalani. Those words you said don't tell me what I need to know right now, do they?"

When she just sat, staring at him with a deer-in-the-headlights look, he exerted more power, spreading her legs wide once again, making sure to brush the apex of her sex. As expected, her panties were soaking wet, contradicting her reticence.

Their eyes locked as Shane trailed his fingers across her bare skin, dipping in occasionally to rub her cotton covered pussy. He kept his motions slow and deliberate, afraid to spook her. She reminded him of a feral colt, just beginning to be tamed. Lucky for her, he was an excellent trainer.

Only when he slipped his finger under the waistband of her panties again did she protest in the worst possible way.

"Red!" she cried out confidently.

Fuck.

Shane released the novice immediately, proving to her the word really did work magic here at Black Light, although he found it interesting it took more control than normal to keep his hands off the innocent.

Disappointed, he leaned back from the beauty, preparing to stand. As fun as it would have been to indoctrinate her into the

BDSM world, he wasn't going to push her where she didn't want to go. Just before he stood, he saw it—her breath hitched, the tears in her eyes, her full lips trembling—regret. She'd been spooked. But why?

"Why did you call *red* if you don't really want me to stop?"

Blood rushed to her cheeks as she glanced away, unable to hold his gaze any longer. She was hiding something. What an idiot. Why hadn't he asked her sooner?

"There's someone else. I'm sorry. I didn't even think..."

"No! That's not it," she rushed to reassure him, confusing him even more.

"Okay, then, what the hell is it?"

How odd he felt unfamiliar insecurity as he waited long seconds for her answer. Shane tried his best not to let being an international heartthrob go to his head—he really did—but the fact of the matter was, women he showed an interest in didn't turn him down... like ever. That Nalani had put the brakes on their impromptu tryst put her in the company of a tiny circle of women who'd rebuffed him in the last few years.

Nalani had been flushed with embarrassed insecurity much of the time he'd spent with her, but when she started taking sips of air while she visibly trembled, he became concerned. Something deeper was going on here than sexual insecurity.

Okay, he really was an idiot. She looked young, but there was no way she was underage. Davidson wasn't stupid enough to hire a kid to work at Black Light or even Runway, for that matter. But... that didn't mean she couldn't be...

"You're a virgin," he stated, sure he'd figured out her secret.

Teary eyes turned back to him quickly, wide with panic as she protested, "No! I'm not... I mean, I'm not a slut or anything, but I'm not a virgin either." She sounded insulted at the idea.

"Then what the fuck is wrong?" he snapped. "Am I that repulsive that you..."

"I have my period, okay? If you must know, I have a tampon

in, and… well, I don't want you to be grossed out or worse, make a mess. These chairs are hard enough to get cum stains out of. Do you have any idea how hard it is to get blood stains out?"

He couldn't stop his bark of laughter. Anyone watching could see her embarrassment turning to anger as he continued to chuckle. He leaned closer, but Nalani was having none of it. The angrier she got at his reaction, the harder she pressed against him, trying to wiggle her way out of the chair and to her feet.

Shane wasn't going to let her escape—not yet. He couldn't let her think he was making fun of her situation. He was laughing at himself for not only not thinking of this possibility but maybe at her for thinking such a thing possibly mattered to him.

She started fighting like a wildcat to be free, and the asshole in him had fun wrestling the beauty into a bear hug to subdue her.

"That's enough. Settle down," he ordered in his most authoritative Dom's voice.

It worked. She stilled in his arms.

He missed seeing her eyes as he hugged her close. What he lost visually, he gained physically. Her perky breasts pressed into his chest as he held her tight. Even through her uniform and his shirt, he could feel her pebbled nipples standing at attention.

The movie behind him had switched scenes. The sound of a woman gagging on a cock as she was face-fucked hard and fast was a sexy soundtrack. He leaned in, placing his lips against the shell of Nalani's ear, darting his tongue out to lick.

"I'm sorry I laughed, but I'm not making fun of you. I couldn't care less about that sort of thing. I can show you a good time, regardless. If you'll let me, that is."

His words hung between them as he started to roam his

hands across her body, wishing the fabric of her uniform wasn't between his fingers and her flesh.

"But… how…"

"Trust me."

He held her tight, caressing her lightly until he felt the hands she'd thrown onto his shoulders start to massage him in small, inviting circles. They stayed in their embrace for several long minutes, silently letting the intimate thread he'd felt tying him to her earlier repair itself until it was stronger than ever.

Had they been seeing each other for a while, tonight would have definitely been an anal domination night, but Nalani wasn't ready for that. They barely knew each other, but still, he was pretty sure what she needed.

Shane moved his right hand, squeezing her sexy body as he moved down. Massaging her left breast through her clothes, placing his palm against her flat tummy while pressing lower… and lower… until he was able to cup her pussy through the layers of fabric in his muscular hand.

Her strangled gurgle against his ear coincided with her hugging him tighter as she thrust her hips forward to increase the friction against her clit. Her gasping breaths as she became more aroused turned him on even more than the sexy aroma of her dripping cunt.

Nalani froze again when he snaked his right hand up under the hem of her skirt to resume petting her pussy through the thin cotton of her panties. Only when she trusted he wouldn't embarrass her by making a big deal out of her having her period did she really relax in his arms.

He knew when she'd finally turned herself over to the scene —her body turned into a pliable noodle, collapsing back against the plush chair with her eyes closed, her breath coming in short pants.

Shane massaged his way down her body, returning his hands to her bare thighs. Unlike the first time he'd been in this position, this time, Nalani let her legs fall apart, opening herself to his petting. Even through her panties, his fingers honed in on her swollen button, pressing it hard enough to bring an untamed groan from the natural beauty writhing with desire in front of him. She cried out louder when he pinched her protruding nipple at the same time he pinched her clit.

The only thing better than watching her coming apart as he played her body like a musical instrument would be watching the passion registering in her eyes as she orgasmed.

"Open your eyes, baby," he ordered just as he felt her body tensing as she succumbed to the pleasure. It took her long seconds to register his request and comply. He wasn't prepared for her to penetrate him with the sexiest glare he'd ever been on the receiving end of as she cracked her eyes open.

Her quiet, "Wow," did wonders for his ego. Hell, he hadn't even got his dick wet, but he felt an odd pride at being able to make someone as beautiful as Nalani literally fall apart.

It was when he felt her tentative touch massaging his own package through his jeans, he balked. God knew he couldn't wait for his own relief, yet hated the idea of her only taking care of his erection out of a sense of quid pro quo.

Shane snapped his fingers around her wrist, halting her fumbling with the zipper of his jeans.

"But I owe you," she protested.

Her words angered him for some irrational reason.

"You don't owe me shit."

"But… you took care of… um… my needs. I can do the same," she replied, still fumbling to get to his zipper.

"Oh, Nalani, baby, you better believe you'll be taking care of me, but it won't be like this." When he was sure she was paying attention, he added. "It was fucking amazing watching you come. Your face was flushed, and you trembled head to toe. And you made the sexiest little tortured moan that went straight to my cock. It makes me want to tie you down and drag another half-dozen orgasms from you until you beg me to stop."

He watched for her reaction to his salacious words. While his observation was spot on, he had an ulterior motive for his dirty rant. Her reluctance, shy embarrassment—she was the textbook dichotomy of innocent reluctance, warring with brazen need.

Recognizing the hidden gem he'd just run across for what it was worth, Shane forced down his current needs, trading them for the longer game with Nalani... Shit, he didn't even know her last name. Hell, he knew almost nothing about her, but he knew this.

She would be in his bed soon... and over his lap, writhing as he paddled her into a frenzy... and on her knees, looking up at him with his cock stuffing those full lips wide... and...

Patience.

"You're going to go home now and peel off all of your clothes. I want you to draw a hot bath and sink inside. Once there, I want you to close your eyes and relive our time together tonight while you touch yourself like the naughty girl I know you are deep down.

"While you do that, I'm going to go upstairs to my suite and strip down as well, only I'm going to crawl into that great big bed all by myself. Only then will I grab my rock-hard cock and stroke myself as I close my eyes and remember what you look like when you climax. I'm going to jack off and shoot my wad all over those nice clean sheets you put on today."

Her breathing was coming in short, shallow pants as he continued with his dirty bedtime story. "And when I wake up in the morning, I'll do it all over again, this time, imagining how you look masturbating in your bathtub while thinking about me."

He waited for her glazed gaze to become more lucid before adding his parting promise.

"When you come to clean my sheets tomorrow, you're gonna find my deposit, and I want you to know you're responsible for that mess. You'll have to think about that as you're cleaning it up, then..."

Shane stopped just long enough to make sure she was really paying attention to him before adding the most important part.

"I'll be waiting for you down here at Black Light tomorrow night at eight. I want you to change into something more comfortable after work and come down. We'll have a drink... get to know each other a bit better... and most importantly, I'll want to hear you describe in detail how it felt to have to clean up my cum, knowing I'd been fantasizing about you when I was touching myself."

Her wide-eyed shock was exactly what he'd been going for. He was going to have so much fun corrupting the reluctant innocent he'd accidentally found.

CHAPTER 3

Shane pulled his sports car up to the valet stand at The Iron Fork exactly ten minutes late, according to the digital clock on his dashboard. That he was here at all was a minor miracle. It had taken all of his efforts not to stay back at the Runway mansion to wait for one sexy housekeeper to show up to work that morning.

It didn't escape him how pitiful it was he was late to a business brunch because he'd been stationed at the tall window of his suite, close to an hour, looking out over the parking lot, hoping to catch a glimpse of the dark-haired beauty who had somehow gotten under his skin—without even trying.

He smiled, thinking about Nalani's face when she arrived to clean his room that afternoon and found the special surprise he'd left for her in his bed. Not only had he left his dried cum as promised, but he'd taken the time to use his finger to draw her name in the sticky liquid he'd deposited while thinking about her sexy orgasm. After he'd done it, he'd felt embarrassed at the almost goofy romance of the gesture. Still, he wished he could be there to see her face when she read his very personal message. He was thinking about what a schmuck he'd been to take things so slow with her the night before.

As he stepped up to the maître d stand, despite several groups of diners waiting to be seated at the popular restaurant, he wasn't surprised to hear, "We've been expecting you, Mr. Covington. Your party is waiting for you at your table. Please, follow me."

Shane weaved through the completely packed restaurant in the heart of Hollywood. Sunday morning was the prime time *see and be seen* time in town. Tourists packed in, cameras at the ready, to snap a photo of their favorite celebrities as they dined with the rich and famous.

It was the last place he wanted to be today.

So, it was with some relief they weaved through the main dining area, through the smaller annex room, past the door to the patio where tables were full of people dining alfresco, and only slowed when they approached the very back booth. It was the only seat in the house that provided a small measure of privacy, which immediately put him on edge.

Only meetings where bad news was to be delivered usually took place back here. Just before they made the last turn toward the corner, he reminded himself he was in the driver's seat of his career. He'd already turned this project down. There could be no bad news since he'd been the one to already deliver it.

I'm just here to eat and run.

That was his last thought as he neared the table, only to find one person sitting at the round table large enough for the eight people he'd been expecting.

"Boeing," he acknowledged first, then turned to the restaurant host. "You've shown me to the wrong table." He resisted leaving off the word *dumbass*. "I'm here to meet with my agent John Graves and a group from Redman Studios."

The maître d looked at the seated man for assistance, clearly confused he'd misunderstood.

Nolan Boeing filled in the blanks as he pushed to his feet. "You're in the right place, Covington." He held his right hand out for a handshake as he reassured Shane. The men shook hands as the restaurant employee slinked off, leaving them to their relative privacy.

"I'm afraid to ask what you're doing here, Nolan."

"Have a seat." The slightly older movie executive waved his arm at an empty chair. "I'll explain over a plate of Eggs Benedict. I've been looking forward to it for days."

The men took seats next to each other, their backs to the restaurant in an attempt to block out the low din of chatter.

"So, which is it?" Shane prompted as a busboy scurried from the shadows to fill his water glass. At Nolan Boeing's confused look, Shane clarified. "You've been looking forward to the Eggs Benedict or this meeting with me?"

The men had known each other for several years. They'd met working on a project several years ago as Shane's career had just been taking off and more recently, had drinks occasionally, sitting at the private bar at Black Light, where both dominant men spent a fair amount of time.

"Definitely the eggs," Nolan answered quickly. The unreadable look on his friend's face made Shane wish he'd canceled the meeting.

"That bad, eh?" he asked as another server deposited a tall Bloody Mary in front of him, a full stalk of celery shooting out at the top.

"I ordered yours with double Grey Goose," Nolan informed him.

Shane took a drag from the strong drink before answering. "I can't wait to hear your pitch."

"Who says I have a pitch?"

"I'm not stupid. They sent you in to change my mind. Let me save us some time here. The answer to whatever you're going to ask is no."

"Hold that thought. You should at least hear me out before you shut me down."

Shane chuckled as he shook his head at the waiter. "I don't need to see the menu. I won't be able to stay for lunch." He held the menu out to the man in uniform, but Nolan Boeing injected.

"Bring him an order of the Eggs Benedict." When Shane gave him a dirty look, Nolan shrugged. "I'll take my chances I can get you to stay long enough to eat. Worst case scenario, I'll take your portion home to heat up for dinner tomorrow night."

The men waited for the server to leave them in privacy before Nolan went to work, trying to change Shane's mind about the movie project at hand. Shane recalled the movie's plot had been solid, but the artistic team they'd put together for the project was a train wreck. Shane didn't want to be even loosely associated with them, let alone the headliner. He couldn't think of one single thing the movie financier could say to him to make him change his mind.

"I just signed on to the project myself last week. Like you, I'd been turning the studio down for over two years on this one."

His friend paused long enough, Shane had to prod him. "And? I'll bite. What changed your mind?"

Nolan grabbed a chunk of baguette from the breadbasket, taking a moment to dip the crusty bread in his plate of olive oil before answering.

"For starters, I made them fire that asshole they had onboard as director."

Shane was impressed. He'd tried to get them to change directors, and the studio wouldn't hear of it. Maybe Nolan Boeing had more pull in town than Shane had given him credit for. Still, it didn't fix all of his concerns.

He could feel Boeing studying him carefully, trying to gauge his body language. When Shane gave nothing away, Nolan continued.

"Next, I told them Amy Parker wasn't a strong enough

female lead for the role of Calista. All they keep talking about is how this project has the ability to take top honors at the Oscars two years from now. I told them there was no way Amy Parker would get them there."

Shane agreed. He'd met the actress several times, and she was a solid performer, but she wasn't an academy award-winning actress, at least not yet. It may make him an asshole, but Shane knew he was at the time in his career he needed to work with only the best, and Amy just wasn't.

"They've replaced her. The new lead signed on three days ago."

News like that usually hit the rumor mill within hours. That it hadn't peaked Shane's interest.

"Okay, I admit. I'm curious who got you to change your mind."

There were only a half dozen names of top-tier actresses Shane thought could pull off this complicated project. Unless one of their names came out of Boeing's mouth...

"Khloe Monroe."

Fuck. She was one of three top leads he wanted to work with. A half-drunk discussion with the man sitting next to him flitted back to Shane's memory. They'd been at Black Light, and Monroe and her Dom, Ryder Helms, had been there that night.

"Bastard. You're using insider info to play me."

"Maybe, but if it puts together a project that will take home up to seven statues, wouldn't it be worth it?"

Shane chuckled. "Khloe's great, don't get me wrong. And let's say, for a minute, I sign on. There's no way in hell *Blessed Betrayal* is bringing home seven statues. Not with the crew they'd assembled."

"The only members of the original project who remain are the screen writer and the costume designer. The studio now has Apollo on retainer for the director slot, contingent on us getting you to say yes. They also hired the same musical director from last year's Golden Globe winner when I pointed out the opportunities for the soundtrack royalties alone on this one. Add to that an upgrade in sound and makeup." Nolan paused before grinning, "And you can't discount my significant influence as the new executive producer for the project."

"Wait. You're producing, not just bankrolling this?"

"That's where we started, but the deeper I got into negations, the more I realized I didn't want anyone else at the helm of this one but me."

Well, fuck me.

Their waiter had just arrived with two huge plates with rather tiny portions of Eggs Benedict. Shane waited until they were alone again to speak.

"Fine, I'm listening," he admitted as he grabbed his fork and dug into the food. He did his best to ignore Boeing's smug smile.

"I'm glad. That was easier than I thought it would be."

"I haven't said yes, yet, asshole, just said I'm listening."

"Fair enough. I talked to your agent. He's probably sitting across the street with a pair of binoculars right now, spying on us. He was pissed at missing this meeting."

"I bet he was. He would sure hate to miss out on his commission if we make a deal around him."

"That explains why he was here waiting for me even though I told him to stay away this morning."

Shane chuckled. "Sounds about right. So, what exactly did you talk to John about then?"

"Your availability for starters." Shane was booked solid for the next fourteen months. "I have Apollo's assurance, he'll wait for you for up to three years if he has to."

"Okay. Not sure how Khloe Monroe feels about that, but it's nice."

"I also negotiated filming on location in Greece and D.C. There's no way to do this exclusively in the studio. That was a deal breaker for me too."

Shit. Boeing was really knocking through his list of objections. There was only one more point of contention.

"I'm not doing a project for less than..."

"Twelve million. That's for each... you and Khloe."

That was higher than the ten million he'd asked for months before. He was starting to smell a rat. "For a standalone film? Don't get me wrong, I like money, but something doesn't feel right. What am I missing? And don't give me the party line. I need the truth."

"You haven't been paying attention to the bestseller lists, have you? This book has been in the number one slot on both the *New York Times* and *USA Today Bestseller's* lists for over a month now. The popularity of the novel has shown the studio the potential they were sitting on by already owning film rights. Lucky for us, they decided to rethink things."

The men took a minute to eat in silence, each thinking through the details of the lucrative project. Shane had followed his gut many times since coming to Hollywood ten years before from the small down in Iowa he'd grown up on. He trusted his gut. That meant one thing.

"Fine. You got me. I'm interested. You can schedule time with my agent to talk about contracts."

Nolan leaned down to grab a folder out of the briefcase he had leaning up against the leg of the table. He pulled a few stray pieces of paper out, waving them in front of Shane.

"I've already put the draft together. I'll send this with you. I'm sure you'll want your agent and lawyer to review, which is fine, but don't sit on these for too long. If you turn me down, I'm gonna have some damage control to do."

"Oh yeah, why's that?"

"Because I promised them all I'd get you to say yes."

"That was pretty ballsy of you. But then again, you've been doing a lot of ballsy things lately."

If looks could kill, Shane would be dead on the floor. Nolan

Boeing was a smart man. He knew Shane was razzing him about the bold move the dominant had made just a few weeks before on Valentine's Day. Shane had been out-of-town filming and had missed the Roulette event at Black Light. Even now, weeks later, the club was still buzzing with gossip about the torrid events of the night.

Stories of Nolan Boeing and Piper Kole were at the top of the gossip pile.

"So, she hasn't called you back yet?" Shane asked, keeping the conversation vague, in case someone was close enough to overhear.

"No, and I don't want to talk about it."

"Ouch. I'm sorry, man. Maybe she's out of town?" Shane tried to smooth his friend's ruffled feathers with what they both knew to be a bogus excuse.

"Fuck that. There's nowhere on the planet where she isn't getting my calls. She puts on this brave face, showing the world how kickass she is, but all she really is a damn coward. Too afraid to pick up the phone and have a goddamn conversation."

Shane couldn't disagree with his friend. He'd witnessed Piper Kole in action at Black Light many times. She was more hardass with her play partners than Shane was on his best day. Before hearing the stories of how Nolan had bid to be her submissive for one night on Valentine's Day, Shane would have said she was all Domme. Now, after hearing his friend's side of their complicated relationship, Shane wasn't so sure anymore.

Shane assumed Nolan would change the subject, but instead, he leaned in to confide in his friend.

"She won't be able to avoid me forever. I've got the inside scoop on presenters for next week's Oscars. She's gonna be back in town. Unless she wants me to meet her on the fucking red carpet, she'd better damn well start talking to me soon."

"You wouldn't confront her in public." It was a statement. Shane was sure Nolan wasn't that stupid.

"Damn straight, I will if she leaves me no choice."

"That's cold, man. You know how private she likes to keep her personal life."

Shane should know. He'd known Piper for years. They'd both been secondary characters in a wedding scene early in their careers. Shane didn't know her well but considered both Nolan and Piper friends, even before bumping into them more frequently since Black Light had opened the year before.

"It's all up to her. She'd better start answering my calls, or she won't leave me any choice."

Before he could second guess himself, Shane pulled his cell phone out of his jean's pocket and started flicking through his contacts list.

"I don't need her number, I have them all," Nolan assured him. "I've called her cell. Her production office line. I've left messages with her assistant, even her personal stylist. Nothing. I feel like a pathetic loser, chasing after the prom date who snubbed him after the dance."

"Interesting analogy."

"There is absolutely nothing interesting about this situation," Nolan groused.

"Have you thought about just walking away?"

Nolan leaned closer, talking softer. "I fucking did that for over five years. I'm not doing it again. There's something there. I know it. She knows it, too. That's why she's avoiding me."

"Okay, okay," Shane held his hands up in a sign of surrender at Nolan's assertive rant. "Then there's only one thing to do."

Shane picked up his phone again and went back to Piper Kole's personal information.

"I told you, I have her number."

Shane pressed *SEND* and held the phone to his ear, listening to the phone ring before he answered, "I know. But she also has your number programmed in her phone. She isn't going to answer for you. She might, on the other hand, answer for Shane Covington."

"Hello? Shane?" Piper's feminine voice came through the phone.

"Hey there, Piper. How's it going?"

"Okay, I guess. It rained all day yesterday, so, of course, we're running behind. It sucks we didn't wrap here before we had to break for award week."

Shane watched Nolan carefully as he listened to the award-winning actress chitchat on the other end of the phone. Conflicting emotions of anger and panic ping-ponged on the producer's face as it sunk in that Shane really was talking to the elusive Piper Kole.

"So, to what do I owe this call? I haven't heard from you in ages."

"Oh, I'm out to brunch with friends, and we were talking about the upcoming award season. I heard you'd be back in town. Maybe we'll bump into each other at Elton's after party again like we usually do."

"Ah… sure. I guess. Other than getting my dress lined up, I hadn't really started to make definite plans yet."

"That's cool. Maybe we'll bump into each other at another club. We can talk about it then," he pumped her.

Several long seconds passed in silence before Piper asserted, "I've canceled my membership to that other club. We won't see each other there again."

"Shit, that's too bad."

Piper wasn't stupid. She was getting suspicious. Nolan was reaching out to grab the phone away from him. He knew if he handed over the phone call with Piper, he'd be burning a bridge with her big time.

Maybe it was the desperation on Nolan's face that reminded him suspiciously of the wimp he'd looked like a few hours before, watching out the window into a parking lot for one sexy housekeeper to arrive at work. Maybe it was the unspoken rules of the dominant man's club, he and Nolan were both members of. Either way, it didn't matter. Shane held the phone out to Nolan. He could hear Piper calling his name through the line, thinking the call had been dropped. Shane stood as Nolan grabbed the phone.

"I need to take a whiz. I'll be back in ten minutes. Good luck."

~

"SHANE? You still there? I think I lost you."

Damn, he'd forgotten how sexy her voice could be when she wasn't raging at him. Nolan needed to get control of his emotions. He'd only had one brief conversation with Piper since Valentine's Day, and it had been a disaster.

"Piper."

God, he'd just said one word, but the anguish in his voice spoke volumes.

A long minute passed. He worried she'd hang up. Words rushed through his brain as he scrambled to figure out what he could say to get through to her. Damn Covington for putting him on the spot like this. He wasn't ready to…

"Nolan?"

His heart raced. That was progress. She'd said his name without screaming at him.

"How are you?" It was a stupid question, considering their history. It surprised him it was what he most wanted to know. She may have ripped out his heart and trampled on it at Black Light with an audience watching, but it didn't matter. He still cared. He still knew at his core, the real Piper Kole was hiding inside the icy shell she'd constructed for the public.

"This is a new low, even for you."

"How do you figure? I care about you. I just want to make sure you're doing okay."

"Oh, I'm just fine and dandy. Now, stop stalking me, or I'm gonna have to..."

"Don't hang up. Please..." Damnit. Now he was begging. Wasn't being humiliated by her during roulette bad enough? "I just want to talk for a few minutes."

"We don't have anything to talk about, Nolan. You fucked-up bidding on me. I fucked-up by not walking out the second I found out. It's over now."

Anger flared. "Nothing is over. We have unfinished business. You've shut me out for five fucking years. I'm not gonna let you do it again."

"Do you even hear yourself, Nolan? Did you ever consider I just don't like you? That I'm not attracted to you?"

"Bullshit. Feel free to play that delusional game with the boys you like to dominate, but it isn't gonna work with me, Piper. We aren't kids with a silly crush. If you think I don't know what a real connection feels like, you're crazy. We have something special." He paused, and when she kept silent, he tacked on, "I don't know why you're pushing me away, but we can work through it."

He'd half expected her to start ranting at him like the last time they'd spoken. Apparently, the call had caught her off-guard as well because he could hear her heavy breathing at the other end of the line. Was that a sniffle? Was she crying?

Nolan closed his eyes, remembering how magnificent she'd looked on Valentine's night. Their connection had been real. She'd literally taken his breath away, right up until she'd left him tied up on center stage while she ran out, crying.

"Please, Piper. Talk to me, baby."

The second the pet name slipped out, he regretted it. He'd used it once in their time together a few weeks before, and she'd fought back at him in anger. But today was different.

There was no shouting. No reminding him Mistress Ice was no one's baby.

"Why won't you just leave it alone?" He had to strain to hear her almost-whisper.

"Because I care. More importantly, I know you do, too."

"What difference does that make?"

"Are you kidding me? Maybe you've felt this way about tons of other men, but not me, Piper. I'm going on record. I've never felt about any other woman the way I do you. Quite frankly, it's been a pain in my ass. It would be a hell of a lot easier if I could just get angry and walk away again, but I can't. I won't. Not again."

"You're certifiable, you know that?" He heard the manic quality of her protest.

"No, I'm not, and if you think about it for even two minutes, you'll know I'm telling you the truth. I'm one of the most level-headed men in Hollywood. I don't get caught up in drama. I don't like to play games, and you know that's the truth. That means you need to take what I'm saying to you very seriously."

He'd been hopeful. She'd been quiet—listening to him.

So, when she jumped in, yelling at him, it caught him off guard.

"Don't you dare lecture me, Nolan! There's so much about this town—this business—you're fucking blind to the bullshit, just like everyone else who has an ounce of power. Who am I kidding? You're part of the problem!"

What the hell was she talking about?

"Tell me about the problems. I can help fix them." He forced his voice to remain calm, refusing to argue with her again, especially since he had no clue why she'd become so angry so fast.

A ragged sob betrayed how upset she was.

"Piper… please… I don't know what's happening, baby, but I promise you, we'll figure it out." Nolan's own heart raced, feeling helpless to understand what had upset her, but for once, he knew it was something bigger than their personal relationship.

"I need to go. Goodbye, Nolan. Tell Covington he's on my shit list. And don't try this again, or I'll just have to change my phone number."

"No! Don't hang up!"

It was too late, she was gone—again.

He was tempted to call her back, but he knew she wouldn't answer. He threw Shane's phone down in frustration before putting his elbows on the table and dropping his head into his hands. Nolan closed his eyes and replayed their brief conversation, over and over again, trying to understand what had happened. His sixth sense told him Piper's anger today had been less about him and more about some larger problem.

But what?

"That didn't last very long. Did she talk to you at all?"

Covington was back. He'd have to think through things later at home. He was missing something. He just didn't know what. Sitting up, he opened his eyes.

"Yeah, she ended up hanging up on me again, but I feel like I made a bit of progress. She said to tell you you're on her shit list, though."

"I figured. I can handle that." Shane held his hand up to signal the waiter to bring the check.

"Don't worry about it. Lunch is on me," Nolan offered.

"Damn straight, it is." Covington had the nerve to turn on that grin that was making him millions and had women swooning wherever he went. "I'll have my lawyers look over the contract. Send over an electronic copy. You've got my email?"

"Yeah. I got it from Graves."

"Cool. Listen, I hate to eat and run, but I have a little someone I'm hoping to be spending my afternoon with…" The heartthrob paused before tacking on, "In my bed."

Without a backward glance, Covington stood and took off

for the exit, leaving Nolan to wait for the waiter to bring the check.

He had to push down the pang of jealousy that Shane's love life wasn't as complicated as his. It would be so much easier if he could walk away from Piper… forget about these irrational feelings he had for a woman who had tried to make it clear on many occasions, she wasn't interested.

Only, it was anything but clear. She was so hot and cold. He'd seen it on Valentine's night, then again on today's call. He didn't know how or why, but Piper was hiding something from him, and he wasn't going to let her push him away again until he figured out what the hell it was.

CHAPTER 4

Nalani's heart was racing a mile a minute. She hadn't been this nervous at work even on her first day.

She'd arrived at the mansion a couple hours earlier and dug into her cleaning duties. She'd been tempted to switch places with her two employees who came in on weekends to help her keep the expansive property in tip top shape. Like normal, sisters Marian and Kelly were downstairs, cleaning the public areas of the mansion while she focused on the VIP suites—six of which had already been completed without any problems.

She pulled her phone out of her uniform pocket and pulled up her housekeeping app, even though she didn't need the app to tell her she had only two rooms left to clean. She wasn't sure which one made her more nervous.

She had zero desire to cross paths with Henry Ainsworth after their disastrous encounter the day before. And as scary as seeing the older man was, seeing Shane Covington again had her even more anxious.

She'd replayed their time together at Black Light the night before, over and over again. If it weren't for the healing cut on her left palm as physical proof, she'd have thought she'd dreamed the whole encounter. Still, she had somehow convinced herself her memory had to be faulty. There was no way the famous actor had flirted with her... taken care of her injury... given her an orgasm... in public!

She felt the heat of her blush as she remembered the amazing encounter, equally dreading and anticipating seeing him again.

Her app told her Mr. Ainsworth had checked out already. Still, if she hurried, maybe she could get Shane's room finished before he came back. She'd tried to be inconspicuous as she'd asked the head of security, Miguel, if Mr. Covington was still on the property. Oh sure, she'd assured him it was only so she wouldn't disturb the guest. Maybe she was just paranoid, but she could have sworn her co-worker had been smiling a knowing smirk as he'd let her know the actor had left the property around eleven that morning and hadn't returned yet.

She opened the door, sticking her head out to peek up and down the hall to make sure the coast was clear before pushing her cart out and toward the Paris suite. With each step she took, she gave herself a pep talk, determined not to act like a silly fangirl, or worse yet, the virginal innocent he'd accused her of the night before. Before she could chicken out, Nalani reach out and rapped her knuckles on the door to Shane's suite.

"Housekeeping!"

When there was no answer, conflicting emotions weighed on her—disappointment she wouldn't get to see his sexy smile again and relief she wouldn't be able to make a fool of herself in front of the sexiest man on earth.

Nalani leaned in to give her scan to unlock the door. Once she'd opened the entry, she called out one more time, careful not to have a repeat of yesterday with Mr. Ainsworth.

He wasn't here. It was for the best.

Pushing down her regret at missing him, she turned and pulled her cart into the room. Once the heavy door slammed closed behind her, an odd sense of trespassing came over her. As a housekeeper, she was in other people's rooms every day, touching their personal belongings. cleaning up the most private of messes.

Today felt different. She wasn't in just any guest's room. She was in *Shane's* room. The pair of jeans hung over the back of the desk chair had been on his body, touching his most masculine body parts. The empty water bottle had touched his lips… the same lips that had whispered against the shell of her ear the night before.

Her heart raced as she let her eyes fall on the empty bed—the mattress he'd slept on the night before. Had he slept naked? And the sheets… is it possible he'd followed through on his dirty promise while at Black Light?

Unable to resist a moment longer, Nalani inched toward the messed bed. Pillows were piled in the most haphazard way, which was expected for most of their guests. The comforter was half on, half off, the bed, completely normal.

Only when she got next to the mattress did she catch her first peek at the sheets. Her heart lurched, shocked as if she'd just been zapped by a defibrillator.

Impossible.

There had to be a mistake, but even as she thought it, a warm fire kindled in her belly, lighting her up from the inside. Thank goodness he wasn't here to see the silly grin that had sprung onto her face. She could feel her cheeks burning as she let her imagination run wild, conjuring how magnificent it would have been to watch Shane Covington lying there, naked… grasping his hard cock in his own hand… stroking himself with his eyes closed.

Had he really been thinking of her as he'd shot the spurts of cum onto the sheets? She couldn't be sure, but she was fairly certain he'd at least been thinking of her while he was scrolling her name in the sticky fluid. She leaned down to touch her name, coming in contact with the dried, crusty deposit, telling her he'd done the deed hours before.

After working at the upscale mansion for over a year, she had thought she'd seen it all, but this was a first. And it was her name… written by *the* Shane Covington—America's heartthrob.

Fighting a pang of longing, Nalani leaned down, picking up one of the luxury pillows from near the headboard—the one that still had the slight indent where Shane's head had rested in slumber.

She pulled the pillow into her arms, holding the cool fabric close to her face, taking a long drag of the masculine scent that was Shane. So many men who partied at Runway reeked of expensive colognes, contaminating the suites with the odor, but not Shane. His scent was clean… virile… sexy as hell.

The sound of the door slamming closed behind her broke her out of her trance.

"Perfect timing. Today really is my lucky day."

Nalani threw the pillow back to the bed as if it had caught fire and was burning her. Mortified… that was the only word that could possibly describe her present emotion. Caught red handed, standing over his bed, smelling his pillow—she wished the floor would open and swallow her so she wouldn't have to turn around and look into the man's eyes.

Too late, she realized by not turning around to greet him meant he'd come to her instead. She felt his arms circling her waist intimately, pulling her back against his hard body as he playfully placed his chin on her right shoulder, peeking down at the bed with her.

"How'd you like my handy artwork?" he teased, hugging her harder, ensuring she wouldn't be slinking away until he wanted her to.

What was she supposed to say to that question? Since she had no clue, she stayed quiet, trying valiantly to think of something she could say that wouldn't embarrass her further.

"Nice penmanship."

That wasn't it! What an idiot! His rolling laughter proved that.

His hands had begun roaming, his right going up to squeeze her breast through her uniform, his left slipping lower, across her tummy, finally cupping her pussy through her clothes as he humped his athletic body against her back. He was strong, holding her tightly from behind as his lips found her ear like the night before.

"You're gonna have to tell me if I'm reading this situation wrong, Nalani. I've thought of almost nothing but you since last night, and believe me, my thoughts are completely X-rated. As much as I'd like to spend the next twenty-four hours in that bed, showing you just how down and dirty I'd love to get with you, I need to ask you what color you are right now."

Her racing brain fought to make sense of his words. She'd gotten lost in her shock at his comments about wanting her in that bed… *his* bed… By the time she finished assimilating the final sentence, she fumbled to remember the rules of the complicated game he'd started the night before.

He wasn't playing fair, surrounding her completely with his larger-than-life presence. Within seconds, she was completely under his spell, wanting nothing more than to be the center of his X-rated fantasies. As afraid as she was of being hurt when he surely dumped her and moved on to his next conquest in a few days, there was almost nothing that would stop her from letting Shane have his way with her. She just hoped the memories she gained with the intimacies would outweigh the heartache after it was over.

"I'm green," she finally answered softly.

"Good girl. Now, I need a few answers, kitten. Have you ever scened with someone at Black Light?"

"No…"

"That shouldn't make me happy, but it does. How about being with a dominant? Someone who likes to take charge."

She had only had a few boyfriends through high school and junior college classes combined, and compared to Shane Covington, they were boys, not men.

"No…"

"My lucky streak continues. I'm gonna have so much damn fun. All you need to do is follow directions. Can you do that for me?"

"Yes…" Apparently, single syllable words were all she could muster.

"That's *sir*. When I ask you a question, you should answer with a respectful sir at the end."

When she hesitated, he squeezed her pussy harder, lifting her whole body off the ground. "Nalani," he growled in the yummiest tone.

"Sir… yes, sir."

"Such a good girl. Now… let's see if I can turn you into my naughty girl as easily."

Emotions slammed into her like a Mac truck. He'd called her *his* naughty girl. It was probably just a careless comment, but it triggered a wave of unexpected longing she recognized for the danger it was.

This is just a fun fling for him. Don't get your heart involved.

She missed his warmth the second he released her, stepping away as he put his hands on her shoulders, turning her, so they were facing each other. He was a full foot taller, so she found it easier to focus on the dark tuft of masculine chest hair showing at the top of his fashionable shirt.

"Eyes." It was a one-word command.

They were close enough to each other, she had to lean her head back to look up at his tanned face with its scruffy day-old stubble. She didn't think she could get more excited, but seeing the look of unadulterated hunger in Shane's slate-blue eyes made her core ignite.

They were close enough to reach out and touch each other. She longed to run her hands through his thick hair or caress those muscular arms that had held her tight, yet she somehow understood Shane was in charge, which meant she was supposed to let him lead.

"I need you naked." When she didn't move, he added, "Like now."

She wanted to protest. Why wasn't he getting undressed too? And why couldn't he just take her clothes off her?

"I thought...." She let her voice trail off when she saw the disapproving scowl that brought out small lines around his sexy eyes.

"You thought what?" he asked sternly, just a hint of a smirk lightening his words.

She wished she'd kept her mouth shut. She'd been here with him for five minutes, and she'd already made him laugh and now, screwed up.

"Nothing..." she said quietly, although a flare of modesty kept her grounded—immobile.

"Do I need to undress you? I can do that, but it will come with a price." His smirk had grown.

What game was he playing? Whatever it was, she didn't feel like she understood the rules.

"What kind of price?" she asked, not sure if she really wanted to know.

"For starters, naughty girls who don't follow directions need discipline. I feel obliged to warn you, disciplining you would bring me great pleasure. I'm trying my best to go slow with you because I know you're a newbie to the lifestyle, but I fucking love your inexperience."

"You do?" Her voice squeaked.

"Don't act so surprised. You have to know how fucking gorgeous you are."

Nalani scoffed out loud. Oh, she knew she wasn't ugly, but there was a big difference between her girl-next-door look and being someone worthy to be on Shane Covington's arm. Still, she could feel her cheeks turning pink from his heated glare and threats of discipline.

Discipline.

Definitely not a four-letter word, but it might as well be. It evoked the same kind of visceral response and had her imagination running wild, fueled by the power exchange scenes she'd witnessed at Black Light. She was a complete novice in practice, but she'd spent more hours than she'd like to admit in her bed with her vibrator, reliving some of the shocking things she'd seen in the last year.

Never in her wildest dreams did she imagine being a participant... and with a man like Shane Covington, no less.

Their stare-down continued until she felt his fingers brushing her chest as he found the tab of her uniform's long zipper and slowly started to pull it toward the carpet, maintaining their eye connection until she felt him reach the end of the zipper.

She held her breath, afraid to move for fear she'd wake up and realize it was all just a dream.

His hand returned to her shoulders, grabbing the fabric of her boring uniform, lifting it up and out until she felt cool air-conditioning wash over her bared flesh. Only when she felt the cotton brushing down her arms, pooling at her feet, did her body visibly shiver.

"You cold, kitten?"

There it was again. She'd had one old boyfriend who had liked to call her *honey* and another who'd insisted on referring to her as his *sweetie*. She'd hated both of them because she had always had a sneaking suspicion they'd used the terms of endearment so they wouldn't have to pronounce her name—the hazard of switching partners like their clothes.

But she loved the way Shane looked when he called her kitten—or even more importantly—his naughty girl, even though she hadn't the slightest idea of exactly what she'd have to do to really earn that title.

The broad grin that lit up his face should be outlawed.

"I'm not sure what you're thinking about, but keep it up. You're blushing beautifully."

Feeling like she'd been caught with her hand in the cookie jar, she panicked, lifting her arms across her chest to hide her body from him.

Shane tsked as he reached out to grab her wrists, pulling her arms apart to expose her body to him again. He raked his gaze down, taking his time as he visually inspected her simple black bra and panties she'd bought online. She considered it a victory today was the one day of the last week where her underwear actually matched.

"So beautiful… so sexy." He took the time to place her hands at her sides and added, "Don't move these."

Her "Yes, sir" surprised her even more than him.

He started at her shoulders, lightly dragging his fingers across her flesh, through the small rounded valley of her breasts, spilling above her size-C cups. She couldn't hold in her giggle when his hands roamed down her sides, finding her ticklish spots.

They stood in silence, her watching his face as she felt his flat palms raking over her flat tummy, outward, light caresses turning into tight grips on her hips.

"Fucking perfect…" His words were soft—reverent.

His hands were suddenly anything but soft as he thrust his fingers into the waistband of her bikini panties, almost ripping them from her body as he yanked them down to pool with her forgotten uniform.

She panicked "I still have my… I mean, it's almost over, but I still…"

"I told you last night that doesn't matter. I have plenty of other dirty ideas for this body that don't include your pussy."

"You do?" she asked incredulously, unable to imagine how they'd possibly proceed, yet pretty sure she'd say yes to anything if it kept that feral look on his sexy face.

"Hell, yes. For starters, let's get this bra off so we can get started on your first discipline session."

"You were serious about that?" she blurted.

"Oh, Nalani, you have no idea just how serious I am."

TRUER WORDS HAD NEVER BEEN SPOKEN. How long had it been since he'd scened with a real submissive? Not a socialite pretending to be obedient just to get in his bed, see their picture plastered in the tabloids, or hopefully, gain access to his bank account. After several back-to-back burns in the romance department, he'd been on a self-imposed hiatus.

He hadn't really recognized he'd been waiting, but as he reached to cup the perky breasts of the woman in front of him, a few things clicked into place. Like how he'd been waiting to find a real submissive to play with. And not just any submissive, but his flavor of choice—*reluctant*.

The longer he'd been part of the underground BDSM scene, the more he'd come to acknowledge dominating a submissive was a turn-on for all dominants, but exercising control over an outwardly good-girl sub who secretly craved being forced to do the dirtiest of things their bodies and minds could conceive—that was Shane's jam.

He'd learned early he didn't have nearly as much fun punishing a masochist who craved the pain. No, he was an asshole. He wanted… no *needed*… real tears. Pushing his sub to a place of tangible fear, shy embarrassment, and reluctance—where despite all the naughty submissive's verbal denials, he knew she craved the debauched, erotic humiliation as much as he did.

He made fast work of divesting Nalani of her bra, letting it fall to the floor. Shane pinched her pert nipples, loving the way they grew long and hard. He let his gaze return to her face as he tested her further.

"Such amazing tits. I bet you love showing them off through thin tops when you go to the grocery store or out to wash your car like a tease. I'm sure you love touching yourself in the dark of the night, thinking about how you wished one of those men you'd been teasing would have shown you what a naughty girl you were."

Her breath caught as her eyes went wide—busted.

"I never..." As expected, she protested with words, but her golden-brown eyes had glazed over with the kind of yearning he knew she'd deny with her dying breath.

Exquisitely reluctant. Perfectly pliable.

"Are you telling me you've never used those probing fingers of yours to touch your cunt until you were gushing slick pussy juice all over your panties?"

She didn't have a chance. He was the champion of dirty talk. He'd barely started, purposefully going slow, so he didn't scare away the rare gem he'd found before he'd had his fill.

Still, he needed to be careful. He was a public figure, a rich one at that. He'd had several disastrous misunderstandings with strong-willed women who'd turned in award-winning performances right up until he'd push them out of their comfort zone.

One particular B-actress had been more than happy to get her fifteen minutes of fame by selling her salacious story of how the one and only Shane Covington had a thing for pet play, forced public diaper usage, and bouts of long-term orgasm denial, courtesy of his impressive collection of expensive chastity belts.

Finding the elusive combination of strength and submission was hard for most dominants, but for the rich and famous with dubious kinks, well, it was near impossible. His wildest sexual fantasies—and he had plenty—required an almost ridiculous level of trust between partners. The raunchier and more dubious the sex act, the higher the intimacy intensified.

That intimacy was his drug of choice and much harder to find in Hollywood than the purest of illegal pharmaceuticals.

He barely knew the young woman blushing beautifully in front of him, but he somehow recognized she was the closest he'd met to a humiliation sub in a long time. He was going to have so much fun testing his theory. His cock was rock hard, anxious to come out and play.

Down boy. We have a long way to go with this one, but I have a feeling she's gonna be worth the wait.

"Now, I'm guessing you've never been disciplined or punished before. Am I right?"

It was a rhetorical question. Her gasping for sips of air as she internalized his words was all the confirmation he needed. Still, he waited since hearing her admit it was half the fun.

"No."

"I'm not right? Or you haven't been punished? Which is it?" he pressed. She was becoming more flustered by the moment.

"I… haven't been punished."

"Not even as a kid, non-sexually?"

"No."

"No, what?" he prodded more sternly, hoping to push her deeper into her submission.

Her eyes darted away, unable to hold his intense gaze as she answered quietly.

"No, sir."

"But you've dreamed about it. Don't deny it. You've closed

your eyes and pictured yourself bent over one of the spanking benches you have to clean down at Black Light, haven't you?"

Their eyes met again, but in her panic, she couldn't hold his stern gaze. Shane crossed his arms, taking a domineering stance. When she remained silent, he pressed her harder.

"I'm waiting for your answer, naughty girl. You've dreamed of being splayed out… naked and on display for everyone to see… while someone spanked your bottom until it was nice and red, haven't you?"

He waited several long seconds, enjoying her tongue darting out to lick her lips while nervously looking at everything around the room except him.

"Eyes when I'm talking to you."

Ah, perfection. His inner asshole cheered at the tears already pooling in her expressive eyes. He had barely touched her, yet her responses had his tool straining for release. Aware she was like the rare, wild animal—afraid to be trapped—Shane forced himself to slow down, afraid he'd spook her away.

"It's okay to admit it. I already know it's true. You've been waiting for someone to dominate you, haven't you, Nalani?"

She hesitated, finally answering, "Not exactly."

He'd bite. "So, tell me. How exactly did you picture it last night when you were masturbating and chasing your orgasm?"

Nalani opened and closed her mouth a few times before finally getting the courage to answer. "I've only pictured *you* spanking me, not just someone."

Holy shit. Who the hell was this chick?

He fought to control his reaction, refusing to let her see she was having the same effect on him, he was on her.

"I wouldn't want to disappoint you, then, would I?"

"I don't know. I'm fine, just thinking about it."

"Oh, I wouldn't want to cheat you out of experiencing your first punishment, now would I? What kind of a Dom would that make me?"

"A nice one?" she offered hopefully.

He couldn't resist pulling her into his arms, holding her naked body flush against him. He felt her trembling as he corrected her.

"Sorry, but no one has ever called me nice in the bedroom."

"What do they call you?"

"Sir. Master. Sometimes, Daddy." He chuckled before adding, "And there's been one or two who preferred to call me asshole."

Despite his joke, a strange look of longing passed through her gaze.

"Never just Shane?"

Her question caught him off-guard. He was so in a D/s mindset, the innocence of her inquiry took him out of the scene. It was his turn to stumble through his answer.

"Not in a long time," he answered truthfully, feeling unusually vulnerable.

"Why's that?" She wasn't letting it drop.

A part of him wanted to recapture the control of their exchange but not before giving her the only true answer.

"I don't know. Maybe because that would just feel too…" He stalled, unsure if he wanted to finish the sentence. She wiggled in his arms, working to be able to look up into his eyes. He waited until they were visually connected to add, "Personal."

"But it's your name."

She was so damn naive, yet her innocent question struck a chord with him.

"It's hard to explain," he defended.

"If you say so." Her sudden confidence not only surprised him but acted like cold water on their scene.

He needed to regain control.

"I think we've talked long enough. I'm more a man of action," he promised, reaching down to palm her flawlessly round ass cheeks in his hands, massaging and squeezing as he ground his hard erection into her.

Nalani's eyes shuttered closed as he lifted her naked body and walked them the few feet back to the king-sized bed, dropping her with a bounce onto the pile of bedding. Her playful giggle reminded him he'd lost the edge of the scene, yet when she grinned up at him, a look of sheer adoration on her face, he couldn't find the willpower to be upset.

"You have dimples when you smile like that."

She groaned, throwing her hands up to her blushing cheeks in an attempt to hide her dimples.

Ah, there was his shy girl. Time to push her a bit more to see if he could figure out where her comfort line was. He looked forward to pushing her up to that line but not an inch farther.

Shane reached down, quickly grabbing her ankles, yanking her body back toward him at the edge of the bed while simultaneously spreading his arms and her legs wide open. The pink on her cheeks quickly flushed to bright red as she realized he was raking his gaze up and down her naked body, inspecting her while towering over her, fully clothed.

Her hands flew up, reflexively trying to cover her nakedness out of embarrassment, but he was ready for her.

"Oh no, no hiding from me. It's important every part of your body will be available to me at all times." He left off exactly how true that foreshadowing promise was, although a little voice in the back of his mind reminded him they were a long way away from him being able to demand that kind of obedience from Nalani.

"Put your hands above your head." When she hesitated, he added, "I can get some rope out of my bag to tie your hands there if it would help."

A cocktail of shock, fear, and longing registered on her face before she reluctantly pulled her hands away from her breasts and pussy, raising them slowly until she was stretched out beneath him like a smorgasbord for the taking.

Time to sample the goods.

She remained pliable as Shane pulled her legs as wide as they would go before moving her knees to bend, bringing her feet together at the edge of the bed. It had the desired effect of opening her cunt like butterfly wings. She was almost completely bare, only a neatly trimmed landing strip pointing to her glistening folds.

He let his thumb graze across her clit just long enough to draw a groan of desire from her. He waited until she was watching before lifting his thumb to his mouth, seductively licking off her wetness.

"Tasty." He paused, enjoying her reaction before tugging lightly on the string of the tampon she was wearing. "I wonder how big of a mess we could make if I pull this out."

Jackpot. While he had no intention of pulling her tampon out, she didn't know that. She broke pose, propping up on an elbow as she reached with her right hand to swat him away.

He caught her hand, "Oh, you moved so quickly. That's very naughty of you. Looks like I need to get the rope after all."

"No! Please!" She begged beautifully, her eyes teary.

"Then you know what to do. Where do your hands belong?"

"But… you aren't going to take it out… right?"

She was at the edge of her line already. With effort, he backed down, unwilling to scare her away. She was a newbie. She needed training.

"Time to remind you of something very important. Are you listening?"

"Yes."

"Don't forget you have a secret weapon and have the power to use it absolutely any time you need to. In fact, I'm counting on you using it."

Her confusion made him glad he'd stopped to remind her.

"What color are you, Nalani?"

Her eyes widened as she remembered the most basic rules of

their complicated game. He could see her thinking through her answer.

"I guess yellow."

"Good girl. That's all you'd need to say to me to let me know I'm pushing you to do something you aren't sure about. It will make me proceed with more caution. What will you say to make me stop a scene completely?"

"Red." She hesitated, before adding, "But… I guess I thought that was just a Black Light thing."

"Not at all." He paused, trying to decide how to best answer. She was a newbie—start at the beginning. "Many people only scene at a club, like Black Light. Others who love the BDSM lifestyle never go to a club at all, preferring to play in the privacy of their own bedroom."

He paused, hoping she'd ask the question she did.

"And which one are you?"

"I guess I'm neither because the location isn't what does it for me. I enjoy the privacy Black Light gives me as a celebrity, but my kinks are way more complicated."

Her dimples were back, and it surprised him to realize how happy he was to see them.

"Complicated, eh? That seems like a slight understatement."

She was teasing him—brave girl.

Still, he used their intermission to add, "Maybe it is, but that's why it's more important than ever you remember to communicate. It's the nature of my kinks. I get off on pushing you out of your comfort zone. Watching you blushing and struggling to obey. I think I'm really good at recognizing when I'm pushing too hard, and I'll back off, but we don't know each other, and you're new to this, so I might get it wrong. When I do, I'm counting on you holding the line."

She hesitated before asserting, "Don't take my tampon out."

"Got it. Tampon is a line," he assured, oddly pleased with the way the conversation was going. Little did she know, he had a hundred other down and dirty deeds his fucked-up brain could come up with that were way worse.

"Now, enough talk. It's time for action. Hands back above your head, naughty girl."

The smirk on her lips as she answered with a simple "Yes, sir" went straight to his cock. Damn, it was gonna be fun playing with this one.

Before Shane could dive in to explore her body again, the ding of a text message coming in sounded. There was literally no one on the planet he wanted to communicate with more than he wanted to play with the toy in his bed. But the surprised panic on Nalani's face threw a damper on their scene.

"That's my phone. Oh God, I'm technically supposed to still be working. What if Madison is looking for me?"

Tangible fear emanated from her, and since he hadn't been the one to cause it, he didn't like it.

"I'm sure everything is fine. I know Davidson doesn't mind employees consorting with the guests."

"Still, I need to get back to work." She attempted to sit up. He was damned if he was going to let her escape so fast.

"Call in and tell them you need to take off early."

"No. I need this job way too much to lie."

He was in no position to force her to do anything, much less risk her employment. Still, he couldn't let her slip away —not yet.

"Fine, we'll go back to our original plan. Meet me downstairs tonight. Eight o'clock."

"Like a date?" she asked innocently.

"Well, if you consider me tying you down on display for all to see, spanking your ass until it's beet red, then fucking you so hard, you're crying and screaming... then yeah... like a date."

He loved her expressive eyes, recognizing he could get lost in them... if he let himself. She'd loved every word of his nasty promise.

Christ, how was he going to last until that night? He was going to have to stroke one off before then. That's when the best idea came to him.

"Hands up above your head again. I need five minutes, then you can get back to work… with a little bonus."

"But…"

"Hands. Above your head. Now."

She snapped to attention, following directions. He leaned down to arrange her nakedness the way he wanted. Thank God, she was flexible. Legs wide, knees flat on the bed, feet together at the edge—she was laid out exquisitely.

She didn't take her eyes off his as he reached for his own belt buckle, the jingling noises as he unbuckled it, telling her what he was doing. Next, he lowered his zipper, unbuttoning the top button and lowering his jeans until he could cup his hand down into his briefs and come out with his hard erection.

Nalani couldn't resist. She broke their visual connection to look down at his package. She liked what she saw and not for the first time, he was happy he wasn't just a pretty face. He had a dick most men envied and he using it to his advantage.

Without a word, Shane grasped his cock at the base and started stroking himself while enjoying the show of her emotions playing on her flushed face. She liked what she was watching. He could see the slight lift of her hips from the bed as she subconsciously rocked, her unsuccessful attempt at getting him to put that cock inside her instead of his hand.

He wasn't going to last long. They maintained their X-rated connection as the slapping sounds of his jacking off edged them both. He glanced at his tool, knowing he was close as the glob of pre-cum that had formed fell to the carpet below.

Shane grunted when the first squirt of jizz finally made its appearance. He stepped closer to the bed, just in time to shoot the sticky fluid onto Nalani's tummy, stray drops making it as far as her left tit. Two more ropes covered her, the last landing directly on that trimmed bush.

It was rather cave-manish, but he fucking loved seeing her marked with his seed. There was only one thing that could make it better.

Still trying to catch his breath, he reached out with his right index finger, manipulating the wet globs on her body until he'd formed S-H-A-N-E in block letters across her tummy.

"There. Let's let that dry a bit. You'll wear it for the rest of your shift to remind you, today, you're mine. You're not to touch yourself while we're apart. No playing with yourself in the shower. No getting out your vibrator to try to scratch that itch I know I'm leaving you with. Got it?"

Her disappointment was tangible. She wanted to come. Little did she know, if she stuck around for any length of time at all, she'd be spending a great deal of time sexually frustrated.

He couldn't wait.

CHAPTER 5

She felt better the second the lock turned on the bathroom door, ensuring she would have at least a moment of privacy. Heaven knows, she needed it after the last hour spent in Shane Covington's room.

Nalani walked to the sink, turning on the cold faucet, hoping a splash of water would wake her up from the dream she had to be in. Only in dreams did men like Shane Covington even notice women like her, let alone show sexual interest in them. He could have any woman he wanted. It had to be a dream. That would also explain the kinky things he'd said and done. Such things weren't real. It was just her subconscious coming up with absurd ideas.

The water flowed down the drain, but she didn't touch it, instead reaching for the zipper to her uniform, pulling it lower to expose her torso, sure it would be clean.

Like the healing cut on her left palm, the proof she was indeed awake was there, in the reflection. The letters were smeared, not having had time to dry before she'd insisted on getting dressed, but there was no denying the actor's mark on her body.

Shane Covington was uber-famous, ultra-rich, and kinky as fuck. Her heart lurched just thinking about all the debauched things he'd said and done to her, and they'd barely spent any time together. She instinctively knew she'd only seen the tip of the iceberg that was Shane Covington. That realization both excited and terrified her in equal measures.

What the hell was she doing?

If she wasn't careful, she was going to screw around and get fired if she kept shirking her duties to spend time with the famous guest.

Worse, she was in real danger of getting her heart hurt when their tryst ended… and it would end. Shane was famously single. If she was to believe the tabloids, he burned through beautiful women faster than the water going down the drain in front of her. So why was he wasting his time with her?

That was the million-dollar question.

She turned the faucet off and zipped up her uniform. There was no time to think about all this complicated stuff right now. She needed to finish cleaning the last suite, then get downstairs to check in with Julie and Maria. She'd left them on their own all day.

It only took her a minute to get back to the housekeeping cart she'd left in the hallway outside of the Paris suite. Just knowing he was still on the other side of that heavy door raised her pulse. She had to press through the urge to knock and return to his bed, pushing her cart toward the double doors at the end of the hall instead.

Even though the computer showed this room had been vacant for several hours, she was anxious not to have a repeat of her error yesterday. Nalani knocked loudly, announcing "Housekeeping" in a loud and clear voice as she leaned forward to supply her retinal scan, which opened the locked door.

Just to be sure, she called out "Housekeeping" a second time as she pushed her cart into the room, letting the heavy door slam closed behind her.

She sighed with relief when she made her way through the foyer into the spacious bedroom, confirming she was indeed alone. The room may be empty now, but there was no doubt it had been well used the night before.

The comforter was on the floor, the sheets almost completely off the bed. Furniture had been moved around, and one chair still had white nylon rope tied to the armrests and legs, bringing back memories of seeing the red-headed woman tied up the day before. Had she been crazy enough to return to the room for a second round with Henry Ainsworth, or had he shared his violent brand of sex with a different unlucky woman last night?

Nalani tried to not think about it, going to work, stripping the bedding and working to put the room back together. When she finished with the bedroom and sitting area, she grabbed the bucket of supplies from her cart and headed into the opulent bathroom.

She was only a few steps into the room when movement caught her attention in the mirror. She looked into the mirror just in time to see Henry Ainsworth rushing her direction from the small room that held the toilet. He was naked with only a towel wrapped around his waist to hide his privates.

He'd surprised her so quickly, she froze, unable to comprehend what was happening. His hands clamping down on her biceps from behind coincided with her brain protesting.

He had checked out. The room was supposed to be empty.

She cried out in pain from the tight grip he had on her arms. Their eyes met in the mirror, him towering over her by at least eight inches. What she saw in his eyes terrified her.

"I've been waiting for you. I'm in need of some of your extra special VIP service."

Nalani may not be as worldly as most of the guests who

stayed at the mansion, but she wasn't stupid. She knew with certainty exactly what kind of *VIP service* Henry Ainsworth was looking for.

She fought down her fear, knowing she needed to keep her wits about her if she was going to escape without making an already bad situation worse.

"I'm sorry, Mr. Ainsworth. My app said you'd already checked out. The room is supposed to be vacant."

"And it will be… as soon as you finish your VIP service duties."

He had started to exert power, pressing her down toward the floor. She instinctively knew he wanted her on her knees in front of him, but he was crazy if he thought she'd go there without a fight.

Nalani lifted her foot, bringing her shoe down onto the bare foot of the man holding her captive from behind. His shout of pain coincided with him loosening his grip on her arms. In their brief struggle, she pushed away from the older man, catching the edge of the towel, exposing his protruding erection.

Like yesterday, the bent pole repulsed her, helping kick her flight instincts into a higher gear. She shoved him as she turned, ready to run to the exit, but he was ready for her, grabbing and holding her captive. For an older man, he was in pretty good shape, making it difficult to escape.

"I love a slut with spunk. Nothing will turn me on more than finally putting you in your place. You've been a naughty girl, bursting into my room yet again without announcing yourself. I'm afraid you need to be punished."

The man was insane—truly.

"I'm sorry, sir, if you didn't hear me calling out my arrival, but you've already checked out. You aren't even supposed to be here." She could see his face turning red in the mirror, a look of raw rage in his eyes.

"Are you calling me a liar? Haven't you heard, the customer is always right?"

He released her left arm and started pawing at her uniform, trying to get his hands on the same zipper Shane had opened an hour before.

This couldn't be happening. It was her worst nightmare. As scary as the idea of being sexually assaulted by a guest was, it was the real possibility of losing her job that scared her the most. If she complained about him, she knew it would turn into *he said/she said* and as awesome as the Cartwright-Davidsons were to work for, she knew she would lose if they were forced to choose between a lowly housekeeper and one of their top paying customers.

Gathering all her strength, Nalani pulled her arm up, then slammed her elbow back as hard as she could into the gut of Henry Ainsworth. Her blow knocked the air out of the movie executive, and he loosened his grip. She took the opportunity to turn and run past him, back out of the bathroom, through the bedroom and foyer, and finally, out into the long hall.

Her first instinct was to stop and pound on Shane's door. Surely, he would protect her from the older man as he had the day before, but seconds before she knocked, she remembered a very important fact.

Shane was an actor, in the same business as Henry Ainsworth. The men knew each other, and while she didn't think they were best friends, could she really take the chance Shane would want to get involved? After all, having one of the most powerful financiers in the industry against you could impact his career.

When the door at the end of the hall opened and a furious Henry Ainsworth appeared in a luxurious Runway robe, she was forced to make her decision.

She turned from the door to the Paris suite and took off at a sprint toward the Runway office, praying Madison or Avery was there. Even if they weren't, the office door had a lock. She could put the door between her and the man chasing her, then… what?

She honestly didn't know how this was going to turn out well for her.

The office was empty when she arrived. The second she slammed the door closed and turned the lock, she felt marginally better. She rested her ear against the door, trying to hear if Mr. Ainsworth had followed her all the way to the office, but it was hard to hear over her pounding pulse.

Only after several minutes went by and there was no knock on the door, she began to relax slightly. But what if he was on the other side of the door, waiting for her to come out?

Worse, how was she ever going to finish her shift? She'd left her cart in the Hong Kong suite. She'd eventually have to go in there and finish cleaning his room. And worse, what about tomorrow… the next day? Next week? The longer she stood at the door, trying to sort through what to do next, the angrier she got at the older man. How dare he put her in this position?

The knock on the door scared the bejesus out of her. She was about to scream at him to leave her alone when Madison's voice called out.

"Hey! It's me. Whoever is in there with the deadbolt on, you need to unlock the door!"

Nalani's brain scrambled to figure out what she was going to say to her friend and boss. Should she tell her the whole story? Or would it just put that bull's-eye on her back for being let go sooner when it turned into *he said/she said*? Only the fear for Madison's safety, out there exposed to Mr. Ainsworth, convinced Nalani to unlock the door and let her friend in.

"Oh, hey, what's going on? I was texting you a bit ago to see what time you planned on wrapping up today. Jaxson called and asked if you could stop by their house on your way home.

Sounds like the twins might have got into a bit of trouble now that they're crawling. He didn't give many details."

Her friend had whisked past her, talking a mile a minute, a fresh cup of coffee in her hand. Only when the club manager got to her chair and sat did she look at Nalani and finish, "You think you can stop by?" Madison had a funny look on her face as Nalani waited near the door. She eventually tacked on, "Hey, you don't look well. You feeling okay?"

She wanted to scream she was anything but okay, but the events of the last twenty-four hours, both good and bad, were starting to close in on her, and she was having trouble focusing. The stress of it all suddenly felt like an eight-hundred-pound gorilla sitting on her chest, cutting off her air.

When Nalani didn't answer, Madison jumped to her feet, approaching Nalani quickly, reaching out to place her wrist on Nalani's forehead to test for a temperature.

"You don't feel warm. Do you have a stomachache?"

How easy it would be to lie and just go home, but Nalani hadn't lied to Madison before, and she wasn't going to start today.

"I just had a scare is all. I thought Mr. Ainsworth had checked out a few hours ago, but I just went in there to clean his suite, and he was still occupying the room. He was in the bathroom when I went in to clean."

"What a jerk. He texted me himself to say he was ready to check out hours ago."

"Well, he changed his mind and…" she let her voice trail off, unsure how much to share. "And he isn't happy with me. He accused me of barging in on him without knocking, but I swear I knocked and yelled housekeeping like always."

"Of course, you did. I can hear you sometimes from the office, so I know you're careful. He's just the pain-in-the-ass he usually is. Don't let him get to you. I'm sure it will blow over by the next time he stays."

Just thinking about having that man in the building again gave Nalani the creeps. It wasn't fair that he had the power to ruin a job that she really liked.

"What are the chances we could refuse to rent rooms to him anymore?" she finally asked hopefully.

"Ha! Don't I wish. He's always bitching about this or that. His newest thing is asking for a discounted rate because of his volume, cheap-ass bastard."

As nice as it was that Madison had a poor opinion of the jerk, it was clear she wasn't inclined to ban him from staying, and as long as Nalani kept quiet about his threats, who could blame her boss. There was a big difference between sexual assault and being a cheapskate.

Nalani needed to speak up. She needed to…

Madison's cell, lying on the desk started ringing. Her face lit up like a Christmas tree, telling Nalani it was Trevor McLean on the other end of the phone.

"Sorry, I need to get this. With the club being closed the next two days, we're trying to take a short getaway to Palm Springs."

Off her boss went with her coffee and phone, leaving Nalani alone in the office again. She relocked the door and plopped down in the chair behind the desk she and Avery shared when they needed to do paperwork.

She had many options, but she didn't like any of them. Should she find Miguel and report Mr. Ainsworth to their head of security? She was pretty sure at least some of the women going into his room were being forced into dubious consensual sexual situations, whether or not they had willingly gone to his suite. What if they were too afraid to speak up? There was a good chance he'd paid them off with money or opportunities, making them unwilling to speak against the powerful man.

Shane had seen Ainsworth angry at her the day before, but she'd made the mistake of entering his room unannounced. And like before, she didn't want to Shane dragged into this mess.

Things were already complicated with him. She didn't need to add this to the mix.

Madison had a good idea. It was Sunday, and the club was closed for the next two days. Only Shane and one other guest were staying over. She didn't need to worry about finishing the Hong Kong room until Wednesday, and by then, she'd figure out how she was going to deal with this whole mess.

She opened the bottom desk drawer and took out her purse. She'd take the elevator outside the office door all the way down to Black Light and take the back exit out to her car. She knew Ainsworth didn't have a key for any of those locations, which gave her a little peace of mind.

She needed to go home, take a long bath and soak while she thought through all that had happened. Her hand visibly trembled as she reached to unlock the door to leave. She wouldn't feel safe again until she was locked in her own apartment.

Nalani was halfway to her car when she remembered Jaxson had wanted her to stop in at their house on the way home. It was the last thing she wanted to do but knew it was her job.

The thought briefly crossed her mind, maybe she should mention the incident with Mr. Ainsworth to the owners, but what good would come from that? He hadn't hurt her, not really. It would still be *he said/she said,* and considering the VIP pretty much paid for her entire monthly salary in the few days he slept over, there was no way the Cartwright-Davidson's would want to open the can of worms her confiding in them would open.

Anger flared that the asshole's actions made her feel unsafe even in her place of employment. Worse… how was she going to feel comfortable coming back in a few hours to meet Shane?

Maybe this was a sign from the universe, telling her what a crazy idea it was to think she could go on a date with the Shane Covington.

CHAPTER 6

Piper should have quit drinking about two drinks ago. Despite her head starting to throb and her near-empty stomach churning, she opened the mini fridge in her suite at The Plaza and pulled out the last two small bottles of liquor.

Aviation gin and Bacardi rum.

She didn't like her choices. She'd already polished off the tiny bottles of Absolute vodka and Jack Daniels as well as her favorite mixers, and there was no way she was desperate enough to drink the Tequila. She'd ruined that drink forever by overindulging on her one and only spring break many years before. She'd have to settle for a gin and seven unless she wanted to phone room service.

She dismissed the idea immediately. She was almost never alone. It had taken way too much effort to arrange for these few days in New York on her own—no assistant, no bodyguards, no publicist, not even one of her many boy-toys she had on speed dial. She hadn't been in the mood to see any of them—not since the disastrous event at Black Light several weeks before on Valentine's Day.

It's how she ended up holed up in her hotel room for the last twenty-four hours, and not even the need for food or booze reinforcements felt like good enough reasons to have to see another human being. Tomorrow afternoon would come soon enough when she'd be forced to rejoin the world and head to her appearance on the late-night talk show.

Tonight, she just wanted to wallow—alone.

She'd been looking forward to the solace after barely holding it together for the last few weeks. This was her 'get her head on straight again' weekend. Her chance to reset back to the Mistress Ice of a month before. Before she'd been foolish enough to sign up for the stupid roulette event, and Nolan Boeing had been insane enough to bid on her, making the dominant her submissive for one night.

What a fucking disaster. Why couldn't he just leave her alone?

Even as her addled brain thought it, the truth burned hot in her alcohol filled brain, refusing to let her forget, no matter how many alcohol units she ingested.

She stumbled to the wall of windows that looked out over Central Park. Even at eleven on a Sunday night, New York City was buzzing below her. From this height, she could look down at the busy street below and see several horse-drawn carriages. They were probably filled with lovers—kissing and holding hands romantically, whispering sweet nothings to each other, proposing marriage. All the things she'd sworn off years before when she'd decided all that mattered was her career. And for the most part, she was happy with her decision.

There was just one problem, and his name was Nolan Boeing.

Piper took another drag from her rock glass, swaying enough, she had to reach out and stabilize herself by grabbing the back of the tall-backed desk chair next to her. The twinkling lights of the city blurred. She told herself it was just the booze, but there, alone in the room, she was having trouble keeping up her lies to herself.

Piper Kole was a strong woman. She didn't cry. Tears were pathetic.

But in a moment of weakness, when no one was there to witness it, she felt her resolve crumble. The tears she'd been holding back spilled down her cheeks, dripping to the carpet below.

This was all Nolan's fault. He snuck in that call that afternoon from Shane Covington's phone, catching her off guard—gotten in under her radar. Despite the almost three thousand miles that separated them, it felt like he was here, in the room with her, ever since she'd hung up on him many hours before.

Because no matter how hard she tried, her brain refused to go more than a few minutes without thinking of him. The bastard had even been showing up in her fitful dreams during the few hours of sleep she managed to get each night since their fateful night at Black Light.

It was unacceptable.

If she couldn't forget him the normal way, she'd have to do it the old-fashioned way—pharmaceuticals and booze.

So, she drank until she'd emptied the glass of gin. Her stomach churned loudly, and for a brief moment, she almost took off for the bathroom, afraid she'd puke up the appetizers she'd eaten many hours before. Only when the feeling passed did she pull the chair over to face the wall of windows, finally taking a seat.

Piper let the tears fall, hoping all she needed was a good cry. Then her life could get back to normal. Once she gave herself permission, it didn't take long for old despair she'd been sure she'd vanquished to resurface, crowding into her already overwhelmed psyche.

She was successful, independent, rich, famous—she had it all.

So why the hell couldn't she just be happy?

The better question was, why couldn't she stop letting shit from the past haunt her? She'd spent a Goddamn fortune over the years, trying to exorcise her demons with a string of therapists. One after the other, they'd told her she'd never move on until she faced the demon head on. She'd been determined to prove them wrong.

Tonight, she knew she'd failed.

She wasn't sure how long she sat in that chair, crying and feeling sorry for herself, but with each passing moment, the unusual solitude she normally relished began to close in on her, reminding her how utterly alone she was in the world. It didn't matter how many millions of people recognized her when she went out in public, not one person out there really knew her—not the real Piper. Hell, she'd done such a great job of reinventing herself, even she wasn't sure who she was anymore.

The wave of loneliness washed over simultaneously with the truth there might be one person who remembered the real her. The woman she was before she'd been forced to turn her life upside down in order to get through the simplest of days. Only she knew the lengths she'd had to go to regain control of her life again.

Control—the tightrope game she and Nolan had played the night of roulette had been their own special brand of tug-of-war. When she had run out of Black Light, she was sure she'd won. Only now was she understanding she had won the battle, but Nolan was winning the war.

She reached into the pocket of the plush robe provided by the hotel and came out with her cell phone. She flipped to the Nolan Boeing contact record, not to phone him, but to look at the profile picture she'd uploaded.

God, she was pathetic, mooning over the picture of some guy thousands of miles away. She wished he'd call again, just so she could scream at him for ruining her 'reset' weekend. Instead of getting stronger, she was getting worse.

It was too easy to push *SEND*. Her hands trembled as she moved the phone to her ear, hearing two rings before her heart lurched.

"Piper? Is this you?"

God, he had the sexiest voice—a tad gravelly and perfectly deep—but it was the yummy, authoritative tone she'd always loved the most. Of course, she'd never tell him that.

Her throat was closed off from the effort trying not to cry. She should hang up but couldn't make herself break their tenuous connection.

Weak.

"I'm glad you called. I've been thinking about you all day."

No way was she going to tell him 'ditto,' which would have been an accurate response.

Piper's silence didn't seem to deter Nolan.

"I'm worried about you."

I'm worried about me, too.

"Where are you? I can come to you wherever it is. We need to talk."

She had to swallow several times before she was able to speak.

"I'm in New York."

"Okay, I'll catch a red-eye. You go to sleep, and I'll be there in the morning. Where are you staying?"

That tone.

"Man, yurr such a fuckin donamant."

"Damnit, you're drunk."

"Wouldn't have called if I wasn't."

His chuckle at the other end of the phone was unexpected. "Yeah, that sounds about right. I'm just glad you did."

"Why, so you can lecture me 'bout how I changed?"

"I've never lectured, but I am concerned. I'm missing something. I know it. And the sooner you tell me the truth, the sooner we can get past it."

"No getting past. It's an immovable roadblock."

"So... there is something. It isn't just my imagination."

He was twisting her words. She could verbally spar with Nolan on her best day. In fact, she wasn't afraid to admit she'd enjoyed their witty banter during roulette. But she was way too tipsy to be able to keep up with him tonight.

"Mistake to call... Gotta..."

"No! Don't hang up. We can change the subject."

It didn't take much to sway her to stay on the line. After all, she didn't want to go back to feeling alone after they hung up. Still, what was there to really talk about?

"So how 'bout that weather," she deadpanned.

God, she loved his laughter. She'd forgotten how much he could make her laugh until he reminded her the night of roulette. Despite the intensity of that night, she'd laughed out loud many times... right up until she'd had to crush him... literally.

"Why are you even talking to me? Aren't you mad at me for..."? She let her voice trail off, unable to sum up just how fucked-up their roulette game had been.

"Mad at you for crushing my balls, both physically and figuratively, only to leave me tied down and screaming at you—begging you to come back? In front of a couple hundred people? Many whom I consider personal friends?"

"Yeah. That."

There was his laughter again. Nolan Boeing was a happy man. She wasn't used to being around people like him.

"I've had time to think about it... a lot. I bought my way into the event, knowing what I was signing up for. You played the game by the rules. I may hate how it turned out, but I truly loved every minute of our time together."

"Liar. You did not enjoy when I stuck that plug up your ass."

"Don't remind me. I'm trying to forget that part."

"I'd have thought you'd want to forget about the very end."

"You mean when you used my cock as your personal dildo, riding me to your orgasm, then leaving me with blue balls, tied center stage?"

"Yeah. That."

"Naw, I loved watching you fall apart when you came. You were even more beautiful than I remembered."

Why did he have to say such nice things? He was making it impossible to stay angry with him.

"I feel cheated. I didn't get to see you come."

"And whose fault is that?"

"Fine. Maybe I had a bit to do with that part."

"Uh huh. Maybe. You owe me an orgasm, Ms. Kole."

"That's Mistress Ice to you. And it might be hard to accomplish three thousand miles away. And anyway, you made a terrible submissive."

"I did not. Your memory is faulty."

Even drunk, her memory wasn't bad enough to forget how confusing it had been to be with such a dominant man like Nolan. It had literally been years since she'd allowed a man to take the lead of her sexuality.

"What are you wearing?" His voice was so smooth—so sexy.

She took a few long seconds to play his game.

"Just a hotel robe."

"Tell me where you are. Sitting at a table? Standing near the window?"

"Don't look now, but you're domming me."

"Damn straight, I am. We aren't at Black Light, and you're drunk."

"What's me being drunk have to do with anything?"

"Because I can dom you tonight, and you'll forget about it tomorrow. We can both get a good night's sleep after having amazing orgasms. Think of it as a win-win."

She hesitated only a second before clarifying, "So, this is just a remote solution. I still get to be in charge in person?"

"If that's your way of telling me there will *be* more sessions in person, absolutely."

"Win-win."

It didn't take much to convince her to play along. She was desperate to maintain the tenuous thread holding them together, and if she got a good orgasm out of the deal, she might finally get some rest.

"Lay back on the bed with your upper body raised up on the pillows. Then open your robe, so your naked body is on display to the room."

"What if it's too cold in here?"

"Oh baby, I'm gonna help you warm up. Do you have a vibrator with you by chance?"

"No," she answered, walking to the bed to do as she was told.

This doesn't make me submissive. It just makes me... horny.

"Too bad. I'd have loved hearing you fucking yourself with it while pretending it was me."

Shit, he was good at this phone sex thing.

"Okay, tell me when you're in position."

"Yes, *sir*," she mocked, only the joke was on her.

"Damn, even knowing you're playing around, that went straight to my cock. As a little mental incentive for you, I'm sitting in my living room, looking out over the L.A. skyline, with my dick in my hand. It's already rock hard, ready to shoot jizz on the carpet, wishing it was buried in your pussy instead. That's what you do to me, Piper."

"Aww, you say the most romantic things."

His bark of laughter calmed her like no pills, booze, or therapy ever could—which pissed her off. Still, in her desperate state of mind, she held onto his voice like a lifeline, afraid she'd drown without him.

"You lying down?"

"Yep." She fought the urge to feel foolish, sitting taking orders like a… Her brain had started to form the word *chump,* but even drunk, she knew it was bullshit. She'd never thought of her submissives as chumps. What they did took great courage—handing over control to a sadistic woman bent on crushing their balls, who actually took pleasure hurting them.

What a bitch she was.

"Piper? Did I lose you, baby?"

"Uh… no. Still here." It took effort to stay focused.

"Close your eyes."

"Trying to put me to sleep?"

"Not quite yet. I need to hear you crying out my name as you come first. *Then* you can go to sleep."

"Pretty overconfident there, Boeing. You're three thousand miles away."

"All the better. We might kill each other if we were in the same room."

"Fair enough."

"Now, be a good girl and close your eyes."

Good girl. She was definitely not that. Still, she liked him calling her that, just the same.

"Now, use your hands to squeeze your boobs. Pretend those are my hands, massaging… pinching those gorgeous tits you love to flaunt in your designer dresses on the red carpet."

"Aww, you noticed? It's impossible to find a good bra to wear with those dresses."

"Focus, baby. I only care about those titties right now. Are they nice and hard?"

"Yeah, but I think it's more because of the aforementioned temperature of the room."

"Damn, even drunk, you're witty." He paused before adding more quietly, "I want to grow old with you, Piper. I can just picture us grey-haired and decrepit in our wheelchairs, still bantering back and forth, entertaining all the old folks around us."

Whoa! Where the fuck had that come from?

"Nolan..." she warned.

"Sorry. But, every word I said is true."

Piper let her imagination run wild, picturing them together and happy, years later with longing. She never looked too far ahead on purpose, afraid of seeing herself always alone. She had to admit, the silly vision calmed her.

"Won't we be the scandalous ones of the retirement home? Insisting on carrying around our crops on our wheelchairs just in case the mood should hit to crop each other."

He couldn't talk for a few long seconds he was laughing so hard.

"Oh, Piper. Thanks for that visual. You'll be the only woman in the whole place who has the orderlies fighting over taking care of you, so they can feel your crop on their ass."

"Maybe they'll give us a discounted rate if Mistress Ice keeps their employees in line."

"Maybe, although I'm pretty sure, we won't need the discount."

"Are you eyeing up my bank account, Mr. Boeing?"

"No, baby. I think you're forgetting who I am. I have my own money, remember? I don't need yours."

Unlike so many of the boys she played with.

He hadn't said that, but it still hung in the air between them.

He doubled down. "I don't need your fame or your fortune. I don't want your house or your damn cars. And I sure as hell don't need that enormous diamond collection of yours."

"You noticed. I love my diamonds. They're a girl's best friend."

"Yeah, well, fuck that. And for the record, that's the only thing I *do* want from you."

He'd lost her.

"I don't get it. You want my diamonds?"

"No, baby. I want to be your best friend."

Holy shit, he was gutting her. This call was such a mistake,

"Nolan…" His name came out as a sob.

"It's okay, Piper. I know you aren't ready to admit it yet, and that's okay. I'm willing to put in the time and wait."

The dam broke. Tears she'd pent up flooded to her eyes, spilling over her cheeks. She tried to keep Nolan from hearing her but failed.

"I'm there with you, baby. Feel my arms around you. Holding you. Protecting you from whatever bullshit you have chasing you."

She had no idea how many minutes went by with him cooing comforting words to her as she exorcized her demons. When her tears slowed, she'd reached for a tissue from the bedside table, blowing her nose with an unladylike honk.

His chuckle brought a smile to her face. "That's a good girl."

There it was again—*good girl.*

"I'm sorry."

"Don't be. I'm glad you trust me enough to cry in front of me."

Fuck me. Why does he keep saying these deep things? She had to try to lighten things up again. She was too drunk for this heavy shit.

"You promised me an orgasm, Boeing. Are you backing out on your promise?"

"Hell, no. Just took a little detour, but I'm ready to push your buttons now."

She didn't say it, but they both knew damn well, he'd already succeeded pushing her buttons.

"Now, hands back on your boobs and start moving them slowly down your chest… across your tummy. Let your legs fall open and dip your fingers into your cunt. Tell me, are you already wet?"

Fuck, yeah, she was, but she wasn't going to tell him that.

He didn't need her encouragement to keep directing her.

"Play with your pussy. Pinch that clitty of yours while you imagine it's my fingers. Press on it, nice and hard like you're humping me again back at Black Light. My cock is long and hard, just for you. You're climbing onboard and gonna take me for a nice ride, aren't you? That's it, baby. Ride me. Take your pleasure."

Her fingers flew across her body, chasing her orgasm, but it felt elusive—until Nolan upped their game.

Piper could hear the slapping of his stroking motion on the other end of the phone. He was jacking off at a fast pace—the exact pace she'd love to imagine him plowing her from behind. Dare she?

"Yes, that's it, Nolan! You have me bent over that fucking spanking bench, and you're behind me. You're squeezing my hips so hard, I'm gonna have bruises tomorrow. You're slamming your cock into me so hard and fast, it hurts."

"Shit… I hope you're close. I'm not gonna last much longer. Ready for my seed, baby?"

Damnit, so hot.

"Nolan!"

She hadn't meant to call out his name, but there it was, hanging in the air as she let the wave of pleasure wash over her, enhanced by the grunting groan at the other end of the phone. The wet squishing as she dripped her own juice out onto the clean sheet was the ideal harmony to his gasping for breath.

They recovered in amicable silence, letting a new blanket of calmness cover her.

"Thank you, baby."

"For what?"

"Calling. Talking. Not hanging up."

She didn't know what to say, so she said nothing.

"Same time? Tomorrow night?"

His question caught her off guard.

"I'll be in the air at this time tomorrow."

"Even better. I'll wait at your house."

"I'm not flying to L.A."

The lie fell from her lips so easily, it scared her. An instant regret took hold, recognizing lying to Nolan came with a price tag.

"Shit, well, I know you'll be home soon. You're presenting next Sunday."

"How did you know that?"

"You do realize I'm in the academy too, right?"

Shit. Maybe she should back out. She wasn't ready to see him again—not yet—she needed to get stronger.

"I need to go."

"Okay, I'll let you off the hook this time. Now, pull the covers up, so you don't get chilled. Sleep well, baby."

Despite his sign-off, the line stayed open, both of them silent for a long minute. Her mind raced. There were so many things she wanted to say.

She finally settled for, "Night Nolan."

CHAPTER 7

"If I didn't know better, I'd swear you were nervous."

Shane didn't need to see who had spoken behind him. He recognized the dungeon master, Elijah's voice as the older man slid onto the bar stool next to him while waving his hand to signal Susie at the other end of the bar.

"Let me buy you a drink on the house. You look like you could use it."

He knew he could use a drink, but he stopped the DM just the same. "Naw, I'm hoping to play tonight, so I don't want to drink another one."

"So, the plot thickens. I can't wait to see who has Shane Covington nervous."

"Fuck you. I never said I was nervous."

"No, you didn't, but you don't normally tear the labels off your beer bottle while glancing up at the entrance every two minutes, either."

Busted.

Okay, if truth be told, he was a little nervous. It had been a long time since he'd met a sub as perfect as Nalani seemed for him. That she was a complete newbie to the lifestyle was a huge turn-on to him. Her shy uncertainty, paired with her reluctant sexual hunger when he pressed her out of her comfort zone pushed every carnal button he had.

That, right there, was the problem. He knew he had the power to really fuck her up and didn't take that responsibility lightly.

He needed to take this slow. She didn't know it, but she'd been thrown into the deepest pool in town, and he didn't know for sure yet if she even knew how to swim. He felt a lot of pressure to be her lifeguard, ready to throw her a life vest, while his dark side hungered to hold her head under water until she came up gasping and sputtering for air.

Fuck, he really was an asshole.

"You haven't heard a word I've said, have you?" Elijah teased as Susie delivered her boss his beer.

"Sorry, man. I'm a bit distracted."

"I see that. Wanna talk about it?"

"Naw, I'll figure it out."

Elijah took a drag of his beer before answering. "If you say so." Shane thought he was done until he tacked on, "But I'm guessing you've finally found someone who might be into the fucked-up mind-games you like to play."

"Asshole. I confide in you, and now, you throw my shit back in my face?" Shane retorted defensively.

"Fuck you. I'm not throwing anything in your face. Have you forgotten what my job is, asshole?" Elijah snapped. The DM stopped to take another swig of beer before continuing, a bit calmer. "It's my job to help members through this complicated shit. We both know a good portion of the members come here for a bit of privacy, and that's fine. Others for a little slap and tickle to feel naughty before they go home to their vanilla life." Elijah leaned in closer, speaking softer, "But there is a group of hard-core members who really take their kinks to the edge. I count you in that category, and that means it gets complicated."

"Complicated is the understatement of the year." Shane stopped short of apologizing to the DM for his defensive outburst.

Elijah chuckled, proving he hadn't taken Shane's comments personally.

"You're doing better than a lot of people around here."

"How's that?" Shane asked, taking the last warm swig of his beer.

"You've taken the time to figure out what makes you tick, what you need. Most people bounce along, trying shit, never really figuring it out."

"So, the fact I know I'm a sick bastard who could do irreparable psychological harm to my subs if I'm not careful is my strength?"

"Whoa there, partner. That seems a bit melodramatic. You're at Black Light, which means anyone walking through that door knows the score. Give her some credit she'll be able to safeword if you go too far."

Shane sure as hell hoped Elijah was right. He looked at his watch for the tenth time in the last hour. Fuck.

"Well, I may be worrying for nothing, anyway. She's thirty minutes late. Maybe she already came to her senses."

"She'll show. Women don't pass up a chance to scene with Shane Covington."

Shane wasn't so sure about that. And why did the word *scene* seem out of place to describe what was going on between him and Nalani?

He was deciding if he wanted to take Elijah up on that next beer or just head upstairs and call it a failed night when Elijah whistled.

"Holy shit. What the fuck is she doing here? Dressed like that?"

Shane followed his friend's gaze toward the entrance, and

his heart lurched. Holy fuck, she'd come. And she looked... different.

Nalani glanced around the social area, finally smiling when she saw him at the bar. He couldn't take his eyes off her as she weaved through the mingling couples between them. She was in an understated little black dress that hugged her curves. The scoop neck showcased her pert breasts, and the high heels made her look taller and more confident.

Elijah stood, preparing to go to her. "I wonder why she's here."

Shane solved the mystery for his friend. "She's my date."

The shocked look on Elijah's face as he turned back to confront Shane spoke volumes.

"Let me guess... your little pep talk about anyone playing with me being able to take care of themselves doesn't apply to Nalani."

"Hell no, it doesn't. She's not a member. She's not even in the lifestyle, for Christ's sake."

"Like you said. It's complicated."

"No. She's off limits," Elijah argued, moving to stand between Shane and the approaching woman.

Unexpected jealousy flared up as Elijah reached out to grab Nalani's arm as she tried to walk past him to get to Shane.

"The hell she is. Who are you, anyway, her father?"

"I might as well be," Elijah retorted as he pulled Nalani closer to him.

"You're old enough, old man," Shane spat like a tenth grader in a schoolyard scrape.

"What's going on?" Nalani broke in between the men.

Hot anger turned Elijah's face red. "You're going home, that's what's going on."

Shane kept his attention on Nalani, watching for any evidence she was reassured at her friend's suggestion. To his relief, she looked angry at her co-worker as she yanked her arm out of Elijah's grasp.

"Why would I do that?"

"You aren't a member. You can't be here," Elijah reasoned.

"So, let me get this straight. You're fine with me coming down here several times a week to clean. You've even invited Madison, Avery, and me down for nightcaps, more times than I can count. But now, tonight the place is off limits?"

Shane was so proud of her. He was seeing a whole new side of his little housekeeper, and he liked it. Maybe she did have the backbone to keep his demons in check.

"It's not the club that's off limits. It's Covington. He's not a good fit for you. You want to learn more about the lifestyle, I'll hook you up. There are a lot of Doms who'd...."

"I don't want other Doms. I want Shane."

I want Shane. It was ridiculous how happy those three little words made him feel.

"You don't know him well enough."

"I know. That's why we're going on a date."

Elijah barked a manic laugh before correctly pointing out, "The fact that you call anything that happens here at Black Light a date means you have no clue what you're getting yourself into with him." Elijah paused before adding, "Nalani, please. I know what I'm talking about here."

Shane had sat on the sidelines, not sure how to defend himself since he'd been thinking the exact same things about himself before the DM had arrived. He was an asshole for enjoying the tortured indecision on her face as she tried to decide which side of the tug-of-war between the men she would end up on. Shane was determined it would be his.

"There's no rule that says employees can't date customers. Not at Runway and not at Black Light," Nalani reasoned with the DM. "So, why are you trying to stop me from doing something that literally every other employee has done in the past?"

"Not every employee…"

"Oh, please. Tyler plays with a different member every week. Susie accepts orgasms as a form of payment for drinks, and I've seen you playing with at least three members. And that doesn't even count Madison dating Trevor. How is what I'm doing any different?"

Damn, she was schooling the DM good. He almost felt sorry for him.

Almost.

Their argument was attracting the attention of those around them. How ironic that Shane got off making his subs do all sorts of humiliating things in public, but here, now, he felt protective of Nalani.

He stood, reaching out to her as she rushed forward into his arms. She hugged him tightly as the two dominant men started their stare down behind her back.

"You hurt her—and I mean really hurt her—and I'll hurt you," Elijah promised. "Got it?"

The Hawaiian beauty was trembling in his arms, reminding him he didn't want to fuck her up any more than Elijah did.

"Got it."

The men had come to a tenuous agreement.

"Maybe we should go somewhere else," Nalani spoke against his chest. "Or upstairs."

Shane was ready to agree when Elijah injected, "No. You should stay down here. I may not like it, but at least I can keep an eye on you down here."

"That's what I'm afraid of," Nalani groaned.

So, his little sub was embarrassed for her friends to see her playing. Shane could make that work in his favor.

Asshole.

Shane nodded at Elijah. "We'll at least start out down here."

Her muffled, "Yes, sir," surprised Elijah even more than it did Shane. With a curt nod, the older DM turned and stalked away from the bar area, heading behind the velvet curtain to the racier areas of the club.

He held her long enough for her trembling to stop before pulling back so he could look into her expressive eyes. She'd applied layers of eyeliner, mascara, and false eyelashes. The smoky eye shadow enhanced her golden-brown eyes, but it was the red lipstick that had his cock standing at attention. He wouldn't rest until he'd wrapped those lips wide around his cock, choking her until tears smeared that mascara.

He shook his head, asking her, "You hungry? Thirsty?"

"No. I ate a while ago. I'm good."

They turned to return to the bar where he helped her onto the tall stool next to his.

Only once they were sitting in silence, each looking forward to seeing the reflection of the other in the bar's back mirror, did it hit Shane how nervous he really was. The encounter with Elijah has made things worse, reminding him just how out of her league Nalani was, yet he was helpless to stop the game —not yet.

"What color are you right now, Nalani?"

"Color? But we haven't even started…"

"Color?" he repeated more sternly.

"Green, sir,"

Before he did anything else, Shane had one final thing to say to the innocent next to him. "Get used to the question. I'm going to ask it often tonight. As much of a prick as Elijah was to butt in, he isn't wrong to try to protect you from me."

Her lips curved up into a smile. "Are you trying to talk me out of this?"

"No, just trying to be fair to you."

"And just what is it you think you're gonna do to me that isn't fair?"

She'd asked so nicely, served it up superbly—he couldn't

resist. Turning to look directly into her eyes, he loosened the reins of his control.

"I'm gonna hurt you, Nalani. I'm not going to stop until you're screaming my name at the top of your lungs between your sobs."

Perfection—her feral fear was tangible, so damn beautiful.

Yep. An asshole.

HOLY SHIT, what the hell had she gotten herself into? Even after she'd calmed down enough from the disastrous exchange with Mr. Ainsworth to decide to keep her date, she'd still almost chickened out several times before she got here. Before arriving, she'd been more worried she'd be a disappointment to the celebrity who could date any woman he wanted. But now, she wasn't so sure.

She hated that Elijah had been right about one thing—she wasn't Shane's date. She wasn't entirely sure what she was to the dominant, but the way he was looking at her, she felt more like a lamb on the way to slaughter.

"I..." She what? She hadn't the first clue what to say to a man who'd just promised to hurt her and make her cry. Thank you seemed wrong. A thrum of fear burned in her tummy, but it was overshadowed by excitement. She felt alive.

"Do you want me to leave?" she finally asked.

He hesitated before answering with a simple, "Hell, no."

"Then, I'll stay."

Shane stood, helping her down from her stool, still acting the gentleman, before reaching down to pick up a black leather bag she hadn't seen on the floor, slinging it over his shoulder. Grabbing her hand in his, he took off for deeper in the club. She had to almost jog to keep up with his long strides.

The music got louder with a strong sexual beat once on the

other side of the velvet curtain. She could feel the bass humming deep inside her, vibrating near the elusive orgasm she was desperate to find. It had taken all of her willpower not to masturbate at home to take the edge off. Nalani was pretty sure Shane would have never found out, but she'd have known she hadn't obeyed him, and since it was one of the first commands he'd given her, she had been determined not to mess it up.

He weaved them through several of the platforms setup for members to play on. It took her self-control not to stare at the salacious scenes on the occupied raised stages. She tugged on Shane's hand to slow down as they passed a woman artfully wrapped in ropes, hanging from the rigging in the ceiling. Even over the loud music, Nalani heard her moans of pleasure as her dominant used a flogger on her exposed patches of skin.

Shane's lips were on the shell of her ear as he leaned down. "You want to be tied up and whipped, little girl?"

It was a ridiculous question she would have laughed at a week before, sure it was a joke. Tonight, it felt more like a challenge. He was testing her.

Be brave.

"The ropes look interesting. I'm less sure about the flogger."

"Don't knock it until you've tried it. If you let me, I can make you fly high with a flogger."

She tore her eyes away from the spectacle to look up into Shane's eyes.

"What does that mean? Fly high?"

His grin was alarmingly perfect, taking her breath away.

"I love how new all this is to you."

She felt blood rushing to her face. Was he making fun of her innocence?

"Sorry I asked," she mumbled, feeling foolish.

"Don't you dare be sorry. I mean it. I love that I get to introduce you to so many things I take for granted. Don't ever be afraid to ask questions."

Nalani searched his handsome face for signs of humor, but all she saw was sincerity.

Before she could come up with a response, he pulled her back into motion toward an empty plush chair right in the middle of the action where they would be surrounded by debauchery.

"Why can't we go to one of the rooms along the back hallway?" she called to him over the music.

He turned as he got to the lone seat to answer her. "I rarely play in the back rooms, Nalani. Can you guess why?"

His voice was so damn sexy—too bad the chill in his words scared her.

Her brain screamed the answer. "You like them to watch you?"

"Not really." When she didn't guess again, he added, "I want them to watch *you* as you struggle to follow my directions. The more they're paying attention, the more it's going to push you where I want you to go."

The look in his eyes warned her she may not like the answer, but she asked anyway. "And where is that?"

"Sometimes, it's heaven… but to be fair, sometimes it might feel like hell."

Holy fuck.

Before she processed the shocking words, he turned and pulled her the last few feet to the chair.

"Now, let's get comfortable. We're just gonna be voyeurs for a bit tonight. Ease into this before we jump all-in."

Nalani pushed down her disappointment. Her brain knew she should be grateful he was taking things slow. Still, it was as embarrassing as hell to know he thought of her as a newbie.

If the shoe fits, wear it.

Shane sat, leaving her standing awkwardly in front of him with nowhere to go. Did he expect her to pull over a chair from another sitting area? She glanced around to see if there even was seating open nearby. Finding none, she looked back at the actor in confusion.

"Kneel." Several intense seconds had passed before he spoke his one-word command.

The word was so simple, but obeying felt anything but. On the surface, there wasn't anything particularly sexual about the request, but knowing where they were—steeped in the sounds of pain and pleasure—she knew it was just the first of what she suspected would be many tests.

She wouldn't fail—at least not yet.

Nalani glanced down before slowly lowering herself to the floor and its industrial grade carpet that covered the seating areas. The fabric didn't give much cushion to her bare knees, but she couldn't think of that now.

Shane had spread his legs wide, motioning for her to take up the intimate place in between. He'd kept his leather bag in his lap, letting her watch as he unzipped it to rummage around and come out with a few items he hid from her.

"Color?"

True to his previous promise, he was checking in with her. She appreciated it.

"Green."

"Excellent. He moved his hands forward quickly, not letting her get a glimpse of what he had in his hand until he was wrapping it around her neck.

"It's what I call a kitty necklace—others would call it a posture collar, but it's not quite thick enough for that."

He buckled the stiff leather into place, the leather fitting her neck as if she'd sat for a fitting as. Wonderfully snug, but it felt heavy on her neck, impossible to ignore—which was probably the idea.

She found it odd to take comfort in the click as he clipped a leash to a hook on her collar, tying them to each other. She liked the idea of being tied to Shane Covington.

The leash had had an effect on the dominant as well. Nalani's heart raced at the feral look in Shane's eyes as he let his gaze move lower to stare at her cleavage before reaching out to cup her breasts through the fabric of her dress.

Many women were naked in the room, others wore fancy fetish gear, but Nalani was the only one whose dom thrust his large hands down the front of her dress, taking a few seconds to kneed her full breasts before pulling them up and out while pushing the fabric lower. The result was her boobs spilling over and out of her dress in an obscene display.

All things considered, she knew it was lame, yet the sudden flash of nudity was so unexpected, she threw her hands up to cover herself reflexively.

"Naughty girl. Time to start learning about my rules."

Shane grabbed her wrists, and despite his censure, she loved that he'd lunged forward to hug her, capturing her arms behind her back as he peered into her eyes from just a few inches away.

"Rule number one, you never try to hide any part of your body from me. Ever. Every inch of you..." He paused before adding, "Inside and out—is mine. To admire. To showoff. To pleasure. And yes, to punish."

With each added promise, her heart rate ratcheted up until she felt herself breathing heavily. She'd assumed he had finished. She was wrong.

"And that rule applies everywhere, not just here at Black Light. Upstairs in my bed... riding in a car... out in public at a restaurant. Understand?"

Her first thought was how exciting it would be to go anywhere with Shane Covington. How nerve-wracking it would be to be on his arm in public, being photographed with him. The thought of being picked apart by the tabloids scared her enough, but then she replayed what he'd said again in her head. He was going to show her breasts in public?

"Um... I don't understand. Why would you show any part of me naked in public?"

"That's a good question. The answer is complicated."

"Okay." She waited for him to explain, noticing he was trying to figure out what to say.

"I won't make you go out in public naked."

What a relief. She'd misunderstood.

"But I will make you go out in public with any number of sexy things going on others won't be able to see... unless they look closely."

Her mind raced to understand what he was saying, but it just wasn't making sense. He must have seen her confusion.

"I don't want to ruin it by telling you ahead since surprising you is half the fun, but... a couple examples might be me inserting a nice fat plug up your puckered ass, then taking you out to dinner. No one but you and I would know it was there, but I'll be rock hard the entire night, watching you shifting uncomfortably in your chair, blushing as you have to ask me permission to use the bathroom."

Holy shit, what? She hadn't even got that image out of her mind before he painted an even scarier picture of her possible future.

"Another favorite you can definitely count on is me inserting a vibrating egg in your cunt, then locking you in a chastity belt. I'll love using my remote control to turn it on and off intermittently while we're out, watching you struggling not to let those around us know you're on the edge, wanting to orgasm in the middle of a packed crowd."

"Oh God..."

"Nope. Just sir."

How could anyone with such a sexy grin have such a dirty mind? They'd barely spent any time together, but she already knew with certainty, he had already changed her. With each encounter, he'd shocked her, pushing her out of her comfort zone in the most unexpected ways. It would almost be easier if she didn't like how he made her feel. Then she could just walk away. But more than being afraid of Shane, she found herself mostly afraid of learning deep, new things about herself.

"You ready?"

"For what?" His question confused her.

Shane didn't answer immediately, looking pensive until he replied, "For more."

Nalani wasn't sure if she wanted him to be more specific. Did it matter? There was no way she was walking out, never to see Shane again, which gave her really only one option.

"Yes, sir. I'm ready."

She hated how her voice quavered. She wasn't even sure if he heard her over the driving beat of the music, but she suspected the sly smile on his face indicated he'd heard.

"Arms up."

Okay, that was a weird command, but one she could follow, at least until he leaned forward to grab the hem of her short little-black-dress and began lifting it up and over her head. The leash tying them together got wrapped up in the fabric, having to pass through the neckline as he pulled her dress off, carelessly tossing it to the floor beside his chair.

It took all her effort not to reach to cover her still exposed breasts, protruding over her black bra. It made her feel more conspicuous than simply being braless would. She was grateful to be facing Shane and not outward, so everyone in the room would see her pebbled nipples.

"Now, I have questions. You have answers. Ready?"

His smile was gone, his voice gruff, the fast swing of his contrasting personalities confusing her—one minute, gentle and protective, the next, sharp and dangerous. Shane was a complex package, so different from his public pretty-boy persona the tabloids painted.

"Nalani, I asked you a question."

"I'm sorry. Can you please repeat it?"

He yanked on the leash, bringing them only inches apart.

"What is it that's scaring you the most about playing at Black Light?"

Literally, dozens of answers jumped in her brain, vying eagerly to be picked.

"I have to choose just one?"

She saw the small curve at the corner of his lips, and it relieved her.

"Let's start with one, yes. Hopefully, we'll have more time to explore the list in its entirety on other days."

Whoa. Did he just insinuate this wasn't just a one-night fling? Nalani refused to give that another thought. Men like Shane Covington changed women like most people changed their clothes.

Her mind raced, trying to hone in what scared her the most about being a participant rather than a spectator at Black Light.

"Pain. I don't understand why some people crave it—either delivering or receiving it."

The woman hanging from the ropes behind her chose that moment to fill the room with a blood-curdling scream. It was the kind of shriek, had they been at the mall, everyone would be calling 911.

Shane's grin was back.

"I'm not a psychiatrist. I can't explain why people love pain, but I know this. You just creamed your panties hearing her cry out, didn't you, dirty girl?"

When she didn't answer, Shane leaned closer, reaching out and clamping down hard on her pussy. Shame washed over her as she felt her own wetness as he ground his palm against her neglected clit.

"Don't look now, but you're soaking wet, kitten."

His probing hands catapulted her to the brink of the orgasm she'd been missing since that afternoon… then they were gone.

She was left hanging over the cliff, unable to fall into her pleasure. It took a few seconds for her to realize the hiss she'd heard had come from her.

"You have a yummy growl, kitten. Sorry, but you don't get to purr quite yet. I need to introduce you to some pain first before you get any pleasure."

Her heart rate doubled at his promise. How foolish she'd been to answer him honestly minutes before. She prayed he wouldn't make her regret her answer.

"I think we should start out nice and simple, don't you? When you think of receiving a punishment, what do you picture?"

"Why do you keep asking me these questions?" His question frustrated her.

"Because I love to watch you blush, embarrassed as you're forced to admit, you have the same dirty thoughts I do. You're just better at hiding them from yourself."

She sincerely doubted that. Even in her wildest imagination, she could have never foreseen kneeling at the feet of Shane Covington, her tits out, talking about kinks.

"Close your eyes. I'll tell you a little story." He waited for her to comply before continuing. "I'm staying here at the mansion, and I leave to go out to an appointment. While I'm out, you come into my room to clean, and you find the stack of BDSM magazines I've left out on the bedside table. Unable to resist, you pick up the top one and start flipping through it, enjoying the photos of the submissives tied in all kinds of nasty positions, on the receiving end of an endless number of punishment implements striping their milky skin. Any number of fat rods are shoved into all of their exposed holes while they cry beautifully for the camera."

Holy shit. The man was a walking porn movie. Her brain ran amok, imagining the picture he'd painted for her.

"Boo."

Nalani almost jumped out of her skin—she'd lost herself down the rabbit hole of Shane's dirty imagination.

"Tell me. Now. What picture did your brain paint for your unfortunate submissive?" When she didn't answer, he pressed her. "Don't think about it too hard. Just spit it out."

She refused to open her eyes and see his handsome face judging her as she blurted her answer.

"She's tied down with her ass stuck up in the air, unable to escape."

"Yes, she is. Is her wet pussy on display?"

Shit, he was barely touching her, but the dirty talk in her ear was feeding the X-rated fantasies she barely acknowledged were her own.

"Yes," she whispered.

"How about her puckered asshole? Does it have anything shoved in it?"

"No!" she answered reflexively.

"Too bad… because watching tight holes be forced to stretch around huge shafts is one of my favorite turn-ons."

They were just naughty words, but damn, they were powerful. Her body shuddered as her mind recreated his vision, her own pucker physically contracting from the visceral fantasy.

"The only thing better than stuffed bottoms are stuffed bottoms with bouncing asscheeks as they are punished with a heavy paddle, turning milky skin to splotchy, red and hot patches that will hurt all over again when I squeeze the punished skin in my hands as I plow my hard cock into the exposed, dripping wet pussy, begging to be fucked."

She felt herself swaying on her knees, her body physically reacting to his indecent narrative. He was there to catch her, lifting her limp body onto his lap. She felt like putty as he manipulated her into a position her brain was not capable of conjuring on its own.

He didn't have her sitting on his lap. She wasn't even laid

across his knees in a traditional over-the-knee position she associated with spankings. Instead, he contorted her until she was straddling his body in the chair, facing away from him and toward the club.

Was she just being paranoid, or was every set of eyes in the club watching Shane dominate her?

It was with mixed emotions she felt him pressing against the middle of her back hard enough, she started to fall forward. Nalani scrambled to hold on to his knees, trying to keep from face planting as Shane's hands clamped down on her hips, holding her tight enough to at least keep her from toppling off his lap.

"Now, it's time for me to unwrap my present." His words were accompanied by the tear of the thin material of her panties. The only positive thing of the odd position was he at least couldn't see her face blushing at the thought of Shane inspecting her now exposed privates.

The whole scene was surreal. Like it was happening to someone else. That was until probing fingers lightly toyed with her clit, teasing her while his words took her submission deeper.

"There it is. Such a beautiful little pucker you have. I can't wait to watch my cock splitting you open here." His fingers moved up, pressing against her bottom hole, slipping the tip of his finger inside, setting off what felt like a firecracker at her core.

"Ah, beautifully responsive. I can tell you want that, too. Don't you, Nalani?"

Did he actually expect her to answer? The quick slap to her right asscheek told her the answer to that question was yes.

"No, sir."

"Liar. I'll have to punish you for that lie. Now, a bit of training. I prefer this position to traditional over the knee punishments for my submissives. I find it infinitely more intimate since it lets me watch carefully how your pussy and asshole are responding to your discipline, not to mention giving me a front-row seat to the damage being done by my punishment implement of choice. From now on, when I say, 'assume the position,' this is how I expect you to respond. Always naked, of course."

She was relieved for once, he hadn't asked her a question because she couldn't have formulated words at that moment to save her life.

"Now, enough talk. Time for action. Hands on the floor in front of you. Lift your head up and look out across the room." He waited for her to slowly comply with his instructions. "Do you see who's over there, watching our every move? He's near the pillar at the pool with his arms crossed, the angry scowl on his face."

She didn't need to follow directions to know who he was pointing out. Embarrassment flamed to her face, realizing her friend Elijah was indeed watching them intently.

"Tell me. Are you an anal virgin?"

His question was accompanied by a renewed pressure at the opening of her most private hole. The sensation of something puncturing her turned her answer, "Yes!" into a shout.

"I can tell. You're so damn tight. I can't wait to fuck you here," he said innocently as he breached her pucker.

"Oh God, no. Please. not there."

"You beg beautifully, Nalani. I can't wait to hear you begging for so many things. Now, kitten, time to insert your tail."

Tail? What the hell?

Cold wetness dribbled into the crevice of her exposed bottom. She felt his fingers massaging the wetness around her anal opening, popping in and out in quick insertions that felt strangely playful—until his fingers were replaced by something hard and cold. Her whole body tensed as the foreign object pressed for entry. Her brain scrambled, on overload as Shane's dirty narration continued.

"I know how much kitties love their tails. Since this is your first time, I'm giving you the smallest plug I have with me in my bag."

What was she supposed to say to that?

"Thank you?"

His chuckle behind her felt out of place with the hardness of the phallic being pressed into her body.

"Oh, stop! It's too big! It hurts!"

But he didn't stop, only pressed harder. The toy at her pucker got wider until she felt her body almost pop as the plug was sucked inside as if it were being welcomed home.

"I didn't hear any colors leaving your mouth, Nalani. I'm gonna let you in on a secret—I love hearing you screaming at me to stop. If you tell me it hurts, I'm more likely to double down than I am to stop. It's how my fucking twisted brain works. I stopped apologizing for it a long time ago, and I'm not always going to keep reminding you. But here. Tonight. Knowing how new you are to this, I'm going to remind you again, the only way to make me stop is to call out a color. Understand?"

Her brain fought to make sense of his words. Red. He was talking about safe words.

"What color are you, Nalani?"

He was cheating. The burn of her stretched hole screamed red, but the throb of her clit as he played with it hummed a big fat green.

"Confused...."

His chuckle had returned. "That's not a color, although I'm somewhat familiar with the word. It means your body loves everything that's happening, but your brain is fighting it."

Damn him, he wasn't wrong.

"Well, if you think you're confused now, just wait until you see what's coming next."

His words excited her, filling her with equal parts of yearning and dread. It was a jumble of feelings she was beginning to recognize as the Shane Covington affect.

The plug in her ass didn't hurt, just felt… weird. His fingers flicking across her clit, on the other hand, felt fucking great. She could feel her own wetness sliding down her inner thigh, she was so turned on. His focused petting of her pussy felt like heaven until…

Holy hell! She heard the crack of leather against flesh a split second before feeling the fire lighting up her right ass cheek.

He'd struck her. With what she wasn't entirely sure of, but it hadn't been his hand. The blossom of pain radiated out from the initial impact. Had it been the only sensation of the moment, she'd have the word red on her tongue, but his probing fingers on her pussy distracted her.

"You're so beautifully wet. You're leaving quite the mess to clean up on this chair, young lady."

Oh God, she really was the one making the mess with body fluids this time, wasn't she? She was just getting her head wrapped around that idea when the burn began on her left globe. She gasped, caught off-guard again by the pain.

She was a novice, yet she instinctively knew he wasn't giving her love taps—at least she hoped not since her backside burned from just two swats. What must it feel like to be truly punished like some of the submissives she'd viewed from the shadows of the club?

"Tell me, Nalani. Do you want to come tonight?"

That was a rhetorical question, right? His teasing fingers in her folds were just hard enough to make her feel crazed with need. She had started humping her hips up and down in an attempt to increase the too-light friction.

"Oh, yes, sir. Please."

"Orgasms come at a price with me, kitten. I don't like to hand them out easily. I find a horny kitten, desperate for some attention on her pussy, is one of my favorite turn-ons. What are you going to give me in exchange for letting you come so quickly?"

Her brain was addled, overwhelmed by the stimulations—both mental and physical. She couldn't form words, but it didn't stop Shane.

"I'll tell you what. Since we're still getting to know each other, I'll make an exception and help you get off, but you'll have to agree to help me do the same. Sound good?"

"Hell, yes." She couldn't wait to have him fuck her from behind. All of this slow foreplay had her hornier than she'd ever been in her entire life.

"Excellent. Now, all you have to do is trust me."

His words were still hanging in the air as the paddle connected with her right cheek with force again. Nalani arched her back, pressing into a pushup as she felt Shane's knees squeezing her body, keeping her from scrambling away from him and the pain.

The next blow came quickly, and the shooting pain left a throbbing agony as his paddle moved between her left and right globes at a steady pace as his fingers thrummed her pussy like he was playing a stringed instrument. Pleasure and pain jumbled together as she felt her body leaning into it all.

She lost track of how long the torture continued. Several times, the word red almost popped out, but she held her breath through the worst of it, letting the warmth move deeper... lower... igniting needs she'd never understood until that moment.

Her bottom had to be beet red by the time she heard the implement he'd been holding fall to the floor. His hand reached for the plug seated in her ass, pulling it out and shoving it back in while his left hand continued to stroke her clit at a fast pace.

Her body was on fire, the flames licking at her until she was shamelessly humping his lap.

"Such a dirty girl. So desperate to be fucked."

Her frustrated growl coincided with his pulling out the plug and shoving it back inside her. That wasn't where she wanted to be fucked. She wanted him inside her pussy.

"Yes! Please!"

Her body exploded the second he pinched her clit. He was being anything but gentle, squeezing her swollen nubbin so hard, the orgasm crashed over her. As heavenly as it felt, a small part of her felt cheated. Once again, he'd played her body without actually fucking her. Her core clenched, wishing it were full of the thick dick he'd showed her in his room earlier that day.

Nalani was vaguely aware of him pulling her up, letting her snuggle against him on his lap. She wasn't sure which part she liked more—his arms wrapped around her protectively or the feel of his rock-hard cock under her still-plugged bottom.

CHAPTER 8

The only thing Shane loved more than pushing a sub to the edge of her comfort zone was catching her after she'd fallen hard. Nalani's trembling in his arms as she recovered from her first scene at Black Light fed his fucked-up kinks. He held her close, the smell of her vanilla shampoo tickling his nose as he cooed soothing words as the natural beauty came down from her sexual high.

It was a bit unnerving how terrific she felt in his arms, her naked body molding against his as she wiggled in his lap, torturing the steel in his jeans. He took a second to unhook the clasp of her bra, the only stitch of clothing she still wore, pulling it off and throwing it to the floor with the rest of her clothes.

As he rested his chin on her head, he glanced out, locking eyes with the dungeon master, still standing guard across the room like a protective father. The standoff lasted a few long seconds until Elijah gave a small nod of approval before breaking the visual connection and sauntering off toward the back hallway.

The only thing keeping Shane from truly enjoying his aftercare was the constant thrumming of his own need, made worse by the friction of the anal plug still lodged in her cute ass. Shit, he'd almost shot his load, watching her tightest hole stretching to accommodate the small plug. He would have to be careful to gradually stretch her before fucking her ass the way he wanted to—hard and fast like a piston.

"How you feeling down there? You thirsty?"

"Uh huh," she cooed softly.

The idea came in a flash. He really was a prick, but then again, he'd never tried to deny it, so…

Shane detached himself enough to reach down to his bag next to the chair and come out with one of the bottles of water he carried and the other supplies his kitten needed.

He could feel Nalani watching him as he jostled until he could reach to uncap the bottle. The second the water started splashing into the metal bowl with the picture of a kitten on the side, he felt her body tense.

Once the bowl was half full, he set the bottle back down on the side table, turning to look down into her wide eyes. She was such an innocent, it was obscenely easy to shock her. He couldn't remember the last time he'd had as much fun playing with a submissive. He held the bowl closer.

"Be a good kitty and lap up your water."

"But… you're joking, right?"

"Do I look like I'm joking?"

"Why would I drink out of a bowl? Just hand me the bottle."

"Kittens don't drink out of the bottle, now do they?"

Still uncertain, she reached out to try to hold the bowl. He held it away from her, cautioning, "Naughty kitty. You don't have any hands."

Her panic grew as they continued their stare down.

"I'm not thirsty anymore."

"Nalani… you need to hydrate. Now."

She blushed beautifully, glancing around the room, clearly worried about how many people were watching.

He almost came in his jeans on the first tiny flick of her pink tongue. She didn't even touch the water with her tentative swipe. He lost himself, watching her next few laps, imagining that tongue licking his balls… the cum at the tip of his hard-on… rimming his own ass like the dirty girl he would enjoy turning her into.

Droplets of water sprayed on her face and her bare tits as she lapped at the water. He couldn't wait to replace the innocent water on her eyelash with a glob of his own cum, taking extra care to smear her makeup.

When she'd quenched her thirst, he set the near-empty bowl aside before roughly grabbing her face in his hands, holding her captive as he rekindled their smoking hot bond.

"Damn, that was sexy. I have a few other places I need that tongue of yours." Her eyes widened as he tacked on, "I hope you're still thirsty. I have something thicker I need you to drink."

Shane released her face, his own growing need helping press her off his lap and back to her knees in front of him. It only took a few seconds to undo his jeans, lifting his ass enough to push them to the floor. He'd come commando, and the open-mouthed 'O' on Nalani's face told him she approved. Anxious to feel that tongue on his flesh, he used her leash to yank her face forward into his lap.

"Stick that tongue of yours back out, kitten. Time to lap up something harder."

Shane wasn't surprised at her first tentative swipes. Blowjobs were pretty standard sexual fare, even outside of the BDSM lifestyle, so the fact she was clearly a novice at even this simple act thrilled him. While most men might grow impatient with her hesitant licks, each shy lap of her tongue flamed his libido until he found himself gripping the arms of the chair, fighting to keep from coming too soon.

He resisted giving her directions until she reached to grasp the base of his shaft with her petite left hand.

"No hands. In fact, put your hands behind your back. Take the end into your mouth and show me how far down your throat you can stuff this big boy."

He suspected she'd deny it, but the beauty on her knees loved his dirty talk. Her golden-brown eyes had a way of glazing over with a smoky haze of lust. He hated to lose their visual connection as she leaned over his lap to suck on the tip of his cock like a lollipop, sucking and lapping at his shaft, creating the sexiest soundtrack.

It didn't take long for Shane to be on the brink of coming. He fought his own body, determined to hold off as long as possible, in part just to make it last but more because he hadn't even started to push Nalani out of her comfort zone. Knowing he was short on time, he thrust his fingers into her thick, dark hair, grasping her head, forcing his erection deep enough to hear her gag.

"Eyes."

It took several long seconds for her to comply, and when she did, she had tears spilling over her eyes from the exertion of the blowjob. At that moment, he was certain there wasn't a more alluring sight in the entire world than this woman on her knees, struggling to accommodate his cock stuffed down her throat. He reached out with his thumb to swish at the tears on her cheek, careful to smudge her mascara, so she was perfectly ruined by him—*for* him.

The panic in her eyes fed his dark side, and it took all of his self-control to use his grip on her head to lift her head off his lap, giving her a few seconds to pant and sputter beautifully.

He pushed her harder, pulling her back down, thrusting deeper until she threw her hands forward, frantically pushing against him, struggling to clear her throat as her body convulsed, gagging. Shane put the face-fucking on a brief hold, pulling Nalani off his cock again, and leaned forward to talk against her ear as she gasped for air.

"I've never seen anything or anyone more stunning than you are right now, kitten. You, on your knees, gagging on my cock—trusting me to keep you safe—it's the biggest turn-on. The only thing that will make this better is watching you in a few minutes as you have to keep swallowing to drink the gallon of jizz I have waiting to fill your mouth, throat, and belly. I'm going to spray some of it on your face and tits, then rub it in, so everywhere you go, you'll smell like me... like us... like sex."

He was too close to see her reaction to his dirty rant, but the low growl that came from her fed his dark kinks.

Enough of a break. This time when he grabbed her head and pressed down, Nalani took him deep, renewing her gagging as she bobbed up and down until he felt the first jet of spunk boiling over. Her panic was real as she tasted him, unable to pull away, courtesy of his hands holding her in place.

He'd edged himself all day, so he had a massive load for his sub. Her throat squeezed his cock as she fought to swallow, choking and sputtering until globs of his ejaculate spilled out and down her chin to drip on her bare tit. Recognizing her panic, Shane pulled out just as a last small jet of cum sprayed on her face, landing on her cheek and forehead.

They each worked to catch their breath from the amazing intimacy they'd just shared. Shane reached out, smearing the white, sticky ejaculate all over her face, taking care to pull his thumb across her lipstick and mascara.

"Fuck, kitten. I haven't even stuck my dick in your cunt yet, and you're already proving to be a filthy little slut."

The anger flashed in her eyes so fast he had to replay his words, scrambling to explain.

"Believe me, with me, being a filthy slut is the highest of compliments, Nalani."

"Yeah, well, I don't like it." Her submission had vanished. She was serious.

So, he became serious too.

"Okay, noted, but I noticed you didn't use your safeword, so..."

"Yellow."

Shit.

"Fair enough. No more *slut,* and I'm guessing *whore* is out too. I get it. We don't know each other well enough yet. All I ask is you keep an open mind, and if at some point, you trust me enough to use those words to describe you during a scene, you'll reconsider and let me know."

She hesitated before adding, "I don't think I will, but if I do, I'll let you know."

He pulled her into his arms, looking down into her cum covered face.

"Congratulations. We just had a successful BDSM negotiation session." When she didn't answer him, he added. "Now, I'd like to negotiate exactly what it's going to take to have you sleeping in my bed upstairs tonight."

IT WAS ODD, the first thought Nalani had at Shane's invitation to sleep in his bed was, she sure as hell hoped he planned on having sex before they slept. As eye opening and exciting as their time together had been at Black Light, a part of her felt cheated.

Maybe she really was the slut he'd called her since all she could think about was having his cock buried deep inside her. There was no way she was going to admit that to him, of course —he already had way too much power over her.

"That could be arranged, but the price I demand is I must

have coffee first thing when I wake up, or I can't be responsible for my actions," she teased, keeping things light.

"Deal. But..." Shane got a mischievous look in his eye, she was beginning to recognize meant he had a filthy idea, no doubt about to shock her. "Do you only need coffee when you wake up after dawn, or do I need to be prepared to get you coffee every time I wake you up during the night to ravage you?"

His hands were roaming all over her body, pinching, squeezing, tickling...

Nalani broke into giggles at his teasing, his playful grin taking her breath away. She'd almost forgot whose arms she was snuggling into, but at that moment, he looked like the larger-than-life hero he'd played in last year's summer blockbuster movie.

The realization slammed into her. How the hell had she ended up here tonight, playing with *the* Shane Covington?

"What's wrong?" His smile was gone.

"Nothing." She tried to smooth over the moment, not wanting to admit how vulnerable she felt.

"Bullshit. Something changed thirty seconds ago, and we aren't moving until you tell me what it was."

She looked away, unable to return his intense scrutiny. He waited, proving he wasn't going to just let it blow over.

"I'm waiting, kitten."

His use of the nickname helped her return his gaze.

"Why kitten?" she spat.

"Don't change the subject."

Shit.

"Okay, fine. Then, why *me*? You're Shane Fucking Covington. You can snap your fingers and have anyone you want in your bed tonight. Why a housekeeper, working her ass off to make her rent each month." She hated the defensive tone in her voice but was helpless to stop it.

"I can help with..."

"Stop! I don't want your fucking money." His cavalier offer annoyed her. She tried to snatch her arm away, but his grip was too tight.

"What do you want, Nalani?" Shane pressed her.

"Right now, I want to know, why me? You can have someone more famous, rich, beautiful..."

It was Shane's turn to glance away for several long seconds. She could see his jaw clenching and unclenching as he contemplated his answer. When he returned his gaze to hers, the intensity in his eyes took her breath away.

"Listen carefully, kitten. I don't give a shit about rich or famous. And as for beautiful, I've never been with anyone even half as beautiful as you are. Not only are you pretty on the outside, but you have this elusive balance of strength and vulnerability that literally pushes every button I have.

"I've spent a lot of time dissecting all the fucked-up things that make me tick, and I stopped apologizing for them a long time ago, but that doesn't change how damn hard it is to find women into the same hardcore things. Women who will trust me enough to do the things you did with me tonight and so much more. More importantly, as a celebrity, I have the added burden of finding this rare gem who also doesn't want to sell the salacious story to the tabloids for fifty grand."

The sincerity of his words calmed her, but she pressed him, "And how do you know I'm not one of those women who'd sell you out?"

His hands squeezed her biceps harder, reminding her they were having this deep discussion in the middle of Black Light while both naked.

"I just know. Just like you know, I'm going to push you to the very edge, but you can trust me to always catch you."

As she internalized his words, she recognized them as the truth. As crazy as some of the things were that he'd done with her, she still felt remarkably safe with Shane.

Around them, the sounds of a nearby couple enjoying pounding sex broke into their intimate discussion. They shared a knowing grin as Shane pulled her into a hug, and she felt his manhood sandwiched between them.

"Please… come upstairs with me. I'm not ready for our night to end yet."

The depressing thought of walking out, maybe to never see Shane again, helped her answer. "Neither am I. And since I have tomorrow off, I guess it won't hurt."

"Isn't the club closed on Tuesday's too?"

"Yes, but I think we should just take things one day at a time, don't you?" There was no way she was going to get her hopes up they'd spend two whole days together.

"If that's the only way I'll get you upstairs, then sure. I'll make Tuesday tomorrow's problem."

God, that mischievous grin of his should be outlawed. She suspected it was going to get her into a lot of trouble.

Shane looked around, waving his hand at someone across the room. When Tyler stepped up next to them, she was jolted back to reality, bringing her arms up to cover her breasts from her co-worker and friend.

"Any chance you can find us two robes?" Shane shouted over the music.

"Sure thing. I'll be right back."

As soon as the dungeon monitor left, Nalani bent down to pick up her discarded clothes. The jolt lit her up, reminding her she still had a butt plug in her ass, not to mention, wearing a collar and leash.

"Can you please take the plug…" her voice trailed off.

"Not yet. Upstairs."

"You want me to wear it after we leave the club?" She was scandalized.

"Of course. I wasn't joking when I said you'll be wearing plugs in restaurants very soon if I have anything to say about it."

She was spared having to come up with a retort by Tyler returning with two plush Black Light robes hung over his forearm, handing them to Shane, then discreetly leaving.

Technically, Runway was still open, so when Shane pulled on her leash and started heading toward the staircase, she panicked.

"I have a code for the elevator we can take straight to the second floor. We shouldn't be seen in Runway like this."

She could swear she saw disappointment on Shane's face at her suggestion. It hit her, knowing what little she knew about him, he'd probably been looking forward to parading her through the mansion on her leash, and she honestly didn't know how to process that. To her relief, once they had all their clothes and toys cleaned up, Shane pulled her by the hand toward the elevator.

Within minutes, they were standing outside the Paris suite. It felt so weird to be there at night. Even knowing Mr. Ainsworth hadn't rented his suite that night, she couldn't help but worry, at any moment, he would come barreling out of the Hong Kong room, yelling at her.

Shane was fumbling through the bag, obviously trying to locate his guest key. Anxious to get safely inside, Nalani stepped up to the retinal scanner and supplied her eye print only available to employees. The lock clicked, and the door to the suite popped open.

The relief she felt the second they were behind closed doors quickly evaporated as the predatory look on Shane's face had her heart racing. He took a moment to take his duffle bag with their clothes and supplies over toward the luggage rack near the desk before spinning to pin her with a devious grin.

"Now…" He rubbed his palms together gleefully. "It seems I have you cornered. I have so many filthy things I want to do to that sinful body of yours, I barely know where to start."

He took a step forward, causing her to self-consciously take a step back.

"I was sort of hoping to start with a shower. Someone seems to have smeared bodily fluids all over me."

"I wonder who would do that?" he grinned, taking another step.

They were in a game of cat and mouse. Step by slow step, he approached, and she took corresponding evasive steps until the hard wood of the door was at her back.

Her pulse raced with excitement. Despite his predatory approach, the only thing Nalani was truly afraid of was how fantastic it felt to have a man like Shane looking at her as if he wanted to consume her.

She waited, her back against the door, while he stalked forward—the hunter after his prey. When he was close enough to touch her, Shane reached out, placing his hands flat against the door, caging her between his body and the unforgiving wood without actually touching her.

His face was close enough for her to feel his breath on her cheek as he leaned in playfully. "What should I do with you now that I caught you, kitten?"

"I hear kitties love to be petted."

"Oh, I'll be petting you, alright—inside and out."

Shit, the things he said should be outlawed.

"I know you mentioned a shower, but I'm not inclined to let you wash my cum off just yet. I love having you marked with my seed. And those lines of mascara from when I face-fucked you are a thing of beauty."

She'd barely known him a few days, but he was already rubbing off on her. That had to be the only logical reason for the thought that came to her brain. Never in a million years would she have said these words a week before, but here… now…

"I'm disappointed," she teased. Surprise registered in his

hazel eyes. When she knew he was waiting for more, she added, "Here I thought you'd be able to produce plenty of cum to replace it if we wash it off, but if that's all you got, well maybe I should go home after all."

Nalani squealed with delight as Shane took the bait, leaning his shoulder down to press it against her tummy and scoop her up and over his shoulder. His palm lit up her tender ass as he took long strides toward the bathroom.

"Such a naughty girl. Challenge accepted. I'm gonna have so much fun keeping you nice and dirty."

His promise went straight to her core. Shane Covington was anything but predictable. A sliver of fear ran down her spine, making her feel more alive than she could ever remember.

A niggle of worry about how much it was going to hurt when this tryst was over and Shane moved on to play with his next conquest tried to push into her brain, but she fought it. There would be plenty of time to wallow about what she'd lost after it was gone. She needed to stay present and try to enjoy all the new experiences now before they were lost.

He headed straight to the walk-in shower with the glass door that was a pain in the ass to clean. Pushing away thoughts of cleaning up any mess they made, Nalani instead focused on how nice it would be to use the spacious upscale room as a guest instead of caring for it as an employee.

Shane didn't even bother taking their robes off before he turned on the faucet. The three different jets of water sprayed into motion. Nalani squealed when the cold water from the rain shower overhead drenched her upside-down head.

"It's cold!"

"All the better to get those tits of yours nice and hard."

The man was incorrigible. She should be outraged, maybe insulted—certainly scandalized—at the things that came out of his mouth, but with each filthy promise, the fire in her girly parts flamed higher.

By the time he'd set her on her feet and was helping to peel off the wet robe, the water had begun to warm. It took only seconds for them to stand naked, the robes heaped in the corner of the shower.

Nalani tried to step out of the direct water, but Shane held her still, looking down into her eyes with longing. Their stare down started to feel awkward, so Nalani closed her eyes and started to turn her face into the stronger jet of water coming from the back wall of the marble shower.

"Not yet. Leave the ruined makeup for a bit longer."

"You seem to have a thing for my makeup."

"Naw," he grinned. "I have a thing for ruining your makeup while doing nasty things to you. You have no idea what it does to me."

They were standing close enough to each other, she could feel the brush of his erection grazing her tummy. Feeling playful, she reached out to wrap her right hand around the base of his cock.

"Actually, I'm getting a pretty good idea of what it does to you."

Shane groaned, wrapping his own fist over hers, stilling her playful strokes.

"You don't want to do that, or we might lose one of those messy loads I'm planning on bathing you in."

She felt like a whole different person than she was a few days before. Never in her life had she even thought of the dirty things flitting through her brain at that moment, let alone say them out loud.

"Promises, promises..."

Shane's self-control snapped like a rubber band. In a split second, he went from playful and sexy to a man possessed—roughly spinning her around and hugging her back to his front, crashing them into the front glass of the shower so hard, it was a wonder it didn't break. His lips were against her ear, sucking her right lobe into his mouth while grinding his hips into her, trapping her body between his hard muscles and the unforgiving glass.

"Look outside the shower. Do you see our reflection in the mirror?"

Nalani's brain fought to hear his words and make sense of them. Her body was like putty in his hands. It took her a few long seconds to look out to the mirror, but when she did, the reflection staring back at her was surreal.

The vision in the mirror was so sexy, it didn't register at first the ruined woman was her. The word he'd used at Black Light came to mind, although she'd never it admit it, but truthfully, the woman in the mirror looked like a well-used whore. Funny how, when her own brain formulated the word, it didn't offend her nearly as much as when Shane had called her one.

His left hand slid down, off her hip, diving in to flick his fingers through her wet folds, teasing her swollen clit. As nice as it felt, his fingers were not what she longed to touch her there.

"Shane..." His name was a prayer on her lips.

"Tell me... Say it."

"What?"

"What does your body need?"

Gone was all softness. His fingers pinched and probed hard enough, it hurt, yet when she got close to tipping into pleasure, he backed off—reading her body perfectly if his goal was to withhold the elusive orgasm.

"I can do this all night, kitten. You, on the other hand, won't be able to walk because I'll frig you raw until you say it. Now," he demanded, "what do you want, Nalani?"

Christ, that tone, those words, the dominant glare in the mirror, his warm breath against the crease between her neck and shoulder—the sexy package that was Shane Covington pushed her to beg.

"I need you!"

"Need me how?" He wasn't going to make this easier on her.

She stammered, so horny she could think of nothing but what she needed.

"Inside me!"

"Getting closer, but I need to hear you beg for what you need."

Nalani whined, frustrated at him pushing her out of her comfort zone. Still, as he edged her higher, she acknowledged she was the amateur—he was the pro. He would win this battle of wills.

"Fuck me! I need you inside me!"

It happened in a split second. One minute her core was cramping, desperate for something hard to scratch her itch, the next, his cock was buried so deep, it hurt. Shane was a man possessed, grabbing her hips and actually lifting her enough to pull her lower body away from the glass.

"Hands flat on the glass. Bend over so you can take it deep like the dirty girl you are."

Nalani had no choice but to comply. She was putty in his hands, letting him maneuver her body the way he wanted while he never missed a beat of his piston action, pounding her hard enough, her forehead banged into the glass with each thrust, warm water flicking all around them.

She had never felt so full—ever. Shane's pole stretched her until she burned, but he wasn't slowing down. She could barely function as she neared her peak, driven higher by the passion of the moment. When Shane yanked the forgotten anal plug from her body in a fast motion before shoving it back in at the same time he was plunging his dick deep, Nalani cried out. Having come less than an hour before, he had excellent staying power, riding her pleasure to her eruption as she arched her back and cried out unintelligible words.

"That's a good girl. I feel your cunt squeezing me as you squirt your juices all over me and down the drain. It's a good thing we're fucking in the shower. You'd be making a hot mess all over the carpet if I'd tried to fuck you bent over the bed."

Oh my God. The things this man said were obscene—and she loved every single syllable. She wasn't sure what that said about her moral fiber, but at that moment, she couldn't have cared less.

"Shit..." His curse sounded legit, but she was too far gone in her rapture to try to understand. "We didn't talk birth control. Please tell me you're on the pill, so I don't need to pull out."

Did he expect her to formulate words at this juncture? His swat to her ass-cheek told her that he was indeed expecting an answer.

"On pill..." was all she managed to get out before her next climax hit hard. The only thing that could make it better was the corresponding growl of satisfaction from the man buried inside her. He hadn't been joking about having plenty of cum—she could swear he shot so many ropes inside her, she felt hot jizz spurting out and onto her inner thighs.

The position was awkward, and once her sexual high crested, her strained legs started to vibrate under her. Nalani was pretty sure she would have toppled over to the marble floor of the shower if Shane hadn't wrapped his arm around her waist to hold her steady as he let his erection die down.

The glass had started to fog over, courtesy of the hot steam and even hotter sex. At that moment, all she wanted to do was finish rinsing off and crawl under the luxurious sheets and take a nap.

After she peed, that was. As she felt Shane's shaft slipping out of her pussy, the urge to pee hit her. Anxious to finish their shower, Nalani leaned back, stretching to get her head under the overhead jet of warm water.

"Can you hand me the shampoo?"

"Allow me."

Within seconds, Shane's fingers were massaging the

shampoo through her thick hair, working it into a lather as she closed her eyes, enjoying the sensations. She lost track of time, enjoying the kneading, so gentle in contrast to the sex just minutes before. Did she imagine things when she heard Shane cooing soft words of how much he wanted to take care of her?

An application of conditioner followed before Shane's slippery fingers roamed her body, pinching and squeezing while pretending to be washing her limbs. Her skin tingled everywhere he touched, enjoying his intimate exploration with her eyes closed.

Only when his hands arrived at her most private parts did Nalani tense. His yank on the butt plug sent a jolt of shock through her body. As full as she'd felt, she didn't like the emptiness left behind after he pulled the hard sex toy from her anal cavity. It made a clunk as he dropped it onto the teak bench at the end of the shower.

When he returned to where she stood under the water, she reached for the bar of soap he'd been using, lathering her own hands before reaching out to glide her palms over the muscular chest she'd been admiring. She felt his heated stare as he turned himself over to her, allowing her to explore his body as he had hers.

She felt like a kid opening the best gift ever on Christmas morning. Working slowly to make it last, Nalani touched first his left arm, up and down his toned biceps, then his right. He was almost a foot taller, so she had to reach up to wash his shoulders, back down his chiseled chest, and through that sexy happy trail of dark masculine hair pointing the way to her promised land.

Wanting to prolong their fun, she knelt on the shower floor, slowly massaging up and down each of his legs, purposefully trying to ignore the semi-erect perfection at eye level.

Nalani may not know much about the movie industry, but she knew this. If his career as an A-list movie star ever tanked, he could make it big in the porn industry. Wonderfully long and thick, the best part of his cock was, the man clearly knew exactly how to use his tool as his most valuable weapon. She had certainly been slain by it.

Even being a bit sore from their play, she felt a renewed pang of desire, wishing he'd just sit down on the bench so she could climb onto of his lap and go for a nice ride.

"I think I've let you explore long enough. You've got me squeaky clean."

She felt his hands on her wet hair, stroking her as she knelt in the center of the shower. She was about to push back to her feet when she felt Shane's pressure, keeping her on her knees. Her heart leapt, assuming he was ready for her to give him another blowjob, but when she reached out to hold his cock again, he pulled his hips back and barked what sounded like an order.

"Eyes."

Nalani did her best to look up from her knees, but she had to shield the left side of her face from the spray of warm water still showering them. They may not know each other well, but she already knew the lust-filled glare in Shane's eyes spelled danger. Her pulse spiked, bracing for what she suspected would be his next dirty request.

"Do you remember my first rule?"

Her brain scrambled to recall their play at Black Light. It was only an hour before, but there was so much happening, it felt like it was long ago.

"I'm not supposed to use my hands when…" Her voice trailed off, self-conscious.

"When what, kitten?" He was enjoying this entirely too much.

"I'm sucking you," she answered softly.

"Good. And what part of me is it you're going to get very good at sucking again?"

The jerk. He didn't even try to hide his lusty grin.

"Your cock."

"Excellent. But technically, it's any body part I ask you to suck." Why did his grin grow at that statement?

"Time for rule number two. I'm guessing it's going to be a bit harder for you to accept, but that's why we're going to get started practicing right away."

Her heart pounding, she wished he'd let her stand up for this discussion. Somehow, being on her knees only inches away from his thick erection made his promise that much more frightening. Leaning down, he took her still dirty face in his hands, holding her tight and leaning in so there was no way to escape his dominance—not that she wanted to.

It wasn't until an awkward silence fell between them, Shane spoke words she'd never dreamed she'd hear in her life.

"I'm gonna love showering with you often, kitten, since God knows, I plan on keeping you nice and dirty as much as possible. But I have a rule for our showers."

His predatory gaze had her overheating as she waited impatiently.

"Neither of us will pee before we get in the shower. Just like your orgasms, I'm taking control of toilet usage when we're together."

His words didn't even register. What the hell did that even mean?

Unaware she was scrambling to make sense of what she had obviously misheard, Shane issued an order.

"Now, crawl over to the drain and squat like the dirty girl you are. I'm going to watch your bright yellow piss wash down the drain, then I'm going to wash my kitten's pussy like a good Daddy."

CHAPTER 9

Perfection. There wasn't a better word to describe the lovely humiliation mirrored back at him from those golden-brown eyes as wide as saucers. His filthy rant had worked flawlessly, shocking Nalani into her role as the blushing innocent about to be corrupted.

He'd learned long ago just how powerful dabbling around with watersports was. It wasn't necessarily he had a kink for pee play like other dominants he knew. To him, it was a means to an end. Few things pushed a reluctant submissive into deep submission better than controlling the bodily functions polite society told them was private—dirty. He'd even given scat play a shot once but now considered it one of his own hard limits.

But Nalani didn't have to know that—at least not yet.

And while scat was out, everything about pissing worked for Shane. In fact, he'd found something as simple as having to ask permission to perform the most basic of human functions—peeing, touching themselves, orgasming—helped innocents like Nalani stay in a submissive mindset.

Taking it farther, forcing a reluctant sub to squat and pee while he watched or better yet, forced to pee in a diaper while in public—hell, that was gold. They were some of the most powerful humiliation tools in his kink toolbox. As any form of watersports was a hard limit for most women, his own pulse spiked as he watched Nalani struggling beautifully to accept his order.

Damn, she was amazing—blushing beautifully while her nipples hardened again to long pebbles, betraying how turned on she was. Oh, she'd deny it to her dying breath, but it didn't matter—his request turned her on.

"I've waited long enough, young lady. I understand you may have never done this before, but you'll need to get used to it."

"I don't think that's possible," she whined, panic raising her voice almost an octave.

He was walking the tightrope without a net, very aware the beauty torturing herself at his feet, trying to figure out if she could obey or not, just might call out *yellow* or worse, *red*, then their fun would end abruptly. He'd been turned down—more often than not—by other play partners when given the same order, but tonight felt ten times more important. He prayed he wasn't going too fast.

Please don't leave, kitten.

He stopped short of saying the words out loud, giving her time to come to terms with his kinky request. He couldn't help but notice how unusually vulnerable he felt as he waited for Nalani's answer to his very personal order, confirming what he already knew.

Nalani was special.

She was going to chew a hole in her bottom lip, biting on it so hard as she blushed at his feet. He felt her temptation. She just needed a bit more help.

"Look at me, Nalani."

He was so grateful he hadn't washed her face yet. A few faint streaks of mascara remained, the ideal accompaniment to her humiliation.

"Push off your knees and squat over the drain right behind you."

That order took her longer, but now that he was using his sternest Dom voice, she slowly moved into motion, following his direction.

"Such a good girl," he praised when she'd complied. He let their intimacy grow as they stared into each other's eyes, noticing her short sips of breath as she waited. "Now, empty your bladder like the dirty girl I know you want to be for me."

Christ, she was adorable. The pink blush on her cheeks turned a bright red just as the first yellow splashed onto the tile around the drain. She started with just a small trickle as she tried to relax enough to piss. Her embarrassment had just started to recede when Shane couldn't resist upping their little game.

Taking his prick into his left hand, Shane aimed, letting his own stream of pee shoot out his shaft, hitting a bullseye exactly where he had aimed—the landing strip above Nalani's pussy.

It was kinda crazy after all the intimate things they'd done with and to each other, but the simple act of peeing on the Hawaiian beauty made him want to yank her up and onto his pole for another ride, all over again. Pink turned back to red as she internalized just how dirty his game was becoming. The acrid aroma made it impossible to ignore the reality of their intimate scene.

When their streams of yellow had finished, he held out his hand, offering her assistance to stand. The second she was upright, he yanked her into his arms, hugging her tight and showing his appreciation for her trust.

"That was amazing, baby."

He felt her wobble on her feet. Maybe she deserved a bit of a reward? Dare he?

Shane shuffled them toward the six-foot long teakwood bench, just out of the spray of the three water streams.

"Be a good girl and kneel on the bench. I want to get you squeaky clean now—inside and out."

Lucky for her, he hadn't come prepared with all of his kinky toys for his stay at Runway. It was probably for the best, anyway. Intellectually, he knew Nalani wasn't ready for punishment enemas and diapers. Still, there was one favorite kink he needed no sex toys to enjoy.

Once he had her situated, Shane grabbed the bar of soap again and lathered up his hands. While he loved to bathe his submissive for the night, he took care washing the last remnants of makeup from her still-pink cheeks. He worked in silence, re-soaping, then moving to her cheeks at the other end of the bench.

Shane started slowly, gently cleaning her ass before sliding slippery fingers through her wet folds, careful to wash off any residue of their urine.

While technically she was perfectly clean, he dragged his finger through the crevice of her ass, teasing the puckered, dipping his finger in and out to tease.

"You're taking your cleaning very well. You deserve a nice reward. When I get finished, I'll let you thank me properly."

"Thank you for what?" she asked adorably, looking at him over her shoulder.

He was helpless to stop, needing to see her reaction. Shane spread her asscheeks wide and leaned down to lap at the tender bundle of nerves, sucking her delicate flesh into his mouth between licks.

He was ready for her to try to buck out of his grasp. Grabbing her hips, he held her steady as he grew bolder, sticking his tongue into her clean hole before lathing all around her pucker, rimming her perfectly.

"Don't! That's gross!"

He replied by cupping his tongue into a point and sticking it into her ass as far as it would go. While it wasn't even close to as deep as the plug he'd just removed, he knew it was more than big enough for his submissive to feel the intrusion.

Nalani started pushing off the bench, thrashing to get away from him as he tightened his hold on her body, riding her flailing body perfectly. When she fought to stand, he easily lifted her bottom half off the bench, suspending her like a rag doll while his tongue never lost contact with her most sensitive flesh.

Shane listened carefully for her to call out a color, but there was none, only beautiful begging for him to stop, followed by involuntary mews of pleasure, mixed perfectly with growls of protest. The lady may protest with words, but her body was on fire—the smell of her arousal proved that.

It would be so easy to reach around and flick her clit, tipping her into another orgasm. Better yet, he could replace his tongue with his—once again—hard shaft and make her cry out from the burn of her virgin ass being breached by his cock.

Instead, he fell back to his favorite kink of all—edging. He may not be locking her into one of the many chastity devices he owned just yet, but Nalani was about to learn just how stingy he could be dishing out pleasure, preferring instead to flame their need until each of them was starving for release. He couldn't wait to see the horny desperation in her gorgeous eyes as he paraded her in public after being denied pleasure for several long days. He'd whisper obscene things into her ear until she was so frenzied to be fucked, she would plead beautifully.

His decision made to wait to edge them until later, Shane deposited Nalani's feet back on the marble, careful to support her with a hug from behind as her legs stabilized, leaning down to talk against her ear again.

"What do you say we dry off and order up a few snacks before the kitchen closes downstairs?"

She answered with a breathless, "Okay."

Shane turned off the water, grabbing several of the plush

towels from the shelf outside the spray of water. He took joy wringing the water from his submissive's hair before wrapping it in the towel, taking the opportunity to explore her curvy body again as he patted her dry, face to feet, enjoying caring for his sub.

It only took a few minutes to dry off and don the plush robes that came with the suite since they'd ruined the ones they'd brought up from Black Light. Once they were back in the main suite, an awkward silence fell. For the first time, Shane realized, besides the smoking hot sex they'd shared together, he knew next to nothing about the woman standing in the middle of the room, looking lost.

"So, any foods you can't eat? Allergies?"

"No."

"You in the mood for something special?" he asked as he opened the leather-bound room service menu. "I've found the chef here is very open to making just about anything as long as she has the supplies."

"That doesn't surprise me. Avery's great."

Shit. Until that moment, he'd conveniently forgotten she worked in the mansion and of course, knew the chef.

Shane looked up from the menu in time to see Nalani looking around the room, her panic growing as she looked lost.

Closing the menu, he took several long strides to close the short distance between them.

"Hey, what's going on, kitten? You look like you're about to cry."

She didn't answer, turning away, refusing to look at him but unable to hide her trembles.

"Are you cold? I can turn the air off."

She shook her head, but still, no verbal answer.

He'd lost her. The tenuous thread he'd built up between them over the last few hours felt like it had been severed. The realization slammed into him hard.

Fuck that, I'm not done with her yet.

Shane reached to hold her chin, forcing her to look up at him. Tears pooled in her eyes, and oddly, he hated them. It surprised him to realize he longed to see her smiling so big, those cute dimples would pop out again.

"Talk to me, baby. What's going on in that head of yours?"

It was torturous, waiting for her to answer him, but he hung tight. Right up until she yanked free of his grasp and took off at a brisk walk toward the leather bag on the luggage rack.

Her clothes were in that bag.

Shit.

It only took a few long strides to catch up to her, yanking the bag out of her hands, holding it out of reach. She only struggled to reach it for a few seconds, giving up when she realized she wouldn't win this battle.

"You want to go? Fine. I'll even drive you home, but not until you level with me. I need the truth. What the hell happened?"

Her panic was tangible. He felt like a prick preventing her from leaving, but he'd never professed to be a boy scout.

"Goddamnit, talk to me."

Nalani glanced up at him several times but wasn't able to sustain her gaze. Almost a full minute went by while he waited before she exploded like a popping balloon.

"I don't even know where to start! It's so confusing to be here—in this room I've been in hundreds of times before, only this time I'm naked… with a famous man who just…. licked my…" She shook her head, refusing to finish that thought. "I'm making the mess instead of cleaning it up.

"Everywhere I look, I'm reminded this is my place of employment, and everyone here is my co-worker, which makes being here with you crazy. Add all the *things* we've done together, and it's insane times ten. I don't know you. Not really. And you know nothing about me. So, where does that leave us? I mean, we haven't even…." Her voice trailed off, trying her best to look away, but he held her chin forcing her to maintain their connection.

His mind raced. Every word she'd said was one hundred percent accurate, but it didn't mean shit.

"Nalani, you're right. We have so much to learn about each other, but that's why I want you to stay. Please, spend the next few days with me."

"Why?" she spat stubbornly.

His mind raced, searching for the right words to change her mind. He knew he couldn't Dom his way out of this standoff. The insecurity he'd felt earlier was back in spades. It had been a long time since anyone, let alone a submissive, had made him feel this insecure, unsure of what to say or even think.

Words escaped him as a burning need like none he'd felt before threatened to consume him. A picture of a caveman throwing his woman over his shoulder, dragging her back to his cave, chaining her down so she couldn't leave him flashed in his brain. If only he could tie Nalani to his bed until she came to her senses, but even he wasn't a big enough asshole to do that.

When he didn't answer, she yanked free and resumed reaching for the bag with her clothes.

Like that caveman hunting his prey, Shane dropped the bag and pounced on Nalani. Struggling in his arms, she swatted at him as he worked to subdue her. There was no way she was getting away. Not before he...

Shane yanked her closer, trapping her in a bear hug, crashing his mouth down on hers in a passionate kiss. The sparks that had been there between them all night reignited, flaming his libido, as Nalani's legs gave out from under her.

Her complete surrender to his kiss fed his ego. When her hands tentatively fumbled between their bodies, reaching under his robe for skin-on-skin connection, he was tempted to pick her up and throw her on his bed to consummate the seduction in progress.

Only when they were both short of breath did he finally pull out of their kiss, holding her tight against him as they rested their foreheads together. Her gasps for air after their passionate kiss were sexy as hell.

"Now… there's no way in hell you're gonna convince me you don't belong here with me. Not after that kiss." He paused, waiting to see if she'd try to keep protesting. When she didn't, he doubled down.

"So, here's my proposal. I'll order up a pizza and some appetizers, along with a bottle of wine and maybe a couple beers. Then, we're going to enjoy our first meal together while we play a little game of *Truth or Dare* to start learning more about each other." He leaned back far enough to see her eyes widen at his suggestion.

"That sounds like a pretty dangerous proposition for me since it's coming from a man I'm pretty sure is fearless when it comes to dares."

She wasn't wrong about that. At least the curve of a smile was back on her lips as she teased him.

"Is that a yes to the pizza?" he pressed.

Victory—a smile big enough to bring out those adorable dimples of hers.

"I'll stay, but only because it's pizza. I've been craving it for days. Just don't put crazy toppings on it."

"Fine," Shane chuckled. "That can be my first question. What are your favorite pizza toppings? Or… would you rather a dare instead of answering?"

"Oh, I think I can handle answering the truth on this one." Her soft laughter was so sexy as she teased him. "I'm not picky. Just no pineapple or anchovies."

It only took a few minutes to place the room service order. Determined to keep things light between them, Shane took Nalani by the hand and led her to the couch near the fireplace. While she got comfortable, he took a minute to light the fire and lower the lights in the room. When he was seated, facing her, close enough to reach out and hold her, he tried to return to their game.

"So, tell me the truth, Nalani..."

"Oh no, you don't. You asked your question already. It's my turn."

"Fine. Ask away. I'm an open book."

He could almost see her brain working overtime to come up with a good question.

"Okay, got it. You don't seem afraid of anything. Have you ever really been afraid?"

What a strange question for her to ask first. Little did she know, he'd been afraid just minutes before when he thought she was going to leave. Still, he knew that really wasn't what she wanted to know.

"I used to be pretty afraid of heights, but then I did a military movie pretty early in my career..."

"Behind Enemy Lines."

He smiled. "You're a fan?"

"It's a classic. I'd have to be hiding under a rock to have not seen it."

"Interesting. How many other of my movies have you seen?"

She blushed beautifully as if she'd been caught with her hand in the cookie jar.

"It's not your turn to ask a question."

"Touché. So, anyway, there were several scenes at the top of rock formations, and while I had a stuntman for the most dangerous stunts, it was becoming a pain in the ass to have him in all the shots. When it came time to film the parachute jump, I decided enough was enough. I hired an instructor and forced myself to jump out of that perfectly fine airplane. Scared the living shit out of me the whole way down, but once the parachute came out and I landed safely, I was hooked. It was truly an amazing experience, and I haven't been afraid of heights since."

"Wow, I don't think I could have done that."

"You can do anything if you have a big enough incentive. Now… my turn. How many of my movies have you seen?" She couldn't hold his stare, glancing away. "You can always switch over to a dare if you'd like…"

"Oh, no. I'm not going to be doing dares if I can help it. God only knows what you'll come up with."

Shane loved the dimples popping through with her broad grin.

"You're stalling."

"Fine. I admit it. I've seen them all, okay?"

"Even the rom-com that flopped a few years ago?"

She looked like she had something sour in her mouth as she admitted, "I've seen that one the most."

"Interesting. So, you're a romantic?"

"How many questions do you think you get here?"

"Is that such a hard question to answer?"

"No, but I want to save it, so you don't think of harder ones."

"Sorry, kitten, but my brain has no shortage of harder questions. I'm just trying to ease you in here."

She mumbled something under her breath that sounded suspiciously like, "That's what I'm afraid of."

"Fine. Your turn, then. Ask away."

He enjoyed watching her think of questions almost as much as her answering them.

"Okay… it's none of my business, but…"

"Maybe I want everything to be your business," he interjected.

"That doesn't make any sense. We barely know each other."

"I have a rule," Shane grinned, unable to resist teasing her. "Once I've rimmed a beauty's asshole, there are no more barriers."

Damn, he loved making her blush. It was almost too easy.

"Well, ironically, that was going to be my question. Exactly how many women's… um… bottoms… have you licked?"

"I don't think…"

"Truth or dare. Answer or you have to do a dare, right?"

Busted.

"You sure that's the question you want answered, kitten?"

"Not really, but it's the question I *need* answered."

He didn't like the sound of that distinction. He briefly thought about lying—he was an actor, he could pull it off—but lying to Nalani felt wrong.

"What if I told you I honestly don't know?"

Her face fell, tears springing to her eyes. He moved closer and despite her slapping him away, managed to pull her into his arms. He held her tight until she stopped wiggling.

"Listen," he whispered softly against her ear. "Early in my career, I let fame go to my head. I'm not proud of it, but I was pretty promiscuous for a couple of years in my early twenties. I had women throwing themselves at me everywhere I went and was too young to understand they were just using me—either for my money or to get their fifteen minutes of fame. But I used them, too, to try all kinds of kinky shit and figure out what I liked and didn't."

"So, all of those stories in the tabloids are true?"

"Fuck no. But they aren't all wrong either. Nothing is ever that black and white, baby."

"Okay." She sniffled before adding, "I asked. It helps to understand where I stand."

Shane yanked out of their hug in a flash.

"Now wait just a damn minute. My answer to that question has nothing to do with where you stand with me."

"Of course, it does. I'm just one of a long string of…"

He clamped his hand over her mouth to keep her from finishing that sentence.

"Let me set you straight. That shit was in my past. I've been focusing on my career for the last several years, and yes, while I've been in a few relationships, they weren't that serious. And for the record… none of the women I would have considered a girlfriend ever let me rim them."

She didn't answer, but he noticed the slight nod of her head to acknowledge his answer. The vulnerable look in her eyes woke a protective side of him he hadn't seen in a long time. He'd started the game, planning to ask her all kinds of sexy questions that would make her blush, but at that moment, a better—more important— question popped into his brain and wouldn't let go.

The knock on the door announced their food and wine had arrived. He decided to drop the question before he answered the door.

"My turn. I'll go get the food while you think about your answer. Ready?"

Nalani nodded, her eyes growing wider as she saw how nervous he'd gotten.

"Nalani… will you go to the Oscars with me one week from today?"

CHAPTER 10

She had to have heard him wrong. There was absolutely no way the playboy, Shane Covington, had just asked her to attend the most important Hollywood event of the year. She sat on the sofa in stunned silence as Shane took the tray from Avery at the door. Nalani was relieved he hadn't let her friend into the room far enough to see that Nalani was there… in a robe… looking well fucked.

Shane carried the large room service tray over to the coffee table between the couch and the roaring fire. The pizza smelled heavenly, and Nalani's tummy rumbled. She hadn't eaten much before heading to meet Shane at Black Light. She'd been too nervous.

Unfortunately, she wasn't any less nervous now. On the contrary, she felt like she was about to jump out of her skin.

"Here you go. Take a few swigs of wine before you answer me."

Nalani did as she was told, gulping half her glass down as he pressed her.

"So? Say, yes."

"I need you to repeat your question. I think I misheard you."

"You didn't."

Nalani laughed manically before replying.

"Won't your current date be a bit upset by you inviting me?"

He grinned slyly, placing the platter of pizza between them on the couch.

"Is that your sneaky way of asking me if I'm dating someone?" He didn't wait for her answer before taking a big bite.

"No. It was my not-so-sneaky way of telling you that you've lost your mind."

She picked up a slice of pizza and took her own bite to avoid saying more.

"For the record, I have no date planned. I'm not that big of an asshole, I'd ditch someone this close to the event if I had a date lined up. I took my mom last year, but my parents had the nerve to go on a cruise this year, so she's not available. I was gonna just go alone."

She vaguely remembered seeing pictures of Shane with his mom on the red carpet as she'd watched coverage the year before.

"Why in the world would you go alone? You could snap your fingers and have a thousand dates tomorrow?"

He took another bite before answering.

"I don't want a thousand dates." He pinned her with a devilish grin. "I just want you."

"You're crazy! You don't even know me."

"I know you blush beautifully when I push you out of your comfort zone, and I know you make this really sexy sound when you come. What more do I need to know?"

That mischievous grin he was flashing her should be outlawed. How the hell was she supposed to keep her wits about her with that?

"Oh, I don't know. Maybe my last name for starters? My favorite color? That I'm not a crazy mass murderer?"

"Okay, I do want to know your last name, but only so I can

have my assistant get all the arrangements made for next weekend. And I'd love to know every little thing about you, including your favorite color, but it's hardly a matter of national security." He snuck another bite of pizza in before ending with, "I'm pretty sure anyone who gets woozy when they cut their own palm on a shard of glass wouldn't be able to handle the blood a mass murder would need to. In fact, I'm feeling pretty confident we can rule out the entire class of felonies where you're concerned."

Holy shit. Her heart skipped a beat at his stray comment. She tried to control her reaction. There was no way he knew shit about her, it had just been a random comment. And there was no fucking way she was talking about that part of her life, not with Shane Covington, and not here, where she worked.

"So?" He pressed her, opening a bottle of beer for himself.

"So, what?"

"Will you go with me?"

"Absolutely not! You're insane for even asking."

"That's bullshit. We'll have fun."

"No, we won't. I'd be a nervous wreck."

"But…"

"Shane, we haven't even gone out to dinner yet, let alone go to one of the biggest events of the year—where hundreds of photographers will be circling like sharks."

"I've never heard a more accurate description of the media circus. Well done."

"So, why would I want to subject myself to that? No, thanks."

She knew in her heart she was doing the right thing, but that didn't stop a small part of her from wondering what it must feel like to attend the Oscars on the arm of someone like Shane Covington, hob-nobbing with the movie industry's rich and famous. She shook her head, trying to get the picture out of her brain. It would be insane to go on the red carpet with Shane.

"Fine, but I'm going to keep working on you this week."

"Didn't you already have to turn in your RSVP?"

"Probably, but I'm Shane Covington. Every once in a while, that has benefits. Now... what is your last name?"

"How many questions do you get each turn?" she teased him.

"As many as I want. Didn't you hear? I'm Shane Covington." God, that grin should win its own gold statue.

"You might have mentioned that," she deadpanned.

"Does that change your mind about next Sunday?"

"Sorry, it's actually working against you, to be honest."

"Ouch. Brutal."

"Yes, that's exactly how the paparazzi would be to me if I showed up with you."

"Oh, you'll wrap them around your little finger. With your beauty, they'll trip over themselves, trying to get the dirt on you."

There it was again. Her heart lurched, understanding for the first time just how dangerous spending time with Shane Covington was for her. Her brain shouted at her to get up and walk out—right now before she fell even harder.

Unfortunately, the rest of her body disagreed with her brain, and her body won the battle. She couldn't leave—not yet.

But she couldn't go out in public with Shane either.

"So, I think you should stick with the easy question. My last name is Ione."

"That's nice and easy. Nalani Ione," he said, trying her full name on for size.

She was desperate to change the subject, taking another bite as she scrambled to come up with her next question.

"I know you get to travel a lot. What's your favorite place you've ever visited?"

"New Zealand. Hands down. It's breathtaking. I'm trying to get back there."

She knew next to nothing about New Zealand other than it was very far away, but seeing the glee in his eyes as he talked about it, well, it made her want to go there too. She'd have to settle for Googling it when she got home.

"My turn." She knew she wasn't going to like the question coming by the gleam in his eye. "What's your favorite thing I've done to your body so far?"

She could feel her face burning red, in part because the fire was making the room extra warm, but more because he'd reminded her of all intimate things they'd done together. She'd thought she hated some of it as it was happening, but looking back, she'd loved every single minute of their time together.

"Nalani..."

"What? You know already I..."

"Loved when I did this...?" He reached across into her robe to squeeze her breast, tweaking her nipple. He abruptly moved his hand lower, opening her robe, reaching for her pussy. "Or did you prefer when I was touching here?"

She closed her eyes, letting her head fall back, enjoying his hands on her body, then those talented fingers were gone.

She opened her eyes to see him grinning again. "Not yet, baby. I need to learn a few more things about you before we get to play another round."

Frustrated, she reached out for another slice of pizza.

"Fine. But it's my turn."

Two hours and dozens of questions later, Nalani had almost succeeded in forgetting she was sitting on the lap of Shane Covington, the Academy Award-winning actor. He'd been true to his promise, opening up to her, sharing everything from his own favorite color, green, to his biggest dreams, and everything in between.

For the most part, she'd been open with him too, only holding back when he'd tried to learn more about her childhood and family. She wasn't ready to share that part of her life with him yet, so she hedged. It wasn't necessarily that she didn't trust him—in spite of all the crazy things he'd done to her body, she did.

She tried to hide her yawn. She was having so much fun, she didn't want their night to end, but she had come to the conclusion it would be too dangerous to sleep over. Having sex and pizza with Shane was precarious enough. Actually sleeping with him… waking up in his bed… just seemed too intimate.

"I should get going."

"Don't you dare make me chain you to the bed. Don't think for a minute I won't."

"Shane…"

"Don't *Shane* me. You have two days off. You aren't leaving tonight. Anyway, it's not safe for you to be out and about. It's almost midnight."

"I don't turn into a pumpkin at the strike of twelve, you know," she said, secretly pleased he was so adamant about her staying. She didn't really want to leave. She just didn't want to get her heart trampled when whatever this was happening between them ended.

And it would end. He hadn't hidden that he'd been with more women than he could count. He was a player, a Dom—larger than life.

She was a nobody—a housekeeper, scratching out an honest living. She didn't doubt Shane enjoyed playing with her since making her blush was a turn-on for him, but that would be all there was to this relationship. They would have some fun, then he'd move on. The best she could hope for was to not get her heart broken.

While she'd been pondering their future, or lack thereof, Shane got busy loosening the tie of her robe, groping and pinching until Nalani broke out into a fit of giggles.

"That tickles!"

His mouth clamped down on her neck, sucking hard enough, she suspected he was leaving a mark. She welcomed it. Like the cut on her palm, his mark would help remind her this fairytale weekend had really happened.

Nalani wiggled, trying her best to make the tickling stop but ended up flipped over Shane's lap on her tummy. She struggled to free herself, but he was too strong, wrestling her into submission without much effort, but then again, she wasn't really fighting *that* hard.

The cool air of the room hit her bare ass a split second before she registered the circle of fire where he'd spanked her right butt cheek, followed by a paired smack to her other cheek.

"Now… it's time to show you how I handle naughty submissives who try to slink off into the night when they know perfectly well they're supposed to be warming my bed. I mean, who the hell is going to suck my cock in the middle of the night when I wake up with a hard-on? That's your duty, young lady."

His fingers moved lower, grazing her pussy and reigniting their chemistry. With each passing second, her resolve to go home weakened until his probing fingers reduced her to a melting pile of goo.

He was an artist, strumming her body until it was humming with need. Then it stopped, and those wet fingers moved in for a different target.

Nalani went wild, struggling as he clamped her tight against his body as his wet fingers breached her private pucker. She'd had the butt plug out just long enough, the new insertion stretched her uncomfortably.

"Please! Not there!" She flailed as best she could, to no avail.

"Oh, kitten, we're gonna have to work on training this hole."

His probing wasn't actually hurting her, per se, but it made her feel uncomfortably full.

"But… it feels weird! And it's—"

"It's naughty, just like you are," Shane cut in, finishing her sentence. "If you relax, I can make it feel so good. In fact…"

She couldn't see his face in this prone position.

"You missed the golden opportunity to ask me questions about some of my more edgy kinks. I thought sure you'd ask me about those."

He had to have at least two fingers inside her ass; she could feel him scissoring them, opening her wider and wider until the uncomfortable feeling turned to pain.

"Shane! It's too much. Please!" she cried out.

"What color are you?"

His question slammed into her. Only then did she remember she was in control.

So, what color was she?

She could lie and call *red*. He'd stop—of that, she had no qualms—but did she really want him to stop? The answer deep down surprised her.

His fingers left her ass just long enough for a volley of quick swats to her bottom, accompanied Shane's lecture.

"I asked you for your color. I need a verbal reply, kitten."

Her "Green" came out as a whisper, but he obviously heard it.

"Good girl. Now, since you didn't bother to ask me this question during our game, I'll just have to give you a bit of bonus content about what makes Shane Covington tick."

His fingers were back inside her, toying with her casually as he ratcheted up his naughty vocabulary.

"I'll start you out nice and easy, but before long, you'll be taking my cock where my fingers are, and you're gonna love every minute of it."

"I highly doubt that," she whined, trying to wiggle her ass to dislodge his digits. Not only did it not work, she felt another finger being inserted, stretching her wider. She resumed her flailing, although it only made him yank her against him harder, holding her securely.

"I'm beginning to think it might be time to pull some rope out of my bag and get to work tying you down. I saw how much you enjoyed watching the Shibari scene downstairs and suspect it's the only way I'm going to be able to make sure all your holes are available to me."

Her face flamed with shame as she internalized his words. She'd love to deny it, but the thought of him tying her up was a huge turn-on—something she'd imagined in the privacy of her own bed when she'd turned off all the lights.

It happened so fast, she didn't know what was happening. Shane thrust his fingers into her thick hair and yanked her head back so hard, she had to arch her back uncomfortably as she laid across his lap. There was a feral quality in his hazel eyes that made her feel like his prey.

"Say it…"

"Say what?" He'd lost her.

"You want me to tie you down, don't you? To take the power away from you, so you can still be the good girl made to do all kinds of dirty things against your will."

When she didn't answer him, he reached out with his other hand to pinch her nipple so hard, it took her breath away.

"No!"

"Liar. Do I need to punish you for lying too?"

"I'm not… I mean… I don't want…" She stumbled her way through several starts to her protests, but they all died before she could get them out. It felt wrong to lie to him. She shivered despite the room being warm, courtesy of the fire only a few feet away. Her heart raced a million miles a minute, making it impossible to form coherent sentences.

Shane Covington was either a damn fine actor, or he really meant business.

"I'll remind you one more time, you can either use your safeword or answer my question. One or the other." He waited a good ten seconds, giving her ample time to cry out red or even yellow, but neither came.

He was on his feet in a flash, carrying her folded over in front of him as she wiggled like a fish at the end of a hook. She couldn't see much through the veil of her long hair, but what she could see, she loved.

Shane dropped her in a heap at the end of the king-sized bed she'd made earlier that day. As soon as she was out of his arms, he started barking orders as he yanked the robe off her body, leaving her naked.

"On your knees. Face down on the bed. Arms behind your back. Legs spread as wide as you can."

"But…"

"Follow directions, sub."

It surprised her how easily her "Yes, sir" fell from her lips.

She was grateful she could hide her face against the bedspread. Despite having her legs spread, Shane picked up first one, then the other as she kneeled, maneuvering her legs obscenely wide. As she was at the edge, her feet jutted out over the end of the bed.

Nalani closed her eyes, turning her head to the left and placing her right cheek against the cool spread, just as she felt something wrapping around her wrists. She'd never had anyone restrain her before during sex, let alone tie her. She waited to feel panic invade, but instead, with each second that ticked by, she felt the weight of the world lifting.

For hours, she'd had to be on her toes—fielding questions, scrambling to make sense of Shane's instructions and her own feelings. Struggling to obey when her brain told her what she was doing with the man who'd just finished making sure she could not move her arms was taboo.

There was something liberating in lying helpless—no more decisions, no more instructions to obey. All that remained was the heated anticipation, almost desperation, to discover what other surprises Shane had up his sleeve.

The smack of his palm against her ass broke her out of her thoughts, returning her to the reality of the moment. She was at his mercy. He could do whatever he wanted to her splayed open body, and apparently, what he wanted was to hear her squeak with surprise when his palm connected with her other butt cheek.

The spanking was slow… deliberate, stoking the heat between them. Nalani closed her eyes, concentrating on the sensations bombarding her—the softness of the bedding, the scratch of the rope at her wrists, the ache of her knees, the snap of flesh against flesh, and the burn… oh, the burn on her ass.

One by one, all sensations faded until the only thing that remained was the fire across her ass and the smoldering heat of her pussy. Only her own wetness between her legs could cool the heat.

Thud!

"Owww!" she cried out when Shane's hand was replaced with something much harder and unforgiving. In the space of a few seconds, her slow burn exploded into hot flames across her ass as she wiggled side to side in an ill-fated attempt to escape.

"Such a good girl."

Thud!

"What the hell is that thing?" she screamed, tears clouding her vision.

"I'm glad you asked. This is The Terminator. It has a way of stopping all naughty behavior."

"But I haven't been naughty!"

"Yet…" Shane connected the wooden paddle with her ass, again and again.

Yellow was on the tip of her tongue until the next swat connected with a splat a bit lower on her sit spot. The tears she'd been holding back burst out. She didn't have enough perspective to understand how she could feel both pain and a new kind of pleasure at the same time.

Nalani flinched as Shane's fingers found her wet folds with his fingers, teasing and pinching with one hand as his other shoved what felt like a single digit into her ass.

The man was obsessed with her butt!

Sensory overload—she was glad she was lying with her head down because, in spite of that, she still felt lightheaded. Only him releasing her completely and leaving her lying there, naked and immobile, could jar her out the almost trance she'd fallen into.

The tip of his cock sliding through her folds woke her further, giving her just seconds to anticipate the feeling of being filled. He was inside her in a second.

"So wet. So hot. So damn tight," Shane grunted.

His hands gripped her hips as he lifted her bent body off the bed to get a better angle for his thrusts. The night had been a production, and they were in the final act. Shane was driving them higher to the grand finale.

Nalani got there first, exploding into a million pieces, held together by the man thrusting his cock hard and fast into her spasming channel. The sound of their bodies crashing together in a sexy rhythm was surreal.

Shane released an animalistic growl as he finally stilled, buried inside her. Nalani loved the feel of his muscular chest as he leaned over her back, hugging her intimately as they tried to catch their breath after their workout.

As his shaft left her body, so did the last glimmer of her energy.

Maybe staying over for just one night would be okay.

CHAPTER 11

This had to be a new low. Submitting to Piper's sadistic whims for the night at roulette had been humiliating enough, but sitting in his dark car, just outside the gate to her canyon property in Malibu at midnight—like a crazy stalker who chased after celebrities—had him questioning his sanity.

Nolan was here on a hunch. It had taken two minutes on Google to find she'd been in New York to appear on the Late Show. With his connections, it had been easy to find out they'd wrapped up taping for the show just before five on the east coast. Assuming she'd at least been telling him the truth that she'd be in the air at the same time they'd talked the night before, Nolan had calculated a window of opportunity to see Piper tonight.

Of course, his entire plan was reliant on the fact she'd lied to him when she'd told him she wasn't flying back to Los Angeles. Knowing she had to be in town in less than a week for the Oscars, he knew she'd be coming home soon if not tonight.

Everything about Piper Kole confused him. He was stuck

choosing which was worse—getting lied to or ignored. He'd concluded it was the latter.

That's how he'd ended up sitting in his car with a cup of stale coffee like a seedy private investigator, hoping to catch her in a lie.

He'd been waiting over an hour when he saw headlights coming up the secluded canyon road. He'd been disappointed a half dozen times already when the cars had turned out to be one of her neighbors passing by. He was half expecting the police to show up, after one of the neighbors reported a suspicious man sitting in his car in the dark.

Nolan's pulse spiked when the car's headlights slowed as they approached the closed gate to Piper's property. He was parked close enough to see the driver of the limo pull up to the small security box outside the gate, reaching out to punch in a security code that got the heavy decorative gates to swing open. He'd never been inside and was somewhat surprised she didn't have on-property security guards.

Anger at being lied to warred with his deep desire to see the beauty hidden behind the tinted windows of the luxury car. Only then did he realize he'd come without a solid plan. So, she was here… now what?

The decision was easy. He pushed the ignition button in his sports car, for once regretting how loud the engine was. He rushed to turn off the headlights that had come on automatically, quickly throwing the car into gear, and driving through the stone pillars, just in time to sneak in behind the limo before the gates closed.

The winding drive to the main house worked in his favor. He was hopeful the driver had been distracted and not noticed they were being followed before turning around a curve. Even as he thought it, he made a mental note to make sure he hired a security firm to come in and beef up the surveillance system for her property. If he could gain access this easily, any dangerous asshole could get to Piper.

The thought made him cringe—tonight, he was playing the role of the dangerous asshole.

Her house was sheltered by dozens of full-grown trees and shorter foliage. It may not protect her from intruders, but it served to give her the privacy Piper needed from the paparazzi and fans, who took the celebrity home tours offered on Hollywood Boulevard. It was why when he rounded the final curve of the driveway and the house came into view for the first time, he was surprised.

So many homes in Malibu had an almost sterile look. It was as if the pretentious, affluent builders purposely built houses that could be featured in magazines, forgetting people actually had to live there.

The two-story stone A-line home reminded him more of a mountain villa in Vail instead of a home on the Pacific Ocean in Malibu. The driveway was stone as well, and the native palm trees closest to the house had been replaced with large oaks and evergreens, artfully lit with landscape lighting that made the property feel like a warm haven.

He was lucky the property was huge, enabling him to pull his car into a side drive, out of the way, yet in position to watch as the limo came to a stop at the front walkway.

He cut the engine, then held his breath, waiting for the driver to open the back door. A tired looking Piper stepped out, throwing a big leather tote over her shoulder and heading up the walkway to the front door under the overhang of what looked like a huge private second story patio.

Why didn't she have security with her? Did she always travel alone? He'd hoped the driver did double duty, but after the man in the black suit rolled the hard-sided suitcase to the front door, he hopped behind the wheel and drove back down the lane.

As soon as he saw the various lights coming on inside, Nolan started to regret his decision. As exciting as it was to be this close to Piper again, he knew without a shadow of a doubt how pissed she was going to be if she found out he was there. If he didn't plan on going up and pounding on the huge wood door until she admitted him, what the hell was he doing here?

He weighed his options for several minutes, seeing Piper's shadow through the sheer curtains covering the wall of windows on the second floor to what he suspected was her master bedroom. The anger she'd lied faded, replaced with longing to hold her.

Before he could change his mind, he used the Bluetooth in the car to call her cell. It rang so many times, he was sure she was going to let it roll to voicemail, so when she answered, he was stunned.

"Nolan? What the hell are you doing calling so late?"

What was he doing calling so late? This was pathetic. Still, she'd answered. He couldn't be the one to hang up this time.

"You looked fantastic for your appearance with Stephen Colbert tonight."

Had she just chuckled?

"You stalking me now?"

Oh, Piper, you have no idea.

"I hardly think noticing you were appearing on a nationally televised show with millions of viewers qualifies as stalking."

"Fair enough. Still, it's late. I'm exhausted."

"I'm sure. Those cross-continental red-eyes are a real bitch."

He heard the hitch of her breath, but she didn't fall for the bait.

"It's three in the morning in New York."

"And midnight here. Your point?" Silence. "I was hoping we could have an encore performance of last night. I haven't slept that good in months."

"Honestly," she sighed before admitting, "I slept great too, but I think it had more to do with the quantity of alcohol I ingested and less to do with who I talked to on the phone."

"Just think how great we'd sleep if we were actually together and not over the phone."

Silence again.

He gave her time, and she finally answered.

"I'm not sure you'd sleep that well. You must have forgotten, I'll be in charge when we're together, which means if you were here, I'd be torturing your cock and balls until you begged me to let you come, which of course, you wouldn't be allowed to do."

"Sadist," he teased.

"Don't look now, but the pot just called the kettle black."

"That's not true. I can't wait to give you so many orgasms, you'll be begging me to stop because your hoo-ha was getting sore."

"My hoo-ha?" Her laughter was like pure gold to him. "And what do you call your cock? Your pee-pee?"

"Actually, his name is The Rock."

"You named your dick?" she asked incredulously.

"Of course, most men do."

"Interesting."

"See how educational this relationship is for you?"

"We don't have a relationship," she snapped.

"Okay. What would you call it?"

She took a few seconds to think before throwing shade. "A disaster in the making."

"That doesn't really roll off the tip of the tongue. I think *lovers* might be best."

"Ha! You're a funny guy. We might actually have to be in the same city before we can make that big of a stretch."

She'd setup the ideal comeback.

"Oh, I'm pretty sure we're plenty close enough." When she didn't respond, he tacked on, "When the doorbell rings in two minutes, don't panic. It's just me." He reached to open the car door before adding, "I'll lose you when I get out of the car."

"Stop!" Her shout kept him in his seat. "Are you fucking insane?"

"Ironically, I've asked myself that same question a few times in the last hour while I was waiting for you."

"Jesus Christ."

"Nope, just Nolan. I'll be..."

"No! Don't you dare come to the door!" She pulled the thin curtains aside and peered out into the dark, glancing around the driveway until he could see her honing in on his location. He turned on the interior lights so she could see him when he waved.

"You look like you could use some help getting out of that tight outfit. I'll be right there."

"You're certifiable. It would serve you right if I called the police."

"Maybe, but you aren't going to do that. You value your privacy way too much."

"Says the man who knowingly broke into my property."

"I resent that. I haven't even got out of my car. I've not broken into anything."

"And yet you're sitting in my private drive, past the locked gate."

"Speaking of which, I'm gonna call this tech guy I trust to come beef up your security. Do you know how easy it was for me to drive in behind your limo? You really should be more careful."

"Seriously? You break in, then try to lecture me?"

"I will repeat, I haven't broken in anywhere. I simply drove up your drive. I'm going to come to the front door like a perfectly civilized human being and ring the bell. All you have to do is open the door. I'll be happy to help you get out of that skin-tight outfit and get ready for bed. I'll even tuck you in after

I give you at least one if not two glorious orgasms. I guarantee you'll sleep like a baby." Dare he? Fuck it. In for an ounce, in for a pound. "Right after I pull you over my lap and paddle that gorgeous ass of yours raw for lying to me, that is."

She would deny it, but he heard her breath hitch at his threat.

"Insane…" It was just a whisper. Interesting she wasn't screaming at him as he'd expected.

"I know we've got a lot of complicated things to work out, baby, but one thing is nice and easy—no more lies. There will only be the truth between us from now on. Got it?"

"Hell, no, I don't *got it*! Who the fuck do you think you are, trying to lay down rules?"

"I think I'm half of whatever the fuck this is we have going on between us, that's who. I don't have a damn clue how it's all going to turn out, but I know this, I'm not going quietly into the night this time, Piper, so you'd better get used to it. You want to dominate me in the bedroom, I'm down with that. What I won't allow is you to run away again or try to lie your way out of feeling whatever it is you're feeling."

"The only thing I'm feeling is anger, Nolan."

"Anger is fine. I'll even let you take it out on me when I get inside."

"You're not coming in here."

He picked up on the almost manic quality in her voice, and it made him pause to rethink his plan.

"Fine. I'll stay out here, but by the rules set out last night, that means I'm in charge again."

Even at the distance through the dark, he could feel her gaze settle on him. It was interesting she didn't have any snappy retort for him at his assertion of control.

Nolan reached into the center console to grab his Bluetooth headset. He inserted it into his left ear and hit the button on the dash to switch the call from the car sound system.

"Now, naughty girl, I want you to go inside and find the biggest vibrator in your collection and bring it back to the window to show me."

"Who says I have any vibrators?"

He didn't bother answering her ridiculous question, letting his laughter answer. When she realized she was caught, she turned with a huff and left the window. Nolan got out of the car and stretched his long legs before walking to the front of the car, leaned his ass on the still warm hood, and waited for Piper to return.

He had just started to worry she was going to ignore him when he saw the curtains fluttering again. God, even from this distance, she was so beautiful, it made his heart hurt. He forced himself to keep things light, afraid of scaring her with how strongly he felt about her.

"Good girl. Open the slider and come out on the balcony." It thrilled him she was obeying him as she approached the wood railing along the balcony.

"Show me that big boy you brought out with you."

"This is stupid…"

"Piper… show me," he barked. It was too dark to see it, but he was sure the confident Domme was blushing beautifully.

Nolan had the advantage of being hands free. Holding her eye contact over the distance, he reached down to unbuckle his leather belt before unbuttoning and unzipping his worn jeans. He reached in to pull out his hard cock in the chilly February night air.

"Take a good look at The Rock, baby. See how hard he is for you?" He stroked himself slowly to stave off the urge to burst in and ravage Piper, settling for giving her more instructions.

"Time to get naked for me."

"It's freaking cold out here," she whined.

"You can solve that by opening the front door."

"Bite me."

"I'd love to. Open the door."

"Grrr. You're incorrigible."

"You mean, adorable. Sexy. And since I'm out here, in charge… strip."

"In your dreams."

"Actually, I do think of you naked in my dreams. Usually tied down in all kinds of compromising positions, your holes on display, dripping wet for me to fuck nice and hard."

"Oh God… Nolan… only…" Something in her tone set off alarm bells. It wasn't her words, it was her desperation. He didn't have to prod her for answers. "Only you have to promise me…"

"Promise you what, baby?"

He saw her reach out and pull a blanket from the back of the patio chair and wrap it around her shoulders. She was going the wrong direction, putting more clothes on instead of getting naked.

"You have to promise me… you can never tie me down with ropes… like ever."

He hated how dark it was out. He could barely see her face through the shadows, but he heard the edge in her voice as she added, "It's a hard limit for me."

He watched her look away, too afraid to maintain their visual connection despite how dark it was out. "Piper, baby… talk to me. What happened to you that you have that as a hard limit?"

"Enough! You need to go. Now. Or I'll call the police. Don't think I won't!"

"Bullshit. No more lies, remember. And you aren't scaring me away."

"I'm not lying. I'm giving you my hard limits. If you don't like them, fuck off."

"You can have whatever limits you need to, and I'll honor each and every one of them. I just need to know…"

"You don't need to know shit. This is stupid. It's never going to work. You need to go."

"Piper, please. Let me come in. I'll open a bottle of wine. We can talk..."

"I don't want to talk about it! For Christ's sake, this is exactly why I had to become Mistress Ice. My boys would never press me like this."

"Of course not." Just mentioning the stable of boy toys she had on speed dial pissed him off. "You've castrated them. Turned them into puppets you can control."

"So, what if I did? Maybe that's what makes me happy. Did you ever think about that?"

God, he hated having this important conversation like this. He could feel her pain. It was tangible. Something... no someone... had hurt Piper Kole, and he was going to make it his life's mission to find out who, when, and why.

"I don't believe that for a minute, Piper. You aren't happy with them. You're comfortable. I scare you, I get it, but I have a news flash for you, baby. You scare the shit out of me, too. Not with your crop or your Mistress Ice routine, but with how much power you have over my own happiness."

"Do you even hear yourself? You sound like a lovesick teenager. We're adults. You need to just move on."

"It's not gonna happen, so put it out of your mind."

"What the hell am I going to do with you?"

"Let me in? I give great back rubs. I bet your shoulders are really tight from the flight."

"Nolan..." He heard the longing in her voice.

"I'm here, baby."

They spent several long seconds, each lost in thought, trying to figure out how to navigate the heavy topics just under the surface. Finally, Nolan opted for trying to get them back on track.

"Now, I think it's time to get you that orgasm you need, so you can get a good night's sleep, don't you?"

"It's too cold."

"Fine, you don't have to get naked. Just take those skinny jeans off and move a bit closer to the railing, then put one leg up on the middle rung."

She humphed with impatience, but followed directions, anyway. Had she been an experienced little, he'd accuse her of being a brat with her bad attitude, but with things as precarious between them as they were, he let it go.

"Now, reach into your panties, and tell me, is your pussy wet?"

She switched her phone into her other hand before dipping her hand lower, into her panties. He loved the involuntary purr she made as her fingers made contact with her clit.

"Tell me, baby," he prodded. "Is that cunt aching to be fucked good and hard?"

"Nolan…"

"Say it, Piper. I need to hear it."

"Yes, alright? I admit it. I want you to fuck me. Are you happy now?"

"Hell, no. I won't be happy until I'm balls deep in that tight channel, hearing you crying out my name as I pound you hard."

"Oh, shit."

"Turn on the vibrator. Hold it against your pussy. Tell me how it feels."

"It feels… shaky."

He couldn't help but chuckle. "Well, I guess that's good. How do you feel?"

"Shaky too…"

"Even better."

"How do you figure?"

"It means I'm having the desired effect."

"You want me to vibrate and tumble over from being shaky?"

"No, I want to rock your world with incredible orgasms while I catch you in my arms. I'm gonna have to settle for watching from a distance tonight."

"You say the...."

When her voice trailed off, he finished for her, "I say the sexiest things."

"I was going to say silly... but you can use sexy if it makes you feel better."

"Focus, baby. Like you said, it's cold out here. I don't want you to catch a chill. Now, is your pussy ready to be stretched?"

"Uh huh..." He could hear the low vibration of the sex toy as she answered with a monosyllable grunt.

Nolan sped up his strokes on his growing hard-on, chasing his own release. He couldn't tear his eyes away from the beautiful sight of Piper naked from the waist down, save her minuscule panties. It took all of his self-discipline to remain leaning against the hood of his sports car, instead of trying to climb the rock and wood of Piper's house in an attempt to bury himself inside her.

"That's it, baby. You're nice and wet. I can hear that vibrator sloshing through your wet juices. Take that shaft and shove it home. I want to hear you cry out as it stretches you so good."

She didn't need to be told twice. The light was just right to see the black dildo disappear inside Piper's snatch as she cried out into the dark night.

It was surreal watching her fucking herself hard and fast as he slapped his own meat to the same dirty rhythm. Several long minutes passed with the only soundtrack heard was each chasing their own satisfaction.

"Shit, I wish I was up there, standing behind you, so I could bend you over the railing and stick this cock exactly where it belongs—deep inside you," he called out to her when he was close.

His dirty rant pushed Piper over the edge. Even in the dim

lighting, he could see her face contorting beautifully as she fell into her *little death*. He wasn't long behind her, spurting his ropes of cum onto the stone driveway.

"Thank you, Piper."

"Why are you thanking me? I didn't do anything," she panted, out of breath.

"Sure, you did. You were gorgeous, even from this distance. Now… I'm gonna head home and crawl in bed and go to sleep, thinking about how sexy it was to watch you tonight. Go in… get warm… and Piper…"

An awkward moment passed by before she finally answered, "What?"

"I'll talk to you tomorrow night, a little earlier this time."

"Nolan! No…!"

He reached to hang up the call. She shouted out to him over the balcony, but he just blew her a kiss and climbed into his car, making the engine roar to life, blocking out her protests. He waved as he put the car in motion, heading for the gate that luckily opened as sensors detected his approach.

He needed to get home and replay everything from their conversation tonight to see if she'd left other clues about what was really going on in her beautiful mind.

CHAPTER 12

The knock on the door interrupted their fun. They'd been holed up for over twenty-four hours, and the only people they'd been forced to see had been the security guards delivering their food.

The smile Nalani flashed was brighter than the California sun shining through the expansive windows of the suite.

"Saved by the bell," she teased.

"That's what you think." He donned his strictest dom face before adding. "You go get it. Naked. And be sure to show that jeweled plug still shoved up your ass when you turn around to come back inside."

The golden specks in her brown eyes disappeared as she internalized his instructions. He saw the indecision warring inside her. He was familiar with her dilemma—he had to maintain his public good-guy persona for the world while balancing his darker side in private. He felt a little guilty, laying the same burden on his little kitten's shoulders.

Her simple, "Red," proved she was up for the task.

"Wise decision, kitten," he said, leaning in to kiss her nose.

"So, why even bother testing me?" she asked, a shred of exasperation bleeding into her tone.

He thought about the question for a few long seconds before answering truthfully.

"Because I need to know I can trust you to hold your personal line. I meant it the other night when I said the last thing I want to do is really hurt you."

He lost himself for several long seconds, enjoying the adoring look in Nalani's eyes. He was supposed to be in charge of this relationship, but at that second, he was reminded exactly how much power she had grabbed from him, and it wasn't just sexual. She'd gotten in under his skin and was burrowing in deeper with each hour they spent together. The realization should make him afraid, but instead, he felt calmed.

The renewed, and louder, pounding on the door interrupted their connection.

"Fine. If you insist, I'll get the food."

He pushed to his feet and reached to grab the soiled towel from the floor to wrap around his waist. If they looked carefully, the security guard delivering their food could make out the dried semen and lube staining the white terry.

He didn't bother looking through the peephole, so opening it to find a scowling Jaxson Cartwright-Davidson on the other side came as a surprise. Shane glanced down and saw the owner carrying a brown paper bag.

"I never knew you were such a hands-on owner. Seems like you have a few other employees who should be in charge of delivering food to your guests."

"I'm not delivering food to my guest," Jaxson groused. The men remained in a standoff before Jaxson added, "I'm doing a welfare check on my executive housekeeper."

Fucking Elijah.

Screw that. "Fuck you, Jaxson."

"No, thanks. I have Chase and Emma taking good care of me

in that department. Now, are you going to invite me in, or do I need to ask Miguel to join us?"

"Are you serious? You think so little of me, you'd get security involved in this shit?"

"This has nothing to do with what I think of you. It has to do with my responsibilities toward my employees."

"Oh, really? You doing welfare checks over at Khloe's house to make sure McLean is treating Madison right?"

"First off, McLean isn't even in the lifestyle, and second, they're taking their personal life off-property."

"So, because I have remodeling going on at my own house, you have the right to barge in here?"

"I didn't barge, I knocked. But honestly, I'm not entirely sure I wouldn't be standing at your front door right now if you were there, anyway. This has nothing to do with your location and everything to do with your kinks."

"You're such a fucking hypocrite, you know that? You talk a big talk about tolerance. You host classes to educate against kink shaming, then show up at my door, judging me?"

Jaxson stepped across the threshold, getting in Shane's face.

"I don't give a rat's ass what kinks you're into. You can practice them to your heart's content in my guest rooms and in my club. What I won't allow is you to use your star power to lure in innocent women who have no experience in the lifestyle whatsoever, then use their innocence to feed your *unique* kinks."

That shut Shane up. As much as he'd like to keep arguing his point, he'd thought the same thoughts a dozen times since he'd met Nalani, concerned he wasn't being fair to her.

In their silent standoff, Jaxson lowered his voice in an attempt to defuse the situation.

"Listen, I'm not here to bust your balls. All I want to do is see Nalani and talk to her for one minute, and we can clear this whole thing up. Then you guys can get back to…"—he paused, smiling slyly—"whatever you were up to before I knocked."

Shane's defensive reflex was to shove the asshole back into the hall and slam the door in his face, but that would just make things worse. He didn't have anything to be afraid of—he'd gone to great lengths to protect Nalani, even from himself.

"Come on in." He took a step back, pulling the heavy door open and waving a mocking arm of welcome to the owner. "You'll find who you're looking for burrowed under the covers of my bed, no doubt hiding from letting her boss see her naked in cum covered sheets."

He really was an asshole but couldn't resist the unique opportunity this encounter would provide to see his innocent little kitten's humiliation of being caught—literally—in Shane's bed.

Jaxson detoured to the table near the window, long enough to drop the food delivery bag. He tried to be inconspicuous, but Shane noticed him scanning the room for signs of anything he didn't like as he walked back to stand at the end of the king-sized bed.

Shane stood back, relegated to an observer while Jaxson briefly took control of his submissive—exactly what Nalani was.

His.

"Nalani, I know you're hiding under there. I need to see you."

"No! I can't believe you're doing this!" Her embarrassed cry was muffled by the layers of bedding covering her.

"Well, believe it. Now, do as you're told, and let me see you."

Memories of how adorable she looked with her ruined lipstick and lines of mascara from her tears had Shane's towel beginning to tent. He'd made her reapply the makeup even though they hadn't left the room, just so he could ruin it. He really was an asshole, but this whole situation was turning out to be a major turn-on for him, getting renewed mileage from their dirty tryst the night before.

It took her almost a full minute to comply, slowly peeling

back the layers of pillows and covers until just her makeup-smeared face appeared. She was beautiful, exactly as she was… that very minute. Like the day before, he felt the pressure in his chest, squeezing him hard as if to get his attention.

Jaxson went into interrogation mode.

"Are you here because you choose to be, or do you want to leave?"

Shane was so proud of the flash of anger in Nalani's eyes at her boss's question.

"Are you kidding me? That's what you want to ask me?"

For once, Jaxson seemed flustered, but he held his ground. "Yes."

"Of course, I don't want to leave. If I'd wanted to go, I would have left already," she said matter-of-factly.

"That's good," Jaxson agreed.

Shane stepped forward, "So, thanks for dropping by, but…"

"Not so fast. You've never played in the lifestyle before, and before I go, I need to be sure you understand what safewords are. That you understand how much control you have in the BDSM power exchange dynamic."

Nalani's tongue dashed out to lick her stained lips, embarrassed to be talking about sexual topics with her boss.

"Of course, I know what safewords are. Shane explained them to me literally within the first hour of meeting me."

Such a good girl.

"I'm glad to hear that. And do you have any concerns Shane won't honor their use if you need to use your safeword?"

Shane's blood pressure was rising by the minute, pissed Davidson and even Elijah had such little confidence in his self-control.

The flash of anger in Nalani's eyes as she chastised her boss helped to calm his own anger.

"I trust Shane explicitly to honor my safeword. You know how I know?"

"No," Jaxson answered.

"Because I used *red* not ten minutes ago when he asked me to get up and answer the door naked. I used *red* to tell him no way, and as you noticed, he's the one who answered the door. Satisfied?"

Damn, she was gorgeous when she was angry. He'd seen it when she'd put Elijah in his place down at Black Light on Sunday night and here again with her boss.

"Fair enough." The asshole had the nerve to smile "I'll leave you two kids to your breakfast then."

He stopped short of apologizing but stopped next to Shane on the way to the exit to add, "Thanks for taking care of her. She's important to us here."

"Yeah, well, she's becoming important to me too," he answered truthfully.

Jaxson nodded his acknowledgment before heading to the door, leaving them alone again.

"I need to go." Throwing back the covers, she bolted from the bed, rushing around the room, frantically looking for the pieces of her outfit that had been strewn about long before. Little did she know, he'd hidden her dress in one of his drawers to make sure she wouldn't be able to slink away from him.

Shane forced a calmness he didn't feel as he walked over to the bag of food, removing the breakfast sandwiches before pulling the cup holder with two venti lattes out of the bottom of the bag.

"Be a good girl and come grab your coffee. Let's sit down and have breakfast."

"I don't want food. I need to go home," she squeaked as she lifted several throw pillows from one of the chairs, no doubt looking for her dress.

He looked back at her to see her stooping over to pick up one of her high heels that had been thrown aside. The glimmer of the jeweled plug in her ass caught the ray of sunshine perfectly, rushing blood to his morning wood. He waited until she stood and turned toward him to drop the towel—score. Nalani's gaze dropped to his erection, where it stayed for several long seconds.

"I'll let you go for a ride in just a bit," he couldn't resist teasing her. "I already plugged your ass, but I need to get that belly of yours full of breakfast before I can fill your cunt with my jizz."

Even after almost two days together, he loved he could still make her blush.

"I don't… I mean, I'm not hungry. I need to… go," she stammered.

"So, you've said." He took a leisurely sip of the hot coffee, not bothering to hide his growing arousal at her uneasy embarrassment. "I happen to know you have today off since both clubs are closed."

Shane didn't take his eyes off her nakedness, making sure she felt like he was inspecting her beautiful curves. With each passing second, he watched her move her hands slowly to cover her pussy and breasts. The second she blocked her privates from his view, he moved with speed, snatching her wrists and yanking them away from her body.

"What is rule number one, baby?"

Nalani's eyes grew wide as she realized she'd subconsciously broke his directive. He'd reminded her often in their time together and was thrilled she'd forgotten again.

"What did I tell you would happen the next time you tried to cover yourself from me?" he asked, injecting an angry tone. She didn't know him well enough yet to know with certainty, his feigned anger was all part of their game.

"But… I need to go home."

"No, you don't need to go anywhere except over to the back of the couch. Remind me what I told you would happen the next time you tried to hide your body from me," he ordered in his best authoritative tone.

Her breath hitched as she glanced around the room as if her missing dress might have appeared from thin air.

"Nalani, look at me, young lady."

God, she was perfect. A dichotomy of innocence and lust danced in her eyes, contemplating between running from the room and throwing herself at him to be properly fucked like the whore he wanted to turn her into.

His whore.

Her naked breasts heaved as she took shallow breaths, the peaks hardening under his stern glare. He didn't miss her rubbing her legs together to deliver a tiny zing of friction to her pussy. She was so lucky he didn't have a chastity belt with him. If he did, that puffy clit of hers wouldn't be delivering that zap of pleasure he saw flashing in her eyes until after he'd had his fun punishing her. But with his filthy mind, he could always come up with ways to have fun, no matter what toys he had in his bag.

"Such a dirty girl. Spread your legs and let that pussy juice dribble down your thighs as you walk over to the couch and assume the position."

"The position?" she asked, her voice a full octave higher than normal.

"Don't pretend you don't know what position naughty subs need to get into before they get punished."

"Punished?" Her single word was a squeak.

He doubted she realized she had stepped backward, trying to put distance between them. Little did she know, he loved a good game of cat and mouse. The thought of chasing her and having to subdue her as she fought to escape took hold and wouldn't let go. He released her wrists as he dared her.

"I'll tell you what. I'll give you three minutes to change my mind. If you can stop me from getting you into position for three minutes, I'll let you off the hook, this one time. But…" he took a second to grin mischievously before finishing. "But if I manage to catch you and wrangle you into position, you'll take double my planned punishment."

He watched her forehead scrunch with wrinkles as she thought about his proposal.

"Fine. But you have to give me my clothes first."

"Nope."

"That's not fair."

"Baby, I never said this would be fair. Believe me, I want to win bad."

"Three minutes?" she prompted.

"Yep."

Little did she know just how long three minutes could be for an innocent. His fucked-up mind could come up with dozens of things to do to her body that would make her feel like it was a lifetime.

He leaned forward to close the distance between them again before uttering a quick, "Go!"

It was as if she were waiting for it. Nalani took off running for the bathroom door a good twenty feet away.

With his long legs, he was able to reach her long before she got close to the bathroom door, but that proved to be the only easy part of his plan. She deployed what felt like a professional defensive move. When he wrapped his left arm around her neck from the back, he expected her to heel quickly, but she surprised him, bending at the waist and twisting, spinning until she was able to get her knee up.

Had he been a shorter man, he knew without a doubt, he would be curled on the carpet in a fetal position, nursing a throbbing set of blue balls. As it was, her knee connected with his thigh hard enough, he might bruise.

Nalani was proving to be a hellcat, struggling against him until he was able to get her back into a bear hug, squeezing her arms tight to her body and lifting her off the ground—her back to his front—letting her legs flail as she tried to kick him.

Shane's adrenaline kicked in, loving the challenge of subduing his valuable catch. And that was exactly what Nalani was at that moment—his prey.

Her flailing jarred his erection between them, providing him with an enjoyable morning workout. It only took a few long strides to get to the leather toy bag near the table. She almost got away again when he took his left arm away to pick up the bag, but he regained control and headed for the straight-backed chair behind the desk.

It was the best location to enact his plan. The chair's back came just a bit higher than Nalani's waist as he set her down on her feet. Within seconds, he thrust her forward, forcing her to bend as he lifted her off the ground, depositing her across the back of the chair with enough force, she groaned from the gush of air leaving her lungs.

Unable to reach the ground, her legs flailed, connecting with his shins and even his thighs. He was careful to not let her kick high enough to hit his family jewels, knowing that would put a serious damper on his fun for several hours.

She proved highly motivated to escape. He found himself winded as he struggled to pull the soft nylon rope from the bag while still holding her down. Only when he moved to the side of the chair and started to tie her left wrist to the arm of the furniture, he truly started to worry she might escape. They were in a race to see if he could get her tied down before she successfully pulled away.

Once he had one wrist secured, Shane had to reset her across the back of the chair. Nalani still struggled to be free, but to her credit, she didn't try to talk her way out of the game they were playing. On the contrary, by the time he had finished securing her right wrist to the chair, he caught a whiff of raw sexual excitement emanating from his subdued captive.

Once he knew she couldn't escape, Shane took a few seconds to catch his breath, enjoying the scenery of a vulnerable naked sub tied in front of him.

"You need to let me down. I need to pee! The back of the chair is pressing on my bladder," she whined, her first words since their game of cat and mouse had begun.

"That is unfortunate, but if you think I'm letting you up now that I caught you, you're nuts."

"Shane, stop!" She let out a screech of frustration as she wildly kicked her free legs. "Let me loose!" When his palm connected soundly with her right butt-cheek, her flailing stop.

Had they been together longer, he would already be tying her legs to the outside of the chair, making sure to expose her pussy as he restrained her, so he could enjoy watching it drip with arousal. Unfortunately, the gentleman inside him forced him to walk around to the front of the chair and squat down, so he was at eye level with his naughty submissive.

Since he wasn't a *real* gentleman, he reached to grasp her thick hair, yanking her head up, so she had no choice but to look him in the eyes as her hair pulled at her scalp. Her ruined mascara and lipstick, from the face-fucking he'd delivered in the middle of the night, made her the most gorgeous woman in the world.

"Now, only because I made a promise to your boss, who was just here to catch you well-fucked and naked in my bed..." He paused to enjoy the embarrassed blush on her face. "I will remind you, despite your current prone position, you are still in control here. While I will love nothing more than to tie your legs wide and punish you with my belt until your gorgeous ass is beet-red right before I fuck you so hard and long, you finally shoot your pee all down the back of the chair when you come..." He paused again to enjoy the utter shock his words had on her before ending his filthy rant. "I feel the need to remind you one last time there is only one word that can stop me from punishing you, and that word is not *stop, no,* or *please*."

Nalani's tongue darted out to lick her lips as she internalized his words. Time stood still as he held her head up uncomfortably, searching her eyes for any indication she was truly upset—any clue she wanted him to stop.

His heart jumped with joy when Nalani looked him in the eyes with determination, uttering two tiny words that sealed her fate.

"Fuck you!"

He knew he was grinning like a goof as he teased, "Oh no, you've got that wrong. I'm going to be fucking *you,* kitten. Right after, I'll introduce you to how much you're going to learn to both love and hate the wide strip of leather I like to wear everywhere." He leaned down, barely able to reach the toy bag, bringing out the soft, leather belt, holding it up so she could get a good look at it.

"I would like you to meet Burn."

"You named your belt?"

"Yep. That way I can mention him in public, and you'll know what I mean. I find it's a very appropriate name as I am going to love blistering your behind with Burn."

"Sadist," she accused, a hint of a smile on her lips.

"Guilty as charged, baby, but I still have some mercy in me. I'm going to make sure you get to enjoy your coffee and breakfast after, although if I do my job right, you'll be enjoying your morning caffeine while lying on your tummy."

He heard her whisper, "Shit" under her breath as he let her head flop back down as he stood. He knew it wasn't going to be comfortable for her, but that was part of the attraction to the idea of pulling her right leg up and out until her knee was next to the right armrest. He made quick work of securing that leg to the chair before moving to her last free limb. Once he had pulled that leg up and out, Nalani was truly splayed open, her pussy and plugged asshole on display.

Only when he had her tied completely immobile, he was able to slow things down, which of course, worked in his favor. Watching Nalani struggle against her bonds was a huge turn-on. Taking several long seconds, he stepped back and admired the view as he stroked his cock to stave off his need.

He had to hand it to the Cartwright-Davidson's. While the suites were not technically BDSM bedrooms, he'd noticed almost every piece of furniture was kink friendly. Headboards with slats made tying down submissives easy. Benches in the shower provided the ideal sex-aide. And today, he noticed the desk chair was the optimum dimension to serve as a spanking bench.

Shane palmed Nalani's bare ass, warming her up with a gentle massage.

"Would you like to make a wager on how many strokes it will take with Burn before I can get you begging me to fuck you?"

"Sure. I bet one stroke," she deadpanned.

"Oh, baby, that would be no fun at all. As much as I look forward to sticking my dick in you again, I really want your bottom to burn me from the heat. So…" He reached and pulled on the plug in her ass just hard enough to bring the widest part out to stretch her puckered hole. "We'll change things up a little. You can make the belt strokes stop anytime you want by calling out, 'fuck me,' but just know if you don't make it to at least twenty belt-strokes, my cock will be going in this dirty ass instead of your pussy, young lady."

She groaned as she flailed ineffectually against her bonds.

"You can consider getting buggered with my cock my second favorite punishment for you, after turning your ass raw. Your choice, of course." He shoved the plug back in as he made his point, watching her wet cunt clench with the need to be filled.

Patience, my kitten. I promise to take good care of my pussy.

Unable to wait a moment longer, Shane stepped back and let the two-inch wide leather belt crack against Nalani's bottom, drawing out a panicked cry from the sub as the pain settled in. His next strike was perfectly placed just below the first. Damn, he loved how she wiggled her cheeks as best she could in her prone position.

Knowing she was inexperienced was a huge turn-on as he enjoyed watching the stripes turning rosy across her bottom. By the fifth lash of his belt, she had begun to cry out for him to stop.

But there was no word *red.*

By the eighth whip of the leather, he heard her first sob.

But there was no word *red.*

By the twelfth stroke of the belting, his own erection was like stone, witnessing perhaps the sexiest scene on his kink-o-meter. The sights, sounds, and smells of the moment conspired to tempt him into aborting the punishment so he could bottom out inside her. It took all of his self-control to slow down between lashes to give Nalani time to absorb each strike.

She fought against her bonds, sniffling as her tears made her nose run, wiggling her cute ass the few centimeters she could, trying to bring herself some relief. She even cried out, "Stop, please," after stroke fifteen.

But still, there was no word *red.*

The litany of the word "Please" started with his sixteenth lash to her now red ass. Over and over, she cried out, but he knew if he pressed her, she wouldn't know herself what she was begging for. He suspected she both hated and loved what he was doing to her body in equal measure.

It's why she was perfect for him. His ability to not balk at her tears and protests was what made him best for her in return.

The nineteenth and twentieth lashes came hard and fast. They were both about to combust from the heat from the belting. With zero finesse, Shane threw the leather to the floor and stepped up behind her, burying his turgid shaft balls deep in one hard thrust. He was grateful the club was closed because Nalani's scream as he bottomed out inside her would have surely drawn his neighbors to pound on his door to find out who had been hurt.

Like a man possessed, Shane used the back of the chair on either side of Nalani's bottom to hold her steady as he pounded her with such force, the whole piece of furniture started scooting across the floor. The fact he'd come more times than he could count in the last forty-eight hours was working in his favor. Despite feeling as if he were ready to explode, he was able to stave off his eruption so long, he began to get winded from the rapid-fire fucking.

And Nalani? She was proving yet again her perfection by releasing the sexiest cocktail of purrs, nonsensical gibberish, and rhythmic cries in tempo with each pump of his cock. The wet sound of their bodies slapping together was only enhanced when her cunt started spasming around him, squeezing his shaft as she fell apart, sobbing incoherently through a massive orgasm.

It was too much. He couldn't hold out a second longer. Feeling a bit like his ancestral cavemen brothers, Shane cried out his own release, shooting rope after rope of cum into her tight channel, then collapsed over her back, completely out of breath from his morning workout.

He wanted to stay like this forever. When she tilted her head back to look up at him, her post-climactic vulnerability took his breath away.

Nalani may be the one who had just been disciplined, but at that moment, he knew he was the one who was truly in trouble.

He was in danger of losing his heart.

CHAPTER 13

"I can't believe you haven't changed your mind yet."

For the tenth time, Nalani regretted opening her big mouth and confiding in Avery and Madison about Shane's invitation to attend the Oscars. It had been bad enough having to fend off his overt attempts to change her mind all week, but since telling her co-workers on Friday, they had gotten downright pushy with her. It was getting harder and harder to hold tight to her decision, considering deep down she really wanted to go.

Only the fear of losing her job kept her in check. Oh, Shane had been not-so-subtly hinting she didn't need to keep working because he would be more than happy to pay her to stay tied to his bed for a living. She'd even admit it was fun joking around with him about the absurd idea. But in the few quiet moments she'd had to herself in the almost week they'd been doing their unique version of playing house, the truth of her situation made sure to slap her back into reality.

She prayed whatever this was they had going between them would last as long as possible. If she was lucky, they'd have a few weeks, on the outside, a few months.

But never… not once… did she allow herself to contemplate forever. If it wasn't forever, that meant she would need to keep her job. And that meant she must never go out in public with Shane Covington. It would take the paparazzi less than a day to track down her sordid history—the mistakes she had moved heaven and earth to put behind her back in Hawaii. The past even the temptation of Shane Covington couldn't erase.

No… she couldn't talk about *that* with her co-workers.

"I told you, there's no way in hell I'd subject myself to that kind of craziness. Anyway, he needed to turn in his RSVP weeks ago. There's no way I could change my mind now, less than twenty-four hours before the show."

Avery leaned across the kitchen island to place a plate of low-cal veggies in front of her and Madison. She'd been teasing them about watching their weight more now that they both had hotties in their beds.

"Well, I'm on record that I think you're crazy. I'd sell my soul to go to the Oscars with anyone, especially Shane Covington."

"Fine, then you go. He can take you." Nalani teased before popping an olive in her mouth.

"Yeah, right," Avery laughed. "I hate to tell you, but that guy only has eyes for you. He couldn't care less about taking anyone else."

Her friend's words comforted Nalani in a strange, possessive way. Warning bells were going off in her head as she reminded herself Shane Covington was a playboy. He'd been with dozens of women before her and would be with dozens of women after. Feeling jealous in any way would only lead to heartache.

She knew with each passing hour they spent together—each night she spent in his bed doing all kinds of intimate debauchery—she was losing herself to *him*, not the larger-than-life celebrity. Truthfully, they never went anywhere where people treated him like a famous person. She treasured he'd made it so easy to forget he was anyone other than just Shane.

Her Shane.

As much as she loved the sex—and she loved the sex—it was the intimacy they shared she knew she'd miss the most. For the first time maybe ever, she no longer felt like a *me*, instead loved being part of an *us*—for however long it lasted.

Strong arms wrapping around her waist from behind startled her. She'd been lost in thought.

"There's my kitten. I've been looking for you. I'm home early."

"Speak of the devil. We were just talking about how insane Nalani is for not going with you tomorrow," Madison interjected, shoving a bowl of the trail mix Shane loved closer to him.

Nalani's brain was still caught up on his statement.

I'm home early.

But the mansion wasn't his home, just where he liked to play house with her until whatever this was between them had run its course. A deep longing took fire in the pit of her stomach as she said a silent prayer she'd be around long enough to at least get to see his real house after the renovation.

Nalani forced herself to snap out of her pensive mood.

"I didn't expect you this early. I should have gone up for a nice soak."

She left off the part that she had started taking long baths in the suite's whirlpool tub to help loosen the sore muscles she had from the exercise her body was getting at the hands of the sex god named Shane Covington. Who needed a membership to a gym when she had Shane to give her the best workout ever?

"I have a better idea," he said, leaning close and hugging her back against him. "Let's head downstairs. We can start out in the sauna, then take a dip in the hot tub before we move on to my favorite kind of watersports."

Nalani couldn't see his face over her shoulder but knew from the scandalized surprise on both Madison and Avery's faces, he was sporting his most dazzling grin, the one he saved for when he said something especially dirty.

"Behave." She threw her elbow back to jab him. "We're at Runway, not…" Her voice trailed off just before she said the two words she should never say while sitting on a bar stool in the mansion's opulent kitchen. There were at least a dozen other people mingling nearby, eager to pick up any celebrity gossip, the favorite pastime of Runway guests.

"I thought you knew by now. I don't know how to behave," he teased, reaching out to snag a handful of the trail mix.

"I'm gonna take my girl here downstairs for a bit. Any chance I can con you into making us a late dinner for when we get back upstairs? I'm planning on us working up a nice appetite."

"Sure thing," Avery answered, smiling mischievously. "Any special requests?"

Shane scooped Nalani off the bar stool, throwing her over his shoulder like a caveman. She almost missed his reply over her involuntary squeal.

"Surprise us with the dinner. Did you get a chance to buy that special something I asked you to pick up?"

It wasn't like Avery not to answer, and her friend's silence made Nalani uneasy about exactly what special something Shane's dirty mind had cooked up. Nalani lifted her head uncomfortably to get a glimpse of her friend, who was looking extremely guilty.

Not a good sign.

"Well?" Shane pressed.

Avery's gaze met Nalani's as she answered, "Umm… yes… I was able to get several of the items you requested."

Shane's voice had an almost gleeful tone as he started walking toward the elevator that would take them down to Black Light. He had to almost shout his confusing instructions back to Avery in the kitchen.

"Be sure to send up the biggest one! Nothing but the best for my kitten."

"Shane! Put me down! I can walk!"

"Maybe you can right now, but if I do my job right, you won't be walking straight in about an hour."

Two hours later, Nalani was more than happy to lean on Shane as they made their way up the back stairs of the club toward their suite. True to his promise, Nalani was not only walking funny, but anyone looking close enough would see her ruined makeup and the lines of drying semen dripping down her thighs. Despite taking a sauna and soaking in the hot tub, she was in desperate need of a shower. She was relieved when they were behind closed doors, a heavenly aroma greeting them.

"It smells awesome in here."

"Yeah, I asked one of the DM's to give Avery a call thirty minutes ago and tell her to send up dinner," Shane answered as he crossed to the desk to drop off his toy bag. "I heard your tummy growling when we were in the sauna, so I know you're hungry."

Nalani walked over to the tray on the table near the fireplace. "I can't wait to see what she…." Her voice trailed off as she lifted the silver cover over the top plate in the stack to display an oddly shaped vegetable of some sort. "What the hell is this? I thought I smelled steak."

Shane caught up to her, and when he didn't answer, she glanced up to see him grinning ear to ear.

"She outdid herself. That's the biggest one I've ever seen."

"Biggest one, what?"

"Let's eat first, then I'll explain."

"No. Explain first, *then* we'll eat."

Shane frowned in what she now recognized was his playful *I'm in charge here* glare.

"Don't be a naughty kitten, or I'll just have to show you before dinner after all. Trust me… you'll enjoy your steak much more if you wait for answers."

Her heart rate started to climb, recognizing the clues the king of kink had something dark and twisted brewing in his gorgeous head. In the last week, she'd learned that usually meant something new and scary was about to rock her world.

The temptation to find out what he'd planned beat out her hunger.

"Shane… tell me… what the hell do you have up your sleeve this time?"

He held up his arm, playfully. "I'm not wearing a shirt, so absolutely nothing."

"Shane! I'm not gonna be able to relax until you tell me."

"Oh, baby, this isn't a *tell* kind of game. This is definitely a *show* opportunity if I ever saw one."

"What does that even mean?" Nalani was so confused. When he didn't answer, she reached to uncover another plate, this one displaying a thick, juicy steak with asparagus spears topped with a yummy sauce Avery made from scratch.

When she looked back up at Shane, he asked again. "Your choice. You want to eat or solve the mystery of the strange delivery item?"

Her brain told her to choose the steak, but impatience and uncertainty won the day.

"What is it?"

Shane grinned as he reached to take the cover off the plate, lifting up what looked a bit like a white tubular potato.

"This, my dear, is a fun little toy I can't wait to introduce you to."

"A toy? It's food!"

"Not tonight, it's not. Tonight, this bad boy is going to make you squirm and cry beautifully."

She didn't know how to reconcile his handsome smile with his almost gleeful boast of how much he loved to make her cry. In moments like this, she knew with certainty, he had cast a spell on her, making it impossible to leave—even though she suspected the smart thing to do would be to run away as fast as possible.

"I don't understand. Is it like an onion that makes me cry?"

"More like hot sauce that burns."

"I don't like spicy food," she reminded him.

Shane's belly laugh made her feel foolish. She didn't have a fucking clue what the hell was going on, but she knew enough to know she hated being made fun of. She yanked her arm out of his grasp and started to move toward the bathroom. That shower was looking better by the minute.

She wasn't expecting the tackle from behind. Shane wrangled her body, thrusting her forward, against the back of the nearby couch until she was bent over the back with her ass in the air.

Fight-or-flight instincts kicked in, and Nalani started kicking to be free. She'd deny it to her dying breath, but she fucking loved it when Shane manhandled her, using his strength to bend her to his will—physically and figuratively. It made her feel less guilty when he *made* her do the perverted things he loved so much.

Cold air met her bare ass as he yanked the robe off her body, using his foot to tap, not so gently, back-and-forth between her ankles, forcing her to spread her legs to an almost uncomfortable stance. She was grateful her feet still touched the carpet.

He left her to walk back to the table, returning with the vegetable and a knife. She moved her hands from the seat of the couch, pushing up to place her hands where her tummy had just been so she could keep an eye on what he was up to.

Nalani tried not to be annoyed when he started peeling the vegetable, letting the shards of skin drop to the floor, making a mess she would inevitably need to clean up later. She was just about to call him out on it when she got the first inkling of what he was doing.

What had started out as a wild jumbled mess was fast being carved up into a smooth, long…

"No fucking way."

He had the audacity to look up and grin, answering with a simple, "Way."

Panicking, she stood up and started to reach down for her robe.

"I changed my mind. Let's eat."

"Oh, we will, but not until we get this bad boy doing his job first."

"And what, exactly, is his job?"

"I told you." He paused, a smirk on his handsome face. "It'll make you cry beautifully."

"I don't want to cry," she complained, exasperated.

"Ah, but you look so fucking hot when you do, and I can't wait to fuck you when this is in your ass."

She had just put her robe back on and was headed back to the table when he caught up to her, wrapping one arm around her waist and lifting her off the ground.

Nalani kicked, flailing her feet and legs in front of her in an attempt to jar loose from his grip, but he only clamped down harder. She was sure he was going to drape her back over the back of the couch or maybe at the end of the bed like he had several times that week.

When he beelined it for the corner of the room, where there was only the linen rack that held extra blankets for the guests, she thought perhaps she'd misunderstood his intentions.

As soon as her feet hit the floor, their cat-and-mouse game

moved to the next level. Nalani attempted to jerk free while Shane doubled-down on his tight grip on her waist with one arm while reaching out to yank the linen off the rack with his other.

Nalani relaxed slightly, incorrectly assuming he'd rethought his planned vegetable attack, right up until he pressed her forward toward the now empty metal rack.

She'd cleaned the rack in the past. She was responsible for the stocking of the rooms with the right linen, yet until the second Shane pushed her forward until her tummy touched the padded top of the rack, not once had she imagined guests using the furniture for anything more than its intended use. Now, she knew she'd never be able to unsee it.

"Bend over like a good girl and take your punishment."

"Why would I do that? Good girls shouldn't get punished. They should get fed."

"Oh, you'll get fed alright. First, this ginger is gonna fill up your pucker, making you feel nice and full. Then I'll feed my snake into your tunnel, and finally you'll get a wet drink of my cum for dessert."

In the time he'd been painting her a dirty picture of what he had planned, Shane had draped her over the padded top of the rack, pulling the robe off her body as he pressed on her back to force her to bend over, ass up.

When had he put those there? Two pairs of handcuffs were attached to the bottom rung of the rack, and Shane wasted no time in securing her wrists to the furniture.

She'd always been impressed by how sturdy the racks were, not understanding why the owners had felt the need to invest in such heavy-duty furniture just to hold a quilt. Now she understood—they were built as bonus sex furniture for their kinky guests.

While her hands were together in the middle of the rack,

Shane used the belt of her robe to tie her left ankle to the outside frame of the rack, leaving her tip-toeing on her right toes to avoid having to put all her weight on her tummy jammed against the padded top. Seconds later, as he yanked her right ankle to the far side of the rack, she couldn't avoid it.

She'd never admit it to Shane, but her heart raced at being manhandled—forced into submission. It was so much easier to let herself go and actually let the intimacy wash over her when she could quiet her brain that kept telling her what they were doing was wrong. It may be dirty and unconventional, but nothing could convince Nalani it was wrong.

She was unprepared for how vulnerable she felt as he dragged the now full piece of furniture away from the corner, into the room a bit more before stepping behind her.

The pulling apart of her asscheeks she'd expected; the feel of his tongue lapping at her pucker she hadn't. It still grossed her out if she thought about it long enough, so instead, she focused on how heavenly it felt right up to when he replaced his talented tongue with the hard tip of the ginger.

She was relieved he took it slow, only inserting the tip before removing it, then pushing in a bit farther the next time. She wasn't sure what part was supposed to make her cry since the coolness actually felt kinda good.

"This is called figging." Shane gave the ginger one final push, and her ass sucked it inside.

Nalani was about to ask what it was supposed to do when the first zing registered in her bowels. Surely… it wouldn't…

Crack.

Shane's palm connected with her ass cheek.

What the hell? Why did the inside of her ass sting worse than where he'd spanked her?

Crack.

The other cheek burned.

Crack. Crack. Crack. Crack.

A fast volley took her breath away.

It was a slow ignition, inside and out. Shane massaged as much as he spanked, edging her higher and higher until the burn on the inside surpassed the surface heat.

"Owie! It's starting to burn too bad. Take it out!"

"Why would I do that? We're just getting started?"

That didn't sound good.

"Shane. Please."

Her brief relief when he pulled the plug out of her ass disappeared when he shoved it back inside. A half dozen thrusts in and out stoked the fire until the heat turned to real pain.

"Take it out! It's too much!"

Through her open legs, she could see Shane walking away from her, back across the room. She tried to focus on him instead of the growing heat inside, which helped keep her mind off the burn until she saw what he held in his hand as he walked back toward her.

The only thing keeping her from calling out *red* when she saw his leather belt was his rock-hard cock protruding proudly as he approached her. Seeing his obvious arousal not only turned her on but gave her pause.

Nalani wiggled as much as her restraints would allow, trying to do anything that might bring her some relief. Instead of helping, the heat only ratcheted up a notch.

"So beautiful. Let's see if we can take you higher."

Thwack.

The wide belt covered plenty of her ass and brought the first hint of tears to her eyes. By the third lash of his belt, the tears were falling to the carpet below. By the fifth lash, the only thing keeping the word *red* from her lips was the new heat burning in her exposed pussy.

How in the world was this turning her on? She didn't understand how her body worked—how something meant to bring pain could also feel oh so good.

"Shane..." It was the only word she could form.

Another belt lash before his reply. "Nalani..."

Did she want him to stop? Truthfully, what she wanted was for him to fuck her with that gloriously big, hard cock dangling between his legs. Each belt lash helped her gain pinpoint focus on the physical sensations tingling at her core. It certainly wasn't a tickle, yet she knew she desperately needed him to scratch her itch.

"Please..." she begged.

"Please, what?"

"You know. I need..."

"Uh huh. You need...? He teased, determined to make her ask for what he wanted to deliver.

"Shane!"

"Ask for it. I love to hear you beg."

It took two more cracks of his belt before she broke down.

"Please! I need you!"

"You need me to kiss you?"

"No!"

He pulled the ginger out of her ass and reinserted it.

"You need me to lick you a bit longer?"

"You know what I need!"

"But I could be wrong. What does my dirty girl want more than anything in the world right now?"

His hands caressed the heat of her cheeks, bringing a small measure of relief. She needed more.

"Fuck me! Please!"

"With pleasure."

His cock was inside her in seconds, her wetness paving the way for him to bottom out on his first thrust, drawing a loud cry from her as her pussy gripped his shaft. The only hitch was the harder she spasmed around his cock, the deeper the burn inside her anus—the perfect dichotomy of pleasure and pain.

The man was truly a sex god. He'd already come less than

an hour before down at Black Light, but it didn't stop him from racing to his next climax and taking her along for the ride.

As sturdy as the quilt rack was, it creaked under her as Shane moved the fucking into a higher gear. The sound of their now sweaty bodies slapping together was joined by the wet sounds of her arousal.

Nalani turned herself over completely to the sensations bombarding every part of her body, her surrender absolute as wave after wave of pleasure consumed her. Shane's fingers joined the fun, pinching her swollen clit and detonating her strongest orgasm yet.

"Christ, you're fucking perfect!" His exclamation was accompanied by a growl as he finally stopped his thrusts, shooting hot cum deep inside her pussy.

They were catching their breath when Nalani's stomach growled loud enough to alert security. Shane chuckled as he pushed off her back.

"Let's get some food inside that tummy of yours, dirty girl." He quickly released her from the restraints, helping her to right herself.

"Um, you forgot to take that stuff out…"

"I think it would be more fun to watch you squirm as we eat dinner."

He had a warped sense of fun.

THE ALARM BUZZING on his phone told him it was time to get up and go. Shane had pushed snooze three times already. If he wasn't careful, his phone would soon be blowing up with his assistant, his agent, and his hired driver for the day all calling.

How did he get to the point in his career he was actually lying in bed, dreading going to the most prestigious of award ceremonies? To be fair, it wasn't that he was dreading going to the Oscars.

It was that he dreaded going alone.

Hell, that even wasn't the truth. Lying there, holding Nalani in his arms as she used his chest for her pillow, he had to be honest and admit that it was leaving her he dreaded. And that thought terrified him. He'd certainly felt close with other women before her, but something about her felt different.

The first text of the day told him he didn't have time to dwell on that. He'd have plenty of time to figure out his feelings later. Right now, he needed to leave.

Shane sighed.

"It's okay. I need to get up and get to work, anyway," Nalani mumbled against his chest, already awake.

"You should sleep in. I kept you up late." He hugged her tighter, placing a kiss on top of her mussed hair.

He loved her playful giggle.

"You mean, you kept me up late and woke me up in the middle of the night."

"Yeah, that too," he admitted, remembering the sexy interlude fondly. He decided to make one last effort to convince her. "Please say yes to at least meeting me after the show at one of the after parties."

"I told you. I don't have anything to wear."

"It doesn't matter for the after parties."

"Of course, it matters! Don't you read the gossip rags?"

"Only when forced at gun point," he groused truthfully.

"Well, I do, and I can just see next week's headline. 'Shane Covington seen kissing woman wearing Target dress.'"

He couldn't help but laugh at her ridiculous joke, although he knew how brutal the gossip rags could be.

"Fine, then take my credit card. Leave early enough to stop and pick up something."

"I told you, I'm not taking your credit card. I have no desire to reenact Julia Robert's famous scene on Rodeo Drive, although the other parallels to *Pretty Woman* are hitting a little close to home."

"Oh? So, you're a prostitute?" Shane joked.

Nalani slapped his chest playfully. "You know what I mean."

"No, I'm afraid I don't."

"Then let me spell it out for you. We've been playing house here at the mansion for over a week now, just like in the movie. Soon, the work at your house will wrap up, you'll move back in, and the spell will be broken. I don't need a new wardrobe to remember you after you leave."

Shane didn't like where this conversation was going. He took charge, rolling them over until Nalani was on her back, and he towered over her. He loved how she opened her legs subconsciously, so his morning wood could nestle against her sticky and well-used pussy.

"Listen up. I don't know any more than you do where this is going, but unlike you, I'm not going to start putting an expiration date on us." He paused when her eyes widened at the last word. "And yes, that's right. There is an *us*, Nalani. So, if you're not ready to come to the party tonight, that's fine, but don't you dare start pulling away from me. You don't want to take my credit card shopping, that's okay too, but know you can go to Marlina's on The Drive any time and tell her who you are and that I sent you. Get whatever you want or need. Got it?"

Nalani frowned. "What? Do you send all your whores there?"

His own flash of rage surprised him. Shane reflexively yanked on Nalani's hair, holding her head still to make sure she was paying attention.

"Don't you dare do this."

"Do what? Call you out on the truth?" she asked fearlessly.

"No, pick a fight with me. I know what you're doing. You're scared of getting hurt, so you're pushing me away. So, listen closely. Marlina is old enough to be my grandmother. I met her working in costumes on one of my earlier films. She was like a mother figure to me at a time when I really needed advice, and I never forgot it. When I found out her dream was to own a shop on Rodeo Drive, I financed her startup. That's it. End of story."

He waited until she finally said a quiet, "Sorry."

"That's not what upset me the most. You aren't my whore, Nalani."

"But that's what you said you wanted to call me."

"Sure, while I'm fucking you and doing all kinds of deliciously devious things to your body, but it's just part of the game. No matter what we do together, I'll never truly think of you as a whore."

"If not your whore, then what am I?" she asked quietly, tears welling in her eyes

That was the million-dollar question. His snoozed alarm went off again as she waited for his answer. He slapped his phone to turn off the buzzing before he tried to lighten things up.

"Saved by the bell." He grinned down at her before adding, "We can talk about the answer to that question later when I call you tonight. I can have my driver on standby, waiting to swing by and pick you up."

"We'll see. Right now, I need to get up and get to work so I can try to get out of here early enough to get home to watch the pre-show on TV."

"Oh? You know you could watch me walk the red carpet, standing next to me."

"No, thanks."

He didn't know why she kept refusing. Most women he knew would jump at the chance to go to the Oscars—just one more reason she was so different.

His phone ringing put an end to their discussion. A glance at his phone told him it was his driver. Shane picked up the phone and answered with a gruff, "I'll be down in five," before hanging up.

He could see the same sadness he felt being separated mirrored in her eyes. Shane leaned down for a long, last kiss.

"I gotta run, but I'll call you later, kitten."

CHAPTER 14

She was running so late. Nalani wished she'd remembered to bring her last clean uniform to Shane's room the night before so she could just hit the ground running after her shower. As it was, she'd need to head down to the employee locker room on the first floor to change.

It was honestly a blessing they'd have that night to be apart. She hadn't been home to her tiny apartment in days. If nothing else, she needed to do laundry and water her plants. She was thinking how depressing that was as she opened the door to Shane's suite and literally ran into Henry Ainsworth, who was passing by.

"Well, what do we have here?"

Nalani's skin crawled where the older man touched her. He had the audacity to pull her against him instead of stepping away like any normal gentleman would. As he raked his gaze over her, she realized how damning this encounter was—an employee, in street clothes, her hair still damp from the shower she'd taken in one of the guest rooms.

"I'm sorry, Mr. Ainsworth. I didn't see you there."

"Oh, don't be sorry. I'm happy to see Covington is done with you. I heard the fun going on in there last night as I walked past and wondered which beauty he'd snagged for his nightly debauchery. Little did I know, it was the goody-two-shoes housekeeper servicing him. I have my room until noon. Let's head there, and you can service me next."

Her heart rate spiked as she yanked as hard as she could, attempting to extricate herself from the older man. He was ready, digging his grip into her arms so hard, it hurt as he held her firmly against him.

"How nice. I love a good struggle. It makes it so much more satisfying when I have to fight to get a whore tied down before I finally sink my cock into her pussy. I don't normally like to take sloppy seconds, but for you, I'll make an exception."

Nalani's panic was palpable. She frantically glanced up and down the long hallway, praying another guest would appear. It was still too early to hope Madison might be in the office down the hall on a Sunday morning. Could she be lucky enough to have one of the guards down in the security office notice she needed help on their monitor?

"I'm sorry, sir, but I need to get to work now."

"Why yes, you do," he said as he started pulling her back toward the Hong Kong suite.

She'd seen and heard first-hand what kind of things happened to women in that suite. If she were honest, they weren't that terribly different from the things Shane did to her nightly. But the portly movie executive was not Shane, and she wouldn't willingly go with him.

"Red!"

"Oh, I'm not into that BDSM game shit." The asshole's laughter mocked her. "I know exactly what you need, and I'm gonna give it to you. You've been a naughty girl, whoring yourself out to guests. Well, it's my turn now, and while I'm at it, I'll be happy to punish you for your transgressions. I'm helpful like that."

Nalani flailed in his arms, fighting to get away. As they neared the door, he had to release her with his left hand to reach into his pocket for his electronic key card. She took advantage of the moment and yanked as hard as she could while lifting her knee, connecting with his junk.

She wasn't sure which one of them screamed louder. Ainsworth finally let go, dropping to his knees, howling with pain as he fell to the expensive carpet, curling into a ball.

Nalani took off running at a full sprint down the hall in the opposite direction. She heard a bedroom door opening behind her but didn't stop to see which guest had come out of their room to check out the commotion.

She ran to the Runway office, praying someone would be there, but the office was empty. Too afraid to return to the hall to get to the stairs to leave, Nalani slammed the door closed and threw the lock, finally stopping long enough to take a few deep breaths.

Her mind raced. What should she do? He was sure to make a complaint against her. There would be a witness back there, comforting him right now, getting his side of the story of how the insane housekeeper had attacked him for no reason whatsoever. She was going to lose her job.

Tears fell down her cheeks as she weighed her options. Oh, how she wished Shane had still been at the mansion. He'd have come out into the hall and kicked her attacker's ass. The tabloids would love to get ahold of that story.

A-list actor fights with movie executive over whore.

The headline made her cringe. Shane's words of warning from just the hour before came back to her. What would he want her to do?

Nalani forced herself to walk to the desk and pick up the office phone, her fingers trembling as she reached out to press the button marked security.

"Hey, Madison, what's up?" the masculine voice on the other end of the phone asked.

She fought down the urge to hang up.

"It's Nalani." She finally choked out. "I need help."

The man at the other end of the phone got serious quickly. "What's wrong?"

Should she say it? She knew her life would never be the same if she did. It would be his word against hers. Who would believe her?

It was only when she realized if she didn't say something, she'd end up having to quit anyway because she would never be able to work in a place where she might run into Henry Ainsworth at any moment.

"I was just attacked by a guest in the hall."

"What the fuck? Seriously?"

"No." Nalani lost her temper. "I just thought I'd play an April Fool's joke in February."

"Sorry. Don't move. I'll be right up."

The two minutes it took for security to knock on the door felt like a lifetime. Her pulse spiked, afraid to open the door, fearing Ainsworth had found her.

"Nalani, I'm gonna use my retinal scan to get in. It's just me."

The guard's voice calmed her slightly.

She'd been holding it together pretty well until the door opened, and it was Roger. The sight of a man she had known over a year and trusted as a friend shattered her bravery, and she melted into an emotional, sobbing mess.

"Hey, there. It's okay. You're safe now."

He held her as she let the fear and anger out. Roger helped her to a chair when her legs felt like spaghetti and grabbed several tissues, handing them to her before squatting down to be at eye level.

"Tell me what happened? Whose ass do I need to go kick?"

Nalani took several deep breaths before being able to speak.

"Henry Ainsworth."

Roger's eyes widened. She knew she hadn't been exaggerating the seriousness of the situation when she saw him evaluate his options. To his credit, he didn't try to change her mind about her accusation.

"Okay, that totally sucks since he's a VIP. Hold tight. I need to call this into Miguel. I'll lock the door behind me. Don't leave, okay?"

Little did Roger know, she couldn't have walked out there, knowing Ainsworth was still on the property, even if she wanted to.

The room was suffocatingly still after the security guard left. She managed to calm down enough, she could listen intently for any commotion on the other side of the door. Five long minutes later, she heard shouting in the distance. She thought she could make out Ainsworth's voice, but there were too many other shouts to know what was being said or by whom.

The phone ringing on the desk right next to her scared the shit out of her. The caller ID identified the caller as Miguel Rodriguez, head of security for the property. She dreaded having to tell her story, but she knew it had to be done. She picked up the phone and heard him calling her name.

"Nalani!"

"Hello."

"How are you doing? Roger's detaining the asshole while we wait for the police to get there."

Police?

"Oh my god, not the police."

"Fuck yeah, that's how this works. Assholes who try to hurt anyone on property, especially one of our employees, get a free trip to the police station."

"But you haven't even asked me what he did."

"Doesn't matter. You've worked here for over a year. I've

seen you handle unruly guests just fine. If you say he crossed a line, that's good enough for me."

"But he's a VIP."

"He's also an asshole. We all know it. I've always told my guys to keep an extra eye on him. Did he…" His voice trailed off before he ended with the million-dollar question. "Did he hurt you? Force himself on you?"

"He just grabbed me in the hall and said terrible things. He was dragging me into his suite when I kicked him and got away. I ran into the office and called Roger."

"Good girl. Just so you know, he's accusing you of coming on to him first and getting angry when he wouldn't give you money. I know it's a total load of bullshit. I have the guys pulling the security footage, so we can take a look at it and hand it over to the police."

What a nightmare.

"Do we really need to involve the police? Can't we just kick him out and never let him back on property?" She was worried about the implications of the story getting out for herself, but she turned the tables and added, "We don't need to have that kind of negative PR."

"I don't know. I'd love to see that asshole spend some time behind bars where hopefully, someone worse than him could turn him into their bitch for a change."

As much as she'd like to imagine that, the thought of having to give an official statement of what happened… about why she was at the mansion so early on a Sunday morning, coming out of another guest's room… Nalani shuddered.

"Please. Just throw him out and don't let him come back. Ever. That's the best thing for all of us."

Miguel was quiet on the other end of the phone while he weighed his options.

"I know you are going to hate this, but I just can't do it. I know this isn't what you want but I take keeping the women on property safe. That includes you and everyone else who works here. I can't have something like this go unchecked."

"But can't you just ban him from the property? Never let him back in?"

Nalani's heart was racing. She hated all of the options available to them.

"Hold on. I'm getting a call from Peter in the security office. He was pulling the tape."

It seemed like she had to wait forever for Miguel to come back to phone.

"Nalani, still there?"

"I'm here."

"There is absolutely no damn way we're letting him just leave. Honestly, I can't believe you're even asking for it. The tape is clear. Even without audio, there is absolutely no doubt that he harassed you and was trying to drag you back to his suite. I'm gonna let the police and D.A. sort this out."

"But… isn't Jaxson going to be angry?"

She was going to get fired. She just knew it.

"Screw that. Jaxson is going to feel exactly as I do when he sees the tape."

"Thanks, Miguel. I really appreciate it. I especially…"

"What?"

"You haven't even questioned my story. I was worried no one would believe me. I mean, he's a VIP."

"So? And you're family. No matter how this shakes out with the police, he's banned from the property. Still, I want someone escorting you to and from your car for the next few weeks. Got that?"

"But he spends so much money here."

"We have a waiting list for the suites every weekend. Anyway, you're more important than money."

The call went dead before she could say thank you. Nalani waited another fifteen long minutes, listening to the angry shouting that eventually got softer as they escorted Henry Ainsworth from the property. She ran to the window in Madison's office that looked out onto the Runway parking lot. She got there just in time to see Roger and another security guard manhandling Mr. Ainsworth towards a black and white police car parked near the front door. Even at this distance, she could see how red his face was as it contorted with anger.

Nalani jumped away from the window when he stopped just before being put in the back seat of the police car. He paused just long enough to glare up in her direction. Her brain knew there was no way he could see her in the sunny reflection of the window, but for a brief moment, it was as if his glare penetrated her.

She'd been so lucky that morning. She shuddered to think about what a nightmare it would have been had he succeeded in getting her back into the Hong Kong suite. She pushed the nightmare aside, grateful for her co-worker's quick action.

The office door bursting open behind her scared the shit out of Nalani. She swung around defensively, ready to fight off an intruder.

"Like, it's just me! Are you okay? I got a call from Miguel in my car on the way here."

It was Madison. Her boss rushed toward her after throwing her big bag onto the floor first. The women hugged while Madison apologized.

"You warned me he was dangerous. I didn't listen last time. I'm so damn sorry. Are you really okay?"

"Yeah, I'm just a bit shaken up. I feel better just seeing him being taken away. I'm just not sure we should have called the police."

"Why not? He deserves to rot in jail!"

"But we don't need this kind of negative attention for Runway."

"Screw that. I'm sure Jaxson is going to agree. I'm gonna call him next."

"No! Please. He's going to be angry."

"We have to tell him. I can't hide something this important from him, and you know it. You should go home now. I can feel you shaking."

"I'll be okay," Nalani tried to reassure the shorter woman. "I'm just so grateful security believed me."

"Believed you? Why wouldn't they?" Madison asked.

"I don't know. So often these things are *he said/she said*. He's rich and powerful. I'm a…"

"A what? You'd better have been about to finish that sentence with 'a treasured employee. Or good friend.'"

Nalani swallowed the words she'd been thinking.

I'm a nobody.

"I don't want to leave yet. I need to finish cleaning the suites first."

"Okay…" Madison looked unsure. "But I'm gonna send up one of the girls from downstairs to help you today." Her friend held up her hand to silence Nalani's objection. "I won't take no for an answer. I want you to wrap up and get out of here early. If you aren't going to go to the Academy Awards, you need to at least get out of here early enough to get home to watch them on TV."

Nalani didn't have any fight left. Madison's plan actually sounded wonderful. So much had happened over the last week. As small as her apartment was, she desperately needed to get home and have some time alone to think through everything.

"Thanks." She hugged Madison. "For everything. I really appreciate it. I'd appreciate help from Julie today. I'm really looking forward to changing into sweats and vegging out on the couch tonight," she added truthfully.

"I still say you're crazy for not going with Shane, but hey, you're a big girl."

It took all of Nalani's courage to walk out of that office and down the same hall where she'd been assaulted. Her brain knew Ainsworth wouldn't be there ever again, and that was a huge comfort, but knew it would take some time before she wouldn't be waiting for him to jump out and accost her, all over again.

~

SIX HOURS and eight clean suites later, Nalani was changing back into her street clothes. Her lack of sleep the night before had caught up with her—combined with the huge relief of knowing she would no longer need to watch out for Henry Ainsworth—resulting in an undeniable urge to take a long nap.

For the briefest of moments, she considered going up to Shane's newly cleaned suite to spend the evening watching on the big-screen TV. She could order room service and soak in the whirlpool. She suspected he wouldn't mind, but as tempting as it was, the horrifying possibility of being there when Shane brought some other woman back to his bed that night after a night out hobnobbing with the rich and famous was unbearable. Her brain said he wouldn't do that to her, but her heart couldn't risk it.

Anyway, her houseplants had to be dying without being watered for a week, and she desperately needed to do a load of laundry. She didn't have that many clothes, to begin with, and on the off chance she changed her mind and actually went out for dinner with Shane one night this week, she wanted to wash her one little black dress that was presently cum stained.

True to his word, Roger walked Nalani to her car. It had been days since she'd left the property. The stale air in her sedan was steaming in the late afternoon California sunshine. Just before taking her seat behind the wheel, Nalani turned to Roger, emotions threatening to overwhelm her as she hugged the tall man.

"I can't thank you enough for your help today, Roger. It means so much to me that you and Miguel… well, everyone, really… you believed me, and I won't have to see Henry Ainsworth ever again."

"I just wish I'd seen what was happening on the monitor as it was going down. I've watched the footage several times now, and I get angrier each time when I see him manhandling you and dragging you down the hallway."

"I just hope the press doesn't get ahold of the story. I'd hate to bring a scandal to our doorstep."

"Who knows, and who cares if they do? We have the security footage and made sure he knew damn well we'd go public with it if he tries to shift the blame on you."

"Wow. You guys did all that for me?" Nalani was in awe of the support she was receiving. She'd always known she worked with wonderful people, but everyone was being so kind.

"Hell, yes. I do hope the news doesn't get out if only because we understand how private you are. I mean, you aren't even going public with the good news about dating Shane Covington, so we know you don't want this to get out."

"Wait. You all know about that?"

"It's a little hard not to notice," Roger chuckled. "Your car hasn't left the property in days, and remember, we do monitor the security feed both upstairs and…" Roger paused before blushing and adding, "Downstairs."

Oh. That was his way of saying the security guys had been watching all the debauched things she'd been up to with Shane at Black Light. She had hoped there were no cameras in the club for security reasons but knew they'd taken risks making out in the elevators that were certainly monitored. She felt the heat rising in her own face as he blushed beet-red.

"We're all really happy for you," Roger rushed to add. "As long as you're happy, that is. All I know is, Covington is one lucky bastard."

Nalani didn't know what to say but managed to squeeze out a simple, "Well, thank you… for today."

"Any time. And just know that the police are going to want to interview you at some point. If I hear anything, I'll let you know. Drive careful."

She rushed to get into her car so she could end the awkwardness that had invaded between them. She tried to put the idea of her co-workers watching her on the security cameras at Black Light out of her mind, focusing on getting home.

She'd forgotten how bad traffic was in town on Oscar's day. The mansion was only a few miles away from the famous venue, and her apartment was even closer.

It took thirty minutes to make a trip that normally took ten. Despite knowing it was ridiculous, she kept looking in her rear-view mirror, worried Henry Ainsworth was going to pop up in the back seat and scare the shit out of her. By the time she got to her block, she was ready to jump out of her skin. She needed to get behind her locked door.

The small parking lot next to the row of shops she lived above was completely full, forcing her to find parking along the busy four-lane street full of tourists looking for a glimpse of anyone famous. She was only about eight blocks away from the main drag in front of the theater. A limo inched by as she locked her car door, and for the briefest of moments, she regretted not being in a limo with Shane right at that moment. Hell, that could be him driving by now.

Nalani shook the thought out of her head as she walked to the nondescript door halfway between the vape store and arcade. As normal, rowdy kids congregated on the sidewalk, but today, they unnerved her.

"Look what the cat dragged in. You go out of town or something?"

She didn't need to turn to know it was the landlord's son and her next-door neighbor, Frank, speaking to her. He was a nice enough guy, but she wasn't in the mood for his normal press to go out on a date.

"Hey, Frankie," she answered as she put the key in the lock of the security door. She didn't have time to turn the lock when the door popped open.

"Hi, Nalani. The kids broke the door again. I called a locksmith, but he isn't gonna be able to get here to fix it until Tuesday."

Normally, it wouldn't bother her, but today, the idea of one less locked door between her and the rest of the world was not a welcome thought. Nalani turned to talk to the man who always had a toothpick hanging out of his mouth since he'd given up smoking.

"Any chance you can call someone else? I don't want to have the door unlocked overnight."

"Oh, baby. What's got you spooked? I'll be happy to sleep over at your place tonight if you need protection."

Frankie was always annoyingly forward, but today, his full-court press as he leaned closer freaked her out. Nalani put both palms against his chest and pushed him away.

He backed up right away, lifting his hands to surrender. "Whoa. I was just kidding."

"Yeah, well, it's not funny today."

"You don't need to be such a bitch about it."

Nalani felt bad for snapping at him. He wasn't a bad guy.

"Sorry, I'm just really tired and ready to lie down for a bit. I'd feel better if you got the lock fixed tonight, though."

"But it's Oscars night. The town is a gridlock. No one will brave this unless it's an emergency. I'll see if I can get them to come tomorrow. I'll let you know."

"Okay." That would have to do. "Thanks, Frankie."

At least the steep staircase was well lit as Nalani walked up to the second floor. There were only two modest apartments in the building. At the top of the stairs, she turned left down the short hall that led to her apartment above the arcade. Frankie had taken the nicer apartment above the vape shop. Thankfully, her place wasn't too noisy except for weekend nights. She hoped the kids below wouldn't interrupt the well-deserved nap she hoped to get in before the pre-show started in less than an hour.

After spending a week living in the opulent Paris suite at the mansion, the stark bareness of her small space depressed her. Sure to lock the deadbolt behind her, Nalani threw her keys on the small table that served as both dining table and office desk. She stopped at the fridge in the galley kitchen to pull out a cold soda before returning to her small living room to survey her withering plants as she first quenched her own thirst. She had just finished splashing the half-dozen pots with water when Frankie knocked on her door.

"Hey, Nalani. I have an update for you."

She peeked through the peephole before finally opening the door. "Hey, there," she greeted her neighbor and landlord.

"I got ahold of the lock service. They'll be out tomorrow at noon. That's the earliest they can get here."

"Okay, thanks for making the change. I appreciate it."

"No problem. So... You want to come over to my place to watch TV tonight? I know you love the award shows, and it would be better to watch on my big-screen."

There was absolutely no one she wanted to watch the show with, let alone Frankie, but she tried to let him down gently.

"Thanks for the offer. I appreciate it, but I'm pooped. I'm gonna crawl into bed. I'm gonna record it, so I can watch it later." That was the truth. She just didn't tell him she was recording it to scour it over and over for a glimpse of Shane and the hundreds of other celebrities.

She'd seen the disappointment of her rejection on his face before—even thought about saying yes once or twice in the past, he was a nice enough guy—but now, she knew Shane had ruined all men for her. The thought of being with anyone other than the larger-than-life actor made her heart hurt.

"Alright, I'll leave you to it then. Talk to you later," he added before heading back down the hall toward his own place.

Nalani closed the door behind him, locking the door once more. She'd just made it back to the TV, about to flip it on, when Frankie knocked again. Annoyed, she went to the door, swinging it open.

"Now what?"

It took a few seconds for the truth to register. The question of what he was doing there merged with her memories from earlier in the day.

Reflexively, she rushed to slam the door closed. She almost succeeded, and for a brief moment, she thought she might have a chance to get the door closed and locked.

But he was too heavy, too strong…

Too angry.

The door came crashing inward, slamming back against the nearby wall. She heard the scream. She knew it was hers as her fight-or-flight instincts took over. Nalani turned, ready to run to the kitchen—there were knives there.

She didn't make it. Arms squeezed her tight from behind, lifting her feet off the ground as she fought like a wildcat. She heard her door slam shut behind them. He must have kicked it closed.

Pushing the panic down, Nalani tried to recall the moves she'd learned in the self-defense class she'd taken upon moving to the city. She wiggled hard, managing to loosen his hold on her enough, she fell forward to her knees hard as he let her go. She took off scrambling on her hands and knees, trying valiantly to get to a knife, but he reached down to grab her ankles, lifting her legs and halting her forward movement.

She rolled, trying to yank out of his grip. She kicked like a wild cat, crawling like a lobster across the floor in her attempt to get away.

They were both out of breath by the time he caught her ankle again. This time, he had a better grip. She sat up, using her nails to claw at his hands, trying to force him to lose his grip. She felt his skin tearing under her nails as he shouted in pain. Unfortunately, he kept his hold with one hand, and now that she was closer, backhanded her so hard, she felt her teeth rattle.

A sharp pain exploded in her head as her neck snapped painfully under the fast strike. Nalani reached up, trying to protect her face as his hand connected with her face again, this time with his fist.

Her brain knew how much trouble she was in, yet some part of her was having trouble reconciling the third hit to her face was actually happening.

Things like this happened to other people, not her. She'd known he was dangerous, but never in a million years had she believed he would break and enter her home. That he'd seek her out outside of the mansion. That he would physically assault her and use her face as a punching bag.

Nalani fought like a wildcat until she finally pulled free, curling herself into a small ball on the floor, throwing her arms and hands over her head in a defensive move.

That was when the kicking began, accompanied by terrifying words.

"No one gets away with disrespecting Henry Ainsworth. All of you… you're gonna pay. And I'm starting with you. I'll teach you a hard lesson right before I end you."

His foot connected with her back… her head. Stalking around her, he kicked at her stomach, connecting with her ribs.

Was this really happening, or was it a nightmare? If so, she hoped she woke up soon.

The assault continued until his voice became distant. She was woozy, tasting the metallic blood in her mouth. She fought not to pass out, knowing that as horrific as this was to live through, being unconscious, available for him to do anything to her unchecked, was a hundred times worse.

He was a man possessed as if years of pent-up frustrations were pouring out of him, directed at her. She didn't have a chance. She did her best to protect her head and organs until the beating slowed. She was too afraid to cry, too shocked to scream again.

The clicking of the lock on the handcuffs, locking her wrists together, broke her out of her shock. She yanked her arms, testing the metal, knowing just how much trouble she was in.

The man towering over her was a stranger, his humanity gone, and in its place was a red-faced psychopath. His evil grin was menacing as he spewed his hateful promise.

"You may not be dead yet, but I'm not going to stop until you wish you were."

Despite lying on the floor, the room started to spin. She struggled to push down her fear, knowing passing out would be the worst possible thing, but the pain across her body married with her fear. White lights filled her vision as the humming in her ears grew louder, drowning out everything until darkness claimed her. The last thought she had was regret—none of this would have happened if she'd only said yes to Shane. Oh, how she wished she were miles away on the red carpet.

Now, she didn't even know if she'd ever get to see him again.

CHAPTER 15

"Hand me my purse." Piper bit out, directing her request to her personal assistant sitting across from her in the stretch limousine. The same limousine they'd been inching forward in for the last thirty minutes.

"You didn't bring a purse, remember? I have everything you need until the after parties."

Bullshit.

"Fine. Then give me my purse for the after party." Piper tried to keep her voice steady between taking sips of air meant to stave off her full-blown panic attack.

"What is it you need? I can…"

"Just fucking give me a Xanax already." Her frustration overflowed at having to explain herself.

When Danielle failed to start digging for the requested drugs in the huge bag on the backseat with them, Piper pinned her with her best Mistress Ice glare.

Unfortunately, an almost identical glare stared back at her.

"Didn't you fire your last assistant for letting you take a Xanax before a public appearance?"

Bitch.

"Maybe, but I fired the one before for insubordination when he wouldn't give me one."

"Fine. I'll be spending my time backstage tonight brushing up on my resume," the PA deadpanned.

Piper's bodyguard for the night sat stoically next to her PA, trying to keep a straight face.

Asshole.

Damn, she was a hot mess. Damn Antonio for running so late, he was going to have to meet her on the carpet. In a last-minute panic, she'd called to change her RSVP from one to two, opting to bring the best-looking eye-candy she had on speed dial. Unfortunately, he was also the most unreliable of the bunch.

"Just hang in there. I can see we're only one car away from the drop-off. Let's review. You and Michael get out. He'll do a short sweep, then reach in to help you out. You'll do a short greet, then hightail it into the arrivals tent. I'll meet you there, and we'll do a quick check of your makeup and gown before you walk the gauntlet. There'll be three short interview stops along the way, then I'll pick you back up at the top of the stairs for a final check before you're seated. Any questions?"

They'd gone over this all already.

"You do realize I've done this before, right?"

"Yes, but I wasn't sure if you remembered all the details due to the aforementioned Xanax debacle."

Double bitch.

"Remind me again. Why did I hire you?"

"Because you need someone to be as ruthless with you as you are with yourself." Danielle's grin calmed Piper.

Triple bitch.

But she was right. Oh, Piper had never used those words with her PA, but they were the truth. That's why Danielle was a keeper.

"Hold off on the resume until we see how the night goes, shall we?"

The attractive older woman chuckled. "I get two calls a week, trying to poach me. I don't need a resume."

"And yet you stick with me. Interesting."

The limo that had been inching forward finally stopped next to a sign, *DROPOFF*. Just before Michael opened the door, Danielle answered.

"I love a challenge, and you, Ms. Kole, are never boring. Now, try to at least have a little fun tonight."

A throng of fans pressed in as closely as the barricades meant to keep them a safe distance would allow. The arrival order of celebrities was carefully choreographed, so she heard her name being called. She took a deep breath and reached to take her bodyguard's helping hand, hoping to exit the limo as gracefully as possible in her glittering, skintight Gucci gown. It was her favorite of the three gowns she'd be wearing that night.

Piper plastered on her showtime smile and stood, waving her free left hand into the air in the direction of the shouting crowd, knowing she was already on camera.

She felt the arm circling her waist just as his words hit her brain.

"You look magnificent."

Nolan.

Her knees literally gave out. She would have face-planted onto the cement if he hadn't been supporting her. His lips brushed the shell of her ear as he leaned in to reassure her.

"I've got you, baby. Just smile and let's head into the arrivals tent."

Like a sheep being led to the slaughter, Piper followed Nolan's lead, trying her best not to let the shock of seeing him register for the cameras. All it would take was a tiny gaff, and the gossip rags would smell blood.

The second they were in the relative privacy of the tent—a

no camera or recording zone—Piper lifted her elbow and brought it crashing down into the washboard abs hidden under Nolan's dashing tuxedo. His corresponding grunt of pain brought her Mistress Ice brain great satisfaction.

"How dare you do that? What a horseshit move," she shouted, drawing attention from the dozen people gathered waiting for their turn on the red carpet.

Nolan recovered quickly. He had the audacity to yank her into his arms, holding her so tight, she couldn't successfully knee The Rock.

Had she really just thought of his dick by name?

"That's enough. Settle down before you make a scene."

"Me make a scene? You blindsided me, damnit."

"I've told you no less than a half-dozen times in the last week, I'd see you at the Oscars."

She fought hard enough to be able to lean back in his arms and look up into his eyes as she retorted.

"See me, sure. From a nice, safe distance. Like fifty rows apart."

"Yeah, I heard about you calling and requesting I be seated in the balcony this year. Thanks. It forced me to go to plan B."

"Plan B?"

"You're costing me a lot of money, Ms. Kole," he grinned. "The sooner you get with the program, the sooner I can start spending my money to buy you more of these diamonds you seem to love so much."

She was obscenely pleased, watching Nolan scanning her ears, neck, wrist, and even bicep, appreciating her ice collection.

"What the fuck are you talking about?"

"Watch your language. You need to play the part of a lady tonight, at least until I get you home and in my bed. Then, the nastier the language, the better."

"Fuck you, Nolan."

"Yes, please." The bastard had the audacity to grin that sexy grin of his before adding, "Are you ready to walk the carpet?"

"Not yet. I need to find my date. He's supposed to be waiting here for me."

"He is." Only after she started to glance around for Antonio, did he add, "I am."

Their gazes snapped together like magnets, and she knew instantly, he was telling the truth.

"Where's Antonio?"

"Seems the only thing he wanted more than being seen with Piper Kole was the one-hundred grand in cash I delivered to him myself."

"The what?" she asked incredulously.

He placed a finger under her slack chin, closing her mouth.

"Don't look so surprised. I spent the same for three hours with you at roulette. The way I see it, we'll be together through the show and the after parties. I'm getting a much better return on my investment this time, so I'm making progress."

The man was certifiable—truly. Still, the fact he'd spent two hundred thousand dollars in the last month just to be in her presence was more than a bit flattering.

"Now, you ready?"

"For what?"

"To unveil us."

"There is no *us*," she spat.

"Oh, baby, there most definitely is an *us*." Nolan's hand moved lower, possessively gripping her ass through the sparkly dress. "I'm proud to say, I'm responsible for delivering over a half dozen orgasms to this delicious body in the last week, and I very much look forward to delivering several more tonight—this time, in person."

"Oh, Mr. Boeing. We weren't expecting to see you tonight… were we?" Danielle showed up next to her, carrying her big bag of goodies. Piper could see her assistant in her peripheral view, glancing back-and-forth between them.

"No, we were most certainly not expecting to see Mr. Boeing, yet here he is. He's like a bad penny—always turning up."

"I resent that. I'm more like a superhero, showing up in time to keep disaster at bay."

Piper let loose a snort that drew several glances in their direction. Only one person in the tent, however, was brave enough to approach them. She saw him coming and verbally attacked as soon as he arrived.

"You're on my shit-list, buddy. See what you started by letting him use your phone last week?"

Shane stepped up next to Nolan, the two men making a damn fine display of Hollywood's finest. The grin on his face told Piper he wasn't fazed in the slightest by her anger.

Mistress Ice sure as hell was losing her touch. It galled her that not one man in weeks had been intimidated by her. While she'd taken a trip to her own pity party, Nolan was quizzing Shane.

"Where's that little someone you've been keeping holed up in your bed this last week? I've been looking forward to meeting her."

"Yeah, well, it seems I've met the only woman in the state who has no interest in being seen in public with me. Go figure."

"Shane Covington has to go stag to the Oscars. That's funny," Piper rubbed it in.

Her old friend smiled brightly, leaning in to talk softer. "Maybe it is, but not quite as funny as Mistress Ice arriving with a Dom as her date."

Nolan stepped in between them to break things up. If only they had been at Black Light—she'd enjoy wiping that sexy grin off Shane Covington's face with her crop… literally.

He was saved her retaliation by someone near the exit of the tent, calling out, "Piper Kole, you're up."

"Seems it's time for me to go to work. We'll have to resume this discussion later, after the show," she promised Shane.

"Oh, I look forward to it. In the meantime, I'd watch your six, Boeing."

She could feel Nolan's attention still on her. She looked up at him and felt her breath hitch from the sexy heat of his stare.

"Oh, she doesn't scare me. Do you, baby?"

Her brain revolted, screaming at her to seize control of the situation. Mistress Ice would never allow Nolan, or Shane for that matter, to treat her like this—call her baby and put his roaming hands on her intimately in public.

Too bad Mistress Ice was nowhere to be found.

"Let's go wow them, baby."

The funny thing was, Nolan was right. She knew they were going to wow the crowd and the international press corp. And why not? She and Nolan made one hell of a power couple.

They were shuffled through the tent toward the exit that led to the gauntlet of reporters and a sea of photographers. Just before they stepped out, Piper leaned closer, pulling Nolan down so she could talk against his ear.

"Don't forget, *baby*. Since we're together, that means I'm in charge."

Nolan's broad grin warmed her from the inside out. "We'll just have to see about that now, won't we?"

CHAPTER 16

On the edge of consciousness, the pinch of a needle sticking her left arm felt like little more than a bug bite. Until a familiar warmth exploded in her veins, spreading what she had learned the hard way was a seductive poison—the poison that had stolen her childhood.

Disoriented, Nalani fought to listen to the far-off voice. Was it her father? No… it couldn't be. He was in prison.

Familiar shame slammed into her, hitting her hard.

She surrendered to the euphoria, letting it wipe away her fear… the pain. God help her, she'd missed this so much. Some small part of her brain still fought to wake up from the nightmare she was in, but the rest of her body seemed to welcome the evil drug like a long-lost friend. It dulled the agony and tamped down the feelings of dread, leaving her languid… pliable.

Nalani fought to open her eyes to see whose hands were ripping the clothes off her body. Whose voice was mocking her nakedness? Whose arms were lifting her from the floor?

The first wave of nausea hit her hard, rolling her stomach in violent waves of protest. The taste of bile in her mouth mingled with the tang of her own blood. Panic raced in, fighting… trying to wake her up. She was in danger, but the poison was too strong. Nalani turned her head, spitting and sputtering.

"Bitch. You'll pay for that."

Her brain wasn't cooperating as she fought to make sense of what was happening, falling deeper into the drug-filled abyss. Her ass hit a hard surface just before whoever it was carrying her dumped her in a heap. Even through the haze of the drugs, a sharp pain exploded in her chest. Was she having a heart attack? If so, this wasn't what she'd thought it would feel like.

There was a new ripping sound she couldn't identify. Then his hands were on her face, holding her head still with one hand while applying something that felt like electrical tape across her mouth. Too late, she realized he'd taken away her ability to scream. Why hadn't she been screaming already?

It took all of her focus to get the message to her eyes to open. When she succeeded, she regretted it.

In her current disorientation, his name escaped her, but her brain recognized he represented danger. The red-faced, angry man had hurt her before. He wanted to hurt her again.

The metal of the handcuffs already restraining her cut into her wrists as she flailed, a lame attempt to get away. It was too late. She was losing the battle.

The ugly man had the nerve to laugh as he easily yanked her arms above her head, walking behind where she couldn't see what was happening. Nalani strained to pull her arms free, but even without the drugs, he was too strong.

Her gaze fell on the water-stained ceiling, choosing to think about the roof leak from the summer before. It was easier to think about yelling at Frank to get the ceiling fixed than acknowledge the truth of what was happening. The stain told her she was lying on top of her one and only table, and he had secured her arms to the legs of the furniture beneath her.

As the intruder came back around into her line of sight, the thought flitted through her brain, she wished he'd tied her face down. At least then, she wouldn't have to see his dangerous anger as he snatched her right ankle and started tying a rope around it.

Nalani gathered up all her strength and kicked, yanking her leg free and lifting it for a direct hit against his face. The blood seeping out of his nose was a small victory, but the unexpected injury only fueled his fury.

For the briefest of moments, she let herself hope she'd scared him away when he stepped out of her line of sight again. Too late, she realized it was to grab his next tool of torture—a stun gun that electrocuted her as he jabbed, holding it against her naked thigh for several long seconds. A burst of fire traveled through her whole body, making her feel like she was about to fall out of her skin. Pain and confusion merged, leaving her limp as she felt his gloved hands back on her ankles.

Her situation went from bad to worse as she felt first one, then the other leg lifted up and over her torso—secured to the legs of the table along with her cuffed wrists—leaving her completely naked, exposed, and subdued.

He'd already robbed her of her mobility and ability to speak. As she vaguely became aware of him taking his own pants off, she knew he was about to rob her of the last shred of innocence she might have. As horrific as the things in her childhood had been, she'd been spared from the most heinous of crimes—rape. With a sad certainty, she knew she wouldn't be that lucky today.

His voice sounded as if he were in a tunnel far away. She was grateful to only catch snippets of his hateful words, but the word Viagra cut through the haze. Even in her fog, it struck fear in her, realizing her ordeal had the potential to go on for hours.

His pole was ugly. Her brain fought to remember where she'd seen it before—at work. He'd been hurting a different woman on that day. The memories were hazy, but regret mingled with fear. Why hadn't she stayed at Runway?

She would be paying a very high price for that mistake.

He pierced her core without ceremony. While his cock was smaller than she was used to, the lack of lubrication drew a scream that was lost in the tape over her mouth. He was a man crazed, pounding her body so hard, the old table beneath her started to creak under the pressure.

Nalani could do nothing to defend herself physically, so she welcomed the drugged haze that dulled her panic as seconds turned to long minutes. She closed her eyes, so she didn't have to see his mocking sneer as he enjoyed violating her body. She let her mind drift, trying to slip away to another place—another time—where she'd been happy and safe.

Shane Covington's face popped into her consciousness, and she fought to hold on to the feeling of safety she felt as snippets of memories started flashing in her brain. Could they be real, or had she just imagined the larger-than-life actor tenderly holding her? Oh, how she wished the memories could be real. As she felt her feminine folds turning raw from their abuse, she fought to hold on to the dream of Shane, instead of the reality of pain.

Her relief was palpable when the pounding thrusts stopped, and her attacker finally stepped away from her body. The sudden silence of the wobbly table highlighted the sound of her own sobs. With the tape over her mouth, she struggled to take deep enough breaths through her snot-filled nose.

Nalani had almost succeeded in catching her breath when the next line of fire hit her raw pussy. Her eyes flew open in time to see Henry Ainsworth's arm in motion, letting the next strike of what looked like a small whip snap out, making contact with her most tender skin.

The tape was effective. It swallowed her screams as two strikes turned to four, then eight. The brutal whipping of her exposed inner thighs, pussy, and even stomach and breasts went on until she could no longer count. The only thing that made it through the agony-filled shroud were his spiteful words like *whore, bitch,* and *cunt*—the hideous names mingled with angry promises of making sluts like her pay for trying to ruin his reputation.

The relief of hearing the whip hit the floor was short lived. His Viagra-filled penis was back inside her, hurting worse than before, thanks to the streaks where the whip had broken open her skin.

Between the meth and pain, Nalani gratefully slipped in and out of consciousness, losing the ability to judge time. When she would pass out, the asshole leaned over her to backhand her face with enough force, she felt her neck cracking from the fast snapping back-and-forth.

She welcomed the bright light after one particularly hard bash to her head, praying for darkness that would take the pain away. She got her wish as she felt herself slipping away.

The sharp pain of her asshole being ripped open jarred her awake. It was unlike any pain she'd suffered before, this new violation so much more personal. Her passage was dry, giving his appendage the evil opportunity to torture her further.

She felt his arms wrapping around her thighs, using her tied-down body as an anchor to deepen his thrusts inside her body. Like her pussy, he was ripping her, raping her with a velocity meant to do maximum damage. She wasn't sure how, but she knew this attack was less about sex and more about getting even with her for daring to report him. He wasn't chasing his satisfaction but was instead racing to achieve his revenge.

Nalani was grateful for the meth making its way through her veins. It was the only thing dulling the pain of the attack. It was also the only thing that made time float, letting her lose herself for long blocks of time, stealing her away from the horror of her reality.

At some point, she became aware the intruder had taken the time to turn on her television. Fragments of sound broke through her stupor, sparking odd thoughts of award shows and walking on the red carpet outside of a theater. Short strains of musical numbers mingled with a laugh track. Somewhere, people were having fun, listening to music and laughing, unaware she was going through hell.

It wasn't fair. She didn't know how, but even in her hazy fog, she knew with a certainty, she was supposed to be there, having fun—not tied to her kitchen table, waiting to die.

But life wasn't fair. As the assault dragged on, her assailant grew even angrier, taking turns between raping her holes and shouting at people on the television. Several times, Nalani wasn't sure if he was calling her a bitch or someone else far away.

After what felt like a lifetime, the portly man, now sweating from his exertion, grew agitated over his inability to climax, blaming it on the sexual enhancement drugs. She didn't give a shit why, she just prayed he'd come soon, so he'd have to stop his hateful assault.

She was only vaguely aware of him taking a short break to put on a condom. By the time he plunged his penis back inside her ass, the passageway was lubricated with her own blood. The final volley of thrusts rammed her body so hard, the table starting wobbling. Her rapist cried out as he finally ejaculated. She opened her eyes just enough to see his ruddy face contorting with grotesque satisfaction.

A tiny ray of hope sparked. She'd survived the worst of it. The only question dancing through her drug-addled brain was if he planned on killing her now that he'd had his fun. She'd seen his face. She knew his name. He may be a monster, but he wasn't stupid.

He wouldn't leave a witness who could identify him.

In the awkward post-attack silence, the sound of people clapping and cheering came from her small TV across the room. "And the award for Best Motion Picture goes to…"

Oh, how she wished she was there. Had Shane Covington really invited her? Was he real, or had she just imagined him looking at her lovingly? It felt like some farfetched fantasy, but she let herself dream of the handsome actor as she watched Ainsworth putting his own clothing back together and his used condom into a plastic Ziploc bag.

One by one, he released her limbs, bringing renewed pain to her extremities as blood rushed back through veins that had been restrained for what seemed like hours.

Only after he'd removed the handcuffs from her wrists and put them into the leather bag, he'd brought with him did her attacker finally address her again after first shoving her off the tabletop, sending her damaged body crashing to the hard floor in a broken heap.

His shoe met with her stomach as he kicked her before crouching down, thrusting his still gloved hand into her hair and yanking her head up until she had no choice but to stare back at his angry glare.

"Don't make me regret leaving you alive. If you so much as mention a tiny part of what happened here today to anyone, I'll be sure to destroy what's left of your pitiful life, you got it? I had my PI work up a file on you. No one will believe a meth addict like you over a powerful movie exec like me.

"And if you try to say I put these marks on your body, I'll be sure to tell the police about all the noises I heard coming out of Covington's suite at Runway this last week. I've heard rumors of the kinky shit he's into. It won't be a stretch for Davidson and the cops to believe it was him who did this to you. I even have photos of him with other sluts, doing almost the same thing. I'll send them to every newspaper and TV station in town. He'll never work in this town again, and neither will you. Davidson will throw you out of the mansion like the garbage you are."

As much as she hated the idea of dying, at that moment, it was preferable to having him walk out of there and get away with the atrocities he'd done to her. Yet she knew she'd never be strong enough to accuse Henry Ainsworth—no one would believe a nobody like her.

He released her head as fast as he'd yanked it up, crashing her forehead against the floor in one final act of violence. Nalani knew she should feel relieved when she heard the door to her apartment closing behind her attacker, but the second she was alone, the panic she'd somehow been suppressing attacked as hard as Ainsworth had.

Heart racing, head pounding, body aching—she fell apart. Her throat was sore from trying to scream. It took several tries to pull the tape off her lips, allowing the first deep breath she'd had since the attack had begun. As her lungs filled, a sharp pain stabbed her. She suspected she had a broken rib or two where he'd kicked her.

She wasn't sure how long she laid on the floor, paralyzed by her own fear. What does one do after being brutally attacked? Somehow crawling to the shower, then bed seemed wrong.

She was supposed to call the police. To report the break-in—the brutal attack. Surely, he'd left behind enough physical evidence to condemn him. Even as she thought it, she dismissed the idea. There was no way she could admit the shame she felt at not being strong enough to fight him off.

Calling the police would mean going to the hospital. She'd be poked and prodded—violated all over again. They'd do whatever it was they did when they performed a rape kit. It would surely involve a blood test. They'd find the meth coursing through her blood. They'd do a background check. They'd find her father and brother were two of the biggest meth dealers in the state of Hawaii... until the day they'd been thrown in prison.

And finally, the police would find how she'd been caught up in the family business at the young age of fourteen. Used by the men she was supposed to trust to deliver drugs for them, and when she'd protested, injected with the very drugs they sold until they'd got her so dependent, she'd do anything for her next hit.

No.

She couldn't relive that part of her life again. It had taken years of treatment to fully recover. She'd just have to move again. Somewhere where she could start all over again. Somewhere where she'd never have to worry about seeing Henry Ainsworth ever again.

A crushing sadness blanketed her when she realized that would also mean never seeing Shane Covington or the friends she worked with again.

Nalani dozed in and out of her stupor, unsure how much time passed before she was finally able to pull herself up enough to crawl toward her small bathroom. She was pretty sure she was leaving a streak of blood across the floor as her knees connected with the cool tile of the dated bathroom.

She couldn't remember when she'd last eaten or drank, but as thirsty as she was, she couldn't find the strength to pull herself up to the sink. Instead, she crawled to the bathtub, taking a full minute to navigate high enough to turn on the faucet and pull the stopper.

She collapsed to the floor again, despair threatening to overwhelm her. Closing her eyes, she took several deep cleansing breaths in an attempt to calm down while she waited for the tub to fill.

She should feel safe now, but some part of her knew... she would never feel safe again. Horrific memories of the attack kept playing on an auto-loop in her brain, gripping her with renewed fear until she felt faint.

By the time the darkness came, she welcomed it.

CHAPTER 17

"This is stupid. I want to go home."

Nolan knew he was on borrowed time with Piper. He'd been walking a tightrope all night, trying to keep things light between them while still trying valiantly to solidify the tenuous thread that seemed to be holding them together.

"I promised Wayne I'd make an appearance."

Piper snagged a flute of champagne from a passing waiter, downing it in one fast swig before slamming the empty crystal back on the tray before sassing back.

"Sounds like a personal problem."

The only thing keeping Piper's unladylike belch from making the gossip rags was the pounding beat of the dance music.

"You're drunk."

"Yep. So nice of you to notice," she said, waving wildly at another waitress carrying a full tray of beverages through the pressing crowd of elegantly dressed celebrities.

Nolan had big plans for their night and scraping a drunk Piper off the floor wasn't part of it.

"Come on," he said, reaching to grab her before she could

pick up her next drink. She tried to yank her hand out of his, but he was ready for her. "You owe me a dance."

"I don't owe you shit," she retorted, yet he noticed she'd stopped trying to get away.

The dance floor was full of revelers. Nolan weaved them through the throng of grinding bodies—several of who were carrying their Oscar statues—finding a pocket of open space near the speakers. Most couples shied away because it was so loud there, but Nolan knew it was ideal for them since they'd struggled to find topics to discuss that didn't end up in their signature verbal bantering. To outsiders, their witty bickering probably sounded like arguing, but Nolan knew the truth.

It was their unique form of foreplay.

The deeper into the night they got, the more certain he was Piper knew it too, and it had her running scared—the more scared she got, the more alcohol she drank.

The upbeat dance song called for wild dancing, but Nolan pulled Piper into his arms, molding their bodies together perfectly as they swayed seductively to the beat of the music.

"Aw… feels like you're happy to see me," she joked, pressing her hips against his raging erection.

"Tease. Don't think I haven't noticed you accidentally brushing your tits against me all night. If I didn't know any better, I'd say you were as anxious as I am to consummate our little game tonight."

"Dream on, buddy," Piper chuckled. "We aren't consummating a damn thing."

"Oh Piper, you're so wrong. We've already finished our first award ceremony together. Walked the red carpet together. Tomorrow, we'll be in every news column… every gossip rag… We've attended two parties together. Now we've had our first dance. And in about ten seconds, we'll be able to cross another first off our list."

"Oh yeah, what's that? My first knee to The Rock in public?"

"Naw, I'd rather save that for another night if that's okay. I had something better in mind."

"What could be better than publicly humiliating you?" she teased, a levity in her eyes he loved.

He knew it was a risky move, but he couldn't have stopped himself if he tried. He'd waited long enough. Nolan tightened his hold on Piper's waist with his left arm, grabbing her coiffed hair with his right hand, finally crashing his lips against hers in a possessive kiss.

She fought to wriggle free for all of two seconds before surrendering herself wholly to the passion of the moment. He was glad he had a good hold of her—Piper's legs turned to spaghetti just as he thrust his tongue into her mouth. He could taste the remnants of the breath mint he'd seen her pop in the car on the way to the party.

She felt like heaven while being hotter than hell. Nolan's heart pounded in his chest as their kiss went on, gaining heat until he was certain they had to be putting off steam for all to see. He let his hand roam, enjoying the feel of her sexy curves, hidden by the satin of her elegant gown.

The good-natured catcalls from the party-going revelers dancing around them finally convinced him to come up for air. While the kiss had been scorching hot, the simple intimacy that followed was more precious. Piper allowed him to lean into her, their foreheads linked as they swayed to the music.

He was afraid to break their amicable silence, so he used the time with her in his arms to memorize the feel of her curves against his body. As the song progressed, he felt her slumping.

"Hey, are you checking out on me?" he finally asked against her ear.

"Aww, you noticed."

Her words didn't match her continued dependency on him to hold her up. He wasn't crazy about her getting drunk, but if that's what it took to break the ice between them, so be it.

She must have been thinking the same thing.

"You're ruining my reputation, you know that?"

"What reputation is that? That you don't play well with others?" he teased her back.

She swatted at his chest. "I tried hard to ditch you tonight. You just kept showing up like a bad penny."

Nolan didn't want to pick a fight, but he also didn't want to let her comment go without notice.

"Yeah, I so appreciated you ditching me for over half of the ceremony by staying backstage after you'd presented. I was stuck sitting with a seat-filler. His name is Clark. He wants to be an actor."

Her tinkling laughter did something funny to his insides.

"Aw, you poor thing. You had to…" Piper stopped mid-sentence. Her eyes opened wide as she lifted her right hand to cup it over her mouth.

"Oh no, you don't. Don't you dare puke on me here on the dance floor."

The panic in her eyes told him she was indeed ready to throw-up on the center of the dance floor.

Nolan got them in motion, using his left hand to clear a path through the grinding bodies, pulling Piper behind him with a death grip to keep them from being separated.

Heading toward the bathroom might have been a safer bet, but he didn't get where he was without taking risks. Tonight, he would be going for broke, which meant he headed for the front door of the crowded banquet hall. Seeing the gauntlet of reporters and paparazzi waiting to catch celebrities doing naughty things for their cameras, Piper yanked on their joined hands to get him to stop.

He stepped in front of her to shield her from the clicking cameras as her complexion took on a chalky-green hue.

"You need fresh air," he offered.

"Not out front," she croaked out, following his plan perfectly.

"Okay, we passed a side exit to the alley. Let's sneak out that way."

They were only a few feet into the alley when a black stretch limo parked along the street flipped on their headlights and turned down the narrow pavement, stopping right in front of them.

Nolan had just opened the door when Piper lost her battle with her stomach, depositing the contents of the appetizers they'd eaten together along with the numerous alcohol units she'd drank on the pavement next to the car.

As she bent down, Nolan held back the few stray wisps of her long, dark hair that had escaped from her up-do from getting sprayed. Unfortunately, he wasn't able to protect the first few inches inside the limo from the same fate.

His driver Thomas got out of the car and seeing the problem, opened the door on the other side of the car as he urged Nolan along.

"You're about to be papped. I'd hurry if I were you."

Nolan looked down the alley and confirmed there were indeed several cameramen with long-range lenses setting up. He reached into his inner pocket to come out with a hankie, thrusting it into Piper's hand before scooping her into his arms.

"We gotta go, baby."

Piper didn't protest as he carried her limp body to the other side of the car, diving into the backseat as the driver slammed the door closed behind them. Once behind the wheel, Thomas gunned the gas so hard, the tires squealed.

Once they were back out on the main drag, safely hidden by the tinted windows, Nolan couldn't help but smile. While he wished Piper hadn't gotten drunk, he acknowledged it might be a blessing in disguise since she was presently sitting on his lap without protest.

He reached to open a bottle of water, holding it up to Piper's lips.

"Drink for me, baby."

The fact she obeyed without protest confirmed she was drunker than he'd thought.

"Mouth tastes bad," she complained.

Nolan reached into the inner pocket of his jacket again to come out with a few breath mints. He held them out, but she didn't take them. When he looked up, he found her eyes closed.

Oh, man, she was gorgeous.

"Open up, baby."

He popped the mints in her mouth as she let herself collapse, snuggling against him as he hugged her closer.

It took almost the entire forty-minute drive back to his house, with Piper snoring lightly as she slept in his arms, to come to terms with the truth.

He wanted more of this. He wanted forever.

Piper Kole, in his arms, was his home.

As much as he'd hoped to consummate their night of foreplay, he suspected it was for the best when she didn't bother to wake up as he carried her from the car to his front door, where his driver was punching in the security code to enter.

"Thanks, Thomas. Sorry about the mess in the back."

"That's no problem, Mr. Boeing. That kinda thing happens more often than you'd think."

The news didn't surprise him.

"Night, Mr. Boeing. I hope Ms. Kole feels better soon."

"Night, Thomas."

He carried her straight to his bedroom—to his bed.

Only when he laid her down and went to take off her high heels, he saw she'd made a mess on her beautiful gown. Nolan rushed to unzip the dress and strip it off her before the mess spread to his comforter. Piper's shoes were next, followed by the diamond armbands, bracelets, necklaces, and earrings the Ice Queen was famous for.

It was a bit like unwrapping a present as he got her down to her tiny panties and the weirdest pasty-things stuck to her boobs where a bra should have been.

If he were a gentleman, he'd tuck her in, but there was nothing in their history that called for being a gentleman. Once he had them both naked, he pulled the covers down and gently placed Piper's head on the pillow. For a moment, he thought she was going to wake up and ruin his plan when she rolled onto her side, tucking her knees up.

Nolan breathed a sigh of relief when she failed to wake up. Crawling into bed, he turned off the lights before rolling until he could reach out and spoon Piper's sexy body. Her soft sigh as he nuzzled against her gave him hope that even if she fought against *them* while she was awake, in her sleep, her body recognized how perfect they were together.

He laid awake, thinking through their extraordinary night together. They'd made great progress, but he wasn't naive. He knew he had a long way to go before he'd win Piper over for good.

He finally nodded off, dreaming about how he'd put the next phase of his plan into motion the next morning.

CHAPTER 18

"You do realize you look like a loser, sitting out here, staring at your phone all night, right?"

The jab had come from his agent, John Graves, but he'd heard the same complaint from numerous women wanting to dance. Even Boeing had given him shit earlier before he'd left with Piper.

Shane shoved his phone into the inner pocket of his suit jacket. He'd changed out of his tux into a more casual suit for the string of after-parties he normally enjoyed. This year, nothing seemed normal. He'd been trying unsuccessfully to get ahold of Nalani for over an hour, and it annoyed him she wasn't answering. It annoyed him, even more, he cared so much.

He pushed to his feet just as his agent sat down in the empty chair next to him. He wasn't in the mood to chitchat. "I'm heading out."

"Aw, come on. Have a seat. I want to talk for just a minute." John patted the seat he'd just vacated.

Shane snuck a peek at his watch—eleven forty-five. Taking a seat, he waved over a roving waiter to snag a bottled beer as he started the timer with Graves.

"You've got ten minutes. My car is picking me up at midnight."

Technically, that was a lie. He hadn't texted his driver yet, but Graves didn't need to know that.

"Why so distracted tonight? You turning back into a pumpkin at midnight?"

His agent's joke fell flat. Shane wasn't in the mood. It scared him to admit it, but it felt wrong being there tonight, hobnobbing with Hollywood's elite when Nalani was home, doing her laundry. He didn't understand her reluctance to be seen with him. He'd never met anyone like her before.

"Hello? Are you even paying attention?"

"Shit. Sorry, man. I'm a bit distracted tonight."

"You don't say. I have to admit, I've never seen you like this."

"What, distracted?"

"No. Smitten. Usually, it's the women chasing you, not the other way around. Care to share names?"

Busted.

"Nothing to share, man. What was it you needed?" Shane pushed to change the subject.

"Right. Well, the studio wants to move the Blessed Betrayal schedule up by two months to accommodate Khloe Monroe's schedule. She had a conflict with the original timeline. I told them I'd check with you, but technically, you could make it work."

"Fuck that," Shane objected. He kept to himself the main reason he didn't want to move the schedule around was it would take him away from Nalani two months earlier than already planned. He didn't think what they had going would have run its course by then, or at least he hoped it hadn't. "You had better have told them no."

"I told them I'd check with you, but we'll have to come up with a pretty solid reason for turning them down."

"Bullshit. Khloe will have to come up with a solid reason

why she can't make the originally scheduled dates. This is on her, not me."

"Maybe, but I get the sense no one wants to go up against Ryder Helms. He can be a real asshole where protecting Khloe is concerned."

"What the fuck does that matter?" This conversation was annoying Shane. "He's her bodyguard and boy-toy. She needs to keep him in line."

Even as he said it, he knew his assertion was bullshit. He'd seen Ryder and Khloe's dynamic in action. She may be the famous movie star, but there was no doubt in his mind, Ryder Helms called all the shots in that little family unit. Still, it wasn't his problem.

Shane pushed to his feet, reaching back into his pocket for his phone and texting his driver to pull the car around. He grabbed his beer, deciding to take it for the limo as he said goodbye to his agent.

"Try your best to keep them on the original schedule. I gotta run, but we'll talk later this week."

Not waiting for a reply, he turned and weaved along the patio, passing a pool full of semi-naked revelers, past a couple making out in a secluded cabana, and down a dark walkway he hoped was a shortcut to the front drive. He texted Nalani again while he waited for his driver.

I WANT you naked and in my bed when I get back to my room. XOXO

XOXO? What the hell? Since when did he sign his texts with hugs and kisses?

He knew the answer—since he met Nalani. A lot of things felt different with his Hawaiian beauty… and she *was* his.

The trip to his home-away-from-home took what felt like forever in the post-show traffic jam. Shane had the time to polish off the beer and move on to finish off the end of the bottle of champagne the limo driver had supplied. He had a nice buzz going by the time he stepped out in front of the Runway mansion. He took the tall steps two at a time, anxious to get upstairs.

He wasn't in the mood for the locked door.

"Fuck."

Shane patted down his pants, looking for his wallet that had his keycard. He was still looking for the card when the front door opened to reveal a burly security guard.

"We've been expecting you, Mr. Covington, although to be honest, I wasn't sure if you'd make it back here tonight or if you'd be out partying. Calling it quits a bit early?"

Shane wanted to tell the asshole to mind his own business, but since he knew all the security staff had to know he was seeing Nalani, he decided to prod the guy for information instead.

"Actually, I'm hoping Nalani is upstairs, waiting for me. Did she get here yet?" he asked hopefully.

"Nalani? No, I've been here since four, and I haven't seen her since Roger escorted her to her car after the Ainsworth debacle."

Shane had started to turn away when the guy had said Nalani wasn't there, but the mention of Henry Ainsworth caught his attention, and he turned back.

"What Ainsworth debacle?"

He didn't like the look on the guard's face one bit as the guy stumbled over his words. "You mean… didn't Nalani tell you?"

"Tell me what?" he snapped, impatient for answers.

"Well… I'm not at liberty to—"

"Fuck that," Shane cut him off, grabbing the guy's arm. "If it involves Nalani, you need to tell me." When the guy kept his mouth shut, Shane added a stern, "Now. Or do I have to call your boss?"

He fully expected the guy to spill the story to avoid getting his boss involved, so when the asshole reached for his own phone and added, "Actually, I think that's a good idea. Let's call him now," his anxiety spiked.

What the hell was going on here? This whole night was fucked-up. Why hadn't he insisted she just come with him? Then they'd be back at the party dancing, or maybe they'd be the ones making out near the pool. His cock stirred, just thinking about it.

The guard talking to someone in Spanish jarred him back to reality. Shane spoke a bit of Spanish, but he couldn't make out much of the conversation, so he was relieved when the guard turned and handed his own phone to Shane.

"Here, my boss wants to talk to you."

Shane held the phone up to his ear just as the guy on the other end asked, "Mr. Covington?"

"Yeah. What the hell's going on? What happened after I left today?" he asked with a growing sense of dread.

"Don't worry, we handled it."

"That's not what I asked. What. Happened?" Maybe the asshole would respond better to a demand.

"I'm not at liberty to say. You'll need to talk to Nalani about…"

"I'd fucking love to talk to Nalani about it, but since she's not here and not answering her phone, I guess I'll have to settle for your side of the story instead."

"It doesn't work that way. If she wants you to know, she'll have to tell you herself."

What the fuck?

"Fine, I'll be happy to have her tell me. I need her address. She's not answering my calls."

The asshole on the other end of the phone had the balls to laugh at him. "No fucking way. If she didn't give you her address herself, there's no way I'm giving it to you."

If he was honest with himself, he was happy to see Nalani's co-workers protecting her security, but he was the last person she needed protection from. Even as he thought it, he knew that was a lie. He'd pushed her out of her comfort zone in their time together. Had he pushed her too far? Was she avoiding him intentionally?

It had been a long time since Shane had felt as vulnerable as he did at that moment. Was it possible he'd lost her already?

The silent standoff continued until Shane gave in. "Fine. I'll wait and talk to her tomorrow. Thanks for nothing."

He ended the call and tossed the phone back to the guard, who almost didn't catch it. He knew he was being an asshole, but he didn't bother thanking the guy or even saying goodbye. Instead, Shane turned toward the impressive staircase and took the stairs two at a time, suddenly in a hurry to get to his room.

He'd texted her. Maybe the guard had missed Nalani's arrival. He let his hopes rise as he neared the door to his suite, sure he would open the door to find her naked and waiting for him.

A dark, empty room greeted him as soon as he swung open the door. He threw the light switch, only to be disappointed again she wasn't waiting in the dark to surprise him.

His level of disappointment annoyed him. How had he let himself fall this hard for a woman? A housekeeper, no less. He embraced his agitation with her, hoping it would help him squash the growing feelings he had for the Hawaiian beauty. As much fun as they'd had together, Shane wasn't ready to settle down or make a commitment and knew that was what a woman like Nalani deserved. She wasn't a Hollywood player or even a groupie.

Determined to ignore his insecurities, Shane went through his bedtime routine—stripping down to his boxer briefs, taking a whiz, and brushing his teeth to wipe the stale booze taste from his mouth.

It was only once he lay down in the huge king-sized bed—alone there for the first time in a week—the certainty something was really wrong gripped him hard and wouldn't let go. Shane forced aside emotional considerations and let his brain think through the night again logically.

There had been nothing in their last twenty-four hours together that hinted she was preparing to bolt. On the contrary, he was certain she'd only been a hair's breadth away that afternoon from changing her mind and going to the Oscars or at least the after parties with him. Even after he'd left, Nalani had been texting him throughout the day, right up until he'd let her know he had to run because his limo had arrived to pick him up at the studio where he'd been getting ready for his public appearance.

He knew it, deep down—what they had wasn't over yet.

That meant there had to be another reason why she wasn't taking his calls.

Maybe her phone was broken, or the battery had died.

Maybe she was out having fun with her friends... or an old lover.

Fuck. He pushed his jealousy aside, praying that wasn't the case.

His thoughts turned darker. What if she was in trouble? The memory of the guard's slip of the *Ainsworth debacle*. What the hell was that about? He thought back to the first moment he'd met Nalani in the hallway a few weeks before, remembering and hating the palpable fear he'd seen on her face as she'd fled the older movie executive.

It only took one minute of lying in bed and mulling things over before Shane knew with certainty he wouldn't be able to get any sleep until he'd talked with Nalani. Grabbing his phone from the nightstand, he hit her number again for the tenth time, once again getting her voicemail. The sweet sound of her voice, letting him know he could leave a message was enough to make him spring to his feet.

Shane stalked to the walk-in closet, throwing on the bright lights as he grabbed a pair of worn jeans from the hanger Nalani had no doubt hung them. Grabbing a black T-shirt from a drawer, he threw it on as he found a pair of casual slip-ons, jamming his feet in, not bothering to fix the part folded uncomfortably under his heel.

He stopped at the desk near the window to grab his wallet and room key before taking off at a near jog—out the door, down the hall, and through the dark mansion. It was odd being in the normally busy club on a Sunday night after closing.

Shane headed through the kitchen toward the back of the club to the door that led out to the expansive patio. Only after he'd pushed through the door did he realize he might be setting off alarms in the security office. Not wanting to take a chance of being stopped, he took off at a jog into the dark night. He was grateful the stone pathway at the bottom of the stairs was lit by dim landscape lighting and the half-moon overhead.

In the distance, he thought he heard a man shouting, but it only made him pick up his pace, weaving through the massive property—around patios, past small gardens with benches for guests to sit and enjoy, cutting through the fenced pool area where he could hear the waterfall feature that was the picturesque backdrop to the parties held there.

Shane was just starting to feel winded when he got close enough to Jaxson Davidson's house to realize how angry the club owner was about to get at being awakened after midnight.

For the briefest of moments, Shane slowed, reconsidering his ludicrous plan.

How long had it been since he'd been so crazy about a woman, he'd contemplated doing anything as remotely crazy?

The answer was never—not once.

The realization he'd fallen in love with Nalani Ione came to him with certainty that couldn't be denied. He welcomed the notion as the truth. It made it easier to push down his reticence and knock on the first door he came to, just past the three-car garage.

Motion sensor lights almost blinded him as they flooded the whole porch area as he alternated between pounding and pushing the doorbell over and over until he saw lights coming on inside the wall of windows facing the pool behind him.

Only after it started moving, he realized there was a camera lens pointed in his direction next to the door. He glowered into it, so Davidson would see it was him and not an intruder. He heard the locks disengaging just before Jaxson Davidson yanked the door open.

"What the ever-loving fuck are you doing pounding on my door at one in the morning, Covington?"

"I need Nalani's address."

"Seriously?" The sound of a baby screaming in the background was getting louder. "You've lost your goddamn mind."

"Maybe, but something's wrong. I know it."

The sound of a second baby crying could be heard down the hall behind where they were standing. The fact Shane didn't even feel guilty for waking them up confirmed he was doing the right thing, despite the fury on the homeowner's face.

"I ought to call the police on you. There has to be something in the law books preventing assholes from ringing doorbells in the middle of the night and waking up infants."

Shane wasn't in the mood for their normal verbal banter.

"What the hell happened with Ainsworth after I left today?" he pressed.

He didn't miss the flash of anger cross Davidson's face just before the club owner swung the door open and turned to walk away.

"Close the door behind you. I'll grab us some drinks."

While he was glad he wasn't being thrown out, Shane wasn't in the mood for chitchat. He just wanted her damn address. Was that so hard?

Jaxson met him in the open great room with a wall of windows that faced the pool and mansion beyond. He had to hand it to the model-turned-entrepreneur. He had a really great thing going here.

A can of soda came into his view before he heard Davidson open his and take a few swigs.

"You should take a seat."

Shane turned on him, practically throwing the still closed can back at his host.

"I'm not here for a social call. I just need her address, then you can go back to sleep."

Jaxson glanced in the direction of the cries coming from deeper in the house before adding, "Yeah, well, it isn't going to be that easy."

For the first time, Shane felt a sliver of guilt. "Sorry, I woke your kids up, but if your security guys had just given me her address, I wouldn't have had to bother you," he accused.

"No, but if they'd given you her address, I would have had to fire them tomorrow. Now, are you gonna shut-up, take a seat, and listen, or do I need to give them a call to escort you off the property?"

The fucker. He really was an asshole. But considering the asshole stood between him and answers, Shane stalked to the nearby couch and took a seat.

The sound of a crying baby got louder, and Jaxson turned his attention to a sleepy Emma in her robe, carrying two crying babies toward them.

"Sorry, baby. I see Chase is sleeping like a rock again. Let me take one of them."

Emma glanced at Shane before approaching her husband, leaning forward so he could take one of the wiggling babies from her.

"Is everything okay?" she asked quietly.

"Yeah, I'm sure it is. Covington is just worried about Nalani. I'm gonna set him straight, then send him on his way."

Shane bristled at the rebuff in Davidson's tone. "Like I said, I just need an address. Then I'll get out of your hair."

Emma rocked the baby in her arms as she answered, "I'm not happy you woke up the twins, but I'm glad you want to check on Nalani. She must be really freaked out."

The mother's words ratcheted up his anxiety. "I'd love it if someone would fucking tell me what happened this afternoon so I can know what it is I should be freaking out about."

He saw the confused glance she threw at her Dom and husband, realizing she might have said too much.

Davidson was having some luck at calming the crying baby in his arms as he rocked with the infant over his shoulder, patting his back gently. It was odd seeing the aggressive Dom looking so domestic.

"It's okay, baby. I'll fill him in. You and Alicia try to get back to sleep. I'll be back with Drew as soon as I can."

"Okay." Emma looked unsure as she turned to retreat. "Don't be too long."

Davidson didn't bother sitting as he launched into his lecture, pacing as he soothed his baby and gave an update. "Like my security team had better have already told you, we don't give out the personal information of our employees to anyone. If Nalani had wanted—"

"I know, I know," Shane cut off Davidson; he'd heard it

all before. "If she'd wanted me to have her address, she'd have given it to me. But I'm telling you, something's wrong. She hasn't answered in hours. She was supposed to meet me back at the mansion. She's not here. She's not even texting."

"So, maybe she's having second thoughts about her relationship with you," Davidson reasoned.

"Fuck that. You've talked to her about us. You know she's all in." Shane hesitated before adding, "Like I am."

"Really. You're all in? What does that even mean?" Jaxson pressed him.

"It's none of your fucking business what it means. That's between Nalani and me."

"And yet, she didn't give you her address, and you're sitting in my living room after midnight, trying to pry it out of me. Seems that makes it my business."

Asshole.

"Fine. I'm in love with her. Happy?" Surprisingly, saying the words out loud came easier than he'd expected. He'd managed to surprise Jaxson, who took a few long seconds to think about the implications of Shane's announcement.

"Actually, I'm not happy at all. I'm irritable. You woke up my family. I have half a mind to call the cops after all and let them deal with you."

"But you aren't going to do that. You like your privacy way too much. Anyway, I'll be out of your hair in one minute once I get answers."

"I'm not giving you her address."

"Fine. Then tell me what the guard was talking about when he mentioned the Ainsworth debacle."

His question surprised Davidson enough, he paused patting the tiny back, bringing renewed crying until he restarted the rhythmic taps.

For a moment, Shane thought he was going to leave empty

handed when Davidson started pacing, but after a moment, the club owner launched into a monologue.

"I'm not sure I should be telling you this either, but if it makes you leave, so be it. This afternoon, after you left for the Oscars, Nalani was assaulted by Henry Ainsworth."

Shane's heart lurched as he internalized the words. Davidson didn't pause, so he had to force himself to listen.

"He attacked her in the hall and tried to drag her back to his room. He threatened her, but she was able to fight back and escape him. She was smart. She ran to the Runway office and barricaded herself in before calling to report the assault to security." He stopped pacing and turned to pin Shane with an intense gaze as he continued. "My guys handled it perfectly. They detained the fucker and reviewed the security camera footage. Once they confirmed what had happened, they called the police. They hauled the asshole off in the back of a squad car in handcuffs."

"What the fuck?" Shane jumped up to his feet. "Why wasn't I called?"

"You weren't called by us because we didn't need your help. You'll have to ask Nalani why she didn't tell you yet, but I'm guessing it's because she didn't want to disturb you during the show."

"Well, the show ended hours ago. That excuse is out the window." Guilt he hadn't been there to protect her when she'd needed him flooded in. Remembering the terrified look on her face weeks before when Ainsworth had bothered her brought renewed guilt. He should have kicked the fucker's ass that day, but he'd let the jerk get away with his harassment, leaving Nalani and others at risk.

"Now more than ever, I need her address. She needs me."

"No. If she needed you, she'd have called."

"She isn't taking my calls." It hurt to admit it, but he didn't have a choice. "But..." Shane paused before adding, "But I'm sure if you called, she'd answer for her boss." When Jaxson looked like he was about to say no, Shane added, "Please. I just need to make sure she's okay. If she doesn't want me to come over, I'll respect her wishes."

Davidson looked conflicted. Shane was grateful when he said, "Stay here. I'll be right back."

True to his promise, Davidson came back a minute later, minus a baby and carrying his cell phone. Shane watched anxiously as Jaxson made the call, placing the phone against his ear. As each long second ticked by, he noticed the worry lines growing on Jaxson's forehead until he finally hung up.

"She's not answering. I thought her phone might be dead, but if that was the case, it would roll to voicemail right away." Jax paused, thinking for a second while pinning Shane with a pointed glare. "Goddamnit, let me get dressed."

CHAPTER 19

Shane resisted fist pumping with his small victory. He'd reserve that for when he knew he'd been overreacting. While Jaxson was getting ready, he started thinking about all the fun punishments he could dish out to his naughty submissive for worrying him—once he made sure she was safe.

Ten minutes later, the men were in Davidson's SUV, driving down Hollywood Boulevard back toward the theater where he'd been just hours before. Jaxson programed an address into his navigation system and then used his Bluetooth to make a call.

"Hello?" A groggy man's voice filled the interior of the car.

"Sorry to wake you up, man, but I need you to call your contacts at the police station. Make sure Ainsworth is still tucked away."

"Why? What's going on?"

"I'm sure it's nothing, but we're having trouble getting ahold of Nalani. Covington is being a royal pain in my ass. In fact, I'm in the car, headed over to her apartment now."

"Shit. I'm sorry to hear that, but I'm sure she's fine. I talked to her today, and yeah, she was a little shook up, but I had her escorted to her car. It's a Sunday. There's no way Ainsworth got a judge to arraign him fast enough that he's out of custody yet."

Shane barged into the conversation. "Are you kidding me? Henry Ainsworth is one of the most powerful men in town. He's a moneyman, and everyone knows money talks. You guys should have fucking called me!"

He was glad Jaxson ran a yellow light just as it turned red, before adding. "I'll be there in a few minutes. I'm sure there's a good explanation of what's going on, but I'd feel better if you'd check in with the police. Let's connect again after we each get a few more answers."

The call dropped just as Davidson pulled into a small parking lot next to a vape shop. The strip of small businesses were all closed at the late hour.

Shane took his lead from the driver, jumping out and following Davidson around to the front of the building as he checked his phone, presumably for the correct address information. After confirming the numbers on the otherwise blank door sandwiched between the vape store and an arcade, Jaxson put his phone in his jean's pocket.

Nalani's boss reached to ring the bell next to the door, but Shane was too impatient, taking a chance and turned the doorknob. He had mixed emotions when the door easily opened without a key.

Shane wished he'd gone in first because he would have been taking the stairs two at a time if he were in the lead. As it was, he had to go up the narrow staircase and down the dingy hallway at the pace Davidson set. Shane pushed in front when they got to a door with the number two painted on it. He couldn't wait a second longer, pounding on the door, calling her name.

"Nalani! Open up, baby! It's just me."

He held his ear to the wood, unsure what it meant that he

could hear her TV playing on the other side. Was she really just sitting there, ignoring him?

Shane pounded louder, getting angrier as the seconds passed.

"Goddamn it, open the door. I can't believe you're making me beg out here like this."

He jiggled the doorknob, at first angry it was locked, then grateful she was safe inside. The sound of a ringing cell phone went off behind the door, mingling with the din of the TV. Shane glanced at Jaxson, who had his phone to his ear again.

Anxiety exploded in his chest. Her phone was there—ringing—but she still wasn't answering, even knowing her boss was at her door.

Something was really wrong.

Shane moved away from the door, preparing to kick it in when he heard another man's voice in the hall. He swung around, ready to beat someone to a bloody pulp, only the guy was in his robe, a baseball bat held as if he were preparing to bash in Shane's head.

"What the hell are you guys doing at Nalani's place?"

"Who are you, and what are you doing here?" Jaxson beat him to it.

"I own the building and live in the other apartment. Hey, are you guys really Jaxson Davidson and Shane Covington?"

Jaxson went into celebrity mode. "Yep. And I'm Nalani's boss. She had a bit of an accident at work today, so we're doing a wellness check on her. You wouldn't have a key to her apartment, would you?"

"I told you, I own the building. Of course, I have a key. I'm her landlord."

"Great. Then you can open the door for us. She isn't answering," Shane pressed.

Anger flashed over the younger man's face. "Yeah, maybe she's sleeping."

The jerk's words and body language didn't match.

"And why would her sleeping get you so pissed off?"

The out-of-shape guy with the receding hairline hedged a bit before answering.

"I invited her to come over and watch the Oscars on my new TV, but she turned me down because she was too tired. She said she was gonna record it to watch later. Then when I came upstairs, she had the volume high enough, I could hear her watching it alone on that dinky little TV she has, instead of sleeping."

Shane wanted to fist pump that Nalani hadn't taken the asshole up on his offer. Not only was she light-years out of this guy's league, but the thought of someone else spending time with her, let alone touching her, enraged him.

Shane snapped out of his train of thoughts, more anxious than ever to hold Nalani in his arms.

"So… go grab the key, or would you rather I kick in the door?"

"Why the hell would you do that?" he asked suspiciously. "Why are you here, anyway? At this hour?"

Why was he here? That was a million-dollar question.

He glanced at Jaxson, who seemed to be waiting to hear his answer as well.

Shane cleared his throat, hesitating only briefly before an urgent feeling in his gut helped him blurt out the truth.

"I'm Nalani's boyfriend."

That was wrong. Too juvenile.

"Her lover," he tacked on.

That didn't feel right, either.

"I love her, okay? And I'm worried about her. I don't know how I know, but something is really wrong."

He watched the emotions on the landlord's face change from surprise to defeat as the asshole realized he was no competition for Nalani's affection against the superstar.

"I'll get the key." He spun and ambled slowly toward his own apartment at the other end of the hall.

Shane wanted to scream with impatience when seconds turned too long minutes. Anxious, he pounded on the door again before holding his ear against the wood to listen for movement.

Was that...

"Maybe she's in the shower. It sounds like water running," Shane said.

"Fuck!" Jaxson's alarmed expletive amped up Shane's anxiety.

Shane glanced back to see Jaxson looking at the floor. The second Shane saw the water starting to seep out from under the door, his heart cramped with fear.

Without a word of coordination, the men both stepped back from the door and lifted their legs in unison, kicking in the old wood easily. A gush of water rushed into the hall, drenching their shoes as Shane rushed inside the small apartment, frantically looking for Nalani—both relieved and terrified she wasn't there. Where was she?

He quickly accessed the space, taking in the toppled chair and the layer of water spreading everywhere like a virus, his brain fighting to process the information. It didn't make sense.

"Be careful if you touch anything electrical. I don't want us to get electrocuted."

At least Davidson was still thinking clearly. Shane's fear threatened to paralyze him, but he forced himself to snap out of it, moving in the direction of the small hallway that had to lead to the bedroom and the bathroom, he could tell was the source of the water. Was it a broken pipe?

He heard the landlord in the distance, yelling at the men for kicking in the door at the moment his shoe connected with the locked bathroom door, breaking it down as easily as he had the first.

The sight of Nalani's naked and beaten body, lying in a crumpled pile on the floor would be forever etched in his nightmares. In one second of terrifying clarity, Shane knew his life had just changed forever. A fear he'd never experienced gripped him hard and wouldn't let go.

She looked so still. What if she was dead?

Thankfully, while Shane was paralyzed, Davidson took charge, barking orders at the other man in the apartment.

"Landlord guy… call 911! Get the police and ambulance on the way!"

Shane finally urged his body into motion, rushing to Nalani's side while Davidson went to the bathtub to turn off the running water.

Dropping to his knees with a splash, he frantically took stock of the visible injuries peppered across his love's beautiful body. With each bruise, every open wound oozing blood, his fear faded—replaced with burning fury.

Henry Ainsworth is a dead man.

Whether the powerful mogul did this to his beloved himself or hired someone else to do his dirty work, Shane knew without a shadow of a doubt, Ainsworth was responsible for the violence against the woman he loved.

Shane reached out to roll her on her back but hesitated. He was afraid to touch her for fear he'd find she was dead. Davidson shouting snapped him out of it.

"Roll her over. We might need to do CPR. Does she have a pulse?"

Jaxson's question told Shane his worry she was dead wasn't out of the realm of possibility. Shane had a hard time finding a place to touch her that didn't have injuries. Her damp skin was clammy and chilled. Reflexively, once he had her rolled to her back, he reached for her wrist, sighing with relief when he felt her pulse.

On some level, he knew he could be doing more damage if she

had spinal injuries, but an irresistible urge to hold her tight hit him. He was desperate to warm her up, comfort her—protect her.

I'm too fucking late for that. She needed me, and I wasn't here.

He pushed the wave of crushing guilt aside—he could wallow in that later—he needed to focus on helping her right now.

Shane scooped Nalani's wet and broken body into his arms, pushing to his feet and retracing his steps back to the small living room. He headed for the couch, one of the few dry places in the place, grabbing the old-fashioned crocheted afghan he passed on his way there.

He was conflicted by the tortured groan of pain coming from the woman in his arms as he cradled her—relief she was alive clashed with loathing seeing her in pain. Like a coward, he avoided letting his gaze sweep over her body—afraid of what he'd find—focusing only on her bruised and battered face.

The sight of the horrific bruises forming was made worse by realizing her left eye was completely swollen shut from the beating she'd taken to her face. The same face he adored watching as he'd brought her body pleasure and pain.

Would he ever be able to look at her again without remembering how epically he'd let her down? He'd just found her. She was his submissive—his love. He was supposed to protect her.

He'd failed.

"The police are on their way. I'll go downstairs to direct them to the right place," the landlord said, seeming anxious to escape the heavy tension building in the room.

Shane brushed the wet hair off Nalani's forehead, uncovering a new bruise. A drop of blood seeped from the corner of her mouth, leaving a streak of red as it trekked down her chin to drip on her chest. It landed on one of dozens of red welt lines crisscrossing her body. Rage blurred his vision as he realized the asshole had whipped her body until he'd drawn blood.

He swallowed hard to keep from throwing up. As the reality of the horrors Nalani had been forced to endure closed on him, Shane felt his own grasp of reality slipping, replaced with a fury he'd never felt before—the kind of anger so deep, it would leave scorch marks on his soul that would never heal.

"I'm going to kill the bastard," he gritted out to no one in particular.

"Not if I get to him first," Davidson promised from across the room where he was taking photos of the crime scene with his cell phone.

Impotent—he'd been rendered helpless, a complete failure protecting his woman.

Shane jumped to his feet, unable to sit still a second longer. Despite Nalani's renewed groans of pain, he took long strides toward the still open door of the apartment, splashing water as he went.

"Where are you going? You shouldn't move her any more than necessary. She could have spinal injuries you're making worse."

His brain knew Davidson was right, but his brain wasn't making decisions at that moment. He stopped in his tracks long enough to turn and pin Jaxson with a determined glare.

"Fuck that. I'm not sitting here, waiting for the Calvary to arrive. She needs medical help now. Are you going to drive us, or do I need to wave down a passing car?"

Indecision turned to action in seconds.

"Fine, I'm not sure this is a good idea, but I don't want to wait to deal with police and fire bullshit any more than you do. Let's go."

Shane hated the cries of pain from the woman in his arms as he rushed down the steps and past the man in a bathrobe, still holding a baseball bat.

Jaxson stopped to bark orders to the landlord. "Tell the

police to treat this as a crime scene. They are looking for Henry Ainsworth. He's responsible for the attack on Nalani."

"How do you know?"

"I just fucking know. He'll have the money and lawyers to contest anything they find, so they need to be extra careful. You got that?"

Shane was rounding the corner and almost to Davidson's SUV when he heard the guy shout, "Alright! I'll tell them!"

"I'm not convinced this is the right move," Jaxson warned as he reached to open the back door. "We're removing evidence by taking her out of the apartment."

Shane took a seat and countered. "We don't need evidence. We know the asshole who's responsible."

"But..."

"Fuck that. I'm not sitting around waiting for the police. It's too late for that. She needs medical attention, and we can get that for her faster than waiting for an ambulance."

"Shit. Fine." Davidson slammed the door closed and ran around to get behind the wheel.

Even in the dim lighting of the interior of the SUV, Shane could see the swelling was getting worse on Nalani's beautiful face, making her almost unrecognizable.

Davidson's phone rang.

"They released the fucker, didn't they?"

"How'd you know?" The voice at the other end of the line filled the car.

"We're on the way to Cedar Sinai. The bastard beat her within an inch of her life. I need you at her apartment... now! Keep a boot up the ass of the investigators. By some miracle, if I stop Covington from killing Ainsworth, I want to make sure we have the evidence to put him behind bars for the rest of his miserable life."

"Shit, you got it, boss." The call dropped.

Despite Jaxson gunning the engine to run a light, he heard her first whisper.

"Shane?"

"I'm here now, baby. No one's ever gonna hurt you again," he vowed. He knew Henry Ainsworth wouldn't hurt her again because dead men couldn't torture victims after they were torn from limb to limb.

"I'm sorry." He could barely hear her over the ringing of a phone call Davidson was making over the Bluetooth speaker.

"What the hell could you possibly have to apologize for, kitten?"

"Ruined Oscars night."

Christ, she was selfless. Even with all she'd been through, she was still thinking of him, instead of herself. He didn't deserve her.

"Nothing that's happened today is your fault, Nalani."

She cried out in pain in response. Despite being wrapped in the blanket and in his arms, she was shivering so hard, it bordered on convulsions.

"Hang on, baby. We're almost to the hospital. They'll be able to help with the pain."

The sound of another man cursing filled the interior of the car.

"What the fuck are you doing calling my cell at this hour, Davidson?"

"Get your fat ass out of bed and get to the Cedar-Sinai emergency room… ASAP!"

"Why would I do that? You get a sliver?"

Shane didn't know who Davidson had called but knew with certainty, it wasn't one of his own employees; they'd never speak to their boss like that.

"Shut the fuck up and listen. Henry Ainsworth assaulted one of my employees this afternoon, and instead of you holding him in a fucking cell where he belongs, some idiot on your department let the asshole go. They didn't even call to warn me."

Jaxson had to stop his rant long enough to take evasive action to avoid hitting a van as he ran a red light. Once through the intersection, Davidson continued his rant.

"The fucker broke into that same employee's apartment and tortured, beat, and raped her within an inch of her life. We're en route to the hospital with her now. You're gonna meet me there, right after you call and wake up your best detectives and the head of your crime scene investigation team and get them over to her apartment immediately to collect the evidence we need to put the prick away for the rest of his life."

"Is that all? Anything else? Want me to get someone to shine your shoes while I'm at it?"

Shane had no idea who the asshole on the phone was, but he was lucky he wasn't there in person because Shane would love to use the fuckers face as a punching bag. Apparently, Jaxson felt the same.

"Listen up, Johnson. I'm doing you a favor, giving you a call to give you a chance to get ahead of this. This story is going to be on the front cover of every newspaper in less than twelve hours. It's going to be the lead off story on GMA in a few hours and will be trending on Twitter in less than that. You guys fucked-up once by letting Ainsworth out of custody. I'll be more than happy to throw you under the bus, right along with him."

"Damn, you have a serious ego problem, you know that Davidson? I agree Ainsworth is an asshole, but why exactly is it you think anyone is going to believe one of your employees over someone with his reach?"

"You're a real fucker, Johnson. So happy to know the Chief of Police cares so much about the innocent women in his district."

"Screw you. We both know Ainsworth is gonna buy his way out of this."

"Not this time."

"I read the report from earlier. She's a housekeeper. The press isn't going to pay any attention. That's not my decision. That's just how this works, and you know it."

Shane couldn't hold his tongue any longer.

"Sorry to have bothered you, asshole. Jaxson, hang up the phone. We don't need the police, anyway."

"Who's that there with you?" the voice over the speaker asked.

"Hang up," Shane shouted, angry Davidson had called the police in the first place. "The police can't help. We're past that now."

"What does that mean? Whoever you are, be warned, you'd better not try to take matters into your own hands."

The men's gaze connected in the rear-view mirror as they passed under a streetlamp. Shane saw the same raw fury glowing in Davidson's eyes, he was sure was in his return look.

"Chief, I did you a favor, calling you to give you a chance to get ahead of this. If you're smart, you'll get to Cedar-Sinai as soon as possible and get your best people on this at the crime scene."

The call ended just as Davidson whipped the car around the corner and pulled up to the main entrance to the Emergency Room of the Trauma Center. For a minute, it seemed as if he planned on driving the car into the building before he finally brought the vehicle to a stop, directly in front of the entrance.

Shane had to jostle Nalani to open the door. Her cry of pain as he pushed to his feet gave him pause, hating that he was bringing her more agony.

Davidson ran around the still-running SUV and shouted, "I'll go in and alert them" as he took off at a sprint toward the brightly lit entrance. Shane followed behind, hugging the broken, shaking, and naked body of Nalani close, grateful he'd wrapped her in the afghan.

He rushed into the brightly lit corridor, glancing around frantically for help—a doctor, nurse, anyone. As he got to the first doorway, all he found was a room full of injured people, waiting to be seen by the overnight emergency staff.

Nalani would not be waiting even a minute. Shane was determined she was about to go to the front of the line, even if he had to make a scene or bribe the staff.

Shane backed out of the room and headed deeper down the hall where he could hear Davidson shouting for help. He blew by a door marked *Emergency Registration* and heard a woman yelling at him to stop, but he barged ahead, determined to get Nalani seen as quickly as possible.

"Sir! Sir! You can't go down there without registering. There's a line!"

Her yelling only made him go faster, rushing around the corner at the nurses' station, almost bumping into Davidson's back. Six medical professionals dressed in scrubs all stood frozen, staring at him, their mouths open.

"What the hell is wrong with you people? Don't just stand there, we need your help!"

The out of breath administration clerk finally caught up to him. "Sir, you'll need to follow me back..." Her lecture died away as she joined the others in standing planted to their spots. "You're Shane Covington."

"Yes, and I need everyone's help. Now."

"But..."

"I promise you, I'll fill out all the paperwork you need me to, but we have an emergency."

Finally, one of the older women in the group seemed to snap out of her trance. Rushing to Shane's side, she pulled back the afghan to take a peek at Nalani's battered face.

"What happened? Car accident?"

She turned on a small spotlight and lifted Nalani's swollen eyelids to check for dilation. Shane struggled to form the words to describe the horrors Nalani had been through. He was grateful Davidson was holding it together better than he was.

"This woman was brutally attacked, beaten, and I'm almost certain, raped by Henry Ainsworth. We found her left for dead in her apartment. As it was only a few minutes away, we drove her straight here. I've already called the Chief of Police, and he's on his way. We need to treat her, of course, but we also need to gather evidence so we can press charges."

"Fuck that. I told you, the police won't be handling this case."

"Shut up, Covington. You're too emotional right now to be thinking straight."

"The important thing is to get the victim the medical help she needs," the doctor interrupted. She turned to a nurse and started barking orders. "Joanne, page the on-duty trauma team. Susan, escort Mr. Covington and Mr. Davidson back to the last exam room where we'll have more privacy. I'll be right behind you."

By the time he laid Nalani down on the waiting gurney, she was convulsing. He tried to cover her body, thinking she was cold, but two nurses pushed him away.

"Stand back. Let us do our job."

He hated to let go of her but did as he was told, stepping back against the far wall as emergency personnel started running in. By the time the doctor arrived, the exam room was getting crowded.

Jaxson leaned closer to let him. "I'm gonna go out and move my car and check in with the head of my security team again."

"I told you..."

"Shut up. I'm furious too. I want Ainsworth behind bars just like you do, but we need to do this by the book."

"Fuck the book and bars. I want him dead." It took all of his self-control to keep from pounding his fist through the wall.

"And I don't? Nalani is part of the Runway family. This started on my property. She's my responsibility."

"The hell she is. I should have forced her to go to the Oscars with me. None of this would have happened if I'd just made her go."

"You don't know that. He would have just waited to get her alone tomorrow or the next day."

Guilt poured over Shane as he admitted, "The first day I met her, I knew the asshole had scared her. I shouldn't have let him near her."

"You can't blame yourself. Thank God, you were a pain in the ass and woke me up. If you hadn't, she'd still be laying there, alone and in pain."

Memories of seeing her crumpled body and not even knowing if she were still alive flooded in, and he had to swallow hard to keep control of his emotions.

"Fine. Go call your security guy, but I'm not leaving her. Not again."

"You'd better not. She'll want you near as soon as she wakes up."

Shane wasn't so sure about that.

CHAPTER 20

Too bright.

Piper despised waking up to sunlight. Her right arm felt like a heavy weight as she lifted it to try to adjust her sleep mask, connecting with her naked face instead.

Her brain was slow to reboot. The low-level throbbing at her temple was her first clue she'd drunk too much the night before… something she'd been doing much too frequently of late.

She squeezed her eyes tight, the only defense against the sunshine. A low groan escaped as she flopped to her back, reaching out to her right for a pillow she could pull over her face, hitting something hard instead.

A deep chuckle coincided with the realization there was a heavy arm wrapped across her waist.

Her brain's reboot wasn't happening fast enough. A panicked disorientation gripped her as flashes of memories from the night before started to come back to her in fits and starts. Each one confused her more, and the glaring sunlight shining right in her eyes wasn't helping.

Reflexively, Piper tried to roll away from the heat source in bed with her, reaching out to find the clicker on her bed stand that would close the sun-blocker curtains across the wall of windows in her bedroom. Instead of a clicker, her hand knocked over what sounded like a glass. She could hear what she hoped was water spilling across the stand and splashing down to the floor.

"Fuck," she groaned, regretting it instantly as her head throbbed.

The arm across her waist tightened, pulling her back tightly against what felt like a solid wall of muscle. She only had a split second to enjoy the embrace before her world crashed in.

"I'd love to." Nolan's deep voice was still husky with sleep as he thrust his hips against her, wedging his morning hard-on against her ass. "As you can see, The Rock likes that idea."

Nolan was in her bed. Holy. Fucking. Shit. What had she done?

First things first. Still keeping her eyes slammed closed, she resumed reaching to the nightstand for the clicker.

"What are you looking for, baby?"

"I'm not your baby. And the clicker. I need to close the blackout drapes."

"I don't have any blackout drapes, but if you promise to wake up here tomorrow morning, I'll have some installed today."

Double fuck.

She had to risk it. Piper opened her eyes just enough to confirm her fear.

She was at Nolan Boeing's house. In his bedroom… his *bed.*

"Jesus Christ," she whispered with exasperation as she snapped her eyes closed again. This time, it was more to try to block out reality than sunlight.

"Nope, just Nolan. I see you're still a morning person."

Asshole. He was way too chipper. What the hell had

happened between them last night? She scrambled to latch on to any memory that would help fill in the blanks.

They'd been at the Oscars. Attended an after party. Multiple after-parties. She'd drunk champagne. Lots of champagne. They'd danced. Shit. They'd kissed. Things were fuzzier after that.

She had to know.

"Please. Tell me we didn't... you know..."

"Sorry to be the bearer of bad news, but we sure did." He paused just long enough for her to realize she actually regretted not having memories of Nolan fucking her when he added. "We danced up a storm."

"Danced," she deadpanned.

"Yep. And..." he paused dramatically before adding, "We even kissed."

"Kissed."

"And for the grand finale, you puked all over the back of your limo."

"Puked?" Piper cringed at that tidbit.

Nolan's chuckle rumbled against her back. "Are you always reduced to single word sentences in the mornings?"

"Only when the sunlight burns my eyelids before I can get up."

"Noted. Will call the drapery installation place right after breakfast."

"Don't bother. This was a mistake."

"You've been making a lot of those lately," he countered, much too quickly.

It was way too early, and she was way too hungover to keep up with Nolan banter. She tried to wiggle out of his embrace, determined to find her cloths, and get the hell out of there. She needed to retreat—she was in no condition to go head-to-head with him under these conditions.

Piper was pleasantly surprised when he loosened his grip on

her waist, allowing her to roll out of the mammoth king-sized bed. A wave of cold air made sure she knew she was buck naked. Squinting in the bright sunlight bathing the room, Piper spun to face-off with the too-handsome man smiling back at her from the bed.

"Where the hell are my clothes?"

"In the shopping bag over on the desk."

"You shoved my designer gown and shoes in a bag?"

"Yep, but to be fair, I only did that after you puked on them. I hope you have a good dry cleaner. If not, let me know, and I'll send them out to the service I use. They were even able to get the blood stains out of the shirt I wore to Black Light the night of roulette."

Piper's brain exploded with memories of the strange night he'd spent a hundred thousand bucks just to spend three hours as her submissive.

"I didn't make you bleed," she defended.

"Oh, maybe not physically, but you sure as hell cut me deep that night." Nolan's smile dipped briefly before he grinned. "But you made up for it last night."

Shit. Shit. Shit.

"What does that mean? What did you do?"

"Don't you mean, what did *you* do?"

"Whatever. What happened? Did we…?"

His smile dimmed as he pinned her with a way-too-serious glare.

"Whatever the hell you think of me, Piper, I sure as hell hope you know I'm not the kind of man who would take advantage of you while you were incapacitated."

A wave of relief mingled with a strange sense she recognized as a foreign feeling of… what? The closest word she could come up with was safety, but that still felt wrong.

She needed caffeine. She needed to stay focused.

"So, where's my bra? And don't tell me I puked on that too."

"I admit I was intrigued when I got the gown off and found those sticky pasties on your tits. They were really stuck on. What did you use, super glue? I hope you don't mind, but I had to use a warm compress to get some of the adhesive off."

Piper felt the heat rising in her face as she realized Nolan had undressed her to find her red-carpet secret weapon for keeping her cleavage looking as pert as her younger peers. Her hands flew to cup her breasts reflexively.

"You can try to hide them now, but I'll forever be grateful I have the sight of those glorious tits of yours forced into submission."

She didn't miss his veiled use of the BDSM analogy. She didn't bite.

"Fine. Are you going to tell me I puked on my panties too?"

Shit. A grin lit up his face. She hated that his smile had the power to make her breath hitch.

"Oh no, you didn't puke on those, but they were so damn wet, I thought you'd be more comfortable if I took them off."

Piper swore she could feel the blush on her cheeks spreading across her entire body as she realized he'd seen the evidence of her arousal from the game of cat and mouse they'd played the night before.

"Asshole," she gritted out.

"Oh, no. You'll be glad to know, I didn't even touch your asshole… at least, not yet."

Unable to come up with a witty response, she growled as she spun around, beelining it for the bathroom.

"I see you remember where the bathroom is," Nolan's voice called out from behind her. "Just let me know if you need any help in there."

For some reason, his taunt annoyed her. She was aware he was reminding her that she'd been there once before. That had been a lifetime ago. Too much had changed since then. She knew what Nolan Boeing didn't—she could never go back to that innocent, naive version of herself.

Piper looked around the bathroom vanity, opening a few drawers to find Nolan's personal bathroom items. She felt like she an intruder rummaging through his deodorant… his beard trimmer… a tube of Ben-gay?

She jumped as he spoke from right behind her.

"If you tell me what you're looking for, I could help you find it."

Their eyes met in the mammoth mirror in front of them. They were barefoot, and he stood an entire head above her, something not many men did. She wasn't a short woman.

"I need to brush my teeth. My mouth tastes like…" She paused, trying to come up with an accurate description. "Like I ate a minty road-kill animal.`"

Nolan laughed out loud as he moved closer to open the cabinet beneath the sink.

"I was with you all night and would have stopped you from eating road-kill. I'm pretty sure the taste is actually the residue of puke mixed with a few Tic-Tacs." Standing, he held out a brand-new toothbrush, still in its package.

Just as she reached to take the toothbrush, Piper realized she now had a front-row seat to Nolan's impressive display of morning hard-on—his perfectly engorged cock jutting from his body like a flagpole waiting for its flag.

Stop looking at it, you idiot.

Her internal chastise came too late. The grin above his chiseled chin, covered in the ideal amount of scruffy beard, told her he was enjoying her checking his body out.

Piper tried to change the subject. "Tic-Tacs?"

"It was all I had with me to help after… well, you know… after you blew chow…" When she failed to respond, he tacked on, "Yakked… vomited… hurled… spewed… puked…"

"Jesus, what are you? A walking thesaurus?"

"When I need to be. It's just one of my many talents."

She snapped the toothbrush out of his hand, spinning back toward the mirror to look around for toothpaste in order to avoid making eye contact.

Without missing a beat, Nolan reached around her to open a drawer, pulling out a half-used tube of toothpaste and holding it out to her, and she snatched the tube. His naked chest brushed her back lightly, sending jolts of electricity through her that pissed her off.

Nolan pinned her with a heated gaze, staring back at her through their reflection.

"I'll clean out a few drawers for you while you take your shower. That way, you'll have room to leave some of your things."

"Why the hell would you do that? Unless you'd like me to leave my smelly gown behind as a token of my feelings for you. Vomit pretty much captures it."

Why wasn't he getting angry? She wanted to make him mad. Better that than his current domineering glare that only made her knees feel wobbly beneath her.

"I'll pass, but I do think I'll keep those panties of yours. I prefer the body fluids on that tiny patch of fabric to your gown."

"Pervert."

"Guilty as charged."

Her hands betrayed her, visibly trembling as she tried to load the brush with paste, spilling a dollop on the otherwise pristine counter.

Already off balance, Piper almost tipped over when Nolan quickly spun her around to face him, the loaded toothbrush falling into the sink as he yanked her into his arms. She could feel his erection sandwiched between them.

"Come on, baby. I think you owe me a chance here."

"I don't owe you anything," she defended, wiggling rather lamely to get free. He only tightened his grip on her.

"I've spent a lot of money to just spend time with you, Piper, and gone to bed with blue balls twice now."

"Sounds like a personal problem."

"Oh, I'll say. Everything about you and me is *personal*."

Despite their proximity, she'd avoided making eye contact until she finally gave in.

"And a *problem*."

"It doesn't have to be. I can make it good."

"Seems you have a pretty high opinion of yourself, sir. Do you really think you can buy me?"

"Fuck no. More importantly, you don't need my money, and I sure as hell don't want yours."

"What do you want, then?" The question was out before she realized how dangerous it was.

"Do you have to ask? I want you, Piper. No, what I really want is *us*. Together. I'm better with you."

"Of course, you are. Everyone is," she said with as much bravado as she could muster. Where was Mistress Ice when she needed her the most?

"Stop. I'm not one of your little boy-toys that will work on. I'm all man and old enough to know exactly what I want."

"You're old enough, alright." Her joke fell flat, her normal verbal defensiveness failing her.

"This goes both ways, Piper. You're a grown woman, not the same naive version of yourself from five years ago." His accurate description of her own thoughts from just minutes before unnerved her. "Isn't it time you go after what you really want?"

"And you think that's you?" She tried to laugh, but it came out as a manic squeak.

"I do, and I know that scares the shit out of you, but it shouldn't."

Piper wiggled to get away from his penetrating glare. To his credit, Nolan released her, but only until she'd turned back toward the sink. Their eyes met in the mirror as he hugged her from behind.

They stood in silence, each scrambling for the perfect witty comeback, only there wasn't one. He'd hit the nail on the head, and they both knew it.

She was petrified of the feelings Nolan Boeing drudged up.

His heated glare was too much. She had to close her eyes. She wasn't sure how long they stood there together—naked. Remarkably, Nolan remained silent, letting her hide in plain sight as she kept her eyes slammed closed, trying to shut out reality. If she were honest with herself, for even one moment, she loved the cocoon of warmth he seemed to wrap her in while he held her against his body. It was that realization that scared her the most.

When she opened her eyes, she found him studying her face… waiting patiently.

"I can't do this," was all she could muster.

"Piper, you can do anything you put your mind to, baby."

Her brain told her to berate him for his continued use of the term of endearment she thought she hated. Somehow, when Nolan Boeing used it, she had to admit she didn't mind it. What did that mean?

With each second that passed of their intense stare-down, her heart picked up its pace until she started to feel lightheaded. Sensing her weakness, Nolan tightened his grip on her.

"I've got you. I won't let you fall."

She understood he wasn't talking about just this minute. Nolan was offering to catch her any time she needed him. Her brain rejected the offer. She was a powerful, independent woman. She didn't need catching.

Only she'd clearly forgotten to copy her heart on the 'independence memo' as it beat wildly in her chest, only too happy to let someone take care of her for once.

God, she was tired. Exhaustion that had nothing to do with

her lack of sleep or caffeine invaded and refused to let go. She felt like she'd been running a marathon for as long as she could remember, and Nolan Boeing was offering to carry her—give her a rest.

But losing her independence and privacy was too big of a price to pay, wasn't it? As convincing as The Rock was, sandwiched against her ass, she knew she needed to leave before….

The ground beneath her started to shift as Nolan let his dominance loose. She'd known this man for years. She'd even seen the heated look staring back at her from the mirror a few times in some of her favorite dreams. They were the dreams she loved while they happened but always felt guilty about in the light of day.

Piper looked away, fumbling to pick up the toothbrush again to avoid the sexual haze filling the room. Nolan swatted the brush out of her hand just before he delivered what felt like the ultimate test.

"Before you brush your teeth, I'd like to get that smart mouth of yours a little dirtier. On your knees, Piper."

It was a command, plain and simple. She was at a precipice, but she just wasn't sure if what he was offering was going to push her over the cliff to her death, or if it was an offer to pull her back to safety.

The fact she didn't yell at him or push away spoke volumes to each of them. To his credit, Nolan didn't gloat. He merely kept that yummy dominant glare on his face while he gave her as much time as she needed.

How long had it been since she'd knelt in front of a man, instead of the other way around? She didn't like where her memories took her, so she changed her internal question. How long had it been since she'd been on her knees and *liked it*?

That one was easier. The irony that it had been in this very house—in front of this very man, five years before—wasn't lost on her.

It wasn't really a decision. Her brain had checked out and left her heart and other needy body parts to fend for themselves.

It was as if he were inside her head, reading her thoughts. The second she decided to throw caution to the wind, Nolan's hands left her arms, his right squeezing her boob while his left jammed into her messy hair, taking hold and yanking her head back hard against his shoulder. In a split-second, his mouth was in the nook of her bare neck, nipping and sucking at her like a man who'd been starved, and she was his feast.

Piper closed her eyes as she surrendered to the tidal wave of emotions she'd been so carefully holding at bay, letting them wash over her. Fear clashed with excitement. Dominance warred with submission. Sexual desire fought through the haze of bad memories, demanding its time.

But it was the intimacy she felt for the man pushing her to her knees she feared the most. It had taken years to hone her Mistress Ice facade. It was the mask that protected her from anyone getting close enough to hurt her again. Nolan Boeing had just torn down the wall between them, contaminating her with emotions she knew would be hell to shake when whatever this game they were playing ended.

He pounced, not giving her a chance to retreat. Thrusting his fingers into her messy hair, using her dark locks as handles, he yanked her face forward against him. Instinctively, Piper snapped her mouth closed, turning her head, so her left ear was jammed against his hard cock.

Her heart thundered in her chest as he growled, "Open wide, Piper."

Three simple words, yet there was nothing simple about obeying. She was so used to giving orders… not taking them.

"Piper… look at me, baby."

His words came out more a plea than a command. She let

him manipulate her head until she was looking up into his handsome, flushed face.

"I hope you know you're safe with me, baby. Always. I'm probably gonna push you hard, but all you need to do is say stop, and I'll stop. Every. Single. Time."

His words were like much-needed medicine, healing wounds she'd thought were long gone. She hadn't even known she needed him to say them, but once she heard his assurances, she knew how very important the words were. Even more importantly, she believed him.

Nolan Boeing was a good man.

Domineering. Exasperating. Smart-mouthed. Honorable. *Good.*

And sexy as hell.

Her mouth popped open without her brain telling it to. Her body wanted what he was offering.

Just this once.

Piper lunged forward, taking the tip of The Rock between her lips. She'd forgotten how vulnerable it felt to be on her knees, working to bring pleasure to someone else. Mistress Ice hadn't been concerned with such trivial things. Some tiny part of her brain tried to think about what a selfish bitch that meant she'd become, but Nolan surging forward far enough to fill her mouth with his cock chased all thoughts of anything but pleasure away.

She'd never heard of a blowjob being compared to riding a bike, but it seemed the art of giving head was quickly coming back to her. Her tongue lathed the underside of his shaft while she took him deep enough, when she sucked hard, he had to reach for the counter next to them to help steady himself on his feet.

"Damn, that feels so damn good. Spread your knees as far apart as you can get them."

The man was insane. What good would that do? She was on her knees. He was on his feet. What was…

"Good girl. Now put your hand between your legs and play with your pussy. Get it nice and wet for me."

Oh.

He didn't have to tell her twice. She'd known she was turned on, but the second her fingers slid through her slick folds, she knew she was ready for his cock. The thought of him inside her pussy helped her enthusiastically take him deeper down her throat. The gagging rhythm of him face-fucking her bounced off the walls of the upscale bathroom, mingling with the slushing sounds of her fingers strumming her clit until she was on the edge, ready to fall into her orgasm.

Nolan's "Stop!" coincided with him pulling out of her mouth, allowing her to gasp for a deep breath before he pulled her up to her feet with one fluid movement, spinning her around to face the wall of mirrors.

She had trouble recognizing the woman in the mirror—the wild, messy hair, the red face, flushed from the heat and exertion, the vulnerable tremble as she reached back to touch him, unwilling to lose her physical connection to Nolan.

His hand was on her back between her shoulder blades, pressing her forward until her forehead bumped the mirror. Nolan grabbed her hips, manhandling her body until he had her laid out the way he wanted.

Piper waited to feel the panic from losing control of the scene, but it didn't come. What did come was Nolan's cock—hard, fast, and deep.

He was a man possessed, grabbing her hips with enough force, she was sure his grip would leave bruises. There was no build up, just his cock's hard possession of her again and again, pounding into her wet tunnel, leaving no doubt between them who was in control.

He lifted her body high enough, her feet left the floor, and the angle of his thrusts changed, the tip of his erection now pounding against her G-spot. Within seconds, her first orgasm detonated like fireworks, exploding to touch every part of her body.

When her arms could no longer hold up the upper part of her body, Piper collapsed to the counter, mashing her boobs against the cool countertop as she laid languid like a rag doll, letting one orgasm roll into another until everything felt floaty.

The crack of his hand spanking her right butt cheek hit her brain, just before the pain from the smack registered through her sexual haze. She didn't have time to protest before the next swat came… and the next… and the next. The only time he slowed his pounding possession was to reposition her so he could pepper another part of her ass with his open palm. Just when it almost hurt too much, the pain morphed perfectly to edge her higher.

Shit, he's really good at this.

"Eyes. In the mirror."

His deep voice sounded far away. It had to fight through the haze of her sexual awakening to register the meaning. She couldn't have resisted obeying if she'd wanted to. Still, she had to struggle to lift her body from the pool of goo she'd melted into.

Their eyes met in the mirror as he continued his possession. His brown eyes were so expressive, she wanted to lose herself in them.

"Nolan…"

"Piper… you're mine. Do you hear me?" When words failed her, he added, "This… right here… is how I want to start every day."

Of course. Just like a man wanting to dip his nib...

"I love watching you come, again and again."

Oh. So, it's not just about him.

Danger bells were going off again as she felt the sting of tears welling in her eyes.

I am not going to cry. I am not going to cry.

The splash of the first tear hit the counter as Nolan cried out his own release, shouting her name as he came inside her. Once the last drop of cum left him, Nolan collapsed against her back, crushing her against the hard bathroom counter.

"You're squishing me," she squeaked.

"Yeah? Well, we can't have that, at least not unless I'm trying to as part of a scene at Black Light."

The mention of the BDSM club jarred Piper out of her sexual haze. Having sex with Nolan in private was one thing, but letting him dominate her in public... her anxiety just couldn't resist ruining the moment as the reality of their complicated history crowded in until she pressed to separate herself from him before the tears she'd been holding off broke loose.

Unaware of her present state of mind, Nolan grinned back at her in the mirror. He looked like a kid on Christmas morning. She didn't have the heart to tell him she'd be canceling his Christmas as soon as she could call an Uber. She needed time to think.

"Guess you can brush your teeth now. Take your time. Grab a shower, then come out for breakfast. I'll have hot coffee ready and make the best eggs and bacon for breakfast."

"I'd rather have pancakes." Her request came out before she could stop herself.

His sexy smile as he hugged her against him made her breath hitch.

"Baby, I'm gonna make you the best pancakes you've ever had. You're gonna want to have them every morning from now on." He placed a quick kiss on her nose, of all places, before turning to retreat.

It was odd, but as Piper watched Nolan grab a robe and leave her alone for the first time in what seemed like days, she had no doubt believing she would enjoy waking up to pancakes with Nolan Boeing every morning.

And that was exactly why she needed to get the hell out of there. Pancakes, among the other amazing things he was offering, were best enjoyed sparingly.

CHAPTER 21

eep.

Beep.

Beep.

The incessant beat of the alarm broke through the fog. Her body felt heavy as if someone were sitting on her chest. Like a defective computer facing the blue screen of death, Nalani worked to reboot her brain. Odd snapshots flashed through her memory as she struggled to hold on to any thought longer than a second.

She didn't know why, but she knew she was in danger. Run! She needed to escape.

Why wasn't her body cooperating? Despite sending a clear direction to her eyes to open, her lids wouldn't obey. The pressure on her chest increased until she was sure when she finally pried her eyes open, she'd find an elephant parked there.

The beeping was getting louder—faster—like the flashes of memories flitting through her consciousness. She was drowning, getting pulled down. Alarmed, she finally succeeded in opening her mouth to take a deep gasp of air. A split second later, her chest exploded in a sharp pain that felt like she'd been stabbed.

"She's awake! Someone get the doctor!"

It took a few seconds to recognize the voice. Why was Madison shouting?

Through sheer determination, she managed to turn her head toward the sound of footsteps nearby, but the shooting agony as she moved even a few inches insisted she freeze.

The slow return to consciousness was a curse. As the flashes of memories lingered longer, reality seeped in. She recognized the drugged fog like a lost friend, welcoming her back home after a long trip.

The excruciating pain was new.

Nalani started to take an inventory of her body, looking to catalog any part of her that didn't hurt, coming up empty handed.

"Miss Ione! Nalani! Can you hear me?"

The voice came from directly above her, close enough, she could feel the warmth of the man's breath against her cheek. When she opened her mouth to answer, her tongue felt like a heavy sheet of sandpaper.

Undeterred by her lack of response, the man above her finally succeeded in forcibly lifting her right eyelid, flashing a bright light directly in and out of her line of vision before repeating on the other side.

"Nurse, do we have the results back yet from her CAT scan?"

"Not yet. I'll call again."

"Good. And tell Sarah she's awake."

Fast footsteps retreated as the first wave of nausea registered. It was upon her in a flash.

"Sick…"

She had told her brain to say the word, but the voice she heard was not familiar. Nalani didn't have time to think about that as her mouth filled with bile. As hard as she tried, she couldn't convince her body to roll. She felt the wetness spilling down her cheek just before something soft patted around her mouth, cleaning her.

"Nalani, I'm Dr. Patel. We're going to take good care of you. You're safe now."

Safe. She knew that was a lie.

From a distance, a deep voice broke through, "...need to interview Miss Ione."

The doctor next to her raised his voice. "I told you that's just not possible. You need to..."

"She's awake. It's possible."

Who were all these people, and why were they all shouting? Had she really just imagined hearing Madison's voice?

"Madison?" Her tongue cooperated long enough to form the word.

"I'm here." She felt the squeeze on her left hand. "We're all here."

So many questions. She started with the most basic.

"Where am I?"

Madison moved closer. Nalani could swear she opened her eyes, but she only saw a sliver of her friend through a slit.

"You're at the hospital. You're safe now. What do you remember?"

There it was again—safe.

What did she remember?

Madison helped her. "Do you remember going home from work yesterday?"

Home. It felt far away. Flashes of her childhood home distracted her. She hadn't thought of that house of horrors in so long. Why did it feel like she'd just been there? She rejected the memories. That was no longer home, yet she struggled to picture her new home.

Runway. That felt like home. But no, that was where she worked, where Madison worked.

The vision of Shane Covington smiling at her with a sexy look on his face flit through her head, and she fought hard to hold on to the dream. Was it just a dream? The explosion of love in her chest as she thought of him was a hint it was more than that.

"Shane…"

"Yes! He's here. So is Jaxson. It's just that…" Madison's voice trailed off.

Nalani whispered, "What?"

"They're talking with the detectives right now."

Detectives. None of this was making sense. Was this just a crazy dream she would be waking up from and laugh about in the morning? She was pretty sure the fact she thought that meant it wasn't a dream.

"Ms. Ione. If you feel up to it, it is critical my partner and I ask you some important questions."

Nalani tried to turn her head in the direction of the voice on the other side of her and became aware of the neck brace holding her head immobile.

Her violent reaction to realizing she was being held immobile surprised her.

Escape. Danger.

Agitated, she finally got her arms moving, flailing to try to get the brace off her neck. The beeping in the room raced as Madison and the unseen woman next to her grabbed her arms to stop her thrashing about.

"Like, you need to lay still. You're gonna pull out the IV, and you could do more damage," Madison warned. Her boss's next statement was directed at the other woman holding her down. "You are upsetting her. You need to leave."

"We just need a few minutes. This is a high-profile case, and every minute is of the utmost essence. You wouldn't want her attacker to get away, would you?"

Attacker. Her brain may be only working at half capacity, but it heard that word and wouldn't let go.

She'd been attacked. At Runway.

No.

Like a wave at the ocean's shore, the vision of Henry Ainsworth bursting into her apartment and raping her crashed over Nalani, dragging her down into the dangerous undertow of memories.

She was back in her apartment, fighting… flailing.

"What's the meaning of this? I told you to wait outside in the waiting room."

Who the hell were all these people? A new female's voice joined the chorus of people around her bed.

"Nalani… My name is Sarah. I'm your nurse. You're safe now."

If one more person tried to tell her that, she would scream.

"Never safe…" she managed to get out.

"That's not true. You've been through a horrific event, but I can promise you, life will get back to normal one day."

What the hell was normal?

The woman named Sarah kept talking. Nalani didn't hear much of what she said, but the woman's composed and steady voice calmed her, nonetheless.

"… completed a rape kit and have sent the results off to the lab. I know it's difficult, but the police and I would like to ask you some important questions if you feel up to it."

Nalani didn't feel up to breathing, let alone talking.

"We just want to get the facts from you, so the person who did this to you doesn't get away with it," the nurse tacked on.

She took her time, forcing out her one-word reply out, "Okay."

Sarah, the nurse, was leaning over her, coming into the sliver of line-of-sight she had. The older woman's small smile and kind eyes comforted her.

"I know you can't see them, but there are two detectives from the Beverly Hills Sex Crimes unit in the room with us. They'd like to listen in to our discussion. Is that okay with you?"

"Madison?"

"I'm still here. I'm not going to leave you. I promise." Her friend's voice was farther away, out of sight.

Knowing her friend was there helped Nalani tamp down her anxiety enough to answer. "Okay."

"Thank you for that. I know this is going to be difficult, but we're all on your side. We just want to help find the facts of who did this to you." When Nalani didn't answer, Sarah continued. "Do you know the name of your attacker?"

An ugly face contorted in anger filled her vision. The nurse gave her the time she needed to answer.

"Ainsworth."

"Henry Ainsworth? Are you sure?"

"Sure."

"Okay, that's good. You're being so brave. Next question. Do you remember what he did to you?"

She didn't want to, but memories invaded—so many horrible things. She summed it up with one ugly word.

"Rape."

"Yes. I know this will upset you, but we've completed several tests while you were unconscious. Would you like to know more about your injuries?"

Would she want to know more?

"Not sure."

"Fair enough. I'll just share that you're being treated for two cracked ribs and a torn labia and anus. You had dozens of open wounds on your torso and thighs that look like shallow knife wounds."

"Whip."

"Excuse me?"

"It was a whip."

"Okay. That will help. It's difficult to get DNA off an implement like that." She paused before continuing, "We've tested you for STD's and administered Plan B, a drug used to prevent unwanted pregnancy."

"On pill."

"Understood, but we don't take any chances. I'm sure you're feeling disoriented. That would be understandable under the circumstances, but your condition is being complicated by the fact you were injected with a dangerous dose of methamphetamine. It's going to take some time to cleanse it from your bloodstream."

That was an understatement. Nalani knew on some level, meth would be with her always, the ugly shadow of her past that would flare up when she least expected it. Even now, she recognized the seductive temptation of shooting up again, just to make the pain stop.

"Is there anything you can tell us that will help the detectives put the facts of the case together?" When Nalani remained silent, Sarah asked a more pointed question. "Do you remember how Ainsworth got into your apartment?"

Memories of her door crashing in on her came back in flashes. She didn't want to think about them.

"Can't do this…"

It was Madison who answered Sarah's question.

"Yesterday afternoon, Ainsworth assaulted Nalani while at Runway. Our security team has videotape of the encounter. They called the police, and Ainsworth was arrested."

"Why not in jail?" Nalani asked.

"He posted bond and got a judge to release him," a voice from behind Sarah answered.

"You're safe here," Sarah reassured her. "I promise you, he can't get to you here."

"Maybe Ainsworth can't, but you need to get the media

under control," Madison snapped. "I had to go through a throng of cameras to get into the hospital."

Her friend's words confused her. Why would the media be interested in what happened to a nobody housekeeper?

Her brain grasped onto a memory.

"Shane?"

Madison squeezed her hand.

"He found you. Thank goodness he woke Jaxson up when he couldn't reach you and made him go to your apartment to check up on you in the middle of the night. I shudder to think what would have happened if they hadn't found you when they did."

"Nalani!"

It was his voice, shouting from far away. Unable to see through her swollen eyes, she relied on her hearing to tell her he was running as he burst into her already crowded hospital room.

Even without seeing him, she knew the second he was beside her, her body collapsing like a popped balloon. She hadn't realized how tense she'd been with anxiety until she let it go.

For the first time since she'd woke up, she believed she was safe when she caught her first whiff of Shane's scent as he pushed in beside her.

"Oh God, baby, I'm so damn sorry."

Why was he sorry? He hadn't done this to her.

"Not your fault," she forced out.

"I should have taken it more seriously when you had that altercation with that fucker the day we met."

Why did that feel like a lifetime ago?

She forced her eyes to open enough to get her first glimpse of the man she loved. Nalani knew she must look like she'd been in a boxing match, but she wasn't expecting to see Shane's right eye swollen, the hint of a bruise forming.

"Did he do that to your face?" she whispered.

"No," Jaxson asserted from behind Shane. "I did."

Why the hell would Jaxson hit Shane?

Her "Why?" was all she could force out.

"Cause he couldn't keep his damn mouth shut, that's why."

"Fuck that shit. I meant every damn word."

"Oh, I'm sure you did. I even agree with you, but that doesn't mean you need to run off at the mouth about it."

She was so confused. What were the men talking about?

"Confused."

"It's nothing for you to worry about, kitten. I was just informing the detectives they'd better find and arrest Ainsworth before I get my hands on him, or they'll have a homicide to investigate as well as sexual assault."

"Will you shut the fuck up? That kind of talk is going to get you arrested right alongside the asshole."

"Fine by me. Put us in the same cell, and I'll be happy to do to him what he did to Nalani, right before I end him."

"This isn't helping Nalani," Sarah broke in. "If you can't refrain from upsetting her, I'll ask the police to remove you."

"You don't need to worry about that." Jaxson didn't back down. "We'll be removing ourselves along with Nalani as soon as the transport ambulance I hired arrives."

"What are you talking about?" the nurse pressed.

"I mean, we can't keep her safe here. We're moving her to our house where we can go on lockdown."

"There's no way Ainsworth is stupid enough to come here," the detective on the sideline threw out.

"It's not Ainsworth we're worried about. The paparazzi are on a feeding frenzy out there," Jaxson replied.

"I assure you that Cedar-Sinai has dealt with this sort of thing before," Sarah retorted. "We have protocols for handing celebrity cases like this."

It was as if everyone in the room had forgotten she was there, talking about her as if she was some kind of a celebrity, which was insane. She was just a housekeeper.

"Don't understand."

"Shane and Jaxson brought you here," Madison answered, still holding her hand. "Shane carried you in. People in the waiting room recognized him and called the press. There are dozens of reporters who were in town to cover the Academy Awards, who are now trying to learn more about the woman Shane carried into the ER."

Oh no, this was her worst nightmare. She'd stayed home from the Oscars to avoid this very thing. Now, not only would the press dig into her past, they'd learn about the things Ainsworth had done to her. They'd pick her and Shane apart until there was nothing good left.

A commotion in the hall outside of her room drew everyone's attention. She could hear someone shouting Shane's name and others yelling for Jaxson to give a statement. The only thing that kept Nalani from melting down was Shane leaning down to put himself between any cameras and Nalani, protecting her from unwanted exposure.

"It's settled," Jaxson said when the shouting died down from the hall. "I talked with Dr. Patel. While he doesn't recommend moving Nalani, he doesn't forbid it either. Sarah, I'd like to hire you to come with us."

"That's crazy. She just suffered through a massive trauma. She has cracked ribs. We need to watch for signs of internal bleeding."

"Agreed, but we can do that at our house as well as here."

"She needs IV fluids. Pain meds. A catheter. Access to specialists."

"We can buy or hire anything or anyone we need to in order to care for her. I'd like you to join the team, but we can find someone else if you aren't up for the task," Jaxson pressed.

"I didn't say that. I'm on duty."

"Dr. Patel will clear you to leave. I'm sure of it."

"Oh, and how do you know that?"

"Because he's the one who suggested you. Get her ready for transport. The ambulance will be here within thirty minutes. Also, make a list of all the medical supplies we should have delivered and waiting for us when we get there."

SHANE NEEDED to plug his phone in. He'd been on calls non-stop since they'd arrived at the Cartwright-Davidson's house two hours before, and he still had a half dozen more calls to make.

He looked across the massive living space and took in the small army Jaxson had assembled in just a few hours. Security guards talked with official police investigators. Doctors and nurses conferred on the best care they could provide their patient. Nalani's friends and co-workers made up a third grouping in the corner, looking grim. Along the wall, the mammoth flat-screen TV had three different channels displayed, keeping tabs on the media coverage as the world woke up on their Monday morning to find out Shane Covington had ended his Oscar's celebration by carrying an unconscious and bleeding woman into the ER, soaking wet and bloody himself.

And in the middle of the room, out of place, the trio's adorable six-month-old twins gurgled and cooed good-naturedly in their infant swings, unaware of the tragedy that had happened the night before.

Beyond them, the sun was up and shining as if the dark horror of the night before had been just a bad dream. The throbbing in his right eye and fist were the constant reminders the nightmare was real.

"She's awake and asking for you."

Shane's heart lurched. He should be relieved to have Nalani safe and awake, but the truth was, he felt ready to jump out of his skin. He'd never felt as out of control, so furious at his core.

He knew with a certainty, no matter how things shook out between Nalani and him, his life would be forever changed.

The worst was the crushing guilt. The day he'd met her, he'd seen the way Ainsworth had treated her. Why hadn't he done more to intervene? Why hadn't he been checking with her to make sure the asshole hadn't bothered her again? Why hadn't he insisted she go to the Oscars with him?

Why?

He had no answers.

"Did you hear what said?" Chase had braved approaching him.

"Sorry, man. I zoned out."

"I get that. I said she needs you."

Shane doubted that.

"The sexual assault nurse, Sarah, is back there with her."

"So? She wants you."

"I doubt that. I fucked this up."

Chase's chuckle was out of place in the serious atmosphere. Shane glanced up to see Jaxson's husband smiling kindly.

"I knew you were gonna blame yourself, which is total bullshit, by the way."

Shane already felt like shit. He didn't need someone else trying to make him feel worse.

"Sorry, man, but I don't think you know enough about this to butt your nose in someone else's business."

"You're standing in my living room. You dragged my husband out in the middle of the night and have him mixed up in the middle of a felony investigation. Nalani is our employee and friend. If not my business, whose?"

The answer annoyed Shane.

"Listen, I've got some calls to make." He went back to searching for a number in his contact list, but Chase wasn't deterred.

"That can wait. She needs you."

Forced to face his own reticence, Shane was brutally honest.

"I can't go in yet. I don't know what I'm going to say."

"Boo-fucking-hoo. This isn't about you. You don't need to say anything. Just hold her while she cries. Tell her you love her while you let her fall asleep in your arms."

Chase made it sound so easy, but he'd already tried to tell Nalani how he felt while still at the hospital, and it had come out as an awkward confession of how desperately he'd let her down.

"I need to call my publicist back. And my mom left me a text after getting calls from friends while on the cruise. And..."

"Those calls can wait. She's only gonna be awake for a bit before the drugs knock her out again."

Shane wanted to tell Chase to mind his own business, but truthfully, he knew what he was saying was the truth. Maybe he should be truthful himself.

"I don't know why she wants to see me. It's all my fault this happened. I knew Ainsworth had bothered her weeks ago. I should have done more then. I should have been following up with her. I should have..."

"Stop! You sound exactly like Miguel. And Madison. And Elijah. Everyone is so damn sure this is all their fault. Well, that's bullshit. There is only one person to blame—Henry Ainsworth. The police issued an arrest warrant for him. They're going to find him and put him behind bars where he belongs. He's the only one who deserves blame."

Shane accepted the words with his brain, but in his heart, he just couldn't shake the fury and guilt.

"I'm not good company for her right now. I need to get my head on straight before I—"

Chase stepped into Shane's personal space. Despite being several inches shorter, the normally jovial guy had no problem schooling him.

"Get your ass back there. Now. I know you're scared. I can

only imagine how I would be feeling if that was my Emma lying back there. Every damn thing you're thinking and feeling is legit, but it's irrelevant. Nalani needs you, so get your head out of your ass and go to her."

People didn't talk to Shane like that. He wanted to get angry and storm out but was man enough to know Cartwright-Davidson had just done him a huge favor.

That didn't mean he liked it.

"Fine. Here. My phone is gonna die. Find a charger."

The men's eyes met. Shane didn't apologize, his nod as he handed off his phone was his only admission of appreciation.

The hallway back to the guest bedroom-turned-recovery room was littered with security guards and a medical equipment rental company employee rolling a wheelchair in from the direction of the back entrance along with a portable oxygen machine.

He had to hand it to Jaxson. Within two hours of making the call, he'd arranged to have the equivalent of a state-of-the-art hospital room setup in their guest room. The club owner spared no expense to make sure Nalani was not only safe but would receive around-the-clock medical care.

He paused outside the door, trying to push down his anger and guilt, knowing those emotions were useless to Nalani right now. She needed his love, his understanding.

Only he didn't understand a damn thing about this. Why the fuck had a man like Henry Ainsworth—powerful and rich—risked everything to hurt an innocent woman?

Unable to stall any longer, Shane opened the door, realizing too late he should have knocked. He stood frozen in the doorway, unable to take his gaze off the broken body of the woman he loved. He'd touched every inch of her, but if he didn't know with certainty it was Nalani in the bed, he wouldn't have recognized her.

Bile rose as his stomach rolled at the sight of the dozens of open cuts peppered across her breasts, stomach, and upper thighs. The nurse, Sarah, was talking softly to Nalani as she applied medicated cream to the wounds. Nalani's whimpers of pain tore at his heart and finally got him moving.

She flinched as she heard him approaching.

"It's just me, kitten."

"Shane. No. I don't want you to see me like this." Her voice was hoarse—that it had gotten that way by screaming out for help broke his heart.

"It's okay, baby. I'm not here to see you. I'm here to hold you."

She accepted his answer as he leaned over, nuzzling in against her neck now visible since they'd taken the neck brace off. Unable to lift her arms without hurting her ribs, Nalani grasped his T-shirt.

"This one is especially deep. I regret not having the doctor stitch it at the hospital. I'd like to stitch it now."

When she didn't answer, Shane pulled out of their embrace enough to look down at her swollen and bruised face. The tears streaming down the outside of her eyes broke his heart. He reached to gently cup her cheek, barely brushing for fear of hurting her worse.

"What do you say, kitten? You can squeeze my hand while she stitches you."

"Okay," she whispered.

He was grateful when she closed the slits of her eyes. He didn't want her to see his own anguish as he watched her suffering through the necessary medical attention.

He had no feeling left in his hand by the time Sarah announced she was finished, and Nalani released the death grip she'd had on it. The nurse pulled the oversized hospital gown down to cover her patient before lifting the light sheet over Nalani.

"I'm going to go see if the oxygen tanks have arrived yet. I'll let you two have a few moments alone."

It was absurd that he was nervous. He couldn't even fathom what Nalani had gone through. So, he took Chase's advice.

Shane toed off his shoes and gently lay down next to Nalani, careful to avoid pulling her IV out. He knew she couldn't roll into his arms with her cracked ribs, so he put his arm over her torso, trying to avoid the worst of her wounds.

He had been so wound up that only after he had his head on the pillow next to her, his lips close to her right ear, he realized how exhausted he was. None of them had got any sleep the night before.

"You're safe now. You should try to get some rest. It will help you heal faster."

Shane thought she might have already nodded off when she didn't answer him for several long minutes.

Her quiet "I'm so sorry" pissed him off.

"What in the world do you have to be sorry for?"

"All of this. You were supposed to be having fun after the Oscars, not taking me to the hospital. I feel so guilty, making everyone do all of this because of me."

An ugly bark of laughter escaped before he could stop it. He felt Nalani tense up again under his arm and was quick to explain.

"Nalani, I laughed because before I came in here, I was spouting to Chase about how guilty I felt. And I've heard Madison and Jaxson saying they feel guilty. The bullshit thing is Chase is right. No one is to blame—no one else should feel guilty—except Henry Ainsworth. So, I'll make you a deal. I'll stop saying how guilty I am if you do too."

He felt her relax under his arm. Although he would never say it out loud, he knew without a doubt, he was going to carry the guilt with him for a long time to come.

Finally, their exhaustion got the best of both of them as they fell into a fitful sleep.

CHAPTER 22

The pancakes were getting cold.

Nolan had suspected Piper would drag her feet in the bathroom, anxious to hide from him. He'd purposefully made several phone calls to put his *'Win Piper Over'* plan into action before starting to make breakfast. Still, the food was ready and waiting for her… just like he was.

Unable to resist, he popped a slice of bacon in his mouth just as Piper emerged from the direction of his master suite. Even wearing an old pair of his sweats and a faded T-shirt from his college days, she was breathtaking—not a drop of makeup, her long, dark hair hanging loosely around her face, still damp from her shower.

She'd never been more beautiful to Nolan, right up until the moment she spoke.

"I can't stay. My phone's dead. I need to use yours to call a car."

Stay calm.

He'd expected this. Nolan turned his back to her, hiding his disappointment as he started the microwave.

"You can stay long enough to eat. Then if you still want to go, I'll drive you home."

"You don't need to bother. I have people—"

He turned, cutting her off, "I know you have people, Piper. So do I."

"Good for you. Then you know you don't need to drive me."

She'd remained standing at the entrance to the open kitchen, most likely afraid to come too far, fearing he'd try to convince her to stay.

She wasn't wrong.

The microwave behind him dinged. He turned his back to her again to grab the plate of fluffy pancakes, turning back to put the platter on the eat-in counter that stretched out like a dividing line between them.

He took a deep breath and moved forward with his risky plan.

Pinning her with a domineering glare, Nolan commanded, "Sit. Eat."

Her eyes widened at his demand, but he took it as a positive sign when she didn't bolt from the room or cuss him out. Lightening his tone, he took his own seat on his side of the counter and invited her again with a wave of his hand.

"Be a sport. I made the whole pound of bacon. My scale will appreciate you eating some of this food."

She took her time answering. "Maybe I don't eat meat."

"I watched you polish off a half dozen hot wings at one of the parties last night. Nice try."

"Fine. Maybe I don't eat pork," she countered, faster this time.

So, Miss Kole wanted to test him already, did she? He'd known they had a lot of tug-o-wars ahead of them.

Let the games begin.

"Piper." Nolan crossed his arms across his chest, pinning her with one of his most intimidating glares. "I suggest you sit that beautiful ass of yours down on the stool in the next ten seconds. If I have to help you sit, I can assure you, your ass will be sore as hell while you eat."

Her eyes widened at his promise, but she hadn't run out yet, so once again, he softened, trying to ease her into their new dynamic.

"Come on, you need to eat. I have food. I have hot coffee. There are two pain-killers there next to your plate and a tall glass of water to help fend off dehydration." He paused to enjoy watching her scan the spread in front of her. "I mean it. If you still want to leave by the time we finish eating, you can go."

Her eyes snapped back up to meet his gaze.

"Oh, I'll want to go, alright."

Not if I made the right phone calls while you were in the shower, you won't.

He resisted celebrating when round one of their breakfast game of tug-o-war went his way as Piper dumped the shopping bag he'd stuffed her things into the night before onto the floor and reluctantly took a seat across from him. He watched as she snapped up the pills and downed them and half the water. He worked hard not to gloat.

When she failed to load her plate with any of the food, he stabbed a few pancakes and flopped them onto her empty plate before lathering a layer of butter on top.

"You like syrup?"

"Duh. Who eats pancakes without syrup?"

She was trying to goad him into an argument. They had a lot of serious things ahead of them. Fighting over condiments wasn't one of them. He let it go.

After loading several slices of bacon on her plate, Nolan went back to eating his own food.

"Do you need me to feed you?" he taunted when she sat frozen,

He had to hide his smile when his question got her to pick

up her utensils and start eating. They ate in amicable silence for a few minutes. He'd expected fireworks, so the quiet stretched out between them awkwardly.

"I can't believe you stuffed a half-million dollars in diamonds in a zip-lock bag," she accused.

He finished taking a sip of coffee before answering.

"Would you rather I'd have let you lose them last night? One of your earrings fell off in the limo when you were… indisposed."

"Indisposed?"

"You know… puking… vomiting…"

"Okay. Okay. You don't need to rattle off like a thesaurus again."

"You sure? I'm really good at it."

"Really? What other words would you use for *asshole*?"

"Oh, that's a complicated one. On the one hand, I'd say fucker, shithead, or prick. Maybe even bastard or jackass. But more intimately, I'd say anus, bud, pucker..."

"Oh, for Christ's sake…"

"Let me use it in a sentence for you. 'I can't wait until I get to fuck Piper's asshole.'"

"You're certifiable, you know that?"

She may be complaining, but Nolan didn't miss the corners of her lips twitching as she worked to squelch her smile.

"Hello? Everybody decent?" The shout came from the entrance near the garage.

Nolan kept his eyes on Piper as she looked around frantically. She resembled a kid who just got caught with their fingers in the cookie jar, trying to turn invisible before someone found her in his kitchen. As soon as Wendy came into view, he didn't miss the hardening of Piper's gaze as she watched his too-chipper personal assistant dump her armload of parcels on the counter near the platter of food.

Piper swung her glare back at him. "Looks like you forgot to tell your girlfriend you were having a sleepover."

He didn't have to defend himself. Wendy did a fine job of filling Piper in on her own with her peel of laughter.

"Fat chance of me ever being *his* girlfriend."

The smile on Piper's face grew victorious.

"Oh, so it seems we may have a quorum for a *Nolan ex club*."

He couldn't resist. "There might be a few I'd put on that list, but neither of you would make the cut."

"Oh, and why's that?"

"For one, Wendy bats for the other team if you get my drift. And more importantly…" He paused, leaning forward to pin her with a dominant glare. "We are far from over, Piper Kole."

He had Piper off base.

"For the other team?"

"Yeah, you know… a rug muncher… a dyke… butch…"

"I've told you a million times," Wendy cut him off. "Those are really offensive, you know? It's a good thing I like this job." Wendy reached into a bag and came out with a green smoothie, placing it in front of Piper. "I've worked for this jerk for three years now. I've explained to him I'm a lipstick lesbian a dozen times. If you get tired of this thing you have going with him and want to give a different kind of relationship a try, give me a call. I'll leave my card."

"Are you hitting on my girlfriend?" Nolan chuckled.

"She's Piper Fucking Kole. Of course, I'm hitting on her," Wendy retorted.

"I'm not his girlfriend. And what's this?" Piper said, holding up the gross looking beverage.

"Bossman told me you might have a wee hangover this morning, so I detoured to pick up my magic cure on the way over."

"What's in it?"

"Don't ask. Truly. Just pinch your nose and drink it down. Think of it as medicine."

Nolan snuck in another bite of bacon, enjoying watching the women meet.

"Did you pick up all the stuff I asked for?"

"I'm here, aren't I? I had to go to two places for the one item. It was a real pain in the ass."

Piper chuckled.

"What's so funny over there?"

"You. You have a type, you know that, Mr. Boeing?"

"Oh? And what type is that?"

"Strong, smartass women."

Nolan looked back-and-forth between Piper and his assistant and chuckled. "You may be right about that, but I can assure you, I only plan on boning one of you."

"Well, that's a relief. I don't swing that way. Now, Ms. Kole…"

"That's enough, Wendy. Thanks for bringing over the supplies I asked for. When are the others going to arrive?"

Piper had just got the question, "Others?" out when the doorbell rang.

"I'll get that," Wendy offered cheerfully. "You two kids eat up. Your pancakes are getting cold."

After she'd left the kitchen, Piper leaned forward and whispered accusatorially, "What the hell? You invite over the whole neighborhood?"

"Not quite, but I can throw a barbecue tonight if you'd like to meet everyone."

"Smartass."

Wendy was back, this time with an older Hispanic man in tow.

"This is Julio," she announced.

"Thanks for coming so quickly." Nolan didn't bother standing. "Wendy, can you show Julio to my bedroom, please?"

"You got it, boss."

Piper turned in her chair and watched the pair leave before turning back to him to pin him with a glare. "Something you want to tell me, Boeing? First, a lesbian. Now you have her taking another man to your bedroom. You need me to leave?"

"Baby, you misunderstood. Julio is here for *you*, not me."

"Excuse me?"

"Sure. I mean, I didn't really specify if they should send a woman or a man. I didn't think it really mattered." He let her confusion last a few seconds. "He's here to measure for the new blackout drapes I'm having installed this afternoon."

"Seriously. You called a drapery installment company before nine on a Monday morning, and they just ran over?"

"Technically, I called Wendy. Wendy called him before nine. You've met her—she can be very persuasive."

"Certifiable."

"You mean, charming."

Less than a minute passed before the doorbell rang again.

Piper's eyebrow rose adorably. "Who is it this time, the pool man?"

"Naw, the pool service came last Thursday."

"Don't bother getting up! I've got this." Wendy called out from near the entrance.

"What a smartass."

"Like I said, you really do have a type."

"Are you admitting *you're* a smartass, Ms. Kole?"

He adored the smile that lit up her face as she teased back, "I refuse to answer on the grounds I might incriminate myself."

"Likely story."

They could hear Wendy talking with someone as they approached the kitchen. Nolan looked up to see Wendy coming in with a burly bodybuilder-type guy trailing behind her.

What the fuck. This wasn't going as he planned.

"I thought I told you to get the best available," he pressed his assistant.

"You gave me exactly thirty minutes. I got you the best available within a ten-minute drive from your house. This is Peter."

Nolan looked the guy over, getting angrier by the minute. He wanted someone to help him pamper her, but he hadn't planned for muscle-boy.

"And what exactly does Peter do?" Piper looked confused as she started making wild guesses. "Install closets? If so, I've meant to redo my master closet for a while now. Can you leave your card?"

Wendy pinned Nolan with a glare he recognized as her 'you really are a jerk' look. "Peter is the best. And for the record, he bats for the other team like I do."

Nolan looked back at the bodybuilder, only to find him making eyes at him, not Piper. He hated how relieved he felt.

"Fine. He'll do."

"And what exactly is it that he is going to 'do' again?" Piper interjected again.

Peter patted the bag he had slung over his shoulder before answering, "I'm going to make you feel very relaxed, Ms. Kole."

"Oh, really? You got some Xanax in that bag of yours, do you?"

Nolan chuckled. "No, but he might have some of those fancy essential oils or some shit like that. He's a masseuse, here to give you a massage."

"A massage. Here. In your house."

"I can ask him to setup out by the pool if you'd prefer."

"Let me get this straight. In the time it took me to shower, you arranged a drape installation and a massage?"

"Don't forget the hangover medicine."

She would never admit it in a million years, but he saw it written all over her face—she was happily surprised.

Score.

"I just want you to relax and feel at home."

Piper hesitated, glancing at Peter and Wendy, then back at him.

"I really should go home."

"Sure. I'll take you after your massage. No sense letting Peter's talents go to waste."

"I know what you're doing."

"Making you happy?"

"Nolan..."

"Piper..."

It only took a few seconds for her to give in. "Fine, but only because I've been trying to fit a massage into my schedule, anyway."

"Of course." He waited for her to stand and turn to leave before he pulled the small gift box out of the top of the bag Wendy had set next to him on the counter. "Wait. Before you go, I have a small gift for you."

Piper turned, glancing between him and the gift-wrapped box he was holding out toward her. It took a few seconds for her to walk back his way and reach out for the present. Their fingers brushed in the hand-off, and he was relieved to feel the electricity still charging between them.

"You shouldn't have. I don't need anything."

"Wrong. You definitely need this."

Piper hesitated long enough, he wasn't sure if she was going to open it or not. When she started ripping the bow and wrapping off, he leaned forward with interest. The second she recognized what was in the small box, her eyes snapped up to pin him with knowing glare.

"I told you it would be something you were gonna need."

"Pretty sure of yourself, aren't you?" she accused as she pulled the sleep mask out of the box and held it up for him to see.

"You can leave it with me," he grinned. "I'll put it on your side of the bed. I'm sure you'll put it to use later tonight when you test out the new drapes."

~

SHANE STARTLED awake sometime later when Sarah placed the nasal cannula into Nalani's nose to give her additional oxygen. He was grateful the movement didn't wake her. She needed as much rest as possible to help her heal.

As tempted as he was to hide in Nalani's room, Shane extricated himself and pushed to his feet. He really needed to make some phone calls. He couldn't rest until they had Ainsworth behind bars.

"I'll be back in a bit."

"That's good. I can tell she is comforted by you being near."

He let her comment go unanswered, leaning down to place a soft kiss on her bruised forehead before picking up his shoes and heading down the hall toward the living room.

If anything, it was more chaotic in the house than before his nap. More police had arrived. Jaxson and Miguel had several laptops open, doing something at the dining room table. Emma and Avery were in the kitchen, making snacks for everyone.

Everyone seemed to have a job doing something helpful except Shane, and he hated it. He felt neutered, unable to assist the woman he loved.

Chase snuck up on him, handing his now charged phone out to him, along with a piece of paper with a list on it.

"Here you go. I've taken some messages for you and made a list of people you need to reach out to. I'd start with your mother if I were you." The men's eyes met as Shane grabbed the phone and paper.

"Thanks, man. I really appreciate it."

They may not know each other well, but at that moment, he

suspected Chase really did have a pretty good idea of what he was going through.

"And FYI, the police chief stopped by. He's ready to kick your ass for not waiting for the ambulance, but he let us know he got a judge to sign off on the search warrant for Henry Ainsworth's estate. They're headed there now. I'll let you make your calls, but let me know if you need anything."

Things were moving along quickly, which suited Shane fine. The room was too warm... too crowded. He weaved his way through the dining area and slid open the sliding glass door to the patio. The temperatures had been in the high seventies in the afternoon, but mornings could be chilly. The brisk February morning was exactly what he needed to wake up.

He was grateful for the privacy the secure estate provided as he made call after call, trying to find someone—anyone—who had seen this violent side of Henry Ainsworth in the past. In his gut, he knew men Ainsworth's age didn't just wake up one day and turn into a violent rapist. He'd heard the gossip of what an asshole he was to work with. Shane used his network to put the word out he was looking for other victims to come forward.

When a Google alert blew up his phone, he hung up on his agent to open the TMZ story titled *Shane Covington carries mystery victim into the ER.* A grainy photo of him carrying a broken and beaten Nalani into Cedar-Sinai in his soaking wet jeans, covered in her blood, filled his screen.

Fuck.

Reading on, his blood began to boil. Despite them bringing her to Jaxson's house and the HIPAA laws, it was clear someone on staff at the hospital had been bought—the reporters knew Nalani was a housekeeper at Runway. While it stopped short of naming her, they might as well have doxed her since there couldn't be more than a handful of housekeepers that worked there.

A picture of his mom replaced the story. He'd avoided

calling her, not knowing how he could explain all that had happened in the last twenty-four hours.

"Hey, Mom."

"Don't hey, Mom me! Why haven't you been answering your phone? What in the world is going on? Are you okay? Are you hurt? Why were you at the hospital?"

"Mom… slow down. Let me get a word in here."

She paused for all of two seconds before urging him, "Well? I'm waiting."

"I'm not hurt. At least not physically."

"What does that mean? How else is there?"

Where the hell did he even start? He hadn't been seeing Nalani long enough to have told his family about her.

"It's complicated."

"We didn't go on the shore excursion, so I can talk all day."

Oh, yay.

"Fine. Just promise me you'll stay calm."

"I'm always calm."

He refrained from calling her a liar.

"I met someone."

"Wait. As in a woman someone?"

"Technically, I meet women every day, but yeah, as in a woman someone."

"She isn't another one of those gold diggers, looking for her fifteen minutes of fame, is she?"

"Ma… please. I'm not in the mood for this."

"Fine. What's her name? And what does this have to do with the pictures of you going into a hospital?"

He shouldn't have answered her call. He wasn't prepared for the third degree. He got enough of that with the police interview.

"Her name is Nalani. And while I was at the Oscars, someone broke into her apartment and…" His voice trailed off.

He didn't want to say the words. It was horrific enough to think them.

"Shane?" Her voice had softened. "Please tell me she's okay."

His heart hurt. Nalani was certainly not okay. What scared him the most was he didn't know how she ever would be again.

"She's alive, but..." Shane's voice cracked with emotion, he hoped she hadn't heard.

"I don't understand. Why wasn't she at the Oscars with you?"

He swallowed over the lump in his throat before he could answer.

"We only met a few weeks ago. She wants to take things slow."

"Oh, goodness, I like her already. None of those girls from your past would have ever done that."

While his mother's observation was true, he couldn't deal with this interrogation right now.

"Mom, I gotta go."

"Wait! What happened?"

"I can't do this right now."

"Shane, talk to me. I can hear it in your voice. You're upset."

Hell, yeah, he was upset. He closed his eyes, and all he could see was the fear on Nalani's face the first day he'd met her—the day she'd run into his arms as she was trying to run away from Ainsworth.

His hands were shaking. There on the quiet patio, with only the sound of the birds overhead, Shane finally let the wave of anguish he'd been trying so hard to hold back crash over him.

His adorable submissive had needed him, but he hadn't been there for her. He let his mind take him back to that tiny apartment above the vape shop where he'd found her—the kitchen chair that had been tipped over, the blood on the table, trailing to the bathroom.

His first sob escaped as he remembered the terror he felt

seeing her crumpled body on the floor, not sure if she was dead or alive. If there was any doubt his feelings for Nalani were genuine, they evaporated as he let himself mourn what they'd lost.

It was insane the word innocence came to mind because the dirty things he'd loved to do to that sinful body of hers were anything but innocent, yet in an odd way, the word fit. They'd been bouncing along, having fun, not realizing how hard life could get.

He rejected the temptation to feel sorry for himself for what he'd lost as he let tears fall for the first time since he was a child. As angry as he was for himself, it was Nalani who'd paid the highest price. The thought of Ainsworth touching her, let alone raping her… beating her…

His heart was racing so fast, it felt like he was having a heart attack.

"Oh, Shane, I wish I was there to give you a hug."

He'd been so lost in his own despair, he forgot his mom was still on the line. He should be embarrassed, yet somehow knowing his mom was there for him did help a tiny bit. He lifted the hem of the T-shirt Jaxson had loaned him and wiped his nose.

He was grateful for the silence she gave him as he worked to pull himself together again. She really did understand him, and that was oddly comforting.

"He hurt her, Mom. Bad."

"Who hurt her?"

"You don't know him. He's a bigwig exec. A moneyman. I'm so afraid he's going to be able to buy his way out of justice."

"So, he's not in custody yet?"

"Not yet. But the cops are moving pretty fast. They have the arrest warrant out and have a search warrant. I feel so damn helpless sitting here, waiting for other people to go out and find him."

"Thank goodness they are. You need to let the professionals

handle finding him. I'm sure Nalani needs you with her, anyway."

"She's finally resting, thank God. Mom, I'm so lost. I don't know what to say to make it better."

"Honey, I don't have all the details, but sometimes, there are no words that can make things better."

"Then what am I supposed to do? I failed her once already by not protecting her. I don't want to fail her again during her recovery."

"You haven't failed anyone, least of all Nalani. You are a good man, and I can tell you love her. The best thing you can do now is tell her that. Show her you love her by holding her when she cries or has a nightmare. Stand by her through the media coverage that is sure to explode as more details get out."

Speaking of media coverage, his phone beeped with an incoming call from his publicist.

"Thanks for listening, Mom. It helped."

"Any time, honey. I mean that. I'm going to talk to your dad. We're gonna come home early. Please call me if anything changes before I get there."

He should feel guilty for them cutting their trip short, but he didn't.

"Will do, and mom… safe travels. I can't take anyone else I love getting hurt right now."

CHAPTER 23

Who knew a massage could relax her better than a Xanax? Peter was one talented masseuse. Piper had nabbed his card before he left. Even when whatever the hell this was happening between her and Nolan had run its course, she'd at least have Peter to show for it.

It took a lot to impress her, but she reluctantly admitted, Boeing had outdone himself this time. As if spending a hundred grand on her the day before wasn't enough, she appreciated his efforts today even more.

Piper took a minute to flip from her back to her front, reaching behind to pull the string to her bikini top so she wouldn't get a mark across her shoulders from the sun. It had been a long time since she'd been able to lounge next to a pool and have people wait on her. As she sunbathed next to Boeing's impressive pool in the late afternoon sunshine, she reviewed her day.

Included in the long line of visitors had been Danielle, her own assistant, with a suitcase of essentials, including the bikini she was wearing. As impressive as the massage, facial, and manicure he'd arranged had been, it was the amazing sex that had started her day she couldn't stop thinking about. The man truly was a sex god.

Piper was no fool. She knew he was manipulating her. The longer she stayed in Nolan's house, the higher the odds were she'd be wearing that sleep mask tonight at bedtime.

On the one hand, it bugged her to let him be right about her staying over again. But the thought of another round of Nolan sexcapades was becoming increasingly attractive the longer she lounged next to his masculine perfection, currently sleeping on the lounge chair next to her.

Don't panic. It's just one day.

"Why didn't you undo that bikini top when you were on your back?"

Correction, his masculine perfection was currently *awake* next to her. A quick peek confirmed his cock was definitely waking up too, tenting his swim trunks.

"Oh, I don't know. Considering we've had a parade of people coming and going all day, I thought it best to stay covered."

"Well, we're alone now. It'll be a sacrifice, but if you need to sunbathe naked to avoid tan lines, feel free."

"You're a real champ, Boeing. Way to take one for the team."

He chuckled before she heard him rolling toward her on his chaise lounge.

"Damn, you're gorgeous."

"Right." It was her turn to chuckle, careful to keep her eyes closed. "I don't have makeup on, and the sun has probably brought out every damn freckle I'm cursed with."

"That's what makes you so beautiful to me, baby."

"So, you have a fetish for freckles? Good to know."

"Only yours. It's the fact I'm privileged enough to see you like this, literally with your hair down. That's what I love the most."

Her trademark snark came easy when they were bantering,

but it had increasingly begun to fail her when Nolan said sappy things.

Several long minutes passed, and she started to suspect he'd fallen back asleep until she heard the creak of the chair next to her, telling her he'd stood up.

"Come on. Let's take a dip."

"Are you nuts? Today may be extra warm for February, but the water will be hella cold."

"Why do you think I have a heater? I swim laps three to four days a week, year-round. No way I could do that without a heater."

Was he serious? At least that explained how he stayed in such great shape.

Piper pushed up her upper body, careful to hold her top over her tits, squinting into the sunlight just in time to see Nolan shedding his swim trunks. His cock was semi-hard, hanging heavy just a few feet away from her.

"Wow, so you just let it all hang out, eh? Bet the neighbors love it."

"Sorry to disappoint you, but I have privacy fences and trees surrounding the property. The only thing that might see those glorious tits of yours other me will be the persistent squirrels I've been trying to get rid of."

"Aw, what did they ever do to you? Maybe they get off watching The Rock getting some sun."

"I see you're enjoying the view."

Stop looking at it.

Piper flopped back to the chair, closing her eyes to avoid his eye contact.

"Have fun with your laps."

She only braved opening her eyes again when she heard Nolan diving into the pool. The rhythmic splashes as he took long, freestyle strokes through the water were oddly comforting. She half expected him to stop after a lap or two, but he kept up the same pace, switching first to the breaststroke, then a half-dozen laps later to the backstroke. He was over a dozen laps in before he switched to the butterfly stroke.

She couldn't pretend to ignore him any longer. The sight of his muscular body working out had her getting wet, and she hadn't even touched the pool yet. Unlike the bulky muscles Peter had displayed earlier, she much preferred the perfection that was Nolan Boeing's hard body. Watching him sluice through the water gracefully, his muscles ripping perfectly in unison with the water, was almost hypnotic.

Piper couldn't resist getting an up-close-and-personal view. Pushing to her feet, she threw caution to the wind, lifting her bikini top over her head and walking barefoot in her bottoms to the tiled steps at the corner of the large pool. The second her toes hit the water, the temperature was perfect—like its owner.

She pulled her sunglasses down from the top of her head, thankful they helped hide how closely she was watching the end of Nolan's workout. Another few laps of freestyle strokes, Nolan finally stopped, hanging onto the edge of the pool, just a few feet to her left.

Only after he'd caught his breath, he seemed to notice her proximity.

"That was impressive."

"Naw, I used to do twice that many laps in a workout."

"Wow. Who are you? Michael Phelps?"

"No, but there was a time in my life I wanted to be. I did the first few years of my undergrad degree on a swimming scholarship at Stanford. It was crazy competitive, and while I may not have won often enough in the pool, I'm grateful that's where I fell into my business degree."

Interesting. Was he really sharing personal tidbits with her? Despite their lack of clothing, she suddenly felt like they were on some kind of a date instead of... what? What the hell were they doing, anyway?

Nolan Boeing confused her—had her off base.

"Sometimes I regret not going to college,"

What the fuck? Why did she confess that?

"I'm sure the modeling money being thrown your way in high school made it hard to pass up."

"Yeah, it didn't help that..." She cut off mid-sentence. What the hell was she doing? He wasn't her priest, and she wasn't in a confessional. So, why did she almost spill some of her most guarded secrets?

"That what?" he prompted. When she didn't answer, he added, "You can trust me, Piper. I just want to learn more about what makes you tick."

"Why? So, you can use it against me?" Her accusation came out like a fight starter.

He didn't bite.

"If I wanted to do that, I have more than enough shit to use already. I just want to learn more about you. If that's too hard, tell me something easier. Like, what's your favorite music? Or holiday? Hell, even your favorite color?"

"Ha! You've obviously fallen behind on your gossip rag reading. You can find answers to all of those questions and more standing in line at the grocery store."

"Bullshit. We all know most of what's in print is wrong, and even the parts they get right are skewed."

"What difference does it make?"

"Do you have to ask?" Nolan closed the few feet between them, crawling up the pool steps on his hands and knees, coming to a stop just inches from her face as his body dripped water onto hers. "I want to know every single thing about you, Piper. That's what people do for the ones they care about."

Her snark had deserted her. The only thoughts her brain could string together involved keeping her eyes on his to avoid glancing down to see if his cock was hard. She wanted to cry bullshit, but the intimacy she felt toward him after just finding out something as simple as he'd been a collegiate swimmer called her a liar.

Intimacy mattered. That was what he was talking about, and it scared the shit out of her. She had too many secrets she'd worked too hard to bury to start getting careless now.

"Fine. I'll tell you a secret." She paused for dramatic effect before confessing. "My favorite color is blood red."

"Ah, the color you see when you rip men's hearts out. Makes sense."

"I can't help it if they're stupid enough not to pay attention when I tell them I don't do relationships." She may have used broad words, but they both knew she was warning him.

"I got news for you, Piper. I don't really want to feel this way about you either. It would be a hell of a lot easier and certainly cheaper to pursue someone else. I'm just playing the hand we've been dealt."

"Yeah, well, I don't gamble."

"The hell, you don't. You take chances with your career. All I'm asking is for you to give me a chance to prove I can make it good."

When she couldn't think of a snappy reply, Nolan took advantage of her silence to lean forward, letting their lips brush lightly before leaning in to nuzzle the crook of her neck, nipping and kissing his way along her shoulder until she visibly shivered. Nolan pulled away, peering down into her eyes.

"Are you cold? I can get you a wrap."

She bit her tongue to keep from admitting she was actually burning up from his proximity. A small warning bell was going off in her head, telling her she should grab her things and get out while she still could, only she couldn't will her body to move.

When he reached out to take her sunglasses off, she felt truly naked in front of him for the first time. There was no more hiding the emotions swirling through her. One look into his eyes and she knew there was nothing that could drag her away from him at that moment.

Nolan crashed his mouth to hers in a passionate kiss that deepened with each second that passed. He lowered his body against hers, crushing her between his hard body and the stone steps at her back. Without taking his lips from hers, he maneuvered her into his arms as he lifted her up to the top step where all but her toes were out of the water.

In one smooth motion, Nolan reached for a nearby pool floaty, putting it under her head as a pillow. She could feel his hardness pressing into her as his hands roamed her body, pinching and stroking her until she could think of nothing else but taking him inside her again.

Nolan had more patience, pulling out of their kiss only to start nibbling her neck, lower to her breasts, her nipples. His tongue tickled as he licked lower, making a quick stop in her navel before she felt his fingers hooking into the sides of her bikini bottoms.

Piper closed her eyes, determined to focus on the physical chemistry between them, instead of the emotional baggage that threatened to ruin the moment.

The only hint Nolan was as anxious as she was to speed things up was when he roughly grabbed her ankles, spreading her legs wide, placing the bottoms of her feet on one of the stairs. The slow trail of kisses he left from her right knee down her inner thigh to her pussy was maddening. She wanted more —needed more.

Anxious to speed him along, Piper lifted her ass higher in an attempt to crash his tongue against her pussy, but he was ready for her, hugging both her thighs as he split her legs open wider, holding her there. Piper cried out in frustration, opening her eyes to see him staring at her with the sexiest look on his face. Warning bells were going off.

"Ask me for it, baby."

"What?"

"What do you want me to do?"

"Oh, for Christ's sake. You need me to draw you a map?"

"No, but I do need to hear you beg. It will be music to my ears."

"Beg? Fat chance… I don't…"

She couldn't even finish her sentence. Nolan had lunged forward and brushed his tongue across her clit. It was a direct hit, and she almost came like an explosive.

And then his tongue was gone. His lips were back, applying soft kisses to her inner thigh.

Piper growled her frustration when seconds turned to long minutes, but his lips never got close enough to recreate the zing from before.

"Nolan. Please…"

His lips didn't leave her skin as he mumbled, "Please, what?"

"You know," she said, wiggling her ass, trying to line up his lips with her needy pussy.

"I'm afraid I don't. You need to use your words. Tell me what you want."

"Why? Is this some kind of sick game you like to play?"

He stopped nibbling her long enough to lean up so their eyes could meet again.

"This is no game, Piper. But I need to know you really do want this. As much as I'd like to turn my inner caveman loose on you, I'm trying to be sensitive to the fact our dynamic is new for you."

The fucker. How could he possibly say something that could make her cry? Unwanted tears blurred her vision of the handsome man only inches away. Closing her eyes only made things worse, spilling the dreaded tears down her cheeks.

Goddamnit, she was ruining everything. Panic rushed in. Damn Mistress Ice for deserting her. Damn Nolan Boeing for wiggling his way under her defenses. Damn her body for needing him.

Nolan's lips on her cheeks, kissing her tears away, were the final straw. Piper reached up to hold on to him for dear life as their mouths crashed together in a desperate kiss. His hands roamed across her, stoking her need higher and higher until she broke their kiss to do the impossible.

"Please fuck me! I need you inside me!"

She expected him to gloat, but instead, he held still above her, peering down into her eyes as she felt the tip of his shaft sliding through her slick slit.

The words "I love you, Piper" left his mouth just as his cock filled her in one strong thrust. It was heaven… and it was hell.

How had she not seen this coming? He wasn't fucking her. There, on the top stair of his mammoth pool, Nolan Boeing was making love to her. If the soft kisses on her cheeks and the crook of her neck weren't proof enough, his words of love and affection sealed the deal.

She wanted to panic. She tried to rally her brain to resist what he was offering, but it felt too damn good. Sure, he was talented in the sex department, but there was something more—deeper—between them. Was this really what love felt like?

Nolan rose up so they could stare into each other's eyes as his hips pistoned in and out, filling her perfectly. Her climax hit her like a Mac truck, leaving her putty in his talented hands.

If only she could just take her pleasure and walk out like she had the night of roulette, but that seemed like a lifetime ago. God help her, she wanted to bring him as much pleasure as he was bringing her, falling apart in his arms as he pushed her to orgasm after orgasm. She stopped lying to herself long enough to admit she couldn't wait to sleep in his arms again tonight… and wake up in his bed in the morning.

She knew he was getting close to coming when his thrusts became erratic, grunting with each stroke.

"Come again, Piper. Come with me," he commanded.

She obeyed.

She wasn't sure how long they laid there recovering, but she eventually became aware of how heavy Nolan was collapsed on top of her.

"You're squishing me again."

Nolan's chuckle made her oddly happy. How strange it was to have fun with a sexual partner, instead of say… torturing his balls—although to be fair, that had been kinda fun too.

He pushed off her and helped her sit up next to him before pulling her onto his lap, holding her tenderly. She was grateful since the sun had started to go down, and it was noticeably chillier than it had been before they'd started their tryst.

"I have a fun idea for dinner. Have you ever ridden a Harley Davidson?"

"As in motorcycle?"

"The same. I invested in a bike a couple of years ago and rarely have a chance to take her out. I know a great Italian place up in the hills about thirty minutes from here. It's family owned. Only locals know about it. I'd love to take you there tonight for some pasta."

"On a motorcycle?"

"Well, we could take the car if you'd rather."

"Oh, no. I mean, I've never ridden a bike before. Are you sure it's safe?"

"I'm sure. I wouldn't do anything to endanger you, baby."

Nolan Boeing was one surprise after another. She was crazy to entertain the idea.

"Alright, it sounds interesting." The words were out before she could stop them.

"Great, let's go inside and get ready. I just want to check the weather. As much fun as a ride sounds, I don't want to get us drenched."

They took a few minutes to pick up the things they'd taken

out to the pool before heading inside. She wasn't sure which unnerved her more—the feel of Nolan's warm cum seeping down her inner thigh as she walked or his grabbing her hand as they weaved through the outdoor furniture past the fire-pit toward the house.

They entered through the long sliding door from the patio to the great room. Nolan went to the side table and grabbed the clicker, switching on the mammoth flat-screen TV above the fireplace.

"You can take the first shower. I'll be right behind you as soon as I make sure we aren't in for rain tonight."

Piper was almost out of the room when the news anchor's report coming from the TV registered in her brain.

She froze in the doorway, afraid she'd hallucinated the words. Her ears piqued as her heart started to race, gasping for air when she realized she'd been holding her breath.

"We repeat, we are interrupting our previously planned programming to report that Hollywood movie financier and Oscar-winning producer, Henry Ainsworth, has been taken into custody while attempting to board a private jet at the Bob Hope Airport in Burbank. State police, along with the Beverly Hills Police Department, are declining to comment further at this time.

"Details are still emerging, and while we haven't been able to confirm the charges with the District Attorney's office, our sources are telling us a female victim was rushed to Cedar-Sinai overnight, accusing Ainsworth of sexual assault and battery.

"Hospital authorities have not been authorized to release information on the victim, but we have learned she is a twenty-five-year-old housekeeper who had previously accused Ainsworth of assault. Sources not authorized to speak from the Beverly Hills Police Department have indicated Ainsworth was previously arrested but later released after accusations from the same woman were not substantiated.

"We now return you to our normal programming. Stay tuned for further updates on this breaking story."

Piper's ears were ringing from the spike in her blood pressure. Behind her, she recognized Nolan was speaking, but she only made out every few words.

"...never liked that guy... creeped me out... buy his way out..."

The room was spinning, unwanted memories flooding her brain, forcing out thoughts of anything except fear and fury. As if the rug had literally been pulled out from under her, Piper fell to her knees, dropping the cup of water she'd been carrying.

As a familiar nightmare started on auto-play in her brain, Piper crouched into a ball, throwing her arms over her head in the crash position. Hands pawed at her as she fought back, screaming for help, but she'd learned—no one would be coming to her aid.

I'm on my own.

Someone called her name from far away. Piper fought back —scratching, hitting, clawing—until arms too strong to fight immobilized her.

She sank deep into the nightmare until soft words started to chip through the haze. The arms entrapping her now rocked her instead. The hard floor had been replaced by a comfortable lap. She gasped for air, trying to push the panic back into its cage deep inside her. Somehow, she managed to squeak out a single word.

"Xanax."

The arms enclosing her loosened. She survived on sips of air taken in fits and starts.

"Open." An order.

A pill shoved into her mouth.

A glass of water to wash it down.

Time passed as she used the breathing techniques she'd

learned to help keep the panic at bay. Why weren't they working anymore?

She had mixed emotions as she started to feel the medicine doing its job. As the panic receded, it was replaced with embarrassment. Slowly realizing where she was and whose arms she was in, Piper grew agitated. She hadn't lost control like this in years and was mortified she'd fallen apart in front of Nolan—in his house no less.

"Talk to me, baby. What happened?"

Nolan pressing for answers was not helping. She swatted at his arms, fighting against his restraint. Her brain knew it wasn't the same thing, but in her precarious state, she couldn't handle being held in place. She needed to get free.

"Let go of me! I need to stand up!"

"You fainted. Let me help you."

"It's too late for that!" the manic version of herself screamed. "No one can help me."

"Piper, baby. It's me… Nolan."

"I know who you are, but it doesn't matter."

Nolan must have realized he wasn't helping, his hold finally loosening. Piper scrambled to push out of his lap, stumbling to her feet and steadying herself by grabbing the back of the nearby loveseat.

She was still naked. Fond memories of their intimate time making love valiantly tried to break through her consciousness, but Piper pushed the memories down. She'd made a mistake coming here.

"I need to go."

"What? No way. I'll order in food. We need to talk."

Right on schedule, she felt her stomach churning. She had to fight the urge to throw-up from the rollercoaster of emotions she was riding.

"Nothing to talk about."

"Are you kidding me? What the hell just happened?"

"Nothing." He'd stood up and was approaching her. She held out her left hand like a stop sign and cried out the first word that came to her.

"Red!"

Piper had a front-row seat to the horror on Nolan's face as he flinched, realizing she'd figuratively pulled the plug on his *us*. Like the honorable man she knew he was, he stood frozen, unwilling to get any closer.

Piper struggled to find the right words. "I know you want to help me, but you can't. No one can. I need to leave. Now. So, either call me a car or I'm going to start walking."

"Don't be ridiculous. I'll give you a ride wherever—"

"No! I need to be alone."

"Piper... baby... please..."

"Fine, I'll walk." She swatted his hands away when he reached for her as she brushed past him, headed for the bedroom.

The Xanax was doing its job, making her feel floaty. She went through the motions of stuffing the few items she'd unpacked back into the bag Danielle had brought over earlier that day. She threw on a pair of jeans and the first top she pulled out, desperate to get the hell out of there so she could lick her wounds in solitude. Her pool flip-flops were good enough shoes.

Nolan was pacing in the great room when she emerged from the bedroom. She could tell he had a million things he wanted to say, but to his credit, he held it all in.

"I wish you'd let me drive you."

"No."

After a few seconds, Nolan dug into the pocket of the robe he'd thrown on at some point and came out with a set of keys.

"Take the Audi. It's in the garage. Are you sure you can drive?"

"I'm sure."

The damn tears were back again. Nolan had made her soft. If ever she needed to channel Mistress Ice, now was the time.

"Thanks for a fun few days, Nolan, but this was a mistake. I'll have Danielle return your car. I'll be changing my phone number, so don't bother calling."

"Just like that?" Nolan's handsome face contorted in anger. "You're gonna walk out of here. No explanation."

"What do you want me to say?"

"I don't know. Maybe the fucking truth!"

"The truth? Fine. You make me soft, and there is no room in my life for that. The truth is, I like being Mistress Ice. Nothing can hurt me that way."

"That's such a load of shit, Piper. You want to lie to me, fine, but do me a favor and at least stop lying to yourself. I don't know what the fuck happened between you and Henry Ainsworth, but I'm gonna make it my life's mission to find out."

"Leave it alone, Boeing. It's none of your fucking business."

"Bullshit. I think I deserve to know why I don't get my happily ever after with the woman I love. You may be okay with throwing whatever this is we have together away, but I sure as hell am not."

There it was again. His declaration of love. For a brief moment, Piper allowed herself to recognize how nice it would have been if she could have reciprocated, but she pushed the feeling aside. She was broken. He deserved better.

"Goodbye, Nolan."

How she got the strange car backed out of the garage and onto the road, she'd never know. She had no plan. As tempting as going home was, she knew Nolan would look for her there. She needed to go somewhere alone, where no one could find her.

She didn't dare try to charge her phone, knowing she could be tracked that way. By some dumb luck, she found Pacific Coast Highway. Just as the final sliver of the sun was setting over the Pacific to her left, Piper headed north, gunning the powerful engine of Nolan's pretty car.

She had no idea where she was going, but that brought her a small measure of comfort since that also meant no one else would ever be able to find her either.

"YOU NEED TO EAT SOMETHING."

Shane didn't need Cartwright-Davidson managing him.

"I'll eat when Ainsworth is behind bars."

"He won't be able to hide forever. The media got ahold of his arrest warrant. They're broadcasting his picture non-stop. It won't be long now."

"That's bullshit, and you know it. He's a moneyman. He can buy himself safe travels to anywhere on the globe."

"Maybe, but at least then, he won't be close enough to hurt the people we love."

Shane glanced to his right to see Jaxson looking across the room, watching Emma as she breastfed one of the twins. The club owner could really be a hardass, but at that moment, Shane suspected the alpha man wouldn't be holding up much better than he was if something happened to his Emma or Chase. The thought brought him an unexpected touch of comfort.

Shane pushed to his feet to check on Nalani. She'd been sleeping the last two times he'd checked on her. The pain medications they were giving her in her IV were finally helping her get some rest. The only reason he'd left her side was there were several nurses and doctors cycling through her room at all times. Maybe he'd curl up next to her and catch a few winks while he waited to hear from the police chief after they executed the search warrant on Ainsworth's estate.

He'd only taken a few steps when his phone rang. He dug it

out of his jean's pocket to see the Beverly Hills Police Department come up on his caller ID.

"Covington here."

"We got him."

The whoosh of air told him he'd been holding his breath while he waited to hear those words. Now that the news he'd been waiting for had come, he realized how anticlimactic it was. While getting Ainsworth off the streets was critical to protecting society at large, Shane had to acknowledge, it didn't do jack shit to help Nalani through her recovery.

"Where the hell was the fucker hiding?" Shane pressed.

"We found a few notes in his home office that gave us a hunch he was planning to rent a charter out of Bob Hope Airport. We had a couple black and whites get there just as he was boarding a charter jet. The pilot had filed a flight plan for Dubai."

"Let me guess. The UAE doesn't have an extradition treaty with the US."

"Bingo. We'll be digging into his financials, but I suspect he's been setting himself up to retire there if things ever blew up here."

"So, it sounds like you're starting to believe that he's a serial abuser after all," Shane pressed the police chief.

"I wouldn't go that far, but let's just say we found some pretty disturbing shit at his house. We've only just begun to process it all, but I'm not gonna lie. I'll sleep better knowing we have him behind bars after what we found."

A small part of Shane wanted to press for details, but he realized that learning about additional Ainsworth victims would only make him feel worse, not better.

"Thanks for calling. Keep me in the loop."

"Will do. I'll let you know when the press conference is scheduled."

"Wait. Press conference?"

"Yeah. This is a high-profile case. There's no way we can get away without having a press conference to announce the charges. It will probably be more like daily until the charges are finalized."

"Fuck. Isn't the media circus already out of control?"

"Exactly. Maybe by answering a few questions, the chaos will calm down a bit, but don't forget, it will help your girl's case if we can get another victim or two to come forward to establish a pattern of behavior. Don't worry about it for now. It's getting too late today. It'll most likely be tomorrow or the next day. I'll have my assistant send you and Davidson a text with the details after I talk to the district attorney."

The police chief ended the call abruptly, not even bother to say goodbye.

Asshole.

Shane turned to tell Jaxson the news only to find everyone in the room had stopped talking to turn toward the huge TV on the wall. A helicopter film crew was hovering over a private jet. The crawler at the bottom of the screen correctly identified the location as Bob Hope Airport, the location the chief had just confirmed.

"Turn it up," Shane asked.

Chase leaned down to grab the remote from the coffee table, turning the volume higher.

"We repeat, we are interrupting our previously planned programming to report, Hollywood movie financier and Oscar-winning producer, Henry Ainsworth, has been taken into custody while attempting to board a private jet at the Bob Hope Airport in Burbank. State police, along with the Beverly Hills Police Department, are declining to comment further at this time.

"Details are still emerging, and while we haven't been able to confirm the charges with the District Attorney's office, our sources are telling us, a female victim was rushed to Cedar-

Sinai overnight, accusing Ainsworth of sexual assault and battery.

"Hospital authorities haven't been authorized to release information on the victim, but we have learned she is a twenty-five-year-old housekeeper who had previously accused Ainsworth of assault. Sources not authorized to speak from the Beverly Hills Police Department have indicated Ainsworth was previously arrested but later released after accusations from the same woman were not substantiated.

"We now return you to our normal programming. Stay tuned for further updates on this breaking story."

"Someone at the hospital needs to get their ass fired for releasing that much information about Nalani," Miguel complained.

"Hey, I'm just glad they left my name out of this report. Let's face it, with Jaxson and me involved, they aren't going to rest until they get all the dirt. It's why I'm so grateful for you hosting us here, where we can have at least a small measure of privacy from the media."

Miguel stood from his seat at the laptop. "Watching that report reminded me, I need to have the guys double and triple checking for drones. I don't want a repeat of what happened at your wedding, boss."

Shane hadn't been in attendance, but he'd heard about the disruption to the trio's unique wedding the previous year when drones with cameras flew over, trying to get a scoop.

The tension that had been building all day seemed to lighten ever so slightly after the news of Ainsworth's capture and arrest. Shane allowed himself a few minutes of relief with the group hanging out in the living room. But now that he knew Ainsworth was behind bars, the exhaustion he'd been powering through started to catch up to him.

Detouring through the kitchen, he grabbed a few chips from the bowl sitting out on the counter, downing them as he headed back to Nalani. He couldn't wait to tell her the good news that her attacker was in custody. Shane knew it couldn't erase her pain or fear, but he hoped it would let her breathe a bit easier, knowing he couldn't get to her ever again.

He'd just finished taking a whiz in the guest bath when his phone rang again. He was tempted to ignore the call, especially when he saw it was Nolan Boeing. He wasn't in the mood to listen to his friend talking about how in love he was with Piper Kole.

He answered the call at the last second.

"Hey, Boeing. I can't really talk..."

"What the fuck happened with Ainsworth?"

The panic in Nolan's voice got Shane's attention.

"Why?" Friend or not, he wasn't ready to start sharing the very personal details of Nalani's attack.

"Just tell me, damnit. I saw the report that he was arrested. And I saw the pictures of you carrying a woman into Cedar-Sinai last night. I'm not stupid. Did he rape your girl?"

"It's none of your fucking business if he..."

"I think he raped Piper, too." Nolan's outburst shut him up. Shane's mind raced as he internalized the words.

"What? She told you that?"

"No, but we were just coming in to get ready to go to dinner. I turned on the TV to catch a weather report, and the news report was talking about Ainsworth's arrest. Shane, she lost it. Like a PTSD breakdown—screaming, crying, flailing. It took a Xanax to get her calmed down, then she just shut down on me."

He mulled the implications of Boeing's hypothesis around in his head. He couldn't imagine Mistress Ice letting any man get the best of her. Hell, Piper was more hard-core Domme than he was Dom on his best day.

"I don't know. That seems very unlikely. Don't take this the wrong way, but she's scary as fuck when she's been at Black

Light. I can't picture any man, especially Ainsworth, getting the best of her."

"That's just it. She wasn't always like that. I knew something had happened. I just didn't have a fucking clue what. I know I'm onto something. I don't know exactly what went on, but I'd bet big money Henry Ainsworth was involved."

"So, put her on. Let's get to the bottom of this."

"She bolted, man. Took one of my cars and ditched me. I have a bad feeling about this. She scared me, Shane. I fucking hate that she's out there alone."

Nalani was recovering in the next room, yet Shane felt the same helplessness he heard in Boeing's voice. Both men hadn't a clue how to get the women they loved through the nightmare Henry Ainsworth had sentenced them to.

Shane hedged on answering Boeing's original question. "You don't want to know the details. Trust me. Just know, I absolutely hate the idea Piper might have had to live through even a fraction of what Nalani is going through right now."

"I'm so damn sorry, man. Is there anything I can do to help?"

Shane knew how lucky they were to have so much help already.

"No, the Cartwright-Davidson's have really stepped up to help. Nalani is their employee, and they're taking it pretty hard. I'll try calling Piper. Who knows, maybe she'll answer for me again like last time. If I hear from her, I'll let you know. Please, do the same if you hear from her."

"Will do."

CHAPTER 24

Piper was going to miss the crashing waves when she left the next day, but it couldn't be helped. She told herself she'd find another rental property on a different beach once she got settled. She'd lucked out finding this Airbnb right on Pismo Beach after leaving Nolan's.

She'd spent the last twenty-four hours trying to get her head out of her ass. Results varied hour to hour on how well she'd done.

In a moment of lucid cogitation, she'd broken down and finally charged her phone. She told herself it was only so she could call Danielle, which she'd done, but then the waves of self-doubt had started crashing in on her like the Pacific Ocean waves on the beach below.

Should she open the CNN app? Maybe flip on Good Morning America to catch the headlines? So far, she'd resisted, but barely, and that temptation was how she'd known what she needed to do next.

The hair on the back of her neck prickled for the umpteenth time. It had been happening all day, urging her to make her next move, sooner rather than later.

Piper spun around three hundred and sixty degrees, looking for the boogieman, relieved when she found she was alone on the balcony. Still, she couldn't shake the feeling she was being watched, which was ridiculous. No one knew where she was, except Danielle, and she'd only told her a few hours before.

The doorbell ringing made her jump. She looked down at her watch, relieved to see it had to be Danielle. Regardless, when she got to the front door, Piper didn't take any chances, peering through the peephole to confirm it was really her assistant. That Danielle was there didn't surprise her. What worried her was wondering if she'd followed instructions and come alone.

She'd have to risk it.

Piper turned the deadbolt lock and pulled off the chain before finally opening the door, so a tired looking Danielle could come in.

"Hey, thanks for coming."

"I didn't think I had a choice," she deadpanned, pulling a rolling suitcase behind her.

"Well, you could have resigned. That was a choice."

"Yeah, I sort of got that vibe."

Piper quickly shut and locked the door behind them, feeling better the second the lock was in place.

"You came alone?"

"No. I snuck Harry and Hermione in under my invisibility cloak." Arriving in the small kitchen of the rental house, Danielle turned and pinned her with a glare. "Of course, I came alone."

"You don't need to be a bitch about it."

"Really? Is that really what you want to say to me right now?" Danielle sassed.

"Well, since you're acting like a bitch, yeah, I guess so."

"That's rich. You wig out and disappear for a whole day,

leaving me to clean up the wake of your tornado without having a damn clue what the hell was going on, and I'm the bitch."

"What tornado? I wasn't supposed to travel this week, anyway."

"Did you forget about the People cover shoot today? And how about the production meeting tomorrow for the project you've just convinced investors to spend seventy million dollars on? And all of that pales in comparison to the boot Nolan Boeing and his assistant have had up my ass every damn hour on the hour. He called me drunk at three yesterday morning, demanding I produce you out of thin air."

Oops.

"Fine. I'm sorry."

"You're sorry. That's it?"

"What do you want me to say?"

"I don't want a damn apology. I want to know what's going on. Why can't you go back to your own house? What happened with you and Nolan? Why did you want me to bring your passport?"

"Stop! This, right here, is why I can't go home. I can't deal with these questions right now. I'm hanging on by a damn thread, and this isn't helping." Piper flailed her arms, trying to avoid eye contact.

Danielle was looking at her funny.

"What? What's wrong?"

"I thought he was crazy, but he was right."

"Who was right?"

"Nolan. He said you were scared. That you're gonna run away. I didn't believe him, but…"

"Would everyone please stop trying to psychoanalyze me? I'm a grown-ass woman. If I want to take a break, then I'll take a break."

"A break. In the middle of filming a movie? And as you're

kicking off one of the biggest productions you've ever led? I got news for you, that's not a break—that's career suicide."

Piper didn't need this bullshit, especially from an employee.

"And so, what if it is? It's my career. I already have enough money to last a lifetime."

"Uh huh. You keep telling yourself that. I got your Xanax prescription refilled. You should have a big enough supply to keep yourself nice and numb. Just know, one day you'll wake up and realize all you threw away."

Piper's head was pounding. She brushed past Danielle to stomp back out to the balcony overlooking the ocean, only to be followed.

The women stood at the railing, looking out over the water in silence. Finally, Danielle broke the awkward silence.

"Tell me what I can do to help."

"I can't talk about it."

"Can't or won't?"

"Does it matter?"

"I guess not. So now what?"

"I'm leaving the country tomorrow. I chartered a plane. I don't know for how long. I'd appreciate it if you'd let everyone who needs to know. I'm aware they'll press you for answers you don't have. Tell them I'm sick and under a doctor's care. Tell them I'll check in with you once a week."

"You'll have to assign someone else to get your updates."

"But..."

"I'm not going to sit around and wait for you to maybe come back. Maybe not. I'll get you through this week's cancelations, but that's it."

"You're deserting me?"

"That's rich, Piper. Last time I checked, you were the one running away here, not me."

"I'll keep paying you..."

"It isn't about the money. Like you, I already have plenty of money to tide me over."

"If not money, then..."

"I never told you why I took the job with you, did I?"

"I assumed it was because I offered it?"

"Like I told you already, I get two calls a week from people offering me jobs. I can get a higher paying job tomorrow. I didn't work for you because of the money."

"Okay, I'll bite. Why the hell did you want to work for me then?"

"I've worked for eleven other celebrities over the last fourteen years. They ranged from nightmares to sweet, but none of them had the drive to succeed as you do. Most were just in it for the celebrity perks.

"I've been honored to represent you. To watch you bring a room full of movie executive men to heel, not with your looks or sex appeal, but through ruthless business dealings. Don't ask me to watch you throw that all away."

Piper hated the words Danielle was saying, but she found it impossible to run away from them. She just wanted to bury her head in the sand, but her assistant had just done a spectacular job of slapping her in the face with all she'd be giving up.

Again.

"Listen, I don't know what happened. I'll deal with everything as you asked, but do me one favor. Please."

When Danielle didn't finish her sentence, Piper turned to see the woman was looking at her. Their eyes met.

"Call Nolan after I leave. He's a good man. Give him a chance to fix whatever he did wrong."

She wasn't going to cry, damnit. She also wasn't going to blame him for something he was as much a victim of as she was.

"Nolan didn't do anything wrong. I was the one who... never mind. Thanks again for coming." Piper reached into her pocket and came out with the keys to Nolan's car and handed them to

Danielle. "Please hold on to these until the day after tomorrow, then if you could, get them to Nolan with the address to this place. He can send someone to pick it up after I leave the country."

"So that's it, then." Danielle looked like she was about to cry too. "I can't change your mind?"

"Nope."

The women had never been touchy-feely with each other, so it caught Piper off-guard when Danielle leaned in to give her a tight hug before stepping back.

"I hope you know what you're doing, Piper. Good luck."

"Bye, Danielle. Thanks again for… well, everything."

Piper heard the rental property's grandfather clock striking three in the morning. She'd been tossing and turning for hours, trying to get a bit of rest before the car she'd arranged would be picking her up to go to the airport at eight. She just had a few more hours to make it through.

She'd been counting down the hours all day since Danielle left. With each hour that crawled by, she'd regretted not booking a flight that would be in the air already. She'd spent her afternoon on the beach, listening to the waves crashing like a metaphor for her life. A tiny voice in the back of her head had been trying to be heard, but Piper had done a good job of squelching it—at least while she'd been awake. Now, in the dark of the night, the voice was echoing louder, shouting she was making a huge mistake.

She'd charged her phone, knowing she'd need it for traveling, but that didn't mean she was stupid enough to turn it on. If she had any hope of keeping her location secret, she'd have to get a new number once she landed in France the next day.

The rumble of thunder in the distance taunted her,

reminding her of the storm brewing. She may be safely hidden tonight, but eventually, she'd have to go out into the storm, and there wasn't an umbrella large enough in the universe to protect her from the shit-storm of media coverage that would hound her if even one reporter caught wind of the secrets she'd carried with her.

In the dark of the night, she finally gave way to her inner angst, reminding her there was someone else—a frightened and beaten woman—who's own shitstorm was just beginning. Piper's heart hurt for the unknown housekeeper if that part of the story had even been correct. She prayed the poor woman had friends and family who would rally around her—believe her.

A bright flash of light was immediately followed by a booming thunder, so close it shook the house. Piper threw the covers off her body, crawling out of bed as if the rumbling had jostled her truly awake for the first time in days. On autopilot, she grabbed her silk robe, sliding it on as she padded down the hall from the bedroom into the main living room of her temporary hideout.

It wasn't really a conscious decision to turn on the flat-screen TV, fumbling with the unfamiliar remote until she was able to stop on CNN headline news.

She didn't dare sit down. She wasn't going to watch long enough to get comfortable, telling herself she was just going to make sure the newest victim of Henry Ainsworth was hopefully recovering, or better yet, the police had an iron-clad case against the powerful movie executive. Any little tidbit could press down the growing guilt swirling inside her and allow her to get some rest was welcome.

The volume on the TV was so low, she couldn't make out the reporter's words, but the candid picture snapped of a disheveled Shane Covington and Jaxson Cartwright-Davidson, exiting what looked like an emergency room surrounded by uniformed police had her scrambling to find the volume on the clicker.

"Our reporters outside Cedar-Sinai Hospital have not been able to confirm the reports the unconscious victim, claiming to have been assaulted by Henry Ainsworth, was carried, naked and bleeding, into the emergency room by Oscar-nominated superstar, Shane Covington. Witnesses in the ER at the time of their arrival are telling CNN reporters, both Covington and Jaxson Cartwright-Davidson were covered in blood and appeared to be soaking wet, dripping water on the floor of the hospital as they screamed for medical assistance for the unidentified woman.

"Requests for interviews to their spokespersons have gone unanswered, but unofficial accounts are coming in that the young woman was an employee at Cartwright-Davidson's popular dance club and hotel, Runway. Multiple witnesses have reported seeing Covington eating dinner with the mystery woman at the club, but as no electronics are allowed on the property, CNN is unable to substantiate these rumors at this time."

The picture above the anchor's shoulder changed from Shane and Jax to a mug shot of Henry Ainsworth, looking as smug as ever.

"A judge today denied Henry Ainsworth bond, remanding him to custody in the Los Angeles County Jail while awaiting arraignment. CNN will have reporters on hand at an official press conference later this morning at ten o'clock local time. The press conference has been called by the District Attorney's office in conjunction with the Beverly Hills Police Department Special Victim's Unit and will be held at the downtown L.A. DA's office.

"In other news..."

Piper turned off the TV, throwing the remote down on the table next to her with more force than necessary. Her brain was exploding with unwanted images. The TV had been on less than three short minutes, yet she knew with a certainty rarely felt, those three minutes had changed the trajectory of her life forever.

Feeling like her heart was about to pound right out of her chest, she started pacing wildly, stomping through the empty and dark house, manically going from room to room and back again. Within minutes, her private refuge felt more like her own personal prison. She was stuck there, alone, with only her nightmarish memories and crushing guilt as a companion.

This wasn't her fault. None of it. She tried repeating that in her head, but her heart was having none of it.

If only I'd been stronger.

Anxiety was closing in. She managed to take sips of air into her lungs as the wave of nausea threatened to have her dinner reappearing. Feeling lightheaded, she knew she needed fresh air.

Piper stumbled through the dark house, out onto the massive balcony overlooking the ocean below. The soundtrack of crashing waves were the perfect duet to the rumbling thunder—heavy drops of cold rain, the appropriate wake-up call for her life.

She forced down the temptation to return to the house to find the bottle of Xanax. While her brain wasn't capable of rational thought, her heart ached with the knowledge the medicine was just a band-aid. For years, it, along with alcohol, had numbed her. But tonight, with rare clarity, she knew the bottles of prescription drugs and years of counseling hadn't cured a damn thing. She'd told herself she'd been healing—improving.

That was a lie.

Piper forced herself to withstand the harsh elements, punishing herself for being weak. By the time the sky started to lighten sometime later, she was cold, wet, and shivering. On autopilot, she stumbled into the house, heading directly into the master bathroom, turning on the shower's water and stepping into the tub, clothes and all.

The burst of cold water took her breath away, but in less than a minute, the temperature turned from cold to burning hot. She welcomed the pain—a small punishment for her many transgressions—letting the water wash the tears that now fell down the drain.

When the water started to cool a long time later, Piper finally turned off the water, stripping off her wet nightgown and robe, leaving them pooled in the tub as she walked back to the bedroom, dripping water as she went.

She hadn't planned it. It just happened. The Apple icon lit up the display of her phone as she pressed power. Within seconds, notifications started pelting her from every app—emails, over a dozen phone calls, even more unanswered texts and voicemails. With each flash across the screen, her anxiety grew.

Most were from Danielle and Nolan. She'd expected those. It was the last text from Shane Covington that gutted her.

~

We need to talk. Boeing says you have info I need. He won't give me details. He's protecting you. I respect that, but you need to call me ASAP.

~

Another text a minute later was short and sweet.

~

Please, Piper. I love her.

~

Fuck.

~

The trio's house was relatively deserted now compared to the last two action-packed days. Still, in the quiet of the night, he couldn't shake the ringing in his ears the nurse, Sarah, had told him was brought on by the stress he was under.

Shane was exhausted, yet sleep just wouldn't come. He'd been grateful to have escaped having to attend yesterday's press conference with the DA's office and the Beverly Hills Police Department.

He wouldn't be as lucky in the morning. Unbelievably, they were coming up on the deadline for the DA to charge Ainsworth or have to cut him loose. The good news was, they'd processed the evidence found with the search warrant and confirmed Nalani's DNA on his shoes and the whip the barbarian had used on her body. The bad news was, the fucker's slick lawyer had the DA spooked, claiming that sex between them had been consensual and had taken place at Runway. Without his DNA or fingerprints found in her apartment, the DA was reluctant to proceed with charges unless additional evidence surfaced.

So, like it or not, he and Jaxson would be attending the press conference later that morning, not only to lend support to Nalani's side of the story but more importantly, make a public plea for additional victims to come forward.

It hurt his heart to think Piper Kole might be one such victim, but that pain hadn't stopped him from texting her to beg her to help them if she had any information that could put Ainsworth behind bars for the rest of his life. It was tempting to be angry at her for not calling him back, but all he had to do was picture her going through what Nalani was going through, and he couldn't be mad.

His brain kept turning over the fast-changing details of the case, preferring to focus on the legal hurdles over the much harder to face emotional mountains that lay in front of him and Nalani.

"Shane?" Nalani's hoarse whisper pulled him out of his spiral of worry.

He flipped the lever of the recliner he'd been lounging in next to Nalani's rented hospital bed, springing the chair forward.

"I'm here, kitten."

The warm glow of the small lamp on the other side of the bed was the only light. Still, the dim lighting couldn't hide the darkening bruises across her beautiful face. Her hand gripped his, squeezing hard to keep him close as her grimace of pain broke his heart. He had never felt as neutered as he had in the last few days.

"What can I get you, baby? Anything."

That was a lie. He knew the only thing Nalani really needed was a time machine so they could go back to Sunday. He'd have made her go to the Oscars with him. Better yet, he'd have stayed home with her. How he wished he could go back to be the one waiting for Ainsworth in that tiny apartment. Of course, then he'd be the one behind bars tonight—waiting to be charged with murder because he had no doubt that if he were in a room alone with Ainsworth for five minutes, he would have absolutely no problem ending him.

"Just need you," she whispered, squeezing his hand harder.

"I was worried I'd hurt you more if I laid next to you."

"Can't hurt me more. Please…"

Shane crawled gingerly into the small space next to her on the bed, being as careful as he could not to injure her more or worse, pull out any of the many medical devices she had attached to her.

"You need to get back to sleep. Rest is the best thing for you right now," he urged once they were as settled as they could be.

"Can't sleep. Hate to close my eyes and remember…"

God, he sure as hell understood that problem.

What might make her feel better?

"You know, he's in jail now, right? He'll never be able to hurt you, or anyone else, ever again."

"He's been there before. He'll get out again."

He hated the certainty in her voice as if Ainsworth getting away with his crimes was a foregone conclusion.

"Not if I have anything to say about it." He bit his tongue from sharing all the horrific deaths he had imagined for Henry Ainsworth. He knew those wouldn't bring Nalani any comfort.

It left them in awkward silence. He was glad they couldn't see each other's faces as they laid next to each other, her on her back, him curled up next to her. He finally broke the silence with a lame confession.

"I don't know what to say."

"It's okay. Neither do I."

"Do you want to talk about it?" he offered, praying she wouldn't take him up on the offer.

"I can't. Not yet."

"It's okay. I'm not sure I'm ready to hear the details yet."

Under his arm, he could feel Nalani's shaking turning into full-out convulsion-like tremors throughout her whole body.

"Are you cold? I can get more blankets."

"Not really," she bit out.

Shane sat up, reaching for the small clicker on the other side of the bed. "Have you hit your pain med button this hour? Remember, Sarah said it won't let you overdose yourself."

"No!" she cried out as he went to pick up the medication delivery button.

"But you're in pain. The meds will help. You're shaking."

"That's not it." She hesitated. Their eyes met, and he saw the anguish in her gaze as she added, "It's the meth withdrawal."

"But it was only one dose. You shouldn't be having such a strong reaction. I'm sure the meds will help."

Nalani clutched his arm, fighting through a fresh wave of pain. He resumed his search in the dim lighting for the button to give her the pain meds.

"Don't want any more drugs," she begged.

"Kitten, that's insane. You need drugs to help you through the worst of the pain."

"Too addictive."

He didn't understand why she was fighting him on this.

"Nalani, you need the medicine to take the edge off the pain. You won't get addicted from just a few doses over a few days."

"It's too late for that."

He wasn't following her reasoning. She wasn't thinking clearly. She needed him to make the hard decisions right now. He was about to press the small button to deliver pain meds when Nalani shouted, flailing wildly.

"No more drugs!"

Her sudden agitation caught him off-guard. His right arm got tangled up in her IV feed and almost pulled it out of the back of her hand.

"Okay. Okay. Settle down. Let's talk about this."

"Nothing to talk about. No. More. Drugs."

"Nalani, baby, you're in incredible pain. You've been through hell. There's nothing wrong with taking medicine to help."

"Maybe for most people, but not for me."

"I don't understand." He truly didn't. He was hovering above her on the bed and could see the anguish on her face—more than pain or fear.

Nothing could have prepared him for her next words.

"I'm a recovering drug addict, Shane."

"Say what?"

Tears flooded her swollen eyes and spilled down the sides of her cheeks.

"You need to distance yourself from me now while you can. The only thing that could make this whole thing any worse is if I end up hurting your reputation. The media is never going to let it go when they find the truth."

Shane didn't think his brain could get more overwhelmed with confusing thoughts and emotions—he'd been wrong.

"I don't understand. I've never even seen you take an aspirin."

"Exactly. I don't take anything. I can already feel myself starting to go through withdrawal. It's going to get way worse before it gets better. I can't let you see me like this."

"You aren't making any sense. Ainsworth only gave you one dose. People don't get hooked on just one dose."

"It's been six years, but this was far from my first time on meth. God, I hate this. I was so sure we'd break up before I ever had to tell you the truth."

"Break up? What the fuck are you talking about?" Shane knew he needed to rein in his anger. He hated the flood of fear he saw shining back at him from Nalani's swollen eyes. He'd frightened her.

"I'm sorry. I didn't mean to scare you. I just don't understand what you're talking about."

"Of course, you don't because I lied to you."

Shane's brain exploded as possible explanations for her words tried to form. Nothing was making sense.

"What did you lie about?"

"Technically, it was more of a lie through omission, not a real lie. Still, it doesn't change anything. You need to get away from me as fast as possible before the media take you down with me."

"You're gonna have to connect the dots for me here, kitten. I'm not following you at all."

Nalani closed her eyes, letting more tears spill down her cheeks as she tried to tell her story.

"My father and brother were the biggest crystal meth dealers in Hawaii for many years. Right up until they went to prison when I was sixteen. They might get out by 2028 if they are granted parole."

What the hell? Her closest family members were in prison? Still…

"Fuck, I'm so damn sorry, but what the hell does that have to do with you taking pain meds?"

"It's only going to take the press a few minutes after finding my real identity to find out I was in prison once too. Well technically, it was a juvenile detention center, but…"

Her words made no sense. She was the sweetest, most innocent woman he'd ever met. There was no way…

"I don't believe you. Why are you saying these things? Are you hallucinating from the pain?"

Her bark of incredulous laughter haunted him.

"Oh, how I wish it was all just a big nightmare, but I'm afraid it's the truth. My family started using me when I was only twelve to help deliver drugs. They knew as a minor, I could go undetected longer, and even if I were caught, it wouldn't be as big of a deal.

"At first, I didn't even understand, but I caught on quickly. When I threatened to turn them in to the police when I was fourteen, they decided getting me hooked on the product was the best way to keep me quiet. Once they made me crave it, they had me. I did anything they asked, just to keep my next fix coming.

"I tried so hard to resist it. I really did, but each time I'd get close to weaning myself off, my brother would hold me down, dad would inject me, and just like that, I was back in.

"Ainsworth hurt me in many despicable ways, but it was the injection of meth that was the most horrible atrocity he did to me. I know the drill. It's going to take weeks, if not months, to put this setback behind me.

"So, no more drugs. I can't risk getting addicted to anything else."

The ringing in Shane's ears got so loud, he worried he wasn't hearing Nalani correctly. What she was saying couldn't be true. It just couldn't. It was too horrifying to think of her being abused by her own family.

Shane's brain was scrambled, flooded with more thoughts than he could process.

"Are you alright?" she whispered.

She was so selfless. She was the one who'd been brutally injured, yet she was more worried about him. He didn't deserve her. Still, her revelations blew his mind. Was he all right?

Shane hugged her tighter as he tried his best to reassure her.

"Nalani, I don't give a rats ass about your childhood, other than I wish I could have been there for you back then. No one deserves to go through what you did with your family, but that has absolutely nothing to do with how I feel about you today. If anything, it makes me love you more. I can't even imagine how hard things have been for you."

"Wait. You love me?"

Her question was so soft he almost missed it. He replayed his words and realized it was the first time she'd heard him say them. He needed to fix that. He lifted up so he could look into her eyes again. Her tears were back.

"Of course, I love you. If I had any doubts, they were gone when I realized how lost I'd be if you weren't here."

"Oh, Shane, I didn't dare even dream you could feel for me the way I felt for you. But you shouldn't. You can have anyone you want in the whole world. Please don't stay with me because you feel guilty, or you just want to protect me. I don't want your pity."

Shane reached up to cup her face gently, using his thumb to swish away a tear.

"Listen to me, kitten. I'm not here out of pity or guilt. And you say I can have anyone in the world I want, then that includes you. I want you. So, I need to ask you. Do you trust me?"

"Of course. I wouldn't even be here if you hadn't found me."

God, he hoped that wasn't true, but they would never know for sure. There was only one thing he did know with complete certainty at that moment.

"Then you need to trust me now that you need… no, wait… you *deserve* to use every tool we can to lessen your suffering. I understand with your history, it's riskier, but let's just take one problem at a time. My first priority is to heal your body and to do that, you need to get good, pain-free rest. Then, if we have to, we'll deal with weaning you off the pain meds. You've done it before when you were alone. This time, you'll have so much help."

The sobs that wracked her body as she hugged him broke his heart. His Nalani had been through so much in her young life. He worried there may be other secrets he had yet to uncover, but tonight, he knew she was the bravest woman he'd ever met. After all she'd been through, then and now, she was still only thinking of others.

The decision was easy. When Nalani's emotional sobs turned to groans of agony as the pain attacked the dozens of wounds on her shaking body, Shane pressed the button, sending the needed medicine into her blood stream, taking only a minute for her to begin to calm. He could feel the tension releasing from her body as the torment in her eyes dimmed, replaced with a soft glaze.

He suspected she would be angry with him later. He rejected the comparison of what he'd just done to her to what her father and brother had done years before, but the truth was, all the men in her life had drugged her against her will. He could tell himself a thousand times he'd done it for her own good, but he hated himself at that moment.

Nalani's breathing calmed until she dozed off into a fitful sleep. He finally laid his head back down on the pillow next to her, letting her long, dark hair tickle his cheek. Her words rattled around in his head, mingling with the horrific visions haunting him.

He wouldn't be getting any rest that night.

CHAPTER 25

It was standing room only in a room clearly too small for the event. The fact the DA had scheduled the press briefing in the downtown district office meant Nolan had spent ninety minutes in traffic to barely make it on time, but nothing was going to stop him from being in the room for this update.

He knew what the herd of news and media outlets lined up with their expensive cameras and microphones didn't. They'd come to hear the Chief of Police and the Assistant District Attorney lay out the charges against Henry Ainsworth, but thanks to details his own private investigators had already turned up, today's news was just the tip of the iceberg.

Nolan wiggled into a small space against the back wall, near the far corner, out of the way of the fireworks that were about to ignite. He patted his suit jacket, comforted by the feel of the small packet of documents he'd brought along that had been provided by the private investigator he'd hired. He wasn't a particularly religious man, but he prayed he would never need to use the evidence they'd dredged up, for many reasons. If the Los Angeles County and Beverly Hills police did their jobs right, the five-year-old heartbreaking story outlined in his pocket would never need to hit the light of day.

He knew with clarity, even if Piper would end up hating him, there was no way he would stay quiet forever if it meant Henry Ainsworth would walk free. That fucker would be spending the rest of his life behind bars, one way or another. Nolan just prayed it wouldn't mean having to go public with a story that wasn't his to tell. A story he knew just the bare details about.

He didn't have to wait long. A line of officials and uniformed officers ushered in from a door behind the platform where a table with a podium and microphone waited. They lined up, looking sober.

At the end of the line of officials was a furious Shane Covington and Jaxson Cartwright-Davidson, accompanied by two other men, both he'd seen at Black Light in the past. He was pretty sure the burly Hispanic guy was part of Davidson's security detail, and the other was a lawyer.

The four men may have been relegated to standing along the sidelines of the stage, but it was a clear statement to the dozens of reporters in the room, they were there to support Nalani's case.

After a quick conference on the stage between the officials, a uniformed police officer stepped to the podium, reaching out to turn on the microphone before speaking.

"Thank you for coming this morning, ladies and gentlemen. My name is Doug Johnson, and I am the chief of police for the city of Beverly Hills. Before I begin our official statement, I want to set some ground rules. I realize there is much media interest in this developing story. Our investigation is only beginning, and therefore, I will intentionally keep my remarks brief. My department, along with the LA County's DA office, will schedule additional updates as further details become available.

"In addition, we won't be taking questions today." The room broke out in a groan. "I'm aware you have many inquiries, but until we are confident we have the right answers, we will hold off on providing too many details.

"What I can share with you is the following. On or around February 5th, Henry Ainsworth allegedly sexually harassed an employee of the Runway club and hotel on Country Club Drive. That unnamed woman did not press charges at the time but did report the incident to her supervisor.

"In subsequent interactions between the accused and his accuser, additional verbal threats were raised until last Sunday, when the Beverly Hills Police were called to Runway in response to a physical attack on the same young woman. Henry Ainsworth was placed under arrest and taken into custody while at Runway by my uniformed police officers. He was then transported to the police station for questioning.

"An official police report was not immediately filed by the woman accuser, and based on Mr. Ainsworth's standing in the community and lack of criminal record, the judge on duty that weekend allowed Mr. Ainsworth to post bond and leave the jail on his own recognizance until such time he could appear in court.

"Later that night, the still unnamed woman returned home after work and was attacked in her apartment by an assailant who pushed himself into her apartment. She has accused Henry Howard Ainsworth of beating and sexually assaulting her for an undetermined length of time, then threatening her to remain silent before departing.

"We are in the process of testing physical evidence collected both at her apartment as well as on her person after she was transported to the Cedar-Sinai Trauma Center. She arrived at the hospital at approximately 2:23 a.m. on Monday morning. While my department will not be releasing the young woman's identity or a detailed description of her physical injuries, I can confirm, she was indeed the victim of a heinous sexual assault."

The chief of police paused, giving the whispers that had broken out in the room time to die down. Before continuing, he looked over his right shoulder at Jaxson and Shane, who nodded slightly.

"There has been much speculation regarding the victim's arrival at the hospital and her relationship to those who transported her there. I have been authorized by the parties involved to confirm the victim was transported in the private SUV of her employer, Jaxson Cartwright-Davidson. Also, in the vehicle was her significant other, Shane Covington. Davidson and Covington had found the victim lying unconscious after breaking into her apartment to perform a wellness check when she failed to respond to their phone calls and texts."

The room erupted into a chorus of questions shouted in the direction of Shane and Jaxson, but the men remained silent, facing forward, refusing to interact with the media circus. Only after the chief got the crowd to quiet down did he continue.

"While I wish the men had waited for the police and ambulance to arrive on the scene, they made the decision that they could transport the victim the few blocks to the hospital faster, thus removing much of the physical evidence from the crime scene without my forensics team processing first. While I initially considered their actions as reckless tampering with evidence, the victim's doctors have assured me, the injuries sustained were serious enough, every minute was critical, and therefore, their actions are to be commended.

"At the present time, Henry Ainsworth remains in custody, pending the outcome of our investigation. I am acutely aware we have only twenty-four more hours to formalize what, if any, charges will be filed in this case. My detectives and forensics teams are working non-stop on this high-profile case and will hold a follow-up press conference tomorrow at the same time in this same location. Until then, that concludes today's update."

The room erupted in questions, again being shouted at everyone on the stage. Nolan hadn't expected much more than this today, but he had thought the DA would at least have the balls to speak about the possible charges they were considering bringing against the movie mogul.

The crowd of officials on the stage were readying themselves to file back out when shouts from the back of the room drew everyone's attention. When Nolan swung around to follow their gaze, his heart nearly exploded.

The chaos in the room hushed. As one, everyone on the stage looked at the door where a stoic Piper stood silently. The crowds parted as if she were Moses, somehow knowing she had something important to say. Why else would the award-winning actress be here in this media circus?

She'd come. As much as he'd goaded her into doing this very thing through his texts, now that the moment of truth was here, he worried he'd made a mistake. What if she wasn't strong enough? What if she broke down in front of the global media?

Nolan's heart hurt, watching her. To the crowd, she looked like her moniker, the Ice Queen, strong as Teflon. She'd dressed in all black, her thick, dark hair pulled back in an all-business ponytail. As she took her first steps forward, she reached to take off the dark sunglasses she'd been hiding behind. Even from the distance, he could see the lines around her eyes, betraying her lack of sleep, and the whites of her eyes were pink, no doubt from crying.

Without a plan, he slowly started pushing through the gaggle of reporters between them, jockeying to get closer to her. He was torn. He wanted so badly to help her through what she was about to do, but he knew there was a pretty good chance he could make things worse for her if she saw him in the crowd.

Unwilling to risk it, he was careful to stand behind one of the larger cameras.

The din in the room increased as everyone whispered to their neighbors, guessing why Piper Kole had just walked up the few steps to the stage. Nolan fought the urge to storm up to the front, placating himself with the knowledge Davidson, Covington, and the head of their security had stepped forward from their sideline perch to crowd in around Piper. He trusted them to keep her safe from anything rowdy that might break out. Sadly, they couldn't do shit to help her through the emotional rollercoaster he suspected she was on.

He couldn't even imagine the kind of courage it had taken her to walk into this building… this room—to willingly insert herself into the middle of the biggest Hollywood media circus of the decade. This was the kind of drama that had TV miniseries written all over it.

There was no way anyone could pick up what was being said by the crowd of officials on the stage, but he recognized the growing agitation on Davidson's and Covington's faces. He fought down his jealousy when they each leaned in to hug the woman he loved. He didn't try to hide his smile when he watched her shoving them away.

She doesn't need hugs, boys. She's about to go to war.

You could hear a pin drop as the DA nodded, and Piper spun in the direction of the center podium. It was subtle, but he saw her square her shoulders before walking bravely to the microphone. Her hands trembled as she took a piece of paper from her jacket pocket and held it in front of her. For a minute, he thought she might back out, then she gripped the edge of the podium and spoke.

"Hello. My name is Piper Kole. I am here to officially inform the District Attorney of Los Angeles County and the Police Chief of Beverly Hills that I am coming forward as a material witness in the felony sexual assault and battery charges being brought against Henry Howard Ainsworth.

"To be clear, I do not have information directly related to the rape and torture of his most recent victim." Piper broke her visual connection with the room to look down at the shaking piece of paper in front of her. For a minute, he thought she might bolt from the room. When she looked back up, he saw the tracks of tears silently streaming down her face. It took every ounce of his self-control to stay rooted to his spot, instead of rushing to her side.

"However, I do have direct knowledge of previous felonies of this nature committed by the same piece of shit, excuse for a human being, Henry Ainsworth."

The room erupted at her accusation.

That's my girl. Stay mad.

"In May of 2015, I traveled to Budapest, Hungary, for on-location filming for the movie I would later win my Best Leading Actress Oscar and Golden Globe award for.

"Over the course of filming, Henry Ainsworth engaged in systematic and calculated sexual abuse of two women. The first was an actress by the name of Mari Lynn Martin. While Mari had only a small role, her excitement for the industry was contagious. She was a bright light on the set… until she wasn't. Overnight, she turned into a fearful, reserved woman who cried easily. When I tried to talk to her about what was wrong, she was terrified. Within days, the rope burns on her wrists and bruises along her neck were impossible to ignore. Without knowing who had been abusing her, I stormed into the production office to report my concern to the producer of the project, Henry Ainsworth and the director, Donald Harrigan.

"To say I was disappointed by their lack of action was an understatement. I threatened to walk off the project if they didn't report the abuse to the local authorities, so an investigation could be opened. They finally assured me in that meeting, the police would be called. I left, feeling I had done the right thing.

"That night, when I returned to my hotel, I was informed there had been a pipe break in the room above mine. Because of water damage, they were upgrading me to a penthouse apartment. I was escorted to that secluded room by the head of security of the Budapest Marriott.

"I share these details because waiting for me in that room was a furious Henry Ainsworth. While the director Donald Harrigan was not present, I have no doubt he had full knowledge of what happened to me over the course of the twenty-four hours because the entire filming schedule had to be modified as the lead actress was not available for filming."

Nolan's heart hurt watching. He wanted to throw his hands over his ears to block her words, but if she were brave enough to say them, he sure as hell would be brave enough to listen. He took his eyes off her for a split second to glance around the room. She had everyone transfixed, hanging on her every syllable.

"Over the next day, I was tied in the most despicable positions. Every part of my body was beaten. He used his belt, the buckle end, to pummel me because he said he loved to hear me scream. His hands strangled me to near death more than once. His feet kicked me until I had three cracked ribs. I wasn't allowed food or water and became dehydrated.

"But the worst were the horrific words and names he spewed as he raped me more times than I can possibly count. No matter how many doctors I've talked to or anxiety drugs I have taken since that time in my life, the memories have dogged me relentlessly. It has impacted every aspect of my life, including my career, my friendships, and my personal relationships.

"Adding insult to injury, by taking horrific photos, framed in a way that made it look like I was enjoying myself, he was able to blackmail me. To silence me when I should have been shouting about his crimes from the rooftop. He repeatedly pointed out that anything that might have happened had been in a foreign country, where the American justice system couldn't touch him, so coming forward to you, the press, would only hurt me.

"I am deeply ashamed I've remained silent all of these years. I want to personally apologize to each and every one of what I worry might be dozens of victims he's abused in the years since I was silenced. I will have to live with the fact that had I been braver back then, perhaps they could have been spared the hell he put them through.

"Before you all leave here and try to use this press conference to gain higher ratings for your news programs or better sales for your newspapers and magazines, I have one favor to ask you, the media. For one minute, put yourself in the shoes of just one of his victims. He preys on naive women who want to trust an authority figure in our lives. Henry Ainsworth took that away from us. When you cover the many victims who begin to come forward, remember that. We are more than just a housekeeper, which is how Nalani is being described. And yes, I am well aware, in spite of her name being withheld, you, the media, have somehow uncovered her real identity and will use it to dog her relentlessly. It sickens me that most of you wouldn't even be here if Shane and Jaxson hadn't come forward with her to somehow legitimize what she's gone through."

Piper's voice broke as a sob escaped. He couldn't hold back anymore. Nolan rushed forward, taking the stairs two at a time to the stage. His movement caught her attention, and Piper looked up, afraid that someone was about to hurt her. The relief in her eyes when she saw it was him gave him hope they might somehow find a way through this mess. She shook her head slightly, waving him off. There was no way he would be leaving her alone on that stage again. Nolan took up his spot next to

Jaxson, nodding to her to let her know he would be standing with her.

Piper finally found her voice to continue.

"I am even more ashamed to admit, I most likely wouldn't be standing here if it weren't for the fact my good friend Shane Covington's heart is broken because the woman he loves has been hurt. Or for the fact, the most recent abuse started at the place of business of my dear friends Jaxson, Chase, and Emma Cartwright-Davidson.

"I have just two more things to add. My assistant, Danielle Chapman, is currently being escorted by several detectives to the local branch of my bank, where they will be retrieving the contents of a lockbox I rented just over four years ago. Inside that box are the photos used to blackmail me, along with multiple pieces of physical evidence that will prove, without a shadow of a doubt, Henry Ainsworth not only raped and tortured me, but he then persisted in terrorizing me over the next six months until I successfully got him to disengage by blackmailing him back. I am aware my own actions during that time may have been criminal in nature, and I will accept any punishment, legal or monetary, that result from the investigation.

"The final thing I will add is, in the safe deposit box is a grainy voice recording of Henry Ainsworth taunting me backstage at the Golden Globes that same year. I recorded him without his knowledge and, again, will accept any consequence of my illegal activity. On that tape, you will hear Henry gloat that he continued to abuse Mari until she felt she had no other option but to take her own life on November 21, 2015. I regret I didn't do more to help Mari at the time, but truthfully, I could barely get through a single day myself without breaking down. I am no longer that scared young woman, and I will no longer stand on the sideline and watch Henry Ainsworth systematically destroy women's lives without consequence.

"Before I turn this press conference back over to the police, I want to speak directly to the scared women at home watching this right now. I know how you feel. I've walked in your shoes. I understand how hard it is to come forward when so often, it will be you who is made out to be at fault. I thought by staying quiet and turning myself into an Ice Queen, it would just go away, but I was wrong. The only way to get our power back is to make the assholes who hurt us pay. So, if Henry Ainsworth has harassed or abused you in the past, I implore you to be brave, come forward. I will stand next to you. If it was someone else who hurt you—a teacher, minister, parent, relative—know that you didn't do anything wrong.

"I didn't start the #MeToo movement, and unfortunately, I don't have the power to make the abuse end either, but Henry Ainsworth has stolen so much of my past from me."

Piper's voice broke as she turned to stare straight into Nolan's eyes.

"I draw the line at allowing him to steal my future too."

His heart exploded with love for the most amazing woman to ever walk the earth.

Piper turned back to the waiting media, and through her sobs, she spoke.

"My name is Piper Kole. I was raped and beaten by Henry Ainsworth. I know without a shadow of a doubt, he is responsible for the same abuse of Mari Martin and Nalani Ione and suspect, of many other women yet to come forward. Thank you for listening to me today."

SHE'D DONE IT. God help her, as she stood there looking out into the sea of shouting reporters being held at bay by a half dozen security guards, the harsh truth of what she'd done slapped her hard. Her life would never again be the same.

Piper's legs turned to spaghetti beneath her. She would have fallen had Nolan not been there to scoop her up into his arms. Like her Prince Charming, he was there to catch her. Only they were living in a nightmare, not a fairy tale. There wasn't going to be a happily-ever-after. After all, she was damaged goods.

"I've got you, baby. Nothing's going to hurt you again."

Oh, how she wanted to believe him as he hugged her close against his chest, heading toward the side door behind the authorities also leaving the stage. It would be so easy to relax into him, to let him wrap her in a cocoon where nothing could hurt her—but not even Nolan Boeing was that powerful.

She'd expected him to whisk her out of sight of the cameras, so when he merely carried her to the edge of the stage, then slowly lowered her legs, Piper was confused. Why wasn't he getting them the hell out of the media circus?

Once her feet hit the floor, he stayed close, holding her until her legs grew steady enough to hold her up. When she focused on the knot of his perfectly tied tie, Nolan's index finger found her chin, gently lifting her face until she had to close her eyes to avoid eye contact.

She'd dug deep to be brave enough to walk to the microphone. She'd done it for Nalani and others like her. And for her friend Shane, and Jaxson, and so many unknown victims she'd yet to meet. But until this very minute, she hadn't realized just how afraid she was of Nolan's reaction to all that had happened in the years they'd been torn apart by Henry Ainsworth. He might not have been physically abused, but Nolan surely was a victim of Ainsworth too.

"Open your eyes, baby." His arm around her waist tightened, holding her close while she felt him slipping away emotionally.

Piper leaned in, placing her forehead on his shoulder. To a casual observer, their embrace looked intimate, but she knew the truth. She needed to pull away, do anything she could to avoid seeing his disappointment and disapproval.

"Please, Nolan. I can't do this. Not here. Not now... hell, not ever."

"Piper, as far as I'm concerned, you walk on water. You can do anything you put your mind to."

"Yeah, right," she scoffed. "I just blew up Hollywood, my career, and our relationship in the space of ten minutes. Aren't you scandalized?"

"You didn't blow up anything except Henry Ainsworth. That bastard better pray he never sees the light of day because I'm positive I'm capable of strangling him with my bare hands for what he's put you through."

He was saying all the right things, but...

"Why didn't you just carry me out of here? I can still hear the cameras clicking. Everyone is getting off on watching us."

"Yep. That's why I put you down. Please. Look at me, baby."

"Why? So, you can feel sorry for me?"

"Now. Eyes." It was a command. She wasn't used to listening to commands.

He waited for her. When she finally peered into his gorgeous eyes, her heart constricted with pain. He was so damn handsome, it hurt.

"Listen up. I didn't carry you out because you are Piper Fucking Kole. You are the strongest, most beautiful, wittiest woman I've ever met. In private, I promise to carry you whenever you need me to. Say the word, and I'll be there. But here... today... you're gonna walk out of here with your head held high. You have nothing to feel guilty about. Not a damn thing to be sorry for."

It took a minute for her brain to process the words he was saying.

"But if I'd been..."

"Stop. You've been through hell. No one in their right mind is going to blame you for any of this."

"Are you so sure about that? I'm pretty sure Shane

Covington is going to blame me for not speaking up earlier, so Nalani wouldn't have been exposed to the devil."

"You aren't responsible for Ainsworth's actions any more than I am, and Covington knows that. You came forward now. You're taking a stand. He'll feel nothing but gratitude for what you've done."

Piper prayed that was true, but were the situation reversed, she wasn't so sure she would.

Nolan leaned in, placing a gentle kiss on Piper's lips before pulling back and smiling down at her.

"Let's go home, Piper."

"Home? Where the hell is that?" She was only half kidding. She was supposed to be on a plane to France… ready to start the next chapter of her life without Nolan—without everything she loved.

And at that moment, she was honest enough with herself to admit, she loved Nolan.

"Baby, home for me is wherever you are. You want to take a trip out of the country, I'll help you pack and will even carry the bags. You want to go to your house… or mine? Either place, we have blackout curtains ready and waiting. All I want is to wake up in your bed next to you every day for the rest of our lives. Don't forget, I plan on rooming with you in the old folks' home."

Memories of their phone call just a few weeks before made her smile. So much had happened since then.

"Better watch out, Boeing. That sounds like a dangerous proposal."

"Yeah, well, I fell in love with Mistress Ice, so danger is my middle name."

"I think I'm the one in danger. You seem to be doing a pretty good job of melting my ice. Pretty soon, I'm going to just be a puddle of water melted on the floor at your feet."

"That sounds like a great scene we can work on next time we're at Black Light. You on the floor at my feet..."

"Fat chance. You'll be the one on your knees, Boeing."

"I can live with that, but I do have one small favor."

Piper could see the mischief playing in his eyes. She was afraid to ask.

"Just one? And what that might be?"

His grin was perfect.

"Any chance I can start getting a discounted price? This spending a hundred grand every week is getting a bit expensive."

Despite how heavy the morning's events had been, Piper unbelievably broke out into a chuckle. She couldn't help herself.

At that moment, the ideal sassy response came to her. Dare she?

"Sorry, Boeing, but you're gonna have to spend a hundred grand one more time, then you can take a break."

"Oh? And what will I be getting for my investment? Think we can squeak out a full weekend this time?"

"Actually, I was thinking a bit longer term than that."

"A whole week?"

"Longer."

Nolan's eyes widened, starting to understand what she was hinting at.

"Piper..."

She had to swallow a couple of times to push down the lump in her throat. For the second time that morning, she found it difficult to find the right words. She could see the hope in Nolan's eyes as he waited.

"I've had my eye on a particularly flawless, six-carat, pear-shape diamond to add to my collection."

"I see. Any particular setting you plan on putting your new ice into?"

Piper was usually the last person to play coy, but nothing seemed usual lately.

"I think I'll leave that up to you, Mr. Boeing. But for the record, my ring size is six."

"I'll have to get right on that. I think while I'm at it, I'll order a nice companion piece. Something else I'm pretty certain you don't have in your collection yet."

"Oh? And what's that? A diamond nipple ring?"

Nolan took her by the hand, and they finally started down the stairs toward the exit as he answered her.

"No, I'll save that for our one-year anniversary. I was thinking about a nice collar you can wear to Black Light, along with a jewel studded leash, so I can make sure you never try to get away from me again."

One-year anniversary, indeed.

Despite the heaviness of the morning's events, as Nolan wrapped his arm around her waist, Piper realized she hadn't felt this light in… well, forever. She was sure a big part of her relief was getting her secrets out into the open as ugly as they were. At that moment, she knew the time was right to share her final secret.

"You know, I do have one more thing I recently realized I've been hiding from everyone, including myself. I wasn't brave enough to confess it at the podium, but I kinda think I should at least tell you now."

Nolan stopped them in their tracks, spinning her so he could pin her with that yummy dominant look of his.

"You can tell me anything, Piper. We can't have any more secrets between us."

"I couldn't agree more. That's why I decided to be brave and tell you…" Piper paused dramatically before smiling. "I love you. Well, technically, I love The Rock," she teased, "But since you're kind of a package deal, I guess I can love all of you."

Nolan's eyes widened with surprise. Within seconds, Piper

found herself scooped up, back into his arms as he took long strides toward the exit.

"I thought you wanted me to walk out of here on my own two feet."

"That was before."

"Before what?" she pressed.

"Before I made up my mind to jump your bones, the second we get into the back of the car. My driver is in for an eyeful."

"That's a great idea, but we should take my limo. It has a privacy screen."

CHAPTER 26

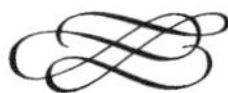

Three Months Later...

"GOOD MORNING, sunshine. Today's the big day!"

Nalani buried her face deeper into the crook of Shane's neck, drawing in a long drag of the scent she loved so much—masculine, sexy—Shane. Like everything else in the past week, she worked hard to commit it to memory.

His excitement broke her heart. To be fair, a lot of things lately broke her heart. He sounded so happy as he droned on, talking about all the decorating decisions he had to make now that the contractors had finished the reconstruction of his massive Brentwood estate. It may only be twenty minutes away, but to Nalani, it might as well be another galaxy.

Shane stroked her shoulder lightly as he held her in his arms, lounging on the bed in the Paris suite at Runway. "The decorator is coming over tomorrow night at seven. I made the appointment late enough, we should both be able to make it home by then."

Home. Such a confusing word for Nalani.

Her childhood home had been a nightmare. She'd bounced around until her small apartment over the vape shop had felt like home.

She was grateful that Shane and the Cartwright-Davidsons had made it possible she would never again have to step foot into the apartment where her life had changed irrevocably. There was just one problem. They'd packed up the belongings she didn't use regularly and sent them to Shane's house, waiting for today—moving day. That meant today was D-day. The day she'd dreaded for the last few weeks.

"I'm gonna go jump in the shower, then we can head out. I thought we could stop and pick up some pancakes on the way. I've been craving them since you mentioned them a few days ago."

Shane started to pull out of their embrace, but Nalani held onto him as tight as she could, refusing to let him leave her.

"Kitten, we need to get a move on."

Words failed her. The only thing Nalani was able to produce on cue these days were tears—more tears. She'd shed enough of those to last a lifetime. Unfortunately, she knew what Shane didn't—there were more tears coming.

"Shane. I..."

"Hey, are those tears I feel on my chest? You have another nightmare?"

So loving. So Patient. A saint.

And that was the problem. The real Shane Covington—the man she'd fallen in love with—was far from a saint. This version of himself was a lie.

Okay, lie was wrong. If he was lying, it was to himself too.

He'd been her knight in shining armor, her Prince Charming—her rock on her darkest days. She'd love him for the rest of her life, and that's why she knew she had to follow through with her plan.

Be strong.

Step one—get the hell out of his bed.

Nalani pushed out of the safety of his arms, rolling to her side of the bed to stand.

Step two—distance.

She needed to put more space between them, taking off for the desk to retrieve the package she'd hidden in one of the drawers.

"Where you going, babe? I thought we were talking."

Stay calm.

Once she had the small package, she took a deep breath and slowly turned to look back at the man who took her breath away—the man she loved more than anything in the world.

The man who deserved better.

Step three—break his heart.

"Shane, I've tried to come up with the right words a thousand times over the last week. I've known this big day was coming…"

"It is a big day. As awesome as it's been living here at Runway together, I can't wait to move into our own home."

"See… that's the thing. It isn't my home. This is." She waved her hands around her to indicate Runway.

"I know you're afraid to leave the security this property provides you, but I told you, I've hired extra guards and invested in a top-of-the-line electronic security system. I promise you, you'll be just as safe there as you are here."

"It's not that. Well, not entirely that. It's… so much more."

"Fine." Disappointment was written on his face. "You aren't ready, I'll stay here too. I can wait to move."

"No." She pushed down her panic.

Just say it. Pull off the Band-Aid.

"You need to move. Not just out, but on. I'll be eternally grateful for having you in my life. I can't even imagine going through what I've gone through without you by my side. I love you for all you've done, but this… you and me… isn't going to work."

"Are you fucking shitting me? You're breaking up with me?" His voice cracked with emotion.

"No, but I am letting you go. You…" She stopped herself from finishing. He'd been so hard on her any time she'd hinted he deserved better than her, yet in her heart, she was certain it was true.

Today was not the day to hold back. She needed to lay it all on the line, so they both could get the closure they needed and move on with their lives… without each other.

Be brave.

"I adore you, Shane, but whether we like it or not, we were always a long shot. As much as I'd love to blame Henry Ainsworth for us not being able to be together, if I'm honest with myself, I know this day would have come, anyway. Hell, it probably would have already happened months ago!"

"What the fuck does that even mean, Nalani? Is this the 'I'm only a housekeeper' argument again? I've never once treated you differently because of your job."

Shane pushed to his feet, pacing around the suite like a caged animal. It made it even harder for Nalani to remain calm. She'd expected this.

"No, you haven't, and I love you for it. But you have treated me differently because of the attack."

He stopped dead in his tracks, whipping his head up to pin her with an angry glare.

"Of course I have! What kind of monster do you think I am? You went through hell. All I've done is try to be there for you."

She was botching this. She had practiced this speech in her head, over and over, grappling to find the right words.

"Shane, you've been perfect. Truly. But don't you see? That's the problem." When he failed to reply, she finally spit out the root of her message. "The Shane I fell in love with is MIA. He's been pushed out by this perfect version of you, who is so loving, caring, attentive."

"Do you hear yourself? Are you really complaining because I'm too nice?"

"Here, now. Talking. No. No complaints. But…" Nalani paused, blushing, yet knowing it was time. "But in bed, at night, the real Shane is gone."

"Oh, for Christ's sake. What do you want from me? You've been through a horrific ordeal. Forgive me for wanting to give you time to heal before I do something that might bring back memories of the attack."

Growling with frustration, she paced to the window, looking out onto the empty Runway driveway, blanketed in the hot May sunshine. It looked like a beautiful day, unlike the storm brewing in the Paris suite.

Taking a deep breath, she turned and pinned Shane with a glare she hoped hid how afraid she was.

"You're right. The strangest things do trigger me. But here's the thing, I'm not sure that's going to end… like ever. Right now, you're happy enough, but I know you, Shane. The real you, deep down, is not gonna be happy playing the Boy Scout in the bedroom forever."

"Is that what this is about? I've been too nice?"

"Stop! Don't twist my words. We both know you have needs… kinks I may never be able to participate in again."

"I think the key word in that sentence is 'may.' You haven't even tried yet, Nalani."

"True, but are you really telling me you're ever going to be able to unleash the real you again? I had to practically beg you to even make love to me again last week."

"God, I hate being wrong." Shane threw his arms up in the air and started his angry pacing again. "Dr. Carlisle warned me this was going to happen, and I was naive enough to tell her we were stronger than that."

"Dr. Carlisle? You've been seeing a doctor?"

Shane froze, pinning her with an angry glare that took her breath away. They'd been so gentle with each other for the last three months, each of them afraid to say or do anything that would break the precarious path to recovery they were both on. The only time she'd seen Shane unleash his anger, it had been directed at Henry Ainsworth.

But today, she had no doubt his anger was definitely pointed squarely at her, and she hated it.

"Of course, I'm seeing a psych! The woman I love was brutally beaten and raped. I found her naked—almost dead—on the floor. I had to carry her broken and bleeding body into a hospital, praying I hadn't found her too late. Forgive me for not being able to just know how to recover from that."

Despite his obvious anger, her heart warmed at his passionate declaration of love, but she needed to harden her heart. It didn't matter that he loved her. What was important was, she loved him enough to let him go.

"I'm so sorry you're going through this hell too, but here's the thing. You don't need to. You saved my life. You've helped me through the hardest three months of my life. We both know this was doomed from the start, anyway. Now that your house is done, it's time for you to get back to your real life."

"My real life? What the fuck do you think this has been? A game?"

"A game, no, but I do think it was a diversion. A detour."

Shane approached her, grabbing each of her biceps and squeezing hard as he yanked her close. She had to crane her neck back to look into his angry face.

"Tell me the truth. How much of this is because I'm famous, and how much is because of Ainsworth?"

"Does it matter?"

"Hell, yes, it matters."

"I know you love me. I do. I love you too—so much, it hurts."

She felt the tears spilling over and down her cheek as she finished. "I just don't think that's gonna be enough."

"This is bullshit. All this time, I've thought you were the strongest woman I knew. Going through all you have with your family as a kid and all that Ainsworth put you through. Are you telling me that was a lie? You're gonna just run away from us?"

Her heart constricted with pain, remembering how supportive and understanding Shane had been when she'd told him every sordid detail from her childhood, growing up with drug dealers for family. He'd listened and held her, supported her. He hadn't looked down on her or condemned her.

"I'm not that strong, Shane. I'm scared every day."

"I know that! It's why I've been gentle with you. Giving you time to heal, and now, you're breaking up with me because of it!"

"You're missing the whole point! I'm not glass. We can't live like this, walking on eggshells… afraid to say something that will trigger the other person. I adore you for being so careful, and you're not wrong. I have meltdowns on a whim. It's just not fair to you."

"I think you should let me decide what is and isn't fair to me. I don't think getting chucked to the curb just because I haven't forced you to your knees to stick my cock down your throat until I choked you is fair either."

His raunchy words shocked her. It was a tiny flash of the old Shane—pre-Oscars night Shane. Nalani waited for the panic to close in, but it didn't come. If she were truthful with herself, the only tangible fear she had at that moment was she was about to make the biggest mistake of her life.

She squared her shoulders, determined to do the right thing for Shane, the man she loved.

"I'm sorry, Shane." Nalani moved her hand up between them, shoving the small box she still grasped into his muscular chest, doing her best to fight back the tears she felt welling in her eyes.

"I just can't do this anymore. I know you think you love me, but this is what's best. I know it in my heart." The tears in his eyes broke her heart. There was nothing left to be said other than

"Goodbye."

Nalani yanked herself free of his embrace, rushing to where she'd thrown her robe over the desk chair the night before, anticipating she might need it to make a quick escape in the light of day.

She half expected him to chase after her. Only when she got to the door and fumbled her way out into the empty hall, she realized she had no real plan. She'd just closed the door on one of the most important relationships of her entire life, and as she stood in the long hall, looking around a place that had been both workplace and home, a wave of sorrow consumed her.

Like she had with Shane, she knew she would need to cut Runway out of her life as well. There would be too many memories to face every day here—good and bad. Leaving would be the only way to move on with her life.

SHANE LEANED out the driver's side window to press the small button on the brick security stand outside Piper Kole's exclusive five-acre beachfront property. He'd only been there once years before and wasn't sure the actress was home, but since she hadn't answered his multiple phone calls or texts in the hour since Nalani had blindsided him, his car had found its way here on its own.

One long buzz broke the quiet of the secluded neighborhood as he held the button down indefinitely.

"What the fuck! Who is it?" Nolan Boeing's voice shouted from the small speaker next to the button.

"It's me, Covington. I need to talk to Piper."

"It's not even eight yet. She's sleeping."

"Correction." A softer, feminine voice could be heard in the background. "She *was* sleeping. Now she's awake and needs caffeine."

Nolan's soft "fuck" coincided with the gates in front of his car swinging open. Shane gunned the engine, determined to get through before Boeing had second thoughts and closed them again.

He parked and spent a full three minutes standing at the huge double doors to the mansion before the lock could be heard disengaging, and a tired Nolan Boeing, wearing a robe, swung the front door open.

"What the hell is so important it couldn't wait until this afternoon? We flew in from New York late last night and planned on staying in bed all day. I had fun plans for this morning if you get my drift."

"Yeah, well, I had fun plans for today too, but they just blew up. It's moving day, and Nalani gave me the boot instead."

Shane hated the pity that filled Nolan's eyes as his friend stepped back from the doorway and used his right arm to usher him in.

"Well, shit, I'll put on some coffee. Sounds like we all need it."

"The hell with coffee. I'll take a shot of whiskey," Shane answered, slamming the front door closed behind him, following Nolan deeper into the luxury home.

"Whoa there. It can't be that bad. I thought you guys got through the worst of it."

"The worst of what?" A sleepy looking Piper met them in the kitchen. It wasn't often Shane, or anyone, got to see the award-winning actress without her makeup or dripping in her signature diamonds. He took it as a sign of their true friendship, she didn't seem bothered in the least.

Shane had to tamp down his jealousy as he watched Boeing hug his fiancée from behind, snuggling in to place a sexy kiss in the crook of her neck, her uncharacteristic giggle filling the space.

This was supposed to be him and Nalani, tomorrow morning in their own kitchen. He was, of course, thrilled for his good friends, but Shane selfishly wanted his own happily-ever-after.

Watching them reminded him he was definitely a fifth wheel. He was tempted to retreat to give them privacy, but a fresh wave of crushing anger reminded him of why he'd come in the first place.

"I need your help," he blurted, grabbing the attention back from the lovers, who almost seemed to forget he was there.

Shane pushed down his guilt. Piper had already helped him more than he deserved. He could only imagine the bravery it had taken her to come forward and publicly accuse Henry Ainsworth. The fourteen additional women who had come forward in the three months since that fateful press conference had helped ease his guilt. Still, it felt wrong to ask her for more.

"What is it?" she asked, popping a bite of melon in her mouth.

He pushed through his guilt. "It's Nalani."

"Yeah, well, I sort of figured. Nothing other than love would get you here before eight," she sassed.

"She broke up with me." He hated to even think the words, let alone say them. "We were supposed to be moving into our new house today, and she waited to spring it on me that she's not moving with me."

"Shit. That sucks, but what is it you think I'm going to be able to do to help?"

"You need to talk to her. Tell her she's making a mistake."

"Oh, is that all?"

He didn't like her mocking tone.

"Yeah, she looks up to you. Like it or not, you two have

bonded over the last few months. I'm so grateful to you for talking with her. Helping her through her recovery."

"And you think that gives me the right to tell her what to do with her life?"

"I didn't say that. It's just… she's not thinking clearly. She's making rash decisions."

"Oh, I see. And you aren't?" Piper accused.

"What's that supposed to mean?"

"Did you even ask if her she wanted to move in with you? Or did you just assume she would move with you when the house was done?"

"Is this a trick question? We've been living together at Runway for three months. Hell, even longer. We'd been together there in the weeks leading up to… well… Oscar night."

"You can't even say it, can you?" Piper asked.

"Say what?"

"Her rape. Her attack. The night she almost died." All of those would be more accurate than *Oscar night*.

"What the hell does it matter what I call that night? It was the fucking worst day of her life. I don't think me using shitty labels that remind us of that will help."

Piper walked to the fridge and took out a small bottle of orange juice, taking a swig before speaking again.

"I need to ask you a question, and you aren't going to like it, but I'm gonna ask it anyway." She waited several long seconds before pinning him with her best Mistress Ice glare. "Would you still be asking Nalani to move in with you if she hadn't been attacked?"

"What the hell kinda question is that? Of course, I would!"

"Really? Are you absolutely sure about that?"

"What the fuck! I didn't come here to have you kick me while I'm down."

"Really? So, why did you come here?"

"I told you. I need you to talk to her and tell her she's making a big mistake."

The Mistress Ice glare softened, but her words were harsh, nonetheless.

"And what if I don't think she's making a mistake?"

"What the fuck? I thought you were my friend."

"I am your friend. And I'd like to think I'm Nalani's friend, too." When Shane couldn't think of a single thing to say, Piper continued on.

"Listen, you two have been dealt a really shitty hand. It was always going to be an uphill battle. The media was bound to crucify you both even before the attack. Put yourself in her shoes for one minute. A young woman who had a horrific childhood… with secrets she was desperate to keep from getting out… dating Hollywood's most eligible bachelor. I speak from experience when I say the media is brutal when it smells blood in the water. You dating a housekeeper was just too salacious a story for them to pass up. Add to it the Ainsworth debacle, and she's looking at never being able to have one free moment of privacy outside of Runway ever again. Staying with you only makes it worse."

"So, that's it? She's too afraid of a little media coverage to stick it out?"

Piper took a seat next to Nolan at the kitchen eat-in island before answering.

"No, I'm saying that was always going to be an uphill battle you'd have to face. Now, that's just the secondary problem."

"Oh, and what is the primary problem, oh wise one?"

"Hey, you came here for my help, remember? I can't help it if you don't like what I have to say."

"Fine." Shane forced himself to take a deep breath to keep from yelling. "You're right. I just need to know how I can make this better."

"That's the thing. You might not be able to, Shane."

"I refuse to believe that. I love her. We have to figure this out."

"Okay, so you love her. You've been living in the mansion. Have you taken her down to Black Light again yet?"

"Are you insane? You of all people should know why I'm not taking her there."

"Oh, I understand, and I even admire you for your restraint, but don't you think she realizes what you're doing?"

"What's that? Loving her? Protecting her?"

"I was actually referring to the fact you've turned yourself into a monk because you somehow think that's what she needs."

"Isn't it? She has nightmares of the attack. And I resent that. I'm no monk."

"Really. So, you two have had sex since the attack?"

"That's none of your damn business."

"And yet you're here,"—Piper waved her hands around the kitchen—"asking for my help before coffee."

"For your information, we made love just last week for the first time since the attack. It went really well."

"Uh huh. It sounds amazing. *Really well.*"

"What do you want? She was scared. I was scared I was going to traumatize her. All things considered, I think it went… fuck… really well," he finished lamely.

"You need to give her more time. And you need to stop assuming you know what she needs or wants. She already feels powerless against Ainsworth and now the media."

"Now you sound like her. She accused me of being too soft."

"Well, are you?"

"Maybe. So, what if I am? I'm just trying to protect her while she's healing."

Boeing got up and poured three cups of the freshly brewed coffee while they'd been talking. As he set the mug down in front of Shane, he jumped into the conversation.

"Piper and Nalani's situations are totally different since

Piper has had years to come to terms with what Ainsworth did to her, but I know a little about what you're going through. Sometimes, it's not easy knowing the right thing to do and say when our women give us mixed signals."

"You do realize I'm sitting right here, right?" Piper interjected.

Nolan turned to answer her. "Case in point. Three days ago, you were in a rare mood, ready to bite every person's head off who came into contact with you. I recommended a nice session over my spanking bench, along with my belt, might relieve you of your stress, but you accused me of being a barbarian.

"I then offered to let Mistress Ice take out *her* frustration on *my* ass instead. I was hoping you'd get whatever it was that was bothering you out of your system, only to have you scream at me that I was a wimp, and you hated it when I let you walk all over me. What part of your behavior that day was not an example of sending me mixed signals?"

"Careful there, Boeing. For the record, I do hate when you treat me like glass."

"Damnit, not you too. Nalani just used those exact words with me this morning, accusing me of treating her like she was glass."

Nolan whistled. "I don't envy you one bit. Piper's had years to recover, and sometimes, I still worry I'm pushing her too hard in the bedroom. I don't know how I would have reacted had I known what she was going through five years ago. I suspect Ainsworth would have been dead, and I'd be in jail."

Shane took a gulp of the hot coffee before verbalizing his real fear with his good friends.

"I've got another problem you don't have, Boeing." He looked up and confirmed they were still waiting for him to continue. "We're all in the BDSM lifestyle. Like you, as a Dom, I feel responsible for—protective of my sub. But as you might have noticed, I have some rather unique and specific kinks I've had to rein in since her attack."

"And Nalani is worried you aren't going to be able to rein that part of you in forever?"

"She pretty much admitted as much this morning."

"And? Do you think she's right?" Piper asked.

Shane wanted so badly to deny it, but he forced himself to be honest. If not with Piper, then at least with himself. "Well... she's not completely wrong."

"And so, the real question you came here to ask me this morning is if there will ever be a time she'll trust you enough to unleash that part of yourself again?"

He hadn't known that was his question, but now that she'd verbalized it, he knew his and Nalani's entire future hung on the answer to that pointed question. He wanted so badly to be angry with Nalani for not giving him the benefit of the doubt, for assuming he wouldn't be able to push down his own sexual kinks in order not to traumatize the woman he loved.

He couldn't be mad that she'd known what he hadn't wanted to face—his unique kinks were part of his DNA. He'd increasingly had to push down the dark memories of Nalani on her knees, his cock down her throat as tears smeared mascara down her face. The entire time he'd made sweet love to her the week before, his mind had remembered how much he loved to hear her scream his name when he'd previously tied her down and fucked her silly.

"Well, will she?" he prodded, not bothering to try to defend himself.

Shane hated the pity he saw in Piper's eyes as she gave him a less than satisfying answer.

"I have absolutely no idea, Shane. And here's the thing. I don't think Nalani knows either. She just knows she's scared and loves you too much to ask you to change who you are."

"So, now what? I just let her walk out of my life? We both pretend we don't notice that half our heart is missing?"

"We see how well that worked for us, didn't we, baby?" Nolan prompted his fiancée.

"Well, I'm not gonna wait around for five years like you guys did, hoping she comes back to me."

"What's your alternative?" Piper asked.

Shane's brain was racing, scrambling to come up with a path forward that would bring Nalani back to him. A solution that would keep her safe… loved… and both of them whole.

"Trust…" he said to no one in particular.

"What?"

"Before, you said the word trust. That she didn't trust me enough to unleash that part of myself."

"Right. After all, isn't that what the BDSM lifestyle is all about, anyway?" Piper added, popping more melon in her mouth.

Shane's brain was exploding with conflicting ideas. He needed to go somewhere where he could just think.

"I need to go."

"Go? You just got here. Nolan can make us breakfast. He makes fabulous pancakes."

"I'll take a rain check."

"But…"

He pinned Piper with a glare. "Thank you."

"But… I didn't really help."

"You helped more than you can know. I need to go."

"If you don't mind me asking, what's your plan to get her back?"

"Who said anything about getting her back?"

"Uh huh."

"Fine. I just need to figure out a way to test how strong her glass is."

"Interesting. Mind if I give you one more piece of advice?"

"Of course. There's no one who can possibly understand what she's going through better than you. That's why I came here."

"Give her a safeword."

"She has a safeword," Shane interjected quickly.

"I'm not talking about *red* for in the bedroom or playing at Black Light. A different word she can use when she's feeling uncomfortable… or afraid or when the nightmare of what she's gone through is triggered by something she hears or sees. A word that will stop things on a dime."

Nolan got up and went to hug Piper from behind.

"We've been using this, and honestly, it's been a lifesaver. Although I'm pretty sure someone used it last night just to get out of a punishment."

"Prove it," Piper teased.

Watching the two of them hugging and laughing together made Shane's heart ache. They had what he wanted. What he knew he could have with Nalani. They'd grown so close together over the last three months. They knew each other's deepest and darkest secrets, and she loved him anyway.

He felt calmer already, realizing with a rare certainty, Nalani was perfect for him in every way.

Now, if only he could convince her to trust him enough to prove it.

CHAPTER 27

Piper weaved her way through the empty rooms of the Runway mansion. She felt like she was trespassing in someone else's home, which in some ways she was. During business hours, when patrons and partygoers were packed into the upscale social club, it was easy to forget the property had started out as someone's home before the Cartwright-Davidson's had reinvented it.

While there were still employees hanging around on days like today when both clubs were closed, Piper had come to see the only person actually living under the mansion's roof.

Peeking out to the expansive stone balcony that looked out over the entire property, Piper found whom she'd come to see. She took a deep breath, and before she could second-guess herself, opened the sliding glass door from the dining area to the patio.

"Jaxson told me I'd find you out here," she called out.

A frightened Nalani spun around in her lounge chair at the sound of Piper's voice, the fear fading quickly as she recognized her friend.

"Hey. I wasn't expecting anyone today."

"Yeah, I had to convince the security guards at the gate to let me in. They're pretty protective of you."

The smile on Nalani's face dipped slightly. "And I do appreciate that more than you can possibly know."

Piper stepped out into the early morning sunshine, approaching Nalani as she replied.

"Honestly, I think I'm one of the few people who truly understands how much you appreciate the protection they provide you."

A light of comprehension sparked in Nalani's eyes. The women had become unlikely friends in the months since the attack on Nalani. Sharing horrific traumatic events had a way of uniting people. Piper just hoped they were still friends by the time she left that day.

When Nalani remained silent, Piper asked, "Mind if I sit down?"

"That depends on why you're here," Nalani hedged, suspicious of the visit.

Piper sat before answering. "You know why I'm here. I'm your friend."

"Don't you mean you're Shane's friend? Don't pretend he didn't call you and ask you to come tell me what a mistake I'm making."

Piper didn't take the anger she heard in Nalani's voice personally. In fact, her anger was a good sign she was starting to heal. The outward signs of the attack had faded weeks before, but Piper knew the wounds she carried inside would last a lifetime.

"I'd like to think I can be friends with both of you. And for the record, Shane came directly to my house yesterday morning after he left here, desperate for me to get involved, but I turned him down." Piper watched Nalani carefully for her reaction to the news.

"So then why are you here today?"

"Because Jaxson called." She paused, picking her words carefully. "He told me you turned in your resignation yesterday. That you're moving away to start over somewhere else."

Nalani broke eye contact, looking back out across the property to the house in the distance where her bosses and their unique family lived.

Silence stretched between them until Nalani answered quietly.

"I just can't stay here. Everywhere I look are memories. Every day, I can see the pity in everyone's eyes as they treat me like I'm made of glass. No one knows what to say. They're all so wonderful and supportive, but..."

"But you wonder if there will ever be a day when they see you, and the first thought they have isn't about the attack or how sorry they are for you."

Nalani turned to Piper, a spark of life in her eyes.

"It's hard enough for me to forget myself, you know?"

Piper broke their gaze to look out over the property herself before answering. "God, do I ever. The last few months, every time I go into the production office or take a meeting for one of the projects I'm working on, I spend the first ten minutes convincing myself not to run out of the room screaming because I hate the pity on everyone's face. Or worse, there have been a few angry men accuse me of lying just for the publicity as if I'd staged the whole thing as one big public relations opportunity."

"I'm so sorry you have to go through all of this. I know it's all my fault."

Piper snapped her gaze back to Nalani.

"Oh no, you don't. You have absolutely nothing to feel guilty about. The only person who is at fault is behind bars—hopefully, for the rest of his life."

"You know what I mean. If it hadn't been because of me, you would have never come forward."

"I'd like to think that's not true, but I honestly don't know. I do know this; going public has been the best thing for me personally. In fact, that's why I decided to come see you, after all."

"I'm sorry. I'm not following you. I thought you said how awful it is now that everyone knows the truth."

Piper wasn't sure she could verbalize her feelings, but she'd made it this far—she had to try.

"Here's the thing, and there's no way around it… Five years ago, I did exactly what you're preparing to do. I told myself I had no one who could possibly understand. No one who could help me through what I was going through. I don't have close family. I didn't have close girlfriends. Nolan and I had barely started seeing each other.

"So, I ran away. Tried to heal as best I could on my own. Built up my icy shell, thinking I was protecting myself from ever being hurt like that again. And for a while, it worked… until I actually started to heal. That was when I realized the most important thing I'd lost the day of the attack."

Piper paused, glancing back at Nalani to see if she was paying attention. Her unanswered question hung silently between them. To her credit, Nalani patiently waited until Piper was ready.

"By running away and closing myself off, I'd lost my shot at true happiness. I traded happy in for safety… traded love in for my need to maintain control. I threw away happily-ever-after with Nolan because I didn't trust him enough to not pity me if he found out what Ainsworth had done to me. Only recently, I realized he's as much a victim—at least psychologically, if not physically—as I am."

"What are you saying? That Shane is somehow a victim too?"

"Well, isn't he?"

Piper took it as a good sign that Nalani didn't answer.

"I would argue that Jaxson, Chase, and Emma are victims as

well. This has totally disrupted their beautiful place of business and brought a lot of negative publicity, not to mention how guilty they feel that one of their employees was hurt because of her job here.

"And what about Madison? She's heartbroken she didn't take your initial reports of Ainsworth's violence more seriously. And the security guards who failed to see the abuse on their cameras and ban the bastard from the property long before your attack."

"You're just proving my point. This is why I need to leave. I remind them all of what happened every time they see me."

"And you don't think they're going to think about this even if you aren't here?"

"They'll get over it faster with me gone."

"Maybe, but I spent five years stumbling through my healing process alone. As horrible as what happened to you is, you are not and never will be alone. You have so many people who care for you. I came here to warn you that running away really sucks. I hope you don't leave, but if you do, please know you can call me any time. Day or night. I'll always be there to listen."

The women sat in silence, the only sound the hum of a lawnmower in the distance.

Piper glanced over to Nalani and saw the tracks of her silent tears on her cheeks. She wished she could wave a magic wand and help her put the horror of what Ainsworth had done behind her.

She should leave. She'd said what she'd come to say, but her intuition kept her in her seat. When Nalani sniffled, Piper reached down to pull a tissue out of her bag, handing it to her to blow her nose.

"I know it's none of my business, and you can tell me to butt out if you want, but I do have one other question I'm burning to ask you."

Nalani looked her way, a wane smile on her lips. "You can

ask anything, but I'm not sure I have answers to anything anymore."

"I know that feeling. Like someone pulled the rug out from under your feet, and you're falling, trying to grab onto anything solid you can to keep from falling farther."

Nalani's eyes widened. "That's exactly how I feel. I never would have used those words, but… I'm so confused. One minute, I'm angry, then I'm crying, then I'm melting down in a panic attack. All within minutes of each other. I can't wait until I can get through a day without feeling like I'm going to jump out of my skin."

"Did I ever tell you what happened the day I found out about your attack?" Piper asked quietly.

"No."

"It was probably the first truly happy day I've had in a really long time. I'd slept over at Nolan's after the Oscar's, and he arranged to have people come in all day to pamper me. A massage… mani-pedi… rest… and other things by the pool. I remember thinking how nice it was to finally feel like I was part of a couple, not just on my own.

"We were coming in to get ready to go to dinner when he turned on the TV, and that's when I heard it. The announcer said the words *Ainsworth* and *sexual assault,* and that's all it took. I was right back in that suite with him in Budapest. My ears were ringing, I dropped to my knees, screaming and holding my hands over my ears, trying to block out the TV. I had the mother of all panic attacks.

"And as awful as it was, for the first time, I had someone there with me. Holding me, comforting me, telling me everything was going to be okay. More importantly, for the first time, I finally believe that."

Piper paused before looking Nalani in the eyes, asking the question she didn't have the right to ask.

"Do you really love Shane?"

Nalani's tears turned to sobs as she ground out, "So much it hurts."

"Then tell me the truth. Are you leaving because of the attack or because he's famous, and you somehow think you don't deserve him?"

"I don't deserve him! He's had to change everything about himself to stay and take care of me. I know he loves me, but eventually, he'll resent me. I'm not sure I'll ever be able to give him the kind of submission he needs."

"Maybe you won't. But… maybe, just maybe, you will. And more importantly, like it or not, this has changed him. Just like our separation changed Nolan. He has always been the alpha man in the room, and I loved that about him. Before the attack on me, he never in a million years would have submitted sexually to me in any way, yet on Valentine's Day, he spent one-hundred thousand dollars to be my submissive the night of roulette, just to get close to me."

"I heard that rumor. I didn't think it was true."

"Well, it is. More importantly, in the last few months, he's become so in tune with my moods, he detects when he can and can't go all dominant on me, both in and out of the bedroom. He's forced me to talk about my feelings more than I ever thought I could."

"What are you trying to say?"

"That you and Shane can find your way through this, too, if you give him a chance. It's true, he may never go back to the same dirty talking kinkster he was, but make no mistake, this will stick with him forever, whether he's with you or someone else. If you're leaving so his life can get back to normal, you're leaving for the wrong reasons. He can't go back to the way he was before the attack, any more than you or I can."

Piper pushed to her feet. She'd said what she'd come to say. The rest was in Nalani's hands. She reached into the outside pocket of her bag and came out with a business card, reaching out to place it in Nalani's lap.

"This has all of my private information. Call me. I mean it. Any time. I'll always be here to listen if you find yourself alone." Piper turned to walk back to the sliding door but stopped, delivering her final words over her shoulder. "I know you're scared, but if you run away like I did, you'll be letting Henry Ainsworth win. I hope you're stronger than I was."

It was crazy that she was tired. She hadn't done anything but sit around, feeling sorry for herself all day, but she was exhausted. Nalani picked up her phone to check the time, only to remember she'd turned it off when she couldn't take one more wellness check.

Her brain knew how lucky she was to have so many people calling and texting to check in on her, but her heart hurt, knowing every one of them thought she was crazy for breaking up with Shane and resigning from Runway. She didn't need them to tell her what a fool she was. She knew perfectly well, but that didn't change a thing.

I love him, and he's better off without me.

And she would be better off not staying where she would be slapped in the face by memories of what they had for a short while, not to mention, the media would always be able to get to her if they knew she was still working at Runway.

The last two days had been depressing but necessary. They were the first two days of relative peace and quiet she'd had since meeting Shane. In the weeks following the attack, she'd been surrounded at all times—police, doctors, nurses, security guards. By the time she'd finally started healing physically, she was convinced her friends and Shane had conspired to arrange for someone to be with her twenty-four-seven just in case her anxiety got the best of her. As afraid as she was to leave the property alone, she knew that it was time.

Nalani's stomach growled, reminding her she had barely eaten that day. With the clubs closed on Tuesdays, the kitchens were also closed, Avery's day off. Even though the thought of leaving the safety of her room to go through the dark mansion scared her, she realized if she couldn't even get food from the Runway kitchen on her own, she'd never make it out in the real world.

Determined to gain some measure of control back over her future, Nalani pushed off the couch near the roaring fireplace in the Paris suite. Walking to the desk, she slipped on the flip-flops she'd taken off there a few hours earlier.

At the door, she took a deep breath, and before she could chicken out, yanked the door open. The sun had gone down, so the hallway was dimly lit. She peered up and down the hall nervously. Her brain knew Henry Ainsworth wouldn't be running out of the Hong Kong suite to chase her as he had in the past, but that didn't make it any easier to step out of the suite.

Thankfully, the grand entrance was well lit when she arrived at the winding and elaborate staircase that would take her to the main floor of the empty dance club.

Spooked, she made sure to turn on each light as she moved room to room—through the library, around the pool table and pinball machines in the game room, past the baby-grand piano and the huge cigar humidor built into the wall.

Entering the mammoth dining room with seating for dinner parties up to fifty, the first sound of voices made it to her. She stopped in her tracks, straining her ears to pinpoint where the sound was coming from. Her pulse sped up with the knowledge she wasn't alone in the mansion as she'd assumed.

She told herself it was just a security guard, doing his rounds, but if so, who was he talking to? Nalani inched forward slowly toward the kitchen, and as she got closer to the open archway, the bright lights of the kitchen spilled into the dining room.

"I think we should just lock her in the Paris suite until she comes to her senses. I can't bear the thought of her leaving and going out there alone without our protection."

What was Avery doing in on her day off, and who the hell was she talking to?

"We can't lock her in anywhere, or we wouldn't be much better than Ainsworth," Chase piped in.

"The hell with that! None of us would ever hurt a hair on her head."

That was Roger's voice from security. He'd taken her attack extra hard since he'd been the one who'd confronted Ainsworth that Sunday back in February.

"Alright, alright. I appreciate that everyone is just trying to help, but Chase, Emma, and I think we came up with the best solution. We have an apartment in D.C. above Runway East. It has state-of-the-art security and a panic room, just like here. We have twenty-four-hour security in the building, just like here. I'm going to offer to put Nalani up there indefinitely until she feels ready to move out. I've already talked to Maxine, and she's thrilled with the idea of hosting Nalani. If, and when, she feels up to it, she can help Maxine with any number of jobs there."

Nalani listened to Jaxson's impassioned plan to help her as the tears she had been holding at bay returned. She was so touched her employers were going to so much trouble to keep her safe and happy. No, they were so much more than that—they were her *friends*.

Before she could chicken out, she resumed her walk, rounding the corner into the crowded kitchen. She'd known several people were there, but Madison and Trevor, along with Emma and the twins were sitting around the U shaped eat-in island.

Even Elijah was there, at the end of the counter with his back to her. When everyone turned to look up, Elijah spun on the barstool.

It was their first time seeing each other since the attack. Madison had confided, for some unknown reason, the dungeon master had really taken the news of her rape the hardest of everyone on staff. Watching his handsome face contort with pity was almost more than she could take.

The chatter of the lively group died down until only one of the twin's good-natured gibberish remained. All eyes turned to Nalani as Elijah got to his feet and approached her slowly. The intensity in his eyes as he made his way closer made her want to look away.

Elijah stopped just shy of taking her in his arms, the normally larger-than-life Dom hesitating as if he were afraid to touch her.

"I'm so damn sorry, Nalani."

There it was. Right on schedule. A fresh dose of pity.

"I know, but you have nothing to be sorry for—"

"You don't understand," he cut her off as he anxiously dragged his hand through his shoulder-length salt and pepper hair.

"What don't I understand?"

"Everything. It's all my fault." Elijah's voice quavered as he broke their visual connection to look away.

"What are you talking about? Absolutely nothing that happened to me was your fault, Elijah."

"He was here because of me. I worked with him on several projects before I retired. I knew he was a fucking jerk, and no one liked to work with, but…"

Nalani turned his words around in her head, trying to make sense of what he was saying.

"I don't understand. You knew he was a rapist?"

"Of course not!"

"Then you knew he liked to abuse women?"

"No, but I knew he was an asshole."

She watched her friend closely, taking in the bags under his eyes and the defeated curl of his shoulders. He genuinely blamed himself for what happened to her. Reaching out, Nalani placed her palm on Elijah's chest. She could feel his heart pounding.

"If we didn't let assholes in, Jaxson, Chase, and Emma would have gone bankrupt by now. This town is full of them. You can't blame yourself any more than I can. The only person who deserves blame is behind bars." Nalani smiled as she recognized she'd just parroted Piper's words from earlier that day.

"Still, I hate the thought of you leaving. You're part of the Runway/Black Light family. You need to let your family help you get through this."

Family.

As Nalani glanced around the room at the faces of so many people she loved, she recognized the truth of the label. They were family. But she knew what they didn't—family just meant they had the ability to hurt each other more.

"What's he doing here?" Avery's question had everyone in the room looking outside to where she was facing.

Nalani turned to follow their lead, and her heart lurched with longing as Shane crossed the patio she'd been sitting on earlier that morning. The same patio where Piper had visited her and given her so much to think about.

"I invited him."

Nalani turned her attention back to the DM, surprised because she didn't think Elijah approved of her and Shane. Elijah answered her unasked question.

"We said we were having a meeting of Nalani's family." He paused, pinning her with a serious glare. "Covington is the head of Nalani's family."

Her tears were back on cue.

"But you said there were better Doms for me."

"I was wrong, and believe me, it pains me to say that." The first hint of levity crept into Elijah's voice. "He's proven to me he's worthy. Give him a chance, Nalani. Hell, give us all a chance to show you what being in a real family feels like."

It felt like time stood still as the entire room held their breath, waiting for her to respond. She felt all eyes on her and braved a glance around the room.

She had expected to find the familiar look of pity, but instead, found love and hope. The sliding door to the patio opening and closing broke the silence, and as one, all eyes moved from Nalani to watch as Shane approached the kitchen.

He looked like a man on a mission. His long strides exuded confidence she envied—confidence she recognized had been absent for some time.

Shane didn't even acknowledge the others in the room, walking past them directly to her. With each step he took, her heart rate increased until she felt lightheaded by the time he dropped the leather duffle bag he'd been carrying with a heavy thud, so he could pull her into a forceful hug.

Nalani burst into ugly sobs at the relief of being in his arms again, hugging him around his waist as hard as she could, burying her face in his chest. How had she ever thought she'd be strong enough to never feel his arms around her again? Never smell his masculine scent or hear the coos of love against her ear as he comforted her?

It had only been two days, yet they had been miserable soul-searching days. She tried valiantly to remind herself she was being selfish—holding onto a Cinderella fairytale she didn't have the right to hope could come true. He was Shane Fucking Covington. He deserved the princess, not the damaged pauper.

But standing in the middle of the Runway kitchen, surrounded by the best friends and co-workers anyone could ever ask for, a final spark of hope ignited inside her. Could they find a path to happiness together?

It was Elijah, who had stayed next to them, who offered her a hankie when her crying subsided. Shane loosened his bear hug enough, she could grab the small cloth and use it to wipe her tears and blow her nose.

She was suddenly very aware she hadn't bothered putting on makeup or even getting dressed before coming down. Yet standing before him in her Runway robe, her hair a disheveled nest, her eyes bloodshot, there was no doubt in her mind, the man looking down at the hot mess she was, loved her anyway, despite her circumstances—in spite of the damage Henry Ainsworth had done to each of them.

Nalani held her breath, scrambling to come up with the right words to say. In her silence, Shane proved he had come up with a plan.

"I'm not letting you go."

So simple. To the point.

"You aren't?" she whispered, unable to remember a single reason why she should argue.

"Nope. And I'm done treating you like glass. As much as I hate that you stood up to me yesterday, I'm so grateful you did. You were right, we never would have made it."

What? She fought down the panic. He was confusing her. Was he just here to offer to be her friend like everyone else? If so, shouldn't she be grateful?

The naughtiest of grins lit up his handsome face, giving her a hint of what he might be saying. She remained silent, too afraid to ask him to clarify, in case she was wrong.

"So, I have a new word for you to learn."

"What? A new word?"

"Yep. I've decided to trust you, Nalani."

What the hell was he talking about? He wasn't making any sense.

"For the last three months, like everyone else, I've been walking on eggshells, too afraid to do anything but shield you from anything that might hurt you, including my true nature. I convinced myself I was only doing what was best for you. And honestly, I'm pretty sure I was in those early days. But Piper and Nolan helped me sort a few things out."

"Oh?"

She couldn't muster anything more than the single syllable around the lump in her throat.

"So, the new word is *time*. As in *timeout*, you need to take a break."

"What was wrong with just *red*?"

"Nothing, and red will work fine at Black Light, but *timeout* is for anytime, day or night, no matter where we are… who we're with… what we're doing. When you feel uncomfortable or afraid, all you need to do is ask for a timeout, and I'll drop whatever is going on and go back into protector mode."

Her brain raced to understand his plan.

"I've been so afraid I would say or do something that would trigger bad memories, I've treated you like the glass you accused me of."

"But I'm not made of glass."

"I know, kitten. But you aren't made of Teflon either."

Truer words had never been spoken.

"So, here is how this is gonna go. I'm gonna do my best to get us back on track. To lead us both through all the bullshit with the media, the police, the DA's office. Sexually, I'm going to push myself out of my comfort zone and drag you along with me. I'm trusting you to speak up when I go too far—with anything. Can you do that?"

Could she?

"I think so."

"Good girl. In fact…" For the first time, Shane stepped back and glanced around the room full of her best friends as they listened to their very personal conversation. "You should use the word *timeout* with anyone in this room. They all love you too, and like me, have been protective of you, but it's time for things to get back to normal around here. That means no more secret meetings to decide what we can and can't say to Nalani. From now on, we all use our best judgment on what we do and say, but we aren't going to hold back if we think she's making a mistake."

There was a short pause, then the room broke out into a chaotic clamor with everyone talking at once.

Madison stepped forward, shushing everyone around her.

"Shane's right. I've been biting my tongue, but you can't leave. Like, you just can't. This is your home."

Emma walked around the end of the counter, Alicia bouncing happily at her hip, approaching Shane and Nalani.

"I know how hard it is to be in love with famous, larger-than-life men. I'm so grateful I never had to go through anything close to what you've been through with the attack, but like you, I tried to run away from the brutal media coverage when the press started picking apart everything about me, from my weight to my lack of money or fame."

"Emma..." Jaxson scolded his wife from across the room. "You'd better not be putting yourself down young lady, or you're gonna be going to bed with a burning bottom tonight."

Jaxson's dominant warning to his wife had Nalani's insides melting. How in the world could she even want such a thing after all she'd been through? Still, there was no denying the thought of Shane spanking her sparked a sexual need she'd worried was dead.

"I wasn't putting myself down at all. I was just repeating the historical facts of early in our relationship... *sir,*" Emma grinned.

Jaxson growled but accepted her answer as the truth.

"All I'm trying to say is how grateful I am I didn't let my fear keep me from following my heart. You and Shane are magnificent together. Anyone close to you can see that. Don't throw it away just because you're afraid."

Nalani's glanced behind Emma, where Shane was watching her with interest. She watched his smile turn into a dominant glare, full of sexual heat.

"I brought a few gifts I want to share with you, kitten. Feeling up to a trip downstairs?"

"Downstairs… now? Tonight? But the club is closed on Tuesdays."

"Exactly. Don't you think it's best if we go there alone to talk about things before we have an audience?"

"Talk about things?"

God, she'd missed his mischievous grin—the smile he flashed when he was cooking up something particularly sexy for them to try.

"Talking to start. I won't complain if it turns into a play date."

Nalani glanced around the room, sure her face was flushing pink with embarrassment, knowing everyone was watching and listening with interest. The heat in Shane's eyes smoldered at her shy blush, reminding her how much he loved pushing her.

It was the first time he'd unleashed this part of himself since her attack. She waited for the fear to creep in at the thought of resuming their true sexual relationship—not the watered-down version they tried the week before—but it didn't come. She'd dreaded this test, but now that it was here, she knew how ridiculous it had been to be afraid.

There was absolutely nothing about Shane Covington that reminded her of Henry Ainsworth. While her rapist may have stuck his cock inside her body, there had been nothing sexual about his act of violence, let alone affection, love, or intimacy. While her attacker had spouted vile and humiliating words—some of the same words Shane loved to use in the throes of their passionate and kinky scenes—the meanings were completely different.

He waited patiently as she'd worked through her emotions at his invitation. Nalani blushed a deeper shade of red as she remembered it wasn't just Shane waiting on her reply. The entire room of her friends and co-workers were waiting too, somehow understanding the importance of her answer.

"I'll go anywhere as long as it's with you, Shane."

He rushed forward, yanking her back into his arms, holding her tight enough, she felt wholly safe for the first time in a very long time.

CHAPTER 28

She'd said yes. Shane held Nalani close, letting the relief of having her back in his arms wash over him.

Anxiety, a familiar companion since the night of the Oscars, threatened to pull him out of his joy. He shoved it aside, determined to follow through with his plan. He knew they were far from home free, but for the first time since he'd found Nalani unconscious in a pool of water and her own blood months before, he felt a small measure of control over their future.

Grabbing her hand, Shane turned to face the group of friends smiling broadly at the lovers.

"Before we head down, I just want to say… thank you. All of you have been the best support system for Nalani. For me. Well, for *us*."

"Yeah, well, there's no accounting for her taste in men, but if you make her happy, I guess we'll have to put up with you," Elijah said from behind him, the good-natured jab making everyone laugh.

Shane turned, and the dominant men's eyes met. He was grateful for the warmth and approval shining back from the older man—a pseudo-father figure to Nalani in this strange family they'd loosely formed.

"Thanks for calling me this afternoon, man. I won't forget it."

"Yeah, well, let's not get all mushy about it. I'll still fuck you up if you do anything to hurt her."

"I'm counting on it," Shane grinned.

With a nod to the group, Shane picked up the duffle bag and pulled Nalani into motion toward the hallway that led to the small elevator.

Enjoying the feel of her tucked tightly against his body, he suspected she was as nervous as he was when they took the ride down to Black Light in silence. When the elevator doors opened, the soft lighting and sexy music he'd asked Elijah to have on greeted them.

Before he'd arrived at the mansion, he'd given himself fifty-fifty odds of making it this far with Nalani. Now that he was here, he realized getting her down to Black Light had been the easy part of his plan. Pushing each of them through their fears of triggering bad memories or worse, a panic attack would be a bit like threading a needle. It could be done, but it needed to be done with precision.

Shane led the woman he loved to the couch waiting for them in the middle of the empty room. He almost chickened out when Nalani moved to take a seat on the leather.

"On your knees, kitten. That's my seat."

Nalani's eyes widened at his command, recognizing it for what it was—a test. If she couldn't handle this simple step, everything else he had planned out in his dirty mind was moot.

Like a flawless sub, she melted gracefully to her knees, facing his empty seat on the couch.

She'd done her part. Could he go through with his?

Shane swung the duffle bag onto the seat next to where he took a seat in front of Nalani. She was close enough, the front of her robe brushed his knees.

"Eyes."

It was a command he'd given her many times before—usually, so he could revel in her humiliation as he pushed her out of her comfort zone. Tonight, it was more so he could keep tabs on her emotions.

She was still with him. With relief, he detected the spark of longing in her beautiful brown eyes.

"Take off your robe. I need you naked."

An adorable smile curled on Nalani's face. It comforted him that she was having fun as she slowly opened the robe and let it fall to the floor, uncovering her full breasts, her nipples pebbling perfectly. Her tiny panties were her only clothing left.

"Something funny, kitten?"

"It sort of feels like we're learning to walk all over again, you know?"

He could appreciate her analogy. "Yeah, well, better to practice walking before we start to run, right?"

"I guess." She hesitated, before blushing beautifully. "But for the record, I've always loved *running* with you, Shane."

He hadn't realized how much he needed her encouragement. He could feel the final tension in his shoulders release, feeling more like himself than he had in months.

Shane took a deep breath and moved forward with his plan.

"I want you to know, the last two days have been hell, kitten, but I truly can't thank you enough for being brave enough to try to break up with me yesterday. It was the exact wakeup call I needed to help me get my head out of my ass."

"It wasn't bravery, Shane. I was trying to run away because I was too afraid to stay and fight. I thought I was doing the right thing, letting you go, but Piper helped me see I needed to trust you more."

He made a mental note to add another reason to his already long list of things to thank Piper for.

"I don't want us to get too wrapped up in talking, but we do need to lay a few new ground rules. I already introduced our new *timeout* safeword, and I want you to know, I'm giving myself permission to use it too."

"You? Why would you need a safeword?"

"Are you kidding me?"

He could see her confusion. She honestly didn't know.

"Baby, sometimes at night, when I close my eyes, all I can see is you lying there on the floor of your bathroom in a broken heap. There was about a minute where I stood frozen, unable to even go to you because you were so still. I thought… worried… you were dead."

"Oh, Shane… why haven't you talked to me about this before?"

"You know why. For the same reason you haven't told me the details of what happened to you that night either. I only know what was in the police report, but we aren't going there. Not tonight. But one day, we're both going to feel strong enough to talk about it all.

"Tonight, we're gonna focus on getting *us* back on track. And to that end, I have a few gifts for you."

Shane unzipped the duffle bag and took out the first small box, reaching out and handing it to the woman waiting on her knees in front of him.

Nalani untied the ribbon he'd wrapped around the box, slowly opening the lid to peek inside. The relief at finding her collar, the same collar she'd given back to him the day before, bolstered him.

Shane reached to take the jeweled leather from the box and lifted it to her graceful neck. The second it was latched, she sighed deeply, visibly relaxing against his knees as if she needed his warmth.

That had been the easy gift. Shane took out the second box he'd brought. When her eyes widened, he realized the small box was the same size as for an engagement ring. As she untied the bow and slowly lifted the lid, he said a silent prayer she wasn't disappointed by the contents.

Nalani reached in and picked up a silver key ring with a single key on it. Turning it around in her hand, she looked up at him, confused.

"To be honest, this is a totally symbolic gift since the entire estate is decked out with keypad and fingerprint locks already preprogrammed for your entry. Still, I want you to know this is the key to what I hope to be our home one day. I know... you aren't ready yet, but it will be there waiting for us. However long it takes you to be ready to leave Runway."

"Shane..."

"It's okay. I understand. I just need you to know we're on your timetable here, not mine. We can stay upstairs as long as we need to."

"Thank you. Truly."

"Hold that thought. You haven't opened the final gift yet."

The final box was much bigger—the size of a shirt box. Nalani's hands trembled a bit as she slowly undid the ribbon and opened the lid to peek in.

He was ready for her confusion.

"What is it?" she asked, pulling the gift out to turn it around, trying to figure it out.

"It's a chastity belt. It's time to introduce you to one of my favorite kinks. One that may actually come in handy."

God, he'd missed that innocence shining back at him. He'd seen her in so much pain since the attack, he'd wondered if she could ever again be his reluctant innocent.

Time to start running.

"I'm going to love fucking you until you scream, kitten. Then I'm gonna insert this dildo in your tight little pussy. It's going to hold my cum inside you." He picked up the box of graduating butt plugs from the box and held them up for her. "And when you're an especially naughty girl, I'll fuck that pucker of yours until you scream, and I shoot my wad deep in your ass. Then I'll shove one of these bad boys' home to hold my cum right where it belongs.

"That's when I'll lock you in this belt that's going to hold the plugs in your holes. It'll remind you at all times who you belong to but will make sure no one else ever touches what's mine again, and that includes you, kitten. There will be no touching of your cute little clitty when you're locked up."

Shane watched her eyes grow wider with each dirty promise. He took her fidgeting on her knees as she tried to get friction to her pussy as a good sign.

"Now, before I can see if this baby is going to fit you properly, we have some work to do, don't we? Let's start with you kneeling up."

Nalani's eyes grew darker as her pupils dilated. As she kneeled up, Shane leaned forward, hooking his fingers into the waistband of her panties, slowly pulling them down. He took the opportunity to lean down and nibble the crook of her neck, catching the first whiff of her arousal.

His sucking her neck hard enough to leave his mark coincided with his left hand cupping her pussy. Her wetness covered his palm, his other hand finding her breast, squeezing hard enough to draw a groan from the woman falling against him.

It would be so easy to rush things, but Shane forced himself to go slow. Moving his mouth from her neck to her ear, he slipped a single digit through the wet folds of her pussy, careful to avoid touching her clit, preferring to edge her higher. Nalani shivered as he sucked her ear lobe between his teeth, nipping at her.

Shane reluctantly broke up their tryst, but only so he could maneuver enough to unbuckle his belt. He hated to release her, but it couldn't be helped. His engorged cock was straining for release, and he was only too happy to unzip his pants and pull his jeans down.

He'd come commando, and the look in Nalani's eyes showed she approved.

"Open wide, kitten. Let's see that throat I'm about to fuck."

Shane forced himself to pay attention to Nalani instead of his growing need, watching for any sign of panic. Not only was there none, she didn't wait for instructions before lunging forward to take the tip of his cock into her mouth.

God, it felt so good to have her tongue lathing him again. He was not cut out to live the life of a monk. Their months of celibacy had taken its toll on him.

Shane relaxed back against the couch, pulling Nalani with him. As she leaned over his body, he thrust his hips up off the couch, forcing his erection deep enough in her throat, she gagged.

He had to push down the guilt for taking what he needed from her, yet if he were honest, her sputtering around his shaft was music to his ears.

"Hands behind your back. I'm not going to restrain you—not tonight—but I'm in control, kitten." His words coincided with him thrusting his fingers through her already messy hair, using it as a handle to control the action. The push of his hips off the leather was erratic, mixing shallow thrusts with deeper plows that drew the gagging he'd missed so damn much.

"Eyes," he demanded as soon as she'd taken every inch of him. He stilled his hips as she opened her expressive eyes that were watering from the excursion. He could see her nose was running, and there was copious spittle leaking out of her mouth, pooling on his groin.

She was a hot mess, yet she'd never been more beautiful to him.

He wasn't going to last long, and as tempting as it was, he wasn't going to blow down her throat, at least not tonight. He'd been saving this load, and it belonged in her pussy—correction, *his* pussy.

Nalani gasped for air as he pulled her mouth off his cock. He didn't give her a chance to recover, moving his hands from her hair to under her arms, lifting her off her knees like a rag doll.

He wasn't going to be accused of being too gentle tonight. He shot to his feet, pulling her with him until he could step away from the couch enough to shove her down against the leather.

It was his turn to fall to his knees in front of her, reaching out to hook his arms around her legs and yanking her until her pussy was at the edge of the couch. He had to dispose of her panties before he could grab each of her ankles and spread her open. Her wetness glistened in the club lighting, encouraging him to lunge forward to taste her.

From one end of her slit to the other, he lapped at her with his tongue, teasing her sensitive nubbin until he could feel it swelling against his tongue.

"Oh, Shane, that feels so good."

On another day, he would chastise her for using his name instead of sir. On another day, he'd remind her to keep her hands above her head unless instructed otherwise, but tonight, the feel of her hands running through his hair as she humped her hips up to meet his tongue only edged him higher.

He'd missed the intimacy of this so much. He'd missed the taste of her. There were other things—darker things—he'd missed that would wait for another day. A day when they were both stronger.

But right now, he'd waited long enough to be inside her.

Shane leaned up, pushing to his feet while still holding her ankles. He stood tall over her on the couch below, bending her open legs back until her feet touched the back of the couch. His erection protruded proudly from his body, making it easy to line up the tip where his tongue had just been.

His brain shouted for him to be gentle, but he remembered

she wasn't glass. He paused, giving her ample time to call for a timeout, but the safeword didn't come.

Their eyes met just as Shane plunged forward, filling her pussy in one hard thrust. Her loud cry of "yes" as he bottomed out inside her encouraged him to set a fast pace. His hips pistoned into her, their bodies slapping together loudly as he took possession of her—once and for all.

"This pussy is mine, kitten, not yours. Say it," he ordered.

"It's yours. Only yours."

"Good girl. And because you've been such a good girl, I'm going to let you come for me tonight."

It was as if she were waiting for permission. He had barely finished his words and could feel her squeezing him as she fell apart in his arms, crying out her orgasmic high.

But Shane wasn't done. He rode her hard through one orgasm, then started demanding another.

"You're gonna come again, baby. This time, with me."

He took her nonsensical mumbles as she came down from her sexual high as a good sign.

She was so light, it was easy to drop her feet and hug her chest to him as he lifted her up—his shaft still deep inside her—retaking a seat on the couch. She had always been thin, but having lost weight since the attack, it was easy to move his hands to her hips, lifting her, then letting gravity slam her body down to impale herself, over and over.

Shane loved this position, not only because it gave her the appearance of being in control, but he was able to look into her eyes as he demanded her next orgasm.

"So close. Come with me, baby."

Shane let the first wave of euphoria consume him as Nalani bounced up and down on his cock until she cried out, collapsing in his arms as she laid spent, each of them trying to catch their breath.

"You look exhausted, kitten. Let's go upstairs where I can tuck you in."

Nalani lifted her head from his shoulder, her warm brown eyes sparkling with love.

"That sounds perfect. Then tomorrow, in the light of day, I think it's time you show me our new house."

Relief washed over him as he corrected her.

"You mean, our new *home*."

THE END.

ABOUT THE AUTHOR

USA Today bestselling author Livia Grant lives in Chicago with her husband and furry rescue dog named Max. She is fortunate to have been able to travel extensively and as much as she loves to visit places around the globe, the Midwest and its changing seasons will always be home. Livia's readers appreciate her riveting stories filled with deep, character driven plots, often spiced with elements of BDSM.

- Livia’s Website: http://www.liviagrant.com/
- Facebook: http://www.facebook.com/lb.grant.9
- Facebook Author Page to Like: https://www.facebook.com/pages/Livia-Grant/877459968945358
- Twitter: http://www.twitter.com/LBGrantAuthor
- Goodreads: https://www.goodreads.com/author/show/8474605.Livia_Grant
- Instagram: https://www.instagram.com/liviagrantauthor/

COMING SOON! BLACK LIGHT: BRAVE

The amazingly talented **Maren Smith** is our next author to contribute a full-length novel for the ***Black Light Series.*** Coming in November, 2019, ***Black Light: Brave***. Fans will remember Maren's amazing story of Kitty and Noah last season in ***Black Light: Fearless***. This year she will complete the story of the Menagerie with Puppy's story. Check out this short excerpt from ***Black Light: Brave.***

Puppy didn't look at the well-known security guard. When Ethen had been the one checking her in and out of this place, it was eyes on the floor, hands at her sides, and silent as a well-behaved Menagerie Girl should be. He did all the speaking. He did all the arranging.

It was appalling how second nature it was to stand just behind Carlson, her eyes downcast and her hands at her sides, just as if he were Ethen and this were just another play night. Her stomach flip-flopped and her knees almost buckled out from under her as she, without thinking, quickly changed places around Carlson. She stood on his left side, and instead of the floor, she looked at the ceiling. Her face flushed. She swallowed hard, hoping neither man noticed because the last thing she wanted to do was have to explain herself.

But neither man did. Danny wasn't even looking at her, not any more than he had the first time he'd checked her in tonight. It was as if he was making a concentrated effort not to.

"Hang on just a moment while I grab my bag," Carlson said, pulling a locker key from his pocket and heading over to his locker.

He was only gone a few moments, but standing in the open entryway with the lockers lined up behind her and the door to the dungeon and lounge in front, she found herself struggling with an all new set of anxieties. She'd never been here when she wasn't Ethen's property. It felt very strange to be doing this, just as if she were any other submissive on the verge of a night of kinky fun. Was this what Piggy had felt the night she'd come here to participate in Black Light's infamous game of Valentine Roulette? Ethen had made it his mission to make her as uncomfortable as possible, just to remind her who's property she was and that her transgressions would not go unnoticed or unpunished. Looking back on it, it wasn't hard to see that was the night everything started to fall apart. It would be months after that before the Aussie broke into Ethen's house, setting the ball in motion that would see the Master of Menagerie arrested and Puppy thrown into this limbo existence between two halves of a life, neither of which felt like something she wanted to live.

Two more months whispered through her mind, spoken in Ethen's voice, and the shiver that went up her back was every bit the same as the one she'd felt as she'd stood quaking before his steely gaze at the prison.

Two more months and then she was going to leave limbo and be right back in hell, with Pony and Ethen, where she belonged.

Two more months, and she would be her parents' legal ward no longer. Because she would have that right to choose, wouldn't she? Oh God, what if she couldn't choose? What if it wasn't that easy? Who would protect Pony from Ethen if she wasn't there to take the brunt of his abuse?

"Ready?"

Puppy startled at how fast Carlson seemed to just appear at her side. She looked up at him, quickly pasting on a smile that she hoped wouldn't show how sick to her stomach she suddenly felt. Yeah. Sure.

"Would you be more comfortable in a quiet spot or one out in the middle of everything?" he asked, his warm hand coming to rest on the small of her back as he gently propelled her out of the doorway and out into the open. Where anyone could and would see her. Not that there were a lot of people here, but every one that she could now see was looking right back at her. The lady bartender... God, Spencer coming out of his office long enough to actually trail in her and Carlson's wake as he gently walked with her past all the tables in the lounge.

"Private," she whispered hoarsely, struggling to keep her panic out of her voice.

It was a mistake. She shouldn't be here. The bartender knew it. Spencer certainly knew it. Was he still watching her? A quick glance over her shoulder said yes, yes he was, and any minute now she knew he was going to place a phone call to Jaxson and Chase and then she was going to be loudly, humiliatingly, irrevocably shown to the door.

"Are you okay?" Carlson asked, startling her from the terrifying direction her thoughts were forcing her to travel.

She looked up at him, nodding. "Yeah... yeah sure."

"Are you lying to me?" he asked.

The craziest tingle ran right up her back, interrupting the shiver that had preceded it. Her breath caught all over again, but not for the same frightened reason it had before.

His tone was so soft, and yet that hint of a warning underlying each word struck her as comforting in a way that--had Ethen ever said such a thing--would not.

She shook her head, another lie.

He tipped his head, searching her face for what, she didn't know, but when his gaze dropped from her eyes to her chest and stayed there, reluctantly, she followed the direction of his stare down to her hands. She had clapped them one over the other on top of her heart between her breasts, pushing hard as if it that desperate press were the only thing holding her together. It wasn't her heart she was trying to keep working, though. It was her lungs. Her chest was tight; her breaths weren't coming in right.

"Are you sure?" he asked.

She was shaking. Puppy stared down at herself, completely at a loss. She hadn't realized how badly she was shaking until she looked down and saw it. She took her hands off her chest and stared at them, watching the wild trembling that refused to hold still.

She looked at him again, at a loss for what to say.

Holding up a finger, he beckoned to her.

Clasping her hands tight over her stomach now instead, she followed him on watery legs to the nearest spanking bench. Laying his bag on the floor, he sat down on top of the bench. When he beckoned again, she swallowed, but crept in to stand in front of him. Perched on the edge of the padded top, he shifted his feet apart and beckoned her closer yet.

Creeping in by the inches, she stood between his feet, her hands pressed over the wild fluttering in her stomach, the craziest riot of tingling dread-filled sparkles of chaotic, was this anticipation? It felt like anticipation; she hadn't felt that in... she couldn't even remember the last time a look from a dom had made her feel anything other than fear. But this wasn't that. This felt lighter, rippling as it was right up the backs of her legs, across her bottom and her belly both. It played in her nipples, and even further down between her legs.

"I'm a dom," Carlson told her. "Admittedly, I'm not your dom, but I still don't like being lied to. Whatever it is that's making you uncomfortable, it's okay. I get it. You don't have to lie to me, and I'd just as soon that you didn't. I want to be able to take every word that comes out of your mouth as the God's honest truth. Because if I can't, then I can't believe anything you say and that makes me very uncomfortable. Right?"

She stared at him, hands gripped tight, her nipples responding to the very nearness of him. The gentle sternness of him.

"Do you want to start over?"

She could barely swallow. She nodded instead.

He held out his hand and for the second time tonight she let her much smaller fingers be engulfed by his. "Hi, my name is Carlson Garvey. It's a pleasure to meet you, Cynthia."

Blurb:

It started with Piggy. It escalated with Kitty. It ends with Puppy.

For almost a year, Ethen O'Dowell has been locked behind bars and yet Puppy is far from free. A legal ward of her parents, she shares her bedroom with Pony, the only part of her old, submissive life that she has left... apart from the guilt, the fear, and the weekly punishments Ethen dishes out every time they visit him. Escape is all Puppy dreams about. Escape and somehow finding the courage to once more become the person she used to be--someone who lived life on her own terms and never let herself be afraid.

Sadly, those days are long over, and as the old saying goes, there's just no getting them back again.

Or is there?

It's a dead night at Black Light when ex-military man Carlson Garvey decides all he wants is a quiet drink and some downtime to practice his Shibari. What he isn't expecting is the petite brunette who plops down at his table, squeaks out a terrified hello, and promptly flees again. There's a story here and although he doesn't know it, Carlson doesn't need to. He recognizes a broken soul when he sees one.

Sometimes the only thing two broken people need is each other.

Coming November 2019!! ***Black Light: Brave***

THERE'S MORE TO DISCOVER IN THE WORLD OF BLACK LIGHT!

Black Light is the first series from Black Collar Press and the response has been fantastic, but we're not done yet. There are many more books to come from your favorite authors in the Romance genre! Including some continuations from the characters in Valentine Roulette, but we won't spoil anything...

If you're new to the world of Black Light, be sure to catch up with the books already released in the first two seasons of Black Light, so that you're ready when the next stand-alone BDSM fueled book is released! Keep in mind that all books in the series can be read as a standalone or in any order.

And be sure to join our private Facebook group, Black Light Central, where fans of the series get teasers, release updates, and enjoy winning prizes. If you are brave enough to become a member, you can find us at Black Light Central.

Black Light Season One

Infamous Love by Livia Grant is the prequel that started it all! It explains how Jaxson, Chase, and Emma get together, fall in love, and fight to stand for their relationship against the forces that would keep them apart.

Black Light: Rocked by Livia Grant is Book 1 in the world of Black Light that begins on the opening night of the club, it follows a rockstar named Jonah "Cash" Carter and his love interest Samantha Stone. Misunderstandings and a dark history have turned this sweet, childhood romance into a dangerous situation – and when Cash and Samantha finally meet again there's only one thing on his mind: revenge.

Black Light: Exposed by Jennifer Bene is Book 2 in the world of Black Light. Thomas Hathaway and Maddie O'Neill would have never met if it weren't for the reporter opening at The Washington Post. But with her dreams on the line Maddie only has one focus: get the story, then get the job. When she lies her way into Black Light on Thomas' arm, everything seems perfect, except that she enjoys the belt and the man who wields it a little too much. Before time runs out Maddie will have to make a tough choice… to follow her dreams, or her heart.

Black Light: Valentine Roulette was the first boxset in the series where for the first time dominants and submissives came to the Black Light BDSM club to spin for their chance at a night of kinky fun, and maybe even love. With eight stories from eight *USA Today* and international bestselling authors, it's sure to heat up your Kindle! Featuring: Renee Rose, Livia Grant, Jennifer Bene, Maren Smith, Addison Cain, Lee Savino, Sophie Kisker, and Measha Stone.

Black Light: Suspended by Maggie Ryan is Book 4 in the world of Black Light. Charlize Fullerton is a tough DEA agent who has worked hard to prove herself, and when she meets Special Agent Dillon MacAllister on a joint task force to take down a drug ring sparks start to fly. When their mission ends he's sure he's lost his chance with her, until they run into each other at the Black Light BDSM club, and Dillon refuses to let her go a second time.

Black Light: Cuffed by Measha Stone is Book 5 in the world of Black Light. Sydney is a masochist that doesn't stick around for Doms who don't push her to the edge. Tate knows exactly what Sydney is after and he's intent on giving it to her, just not until she begs for it. One snag, there's a murderer in town and it's their job to make sure they get the right guy and keep him behind bars. But when the case starts to hit a little too close to home can Tate and Sydney work side by side without losing each other in the fray?

Black Light: Rescued by Livia Grant is Book 6 in the world of Black Light, and we're right back with Ryder and Khloe from Black Light: Valentine Roulette. Saying goodbye after Valentine Roulette had crushed them both, but Ryder Helms is a realist. He knows his CIA covert career will never allow him to be with a superstar like Khloe Monroe. But when things go sideways for both of them, it's not just their lives at risk, but their hearts as well.

Black Light Season Two

Black Light: Roulette Redux by eight talented authors was Book 7 and our second boxed set in the Black Light world. Our couples are back to their naughty shenanigans on Valentine's Day by being randomly paired and made to play out scenes decided by the turn of the wheel. Are you brave enough to roll?

Complicated Love by Livia Grant is the follow-up to the prequel, Infamous Love. It gives Black Light fans another look into the complicated lives of the trio, Jaxson, Emma, and Chase as they try to live their unconventional love in a sometimes uncompromising world. This book is a must read for MMF menage fans!

Black Light: Suspicion by Measha Stone is Book 8 in the world of Black Light. Measha is back with another fun dose of suspense and sexy BDSM play combined Sophie and Scott work together to solve crimes by day and burn up the sheets by night. When Sophie is in danger, there is little her Dom won't do to keep her safe, including warming her bottom when she needs it.

Black Light: Obsessed by Dani René is Book 9 in the Black Light world. Dani's first story in the series is also the first Black Light book set on the West Coast new club. He might just be a little obsessed with his new submissive, Roisin. Does he go too far?

Black Light: Fearless by Maren Smith is Book 10 in the Black Light world. The talented BDSM author, Maren, is very familiar to Black Light fans since she has had short stories in both Roulette boxes sets. In fact, fans of her short story Shameless will recognize the beloved characters in this full-length follow-up novel. This is a must read Black Light book!

Black Light: Possession by LK Shaw is book 11 and the final book of season two. It brings the action back to the East Coast and gives us a glimpse of another fantastic menage relationship set in the middle of danger and intrigue. It is the perfect ending to our second season as we move forward into season three with Celebrity Roulette.

Black Light Season Three

Black Light: Celebrity Roulette by eight talented authors is Book 12 and our third annual Valentine's Day boxed set in the Black Light world. New couples are back to their naughty shenanigans on Valentine's Day by being paired, this time with a celebrity auction, and made to play out scenes decided by the turn of the wheel. Come see how the celebrities play on the West Coast!

Black Light: Purged - A Black Light Short by Livia Grant is a bit unique in the Black Light world. It is a short glimpse into the lives of some of our beloved recurring characters, Khloe Monroe and Ryder Helms. It is a dark and realistic view into the lives of someone living with an eating disorder and how having someone who loves you in your corner can make all the difference in the world.

Black Light: Defended by Golden Angel is book 13 in the series. It takes us back to the East Coast for a delicious, and our first, full-length Daddy Dom book. If you've ever wanted to explore this unique kink, this is a fun introduction and you will love Kawan and Melody.

BLACK COLLAR PRESS

Black Collar Press is a small publishing house started by authors Livia Grant and Jennifer Bene in late 2016. The purpose was simple - to create a place where the erotic, kinky, and exciting worlds they love to explore could thrive and be joined by other like-minded authors.

If this is something that interests you, please go to the Black Collar Press website and read through the FAQs. If your questions are not answered there, please contact us directly at: blackcollarpress@gmail.com

WHERE TO FIND BLACK COLLAR PRESS:

- Website: http://www.blackcollarpress.com/
- Facebook: https://www.facebook.com/blackcollarpress/
- Twitter: https://twitter.com/BlackCollarPres
- Black Light East and West may be fictitious, but you can now join our very real Facebook Group for Black Light Fans - Black Light Central

Made in the USA
Columbia, SC
18 January 2020